James Barnett

The Firing Squad

Futura
Macdonald & Co
London & Sydney

A Futura Book

To Martin and Glenn

First published in Great Britain in 1981 by
Martin Secker & Warburg Ltd

First Futura edition 1982

ISBN 0 7088 2198 7

Reproduced, printed and bound in Great Britain by
Hazell Watson & Viney Ltd, Aylesbury, Bucks

Futura Publications
A Division of
Macdonald & Co (Publishers) Ltd
Maxwell House
74 Worship Street
London EC2A 2EN

James Barnett was born in 1920 in Glasgow and was educated at Glasgow's Calder Street School. He joined the Territorial Army in 1939 and served in France and later in the Middle East, Italy and Austria. He joined the Metropolitan Police in 1946 and retired in September 1976 with the rank of Commander in the CID. During this time he was awarded the Queen's Police Medal for Distinguished Service. *The Firing Squad* is his fourth novel. He is married with two sons.

Part One

Death and Detectives

One

◆◆◆◆◆◆◆

He had resignedly accepted, without question, that both were what they said they were when they picked him up outside the Customs hall at Gatwick Airport. One of them in particular, the lean one, displayed the confident assurance of long authoritative years, taking him firmly by the arm, flashing an embossed I.D. card in the palm of his hand, and saying crisply, 'Special Branch. You're coming with us.' The frozen finality of his statement stilled any protest. Not that the numbing weariness of flight after flight had left him with the will to protest. His nerves had peaked too many times during the last ten days, during the last ten minutes, to react in any positive way, to react with anything other than a dull acceptance of inevitability. And he had nearly made it. Rio to Paris. Paris to Madrid. Twenty gold Kruger Rand to Eckert's man. Madrid to Malaga. Five gold Kruger Rand to the package holiday courier. Why did they call it a package holiday? To denote the manner in which they crammed those awful people into the aeroplane? 'Just go through with the crowd,' the courier had said. 'Not too fast. Not too slow. Keep in the middle. Pity you haven't a wife with you, looks more natural. Still, there are four or five single-handed poofters going back on this flight. If you waggle your bum a bit going up to Passport Control you should have no problem. What's that, squire? Oh, no offence intended, squire. A word to the wise, eh.' Loathsome scut.

Nevertheless he had minced up to the desk, emulating the walk of a willowy blond youth in front. The Immigration Officer had laughed admiringly. 'If more people took the mickey out of them, maybe the bastards wouldn't be so brazen.' Waved him through, hardly a glance at his passport. And he had been so worried about the stitching. Not all that clever. But another high peak surmounted. Case collected. Straight into the Green Zone. Two lounging uninterested Customs men; a slip, a lurch, a momentary warm trickle as one snaps forward, 'Please come over to the side.' But not to him; to the heavily laden couple in front.

Through to the main terminal, nerves sagging, standing in a stream of rushing, barging, suitcase-heaving, trolley-pushing people. Dithering! Was it Paddington Station or Waterloo for Taunton, to a cottage in Somerset? Christ, why couldn't he remember? Was Constance still alive? Could he risk making contact? The shock? Yes, in time perhaps. Before she died. Before they both died. Not much time left for either of them. No. Be damned if he would succumb to age. Already he could feel the invigorating crispness of the spring air. An English spring. English air. A surge of elation. Temptation. Anticipation. Overnight in London? The Ritz, Savoy Grill, the Café Royal, the Cav Club? Would any of the old crowd still be around? Old crowd indeed. Would any of the old crowd still be *alive*? Don't be an idiot, no living in the past, think of the future. A cottage near Porlock . . . Exmoor and the sea. Might get a reasonably decent hack. The future? At your age you don't have a future, only a past. He had felt the tremors growing at the base of his spine and had just swallowed the Nivaquine – when the hand gripped.

The thin Special Branch man held the door open. He tried to formulate jaunty defiant words but all that came rattling out of his dry throat was, 'I am over sixty-five, y'know, and fit as a flea.' Inane. A lie. A subconscious plea for pity? Only a thin smile in response. A thin knowing smile. 'We're all getting on a bit. Get in.' The opulence of the car surprised him. A Daimler Jag! The old country supposed to have gone to the dogs, yet here were policemen, albeit Special Branch, riding around in Daimler Jags! Vague doubts about their identity dripped into his mind. Stiffening to icicles. He shivered again, a low involuntary moan slid from his lips. He turned to bury it in the deep cushioned leather. Were they Mossad – Israeli intelligence? Or agents of *Der alt Jude*? Had Schellenberg lied to him? Was his S.D. file not destroyed with the others? Yet even if it still existed, he had had no real part in the removals, was never greatly involved in the liquidations. At least, not those. But he had done courier work, to and from Eichmann before they snatched him. He had shaken hands with Heydrich, been photographed with Himmler, worked alongside Pieter to reduce the Russian and Polish excess. K.G.B. people? No, surely not. Not in a Daimler Jag.

Brazen it out. Poofters? After all, Pieter had brazened it out right in his own back yard. Back yard? In his exotic estate right in the middle of his own country. Brazened it out? *Bought* himself out! Dammit, he should have brazened it out himself. There were people who could have helped. Should have helped! Pinkie, nearly in the cabinet when they met in Lisbon back in '53. 'Best forget it, old chap. Only put both our heads in the noose. Give it a few more years. Paraguay's not so bad, is it? They tell me Rosario is a pleasant little place. And you're getting about quite a bit. Down to B.A. now and again, over here to Lisbon, to Madrid. Give my eye teeth for a nice carefree life like yours, travelling about, seeing the sights . . . You're a great asset to them. You can get about; you're not listed. No. It doesn't prove there is nothing on you. It may suit our people to have you on the loose. I hope you realize the risk I'm taking in agreeing to meet you. You know what they're like. All right, you don't. I do. They exist by deception, subterfuge. Oh yes, they would lie, even to me. You come back and before you know where you are you've got a seat at the far end of the rifle range in the Tower. And I and several others will be getting the Lord-have-mercy-on-your-soul bit from the old boy in the black cap.' Solemn, serious, grave. A beseeching hand on his wrist. 'It would bring the Government down. They would never forgive me for that.' Sincerity. Cajolery. 'Give it a few more years, old friend. You really don't know what it's like at home. You're far better off where you are.' Bastard. Took up the hereditary ermine and went waffling on about Britain's declining role. A plum-duff patriot. Never lifted a finger. Left him on the ground like a dung beetle to roll a ball of shit around the world forever. Never should have listened to him in the first place. Back-stabber. What was it Sybil had so maliciously and gleefully told him Pinkie had said of him just before the war? 'Antony was a great natural bounder. Bounded along on his father's money, his uncle's title, Rosalind's horses and Rosalind's titties. Now, since both his pate and his pater are broke, the cousin's inherited, Rosalind's taken up with a Socialist, the fellow's become a natural bouncer . . . of dud cheques.' Recollection brought a wan smile. There was a time when recollection brought a swelling anger in his head. But not now, it was all so long ago. What did it matter?

Who were these confounded people with their Daimler Jags? Eckert had been right. Eckert was always right. So cynically, imperturbably wise.

'I think you are making a serious error of judgement, Antony, in going home. You should not assume attitudes have changed because of one man. And you're not in the same intellectual league. Nostalgia can be a fatal disease, Antony. You think it does not affect me, this homesickness? *Heimweh nach meiner Bayerischen Heimat*. Oh, Antony, how I suffer. But with you it is a death-wish; incurable. So you will go anyway. Mind the old Jew does not get you. I don't know why the man is so implacable. The Jews should say kaddish for us. We gave them a sanctity exceeding that of the most devout Christians. Provided them with multiple Calvarys. Gave them six million emaciated saints recorded for eternity on holy celluloid. Shadows. Making the Pietà in Rome and all other Christian statuary mere lumps of cold marble. Out of the furnace chimneys we gave them a Resurrection, a new life, a new nation. You would think the Jews would be grateful, Antony. For the first time in history they have an acknowledged moral superiority over Christians . . . grudging and resented though it be. When the Christian asks, "Have you seen our magnificent twelfth-century cathedral at Chartres?" the Jew can quietly smile and reply, "No, have you seen our miserable twentieth-century mausoleum at Belsen?" '

Could they be from Mossad? No. It was nonsense, he was nothing to them. They only went after the P.L.O. Wogs. British Intelligence! That was the answer. He relaxed into the cool leather. Surrendered to a placid equanimity, and the gentle illusions of false lucidity and logic, with warm comforting conclusions pre-ordained. Effortlessly the facts assembled themselves. Whereas the thin authoritative man seems ill at ease in the luxury of the car, the other – older, softer, flabbier – wordless, nervous and uncertain at the airport, was now self-assured and confident behind the wheel. A man who matched the car, the car of a soft flabby successful man. His own car. A secure undisputed chattel on four wheels, completely responsive to his demand and will. Yes, the man was one of those few discreetly powerful figures in the Permanent Civil Service. Possibly a senior officer in British Intelligence. One with his own money. A gentleman. Tie was a bit off, though? Still, quite on the cards Intelligence would be interested in him. There was a lot he could tell them. You scratch my back and I'll scratch yours. Play the game with me and I'll play the game with you. My God, what had prompted those hoary banalities? Something familiar about this lean chap next to him. Seen him before some place . . . He wandered back through the years searching for him. Rio . . . Asuncion . . . Buenos Aires . . . Montevideo . . .? No sign of him. Madrid . . . Lisbon . . .? Nothing. Leopoldville just after the war? The war? The Army? Obscure images drifted hazily, young forgotten faces, without shape or form, receded into a troubled darkness. He plunged after them, trying to get closer, to see them more clearly. But the faces had been too hurriedly buried in the past to be remembered now.

'Gone out like a light,' said the lean man to the driver.

'If you're sure, there'll be no need to put the hood over his head.'

'I'm quite sure.

'Must be the first helpful thing he has ever done for us.'

He woke to find himself in a cellar; windowless, with steps ascending to a solid wooden door. Apart from the camp bed on which he lay, the other furniture consisted of a table and chair. Illuminated on the table by a green-shaded reading-lamp were a vacuum flask and a bowl containing bread, cheese and fruit, and something else; a notebook. A thick old-fashioned notebook, with tattered red cloth covers. Walls whitewashed, blank, except for a deep porcelain sink below exposed pipes leading to the water taps. His suitcase open and with the lining slit, lay on the floor. His personal papers were gone but the body belt holding two hundred gold Kruger Rand lay almost contemptuously intact on top of his clothing. He hauled himself up the steps to the door and pulled and pushed at the handle. The lock was solid and unmoving against the mortice. Twice, with the heel of a clenched fist, he hammered on a thick panel. The sound returned dull and empty.

Recollections of his earlier dreamy thoughts came back. British Intelligence. This would be a safe house. Not necessarily a bad sign. Indeed it was considerate of them to allow him to sleep. The opposite was usually the case. 'Keep the bastard awake and on his feet until he decides to open his mouth.' He gave the order aloud, voice booming in the empty room. Stupid. Must keep a grip. They probably have the place wired. Act in a controlled formal manner. He went back downstairs, ignoring the food, to retrieve his toilet bag from the suitcase. First a wash, shave, a change of clothes. Then he would eat.

The coffee in the flask was strong, black and richly sweetened. Just the way he liked it. You have to give it to British Intelligence, they must have quite a dossier on him. Had they? Had they?

He sipped the coffee wondering how many of the expatriates he had met in S.A. had actually been working for them. All submitting weekly reports on him. Which of them? Pointless to try and guess. Well, it was a good sign. If they had wanted to do anything about him they would have done it years ago. Certainly before he ever got back. Now he was back . . . he was an embarrassment! That was it, they wanted to make a deal. 'Keep your mouth shut and we'll play ball with you. We don't want any skeletons dragged out of cupboards now.'

'That's all right, old man. Had no intention of opening old wounds. Just want to finish my days at home. Bit of fishing. Bit of a canter well behind the pack. Rely on me. Not proud of what I did. Thoroughly ashamed. Led astray by my elders and betters. Do you want their names? No? Old sores, eh? Bet you know them anyway. Knew them all along, eh? Always admired you chaps. Pretty nearly won the war for us, eh?'

For us?

As he munched on a piece of Cheddar, his eyes rested on the large notebook lying just beyond the pool of light from the reading-lamp. He reached across and pulled it over. A separate sheet of typewritten foolscap was inserted between the pages. Putting on his spectacles, he withdrew the paper and read . . .

Field Court-Martial of

Captain Antony Pyrnford, Royal Army Service Corps.

CHARGES AND SPECIFICATIONS

He stared unbelievingly at the document. Aware his left knee cap was quivering violently, he placed a restraining hand upon it and read on.

CHARGE (1).	High Treasons, under Section IV of the Treason Act, 1351.
Specification.	Whilst on Active Service and holding a Commission from the Crown, between 3rd September, 1939 and 7th May, 1945, your country being in a state of war with Germany, were adherent to the King's enemies

giving them aid and comfort in his realm or elsewhere.

CHARGE (2).   Murder.

Specification   Whilst on Active Service and holding a Commission from the Crown, on 24th May, 1940 at the Quai Maritime, at Dunkirk in France, did murder Driver Samuel Quarrie, R.A.S.C., a member of His Majesty's Forces.

Note for information of the Accused:— You are hereby informed that should a verdict of 'Guilty' be returned on one or both charges, a sentence of death will ensue.

You are therefore advised to study the contents of the journal wherein this indictment has been placed, as it details the evidence upon which the prosecution's case is founded.

Despite the pressure of his hand, the left leg, from hip to toe, was jerking uncontrollably to such an extent that his foot beat a rhythmic tattoo on the floor. He added his other hand and pressed on the jerking limb with all his strength. Even then the tremors continued. He had to stop it, control it, get his eyes away from those awful words, hypnotic. All you've got is a past. Think. Surely after all these years they couldn't . . . Officially? Where was he? Some dungeon in the Tower . . . Too bizarre. That cowardly Driver who abandoned his gun. Had to shoot him. Was his name Quarrie? Had to shoot him. No other reason? Quarrie? Couldn't remember. Couldn't remember any of them. Names, faces. Nothing. That Sergeant! Too damned clever by half. Sergeants learn by rote and repeat what they learn like parrots. They do not quote Clausewitz, Fuller and Liddell-Hart, or discourse on the Schlieffen Plan like someone of field rank passed out of Staff College. Jumped-up working class Bolshevik. What was his name? A face? Nothing. Just vague anonymous shapes in coarse battledress. Whiners, with malevolent shifty eyes and stupid stolid solid dumb insolent faces. Why couldn't he remember one single face? The one he had shot? Something there! Teeth, snarling up at him as he cringed beneath the rear wheels of the Ack-Ack Bren truck. Coarse Scotch guttural howling, 'Please, sur, No, sur. No, sur. The serjint tel't me tae take cover.' Had to be done. The platoon was on the verge of panic. Stiffened them up. No other reason?

His eyes fell on the sheet of paper again. Damn it, what was he doing? Preparing a defence to this . . . this nonsense. And it was a nonsense. There was nothing official about this . . . jargonistic rubbish. He had attended Courts Martial in his time. This nonsense bore only a pseudo-resemblance to proper form and procedures. What on earth was going on? Who had their hands on him? Whoever they were they were not official. British extremists acting on behalf of the K.G.B? Not in a Daimler Jag.

He got to his feet, trying to stamp the uncertainty out of his knee, glancing from time to time at the dubious document. Then he crushed it in his hand and flung it into a corner. He went back to the table, opened the red-covered notebook and began to read. Names appeared. Faces took shape, features formed. His left kneecap began quivering again, unrestrained. For the words he read had the intense fascination of his own life as seen by another's eye.

Two
++++++

The man in the tracksuit with a towel round his neck had been running at a steady pace for five miles, and the rhythmic slap of his feet on the road had gradually induced a hypnosis rendering him oblivious to the shrilling birds and the advent of dawn. His head was down, his only thoughts concentrated on the length of each stride, the height of each lifting knee, sadly aware that the steps were now shorter, the knees lower and the legs heavier, as though he still ran in the sand-filled gaiters he had worn in the early days to strengthen them.

For his legs were more important to him than those of ordinary men. He was Joe 'Bim Bam' Bailey, middleweight boxer, and his next fight was a final eliminator for the British title. Until recently they had said he was over the hill – actually, he had never made it halfway up the slope – an eight- or ten-round filler on the big bills; good for a head-down crowd-pleasing two-handed attack over the distance, but more often than not winding up a points loser, bloodied, cut and scarred. Then eighteen months ago it had changed. They had put him in as a substitute against a highly rated young contender looking for an easy pre-title warm up and he had flattened the kid in the seventh, despite another badly cut eye and a flayed lip. When the fight reporters came to see him afterwards, uttering cynical praise, enquiring how he had pulled it off, he had replied with a spontaneity inspired by elation, 'Well, I bim bammed him, didden I?' Much to his own delight and that of his manager, Alfie Joss, he was captioned in the half-column reports on the fight as 'Bim Bam' Bailey. Three further fights followed against increasingly good opposition. In all of them he bim-bammed his way to victories, bloody but inside the distance. Now, after nine years in the game he was within sight of the summit, in with a chance of making some real money . . . If his legs held up!

He saw the red postbox that was his marker and its significance snapped him out of the trance. Glancing down at the stopwatch he noted with dismay he was nearly a minute slower than at the beginnning of training. Every day over the past week he had been getting slower, his legs heavier and heavier. Maybe he was over-training? But the fight was still a month away, he couldn't taper off now. Every stride was becoming an effort of will – the legs wouldn't carry him fifteen rounds – but he plugged on, fierce in his resolve. The fight wouldn't go the distance, he would bim bam the bastard inside ten . . . He saw the champ's grinning face in front of him and slashed at it with a fast left hook, following it in with a heavy right under the heart. The smooth working of hands and arms dispelled worries about his legs and he trotted along for a hundred yards, arms swirling in a series of fast combination punches. He felt good again; the birdsong came through to him and he whistled a tuneless reply in time to each jogging step. Yeh, his wind was as good as ever it had been; so long as he had his wind and his fists he could take the guy with both ankles broken.

Jesus, this was a good time to get in roadwork, nobody about to gawk at him. No traffic. Just them birds singing their throats out. Another half-mile and he would be up on the Common where he could take a breather – not that he needed one, just that it was nice in that little glade with the fallen tree, where he could lie down with his legs propped over the trunk, feeling the leaden blood draining out of them. He always looked forward to that part of it, looking up at the sky, thinking about the big purses to come, maybe buying one of them big houses up here for Shirl and the kids.

He had lain on his back for several minutes watching the sky change, seeing the greyness thin and fade before a spreading blue. The birds were quiet now and all he could hear was the hissing tinnitus inside his battered ears. It didn't worry him none, he was used to it. Alfie had said he would get used to it and he wasn't to mention it to anyone else, particularly the Board's doctor, and he could still hear well enough . . . Just as he heard now . . . Distant words, vague, yet sharp incisive words, like a referee on a count to ten . . . A rattling metallic sound . . . Another sharp word . . . Break? . . . Then a sudden thudding, crackling moment of penetrating sound crushing and compressing the silence upon his ears with sharp unexpected impact, setting the branches strumming – until he realized it was the birds, wings fluttering as they fought clear of the leaves to gather in the sky, screeching and cawing in raucous protest.

Bailey pressed himself tight against the trunk. He knew that what he had heard had been shots and wondered if they had been directed at him. When he had taken that kid, the big spielers had had a lot of money laid against him, even though the kid was eight to one on. There had been threats. But the threats had turned to offers – to take a dive on the next one. He had ignored the threats and spurned the offers, even though Alfie had wanted to go along; particularly on the last fight where they had put up five grand. He told Alfie they could stuff it; he was 'Bim Bam' Bailey, next middleweight champion of the world . . . They were trying to put the frighteners on him? Yeh, that was it . . . The bastards . . . Silence again, but in his head the hissing was now an incessant buzz, obtrusive and persistent. Angry, he rose, but no higher than his favourite fighting posture, a low crouch with left arm probing forward, his lethal right tucked in close. Thus positioned he sidled forward, bobbing and weaving round the pines towards the source of the shots, to emerge at the edge of a deep sandy basin in the middle of the Common.

At the bottom, fifty feet below, wisps of blue smoke layered the still air; wreathed in the smoke was a heavy wooden chair with a man straddled across it, chest into the back of it, arms stretched down the sides, head lolling over the top, blood dribbling from his mouth into the receptive sand. As Bailey looked closer, he saw the ropes binding the man's body into the chair, the arms lashed down to the back legs, ankles tied up to the front, feet just clear of the ground. Movement drew his eyes to the far side of the basin and in a blur he saw four men – no, five – climbing slowly upwards. Each carried a long gun of some sort, three of them using the butts to lever themselves to the top where another man stood, extending a hand to each in turn, pulling them over the edge.

As the men gained level ground, none gave a backward glance; each one filed into the trees, fading from his sight. Only the sixth man who had helped the others over the top remained, looking downwards at the body in the chair. Bailey saw him raise his hand in salute. A salute, that because of its exaggerated slowness seemed to be a mocking and contemptuous farewell. Then like the others, he also turned and vanished into the trees.

Bailey tried to think what best to do and found the process difficult. Shuffling about on the lip of the basin, he threw short indecisive punches at his quandary. Why hadn't Alfie come with him? Got a bleeding cold! The lying git. He had been out on the piss with that bastard bookmaker. Should he phone the law? Fuck the law. They had done him once years back when he was making a few readies as a club bouncer . . . an' that loud-mouthed git . . . They had done him for G.B.H. Just for doing what he was paid for. He would have gone inside if Alfie hadn't come up with two ton and paid the fine . . . Yeh, that was it, he'd nip up to the railway station and get the first train back down the line. Go and see Alfie. Best be guided. Alfie would know what to do.

'You done dead right, son.' Alfie Joss sat on the edge of his bed and tried to give Bailey a reassuring smile. He had made his boy repeat the story twice. The first time he heard it, it frightened him, not because of the circumstances but because he thought the boy's brains were scrambled. When he heard it for a second time he knew it was true; and the fear remained because it was true. 'You done dead right, son,' he repeated, more for his own benefit than Bailey's. 'Last thing we need is to get mixed up wiv the law.'

'But supposin' they come askin' questions, Mr Joss? I mean, I been doin' my roadwork up along the Common for a few years now. Plenty of Old Bill know I work along there – I mean in the cars, like. They used to give me a pull now and again before I hit the big time.'

'You want to stay in the big time, doncha? Nobody saw you this morning did they?' Joss waiting anxiously for an answer.

Bailey shook his head 'Don't fink so, Mr Joss.'

'Then stay schtoom. If the law does come round, you didn't go near the Common. You turned left up towards the railway station, and come straight back here.' Joss got up and fumbling with his pyjama cord went through to the lavatory on the landing. Bailey listened to the sound of his manager's bladder emptying into the bowl. He was still concerned about the police and called out above the noise. 'Are you sure there won't be no bothers, Mr Joss? I don't want no aggravations.'

Joss came back into the bedroom, scratching at his belly. 'Listen, aggravations we got already. The mere fact you saw what you saw is aggravations. That's why it's got to be total schtoom on this.' He transferred his scratching fingers to his sparse hair. 'Apart from the law we have the people themselves to worry about.' He brought his fingers slowly down his face, tearing into the stubble on his cheeks. 'Who do you reckon them to be, son?' It was not a matter Bailey had considered and he simply spread out his empty hands by way of reply.

'Could be a firm of south London villains cuttin' down a grass.' Joss supplied himself with a speculative answer. 'Or they could be I.R.A? Christ, yes, it sounds just like them Micks. Either case, the law's the least of our worries. We stay schtoom, old son. That's the policy, we stay schtoom.'

'It's a funny thing, Mr Joss. I don't think it could be a firm or the I.R.A. Y'know, well, they moved . . . the way they moved . . . they was like old men, stiff like. Couldn't be sure, me eyes ain't that good over a long way, but they moved like old men.'

Joss waved aside Bailey's vague conjectures in a gesture of irritation. 'It don't matter none how old they were. They shoot people, don't they?' He stuck a threatening finger into the boxer's ruined face. 'So you keep schtoom on this, you hear? An' another thing, keep schtoom on those dodgy minces of yours as well. You want to lose your licence?'

Three

◆◆◆◆◆◆◆◆◆

Smith answered the radio demand with his call sign. The M.P. despatcher came back with the message. 'Oboe Delta Five-Five – Location reference three niner-Foxtrot five. Meet your D.C.I. at road junction upper left with names beginning S-Sierra-B-Bravo. Most urgent. Over.'

Smith gave a brief 'Received. Over and out' in reply and pulled into the side to consult the police street guide at page 39 and square F5. The junction was at Sandpit Lane and Birbeck Avenue, Cobb Common, right on the edge, not only of his district but of the Metropolitan Police Area. Green belt, a wooded common, a few scattered houses, money manors, all swimming-pools and tennis-courts.

He palmed the stick into gear and swung the car round. Most urgent, eh? Could only be a murder. O'Brien, the local Detective Chief Inspector, would only use a map reference in an effort to hold off the media earwigging on the police bands in search of a story. Probably meant the victim was lying out in the open. Well, it wasn't too bad. Here he was, posted out of the Yard only two days previously to Outer District Five, where they assumed he would have no aggravation – and above all, cause no aggravation. And already he had a murder! If it was on the Common . . . almost bound to be a rape murder? Perhaps a child? He hoped it wouldn't be a child. Still, nice to get the call at this time of day, just as he was on his way to the office. Beats being dragged out of bed at three or four in the morning; gives you a chance to get an investigative team together . . . all nice and fresh. And they had a fairly new Divisional station in the small town of Cobb Common. Plenty of space to set up a Murder Room – that is, if it was going to be a long job. Maybe it would all be on top . . .? A domestic! In that case he would let O'Brien get on with it. Do him a bit of good as a newly promoted D.C.I. to be in charge of a murder enquiry. Have to keep an unobtrusive oversight on it though, O'Brien was inclined to be a bit slapdash. Still, if you had to have a murder it was a good time of day to have it. He slipped into the westbound lane on the throughway, singing quietly to himself, 'When I was a lad I spent a term . . .'

He saw the unmistakable slouching outline of O'Brien standing on the corner. He would have to have a word with him; O'Brien was getting beyond being fat, he was becoming obese. No wonder it took four appearances on the Promotion Board to get him made Chief Inspector. In the end they probably only made him because they were fed up with the sight of him. And O'Brien was not looking cheerful, but then he rarely did first thing in the morning. He stopped the car at the kerb.

'Morning, George, don't look so bloody miserable. What have we got?'

O'Brien did not give an immediate answer, but directed him to the nearby car park serving the Common. The small compound was packed with Police cars. Smith saw, with some surprise, the District Commander's Princess and the Talbots of lesser breeds, together with three blue and white Pandas. 'What have we got, George?' he said again, beginning to feel a little disturbed.

O'Brien shook his head mournfully. 'You never saw anything like this, Guv. Wait till you see it; just up through the trees.'

He followed O'Brien through the dark pines until they reached the top of the basin. His eyes went directly to the body in the chair and dwelt on it for a time. O'Brien watched expectantly as his gaze wandered round the scene below. The District Commander was there chatting with the Chief Superintendent of the Division. Two uniformed Inspectors hovered nearby. Six P.C.s strolled about, casually scuffing the sand with the toes of their boots. O'Brien waited for the blast.

'What the hell is going on down there, George? A Greek tragedy? You been selling tickets? For Christ sake why did you allow that bunch of blue woollies to fuck up the scene of a crime?'

O'Brien took it with a sad philosophical smile. 'They were all here before I was, Guv.'

'What?' Disbelief contorted Smith's face.

O'Brien's sad smile deepened, falling upon Smith as if on an ignorant child. 'You've been up at the Yard too long, Guv. Out on District our uniform colleagues are our guides and mentors in all things. To refer to them as woollies is almost an offence under the Race Relations Act.' There was no humour in his reproach. He went on with the fatalistic air of a man who has learned to accept immutable change. 'The sequence of events was that a call came in just after five this morning, from one of the houses round here; about somebody out shooting on the Common. The beat man came up, found the body and called the Duty Officer, who called out the Divisional Chief, who directed they inform the Commander . . . Then they let me know. Well, by the time I get here from the other side of Croydon they were all on scene and dealing.'

'Hulloooo Owen!' The greeting was loud and prolonged. Carey Hessen, the District Commander, was a big man with a matching voice. Smith raised an open palm in reply to the semaphoring arm. He had no personal knowledge of the man below but had, as a matter of course, made it his business to see what the fellow was made of prior to arrival on his District.

Hessen was young for the rank, even for these days. In his mid-thirties, a university entrant, rugby colours, he had skittered up the promotion ladder with feet barely resting on any rung, each step giving added momentum to his upward progress. Into everything and always at the front. A dry-sherry drinker, whose bottles lasted a long time. A day and night man, just as liable to walk into one of his nicks at three in the morning as three in the afternoon. His districts had the lowest sickness record in the Metropolis, because as soon as one of his men reported sick he was round on the doorstep with a bunch of grapes and a long sympathetic and encouraging chat. Nobody now went sick on his district with anything less than double pneumonia or a fractured skull. Hessen was an assiduous student of man-management. He served on every welfare, sports and police training committee that existed.

Smith fervently hoped all these activities would keep Hessen well out of his hair, but there he was waving his arms about at the bottom of a sandpit, making a right mess of the scene of his crime. His early exuberance had vanished; what was down there had all the signs of a right sticker . . . the sort of job that when the D.I. asked if there was anything special he should put in the murder equipment box, you replied, 'A bottle of scotch and a prayer mat.'

He made his way down the slope and, ignoring Hessen, stood looking at the body in the chair. The bullet-holes in the back of the shirt were easily seen as there was little blood-staining. That had all come out the front.

'Sub-machine-gun, I would say, wouldn't you?' Hessen's voice came from over his shoulder; tentatively offering to consider any reasonable alternative. Smith's answer was an offhand jerk of his head and a dubious pout.

'Not at short range though,' Hessen continued earnestly. 'Powder marks would be noticeable on a white shirt like that . . . if it was at close range . . .' His words trailed momentarily as if realizing he was on uncertain ground. 'At least, according to old Tom Palmer. You know, the Principal Scientific Officer on ballistics at the Lab?' Self-assurance surged back into his voice and he conferred on 'old Tom Palmer' a familiarity intended to indicate that they discussed ballistics at frequent intervals. 'Did you ever hear old Tom's lectures at the Police College? I remember them well.'

Probably the only occasion he had ever met old Tom, thought Smith. 'You must have missed the bit on preserving the scene of the crime?' He managed a sour smile in an effort to take the edge off his words.

'No one has touched the body, Owen.' Hessen's indignation was quick but restrained. 'When the divisional surgeon came to certify death, I wouldn't even allow him to touch it with his stethoscope. He was satisfied from external appearances.' The sanguine display of superiority by Hessen not only of rank, but of expertise, fell like a hot coal on the powder of Smith's resentment. While at the Yard he had given little sympathy to the complaints of colleagues on District about uniform interference with major crime operations, about sudden interchange, and tight control of C.I.D. administration and operations. But now he himself was on District and he was finding out . . . He didn't like it.

Turning to the corpse slumped in the chair, he spat angry words at it. 'Bugger the body!' And swinging back to Hessen, said, 'I'm talking about the scene of a crime.' With a wide gesture he encompassed the sandy basin and beyond. 'Every inch of this place is important to me. There are bullets buried in the sand, cartridge cases maybe, that have to be found. There are footprints, or would have been before all these . . . people began tramping about.' Turning again to the corpse, he repeated in a vehement hiss of morose petulance, 'Bugger the fucking body.'

Throughout his angry tirade Hessen's relaxed frame had been

stiffening upwards into a monument of rigid severity. At six feet four inches and sixteen stone, Hessen had, despite a youthful unlined face, a posture appropriate to his rank. Commanding. His eyes fell imperiously on Smith and his words smote him about the ears.

'This is *my* district, Mr Smith, and no part of it may be regarded as the sole preserve of detectives. The scene of a crime will no longer be regarded as holy ground on which only the high priests and acolytes of the C.I.D. cult may tread, to indulge their secret rituals and enhance their mystique. There will be no esoteric C.I.D. ceremonies on *my* district. That is a fraudulence that is, thank God, being done away with.' As if to enhance his height, Hessen climbed a few feet up the side of the pit before addressing himself further to Smith — and everyone else.

'And by the way, whilst homosexual necrophilia may appeal to you as a forensic possibility, please bear in mind I will not tolerate foul language in my presence. When every endeavour is being made to forge a thrusting spirit of Christian morality within the police service, it ill behoves officers of your rank and position to descend into the filth of the gutter. The English language is a gift of God and should never be abused.' Hessen's voice boomed about the natural amphitheatre, bringing all movement to a halt as his eyes flashed round seeking a challenge. None was offered, although over on one side, out of range of Hessen's peripheral vision, Smith saw one of the older Inspectors bring his hands together and offer him the solace of mock piety. 'Jesus wept,' he muttered sadly to himself.

Hessen descended from the slope and called his Divisional Chief to his side. 'Work to do, Peter, work to do.' Then, striding away for a few paces, he came to a contemplative halt, went back to Smith and said in wounded but conciliatory tones, 'I will leave you to your crime scene, Owen. If you require any assistance from District resources, you have only to ask . . .' He waited patiently for Smith's answer.

'I would be grateful if an Inspector and the P.C.s could remain, sir,' said Smith with all the humility of professional hypocrisy.

'Mr Packer.' The words rolled peremptorily over Smith's lowered head. The old inspector of the pious hands lost a grin from his face and came awkwardly to attention. 'You and the six P.C.s remain on scene to assist Mr Smith.' The inspector returned a forthright bark: 'Yessir.'

Hessen returned his gaze to Smith, stern righteousness in his

20

youthful face softening to a momentary sadness that in turn vanished in the glow of a slow forgiving smile. A long muscular arm encircled Smith's shoulders and he was heaved along at Hessen's confiding side. 'Y'know, Owen, all this uniform – C.I.D. antipathy that used to exist has got to be completely eradicated. All vestiges of it removed.' The grip tightened on Smith's shoulder. 'I know it's difficult for an old C.I.D. warhorse like you to accept change, but accept it you must. What the Commissioner wants for the entire force, and what I certainly demand for this district, is everybody working together, harmoniously . . . All dedicated by example to securing the moral and spiritual regeneration, not only of the service, Owen, but of the nation itself.'

'It's an enormous task, sir,' said Smith gravely.

'We can do it, Owen, we can do it.' He looked up and saw Hessen's proud chin thrusting heavenwards and realized he was not necessarily included in the plural. Hessen's arm slid from his shoulders to allow a great hand to curve its fingers into a weapon of serious debate. 'If you consider it, Owen, you are privileged to be one of the new *thinking* police. Thoughtful. Socially aware. Publicly involved. Morally impregnable. Our image will be summed up in two words . . . Think Clean . . .' He paused to allow the significance of his revelation to penetrate Smith's mind, almost anxiously seeking a visual reaction. The look of wonder on Smith's face did not disappoint him. 'If I . . . Should I . . .' A deprecating, almost apologetic smile interrupted the flow. 'Should I,' he modestly re-emphasized the remoteness of the possibility, 'ever gain the Commissionership, I will do my utmost to have these words adopted as the force motto . . . Think Clean . . . *Noli Putare* . . . No. *Noli mala Putare.* How's that?' Smith shook his head to indicate sublime ignorance. Hessen took full advantage. 'Yes, that should just about fit . . . *Noli mala Putare.*' Raising an arm, he allowed a friendly fist of absolution to fall on Smith's melancholy shoulders. 'Think clean, Owen,' he said by way of parting.

'I'll remember those words, sir,' Smith called after Hessen's large frame as the Commander bounded effortlessly up the slope, with his Divisional Chief struggling behind. O'Brien approached him, a rueful smile on his face indicating that tokens of sympathetic commiseration were about to be offered.

'Don't say a bloody thing, George.' Smith punched his words into O'Brien's face. 'Just give me straight answers. Photographer?'

'On way.'

'Lab team?'

'Ditto.'

'Pathologist?'

'Thought you would want Simonson. He'll do it, but can't get here before one.'

'We can't leave him out in the sun for another three hours. Even if we put the tent up over him, it'll get as hot as hell inside.'

'I told him that. He says it's a straightforward shooting and as the shots were heard, we've got a time of death. So there's not much point in his coming to the scene. He wants it taken, just as it is, direct to the mortuary. I asked him how we were supposed to do that without disturbing the body too much. He said something about making a sedan chair out of it. Do you know how to make a sedan chair, Guv?'

'That's the least of my worries. Where's the murder box?'

'Up on the top. I had it fetched.'

'Mr Packer!' The Inspector had taken off his tunic and was rolling up his sleeves in a workmanlike manner. Any inclination to jocular comment on his part was stifled by the look on Smith's face. He contented himself with a polite, 'Yessir?'

'There will be some rolls of white tape in the murder box. I want the entire ground area around the bottom here marked in a grid of two-metre squares. Each square will be searched systematically. When the lab team arrive they should have a couple of metal detectors on board. There are at least five bullets somewhere in this ploughed-up mess. I want every one of them found and anything else that is foreign to the place from fag ends to French letters.'

'Cartridge cases, sir?'

'I doubt if even the thundering hooves of the herd of bison that has already been across here could have missed them, so they've probably been picked up by the killers. But I will be grateful for anything. And don't forget to make a note of the grid square in which any find is made.'

'We'll do our best, sir.'

'Mr Packer.'

'Yes, sir?'

'Your best had better be at least finding the bullets or it will be shovels and fine sieves until you do.'

Packer went up the slope to find the tapes, Smith to kneel beside the seated body, examining chair and corpse with his eyes, like a worshipper ensuring that a sacrifice had been well made and received. Gently, he reached out and felt the trouser pockets. Nothing. No identification. No origin. No place to begin other than here in this pit with a corpse in shirt, trousers and shoes. With a chair and some rope. Eventually, a few bullets. O'Brien stood by patiently until Smith got to his feet, brushing away sand from his knees.

'I.R.A., Guv?' O'Brien tried to be helpful. 'They're about the only people who would use a sub-machine-gun and set up a scene like this.'

'It wasn't a sub-machine-gun, George,' said Smith with flat finality. 'No S.M.G. has the muzzle velocity to rip right through like that. Look at the way a couple of shots have torn through the bar of the chair. This was high-velocity stuff.'

'Something like an Armalite on automatic? The I.R.A. have plenty of them.' O'Brien still clung to the I.R.A., wanting the comfort of a reasonable source. Smith shied away from it, partially out of pique because it had been Hessen's suggestion in the first place, but mainly because it didn't seem to fit. He voiced his reasons for the benefit of O'Brien and himself.

'The I.R.A. wouldn't go to all this trouble. Not here, it would be too risky. And it wasn't an Armalite on automatic, the wounds are too widely dispersed for a short burst; it wasn't even an Armalite. Or any of the small-calibre super-high-velocity weapons. His back would have been blown to bits. Same thing would apply to a magnum pistol.'

A small storm in O'Brien's mind brought ripples across his forehead. He sought refuge in sarcasm, looked at the surrounding trees, and shrugged. 'All right then, bows and arrows?' He expected abuse for his levity but all he got from Smith was a ruminative lecture.

'Modern military history makes fascinating reading, George. During the first war when the occasional squaddy failed to see much point in walking through a crossfire of Maxim guns and took a walk in the opposite direction, it was a quick court martial and the firing squad. There was none of this standing nonchalantly against a wall, waving away the blindfold, and having a last fag bullshit. The N.C.O.s in charge of the execution knew what it was all about. There but for the grace of God went some of them. They would get the poor sod so stupefied on issue rum he couldn't stand. Then they tied him in a chair, just like chummy here, and did the job on him.'

The thought of it had made Smith angry again. Prodding O'Brien's chest with a fierce forefinger, he accentuated his words. 'That's what we've got here, not one man with a sub-machine-gun, we're looking for a fucking firing squad of at least five riflemen.'

'Think clean, Guv,' said O'Brien anxiously as he reeled back from the prodding finger.

'Make it "Think Clear" and I might join.'

Smith looked up in answer to a call from the top of the basin. The photographer was up on the rim with his heavy box of equipment looking for an easy way down. Smith told him to set up where he stood: for starters he wanted a wide-angle shot of the bottom with the grid squares laid out undisturbed. And bearing in mind the reading of the day's first lesson, he made a loud but polite request to Inspector Packer and his men to kindly hurry with laying out the tapes please. Somehow it sounded more insulting than his original inclination to shout out, 'Get a bloody move on for Christ's sake.'

Behind him, O'Brien was now studying the face of the corpse. 'He's no chicken, Guv. But he ain't old enough to be a First World War deserter.' His tone was half jesting but at the same time puzzled and plaintive.

'The chair method became quite popular, George,' explained Smith patiently. 'They used it to execute spies during the Second World War. By then it was not so much that the victims were pissed on rum, just that it was easier on the firing squad to shoot at a man's back.' He changed the subject abruptly. 'How many men have you got out on house-to-house?'

'Only three, Guv. There's no more than a dozen houses within a mile radius of this place. I thought that would be wide enough to begin with.'

Smith agreed and said he would go back to the station and see the initial results. He told O'Brien to supervise the photographer and the lab team then get the body to the mortuary. And finger-prints! He wanted the fingerprints rushed to the B13 computer. An ident, a place to begin, somewhere beyond this damned pit. He wanted it badly. He wanted it fast.

'Just one thing before you go, Guv.' O'Brien's words stopped him half-way up the slope. He looked down enquiringly.

'How do I make a sedan chair?'

Smith told him to get two long poles and what to do with them.

When he got to the Divisional Station and entered the long narrow office set aside for major incidents, he was surprised, pleasantly surprised, to see that the System was set up and in operation. Generally the first few hours of a murder enquiry were a bit chaotic, with all interest centred on the scene, with spasmodic and uncoordinated action and reaction from junior officers going in various directions; acting on whatever information was immediately available. Jumping to conclusions, sometimes correct, but more frequently erroneous. If their conclusions were correct, they were praised for initiative. If wrong, they were damned for precipitate and unauthorized presumption and removed from further participation in the enquiry.

There had been little initial information emanating from the scene of this particular murder. Someone must have assessed that fact at an early stage, seen it was going to be a long-drawn-out enquiry, and set up the System. The Scotland Yard system for all major investigations – The System. A growth centre for investigative fact, its indices on names, descriptions, suspects, vehicles, places, times, and all the other relevancies and peculiarities of a particular investigation, cross-referenced in minute detail. Fed from an accumulation of statements, messages, and information from every available source. They had tried to computerize it and failed, because a computer has no instinctive suspicion, no emotive reaction to the truth, or the lie, its so-called memory merely an act of regurgitation. It took a good man – or woman – to run the System. One who would nourish and cherish it; closely supervise its diet of fact and purported fact, distinguish accuracy from inaccuracy, be capable of both objective and subjective thought because in all crime, and particularly murder, detachment and emotion are inseparable. The purpose of the System is to generate action, be it positive or negative, for both are equally important. The first may lead simply from fact to fact to prove irrevocable guilt; the second, more subtle and complex, may destroy a web of lies and convert each strand into a prison bar.

So Smith was not unnaturally interested in who was going to run the System for his investigation. He would either approve or disapprove. It was his decision. He called for the Action Book, which was not only the product of the System, but one of its many sources of regeneration. The book was brought to him by a man in his middle years, or older? He found it difficult to tell, for there was an air of alertness about the man. Alert and . . . neat, was Smith's immediate impression. The man was not overly tall but slim, erect . . . and neat; the impression was difficult to remove. The man was not wearing a jacket but his waistcoat was tightly buttoned and matched his well-pressed trousers, his tie was a subdued maroon in colour, held by a small precise knot against the perfect inverted V of a stiff white collar. The cuffs on his shirtsleeves were fixed by yellow metal studs. Maybe rolled gold thought Smith, but . . . neat, like his shoes, highly polished, under old-fashioned trouser turn-ups. An old suit, cleaned and pressed many times, but . . . neat, like his hair, iron grey, with an old fashioned centre parting bisecting his scalp from forehead to crown with absolute precision . . .

'Good morning, sir,' the greeting was formal but the man offered no hint as to his identity or position. Smith was not offended, he was the District Detective Chief Superintendent, and it would be assumed he would have ascertained who was who and what was what before arriving at any C.I.D. office on his district. It would have caused offence to have thought otherwise. But he hadn't had the time to brief himself . . . Still, that wasn't this fellow's fault. Nevertheless, he enquired bluntly, 'You are?'

'John Marrasey, sir. I'm the civilian clerical officer.' The neat man saw Smith's raised brows, gave an understanding nod and an explanation. 'I was D.I. at the District station until I retired on age limit eight years ago. The job of clerical officer was going out here. I applied and got it. I thought you would want the System set up and as everybody else was out at the scene or on house-to-house, I got cracking.'

The explanation was, as Smith somehow expected, concise, succinct. He responded with a non-committal smile and sat down with the Action Book. The serially numbered entries on all the preliminaries had been written up in the upward fine lines and downward broad strokes of a copperplate master, immediately legible. From the first irate calls about shots being fired on the Common – D.S. Passmore deputed to obtain statements – to O'Brien's radio request for two eight-foot lengths of stout timber to assist in removal of victim. The 'Remarks' column noted the dispatch of the police van to a local timber yard with the driver instructed to afterwards report to D.C.I.. O'Brien at scene and convey body to mortuary. Smith, envisaging the difficulties in carrying the seated corpse up out of the sandpit hoped that part of it would be done . . . Neatly?

Two telephone engineers were installing additional outside lines. And there it was – Action No. 7 at 0905: initiated by Mr

Marrasey . . . Initiative? Or presumption? Smith watched him as he supervised the siting' of the handsets, quietly and politely authoritative. It was initiative all right. The extra lines would be needed.

If the man had retired on age limit of fifty-five, eight years ago, that would make him sixty-three. Marrasey was previously unknown to him, which was unusual, for even with more than four thousand detectives in the Metropolis, you got to know most of them over the years, at least the D.I.s and above. Marrasey had obviously been one of those outer-district limpets who accepted limited promotion to cling to the steadfast rocks of suburbia, where no doubt he had a neat little bungalow or semi-detached within ten minutes of the nick; where he could nip home for a couple of hours every afternoon and tend the roses or water the tomatoes. Not that such officers were to be despised. Years of accumulated local knowledge, not only of resident criminals, but of residents *in toto*, made them accepted, respected; sometimes feared . . . and not only by the villains. And when the occasional crunch situation occurred on the ground, they beavered day and night to clear it up, affronted by the intrusion of outsiders, outraged by the temerity of their trespass. The condition of such detectives had long been recognized by administrative power as tending towards major complacency and minor corruption. Their ordered lives would suddenly be shattered by a thunder-clap transfer, posting them to an inner district or to the Yard itself. Not that they found the work more onerous or demanding; a high incidence of major crime soon becomes commonplace. But no longer could they nip home for lunch or slide away for an hour to deal with some domestic crisis. Their contacts, personal and professional, withered like their roses, distanced from them. Their positions and postures within the locality were usurped by those who replaced them. Only a very few, uninterested in promotion yet supremely effective and efficient, were allowed to remain undisturbed. Provided they were fortunate enough to have some strong-minded senior officer on district with sufficient muscle to plead a special case successfully. Regarded as indispensable and irreplaceable, worthy of fighting hard to retain in post, because these very qualities were used by the senior officer himself to enhance his own career.

On the evidence so far available to Smith, Marrasey seemed to be within that category. As if to support that finding, Marrasey emerged from a small annexe at the end of the office bearing coffee on a tray. A stupid conclusion, based on very slim evidence, thought Smith, critical of himself. Yet there was nothing ingratiating about the way Marrasey punctiliously served cups to the two typists before pouring one for Smith. The girls thanked him, calling him, respectfully, Mr Marrasey. It was that fact more than the appearance of the coffee that convinced Smith, Marrasey was that rare creature, 'a special case.' Marrasey waited until Smith had taken a couple of sips from his coffee cup then asked, 'Would you consider having me run the System, sir?'

Smith could see the request coming even before it was made. He had been right about Marrasey, he was a dedicated outer-district man, parochial, concerned only about his own manor, but concerned to see it was not abused or despoiled by uncontrolled crime. A man so involved with the ground he had worked that he could not fully surrender his grip on it. Maintaining contact by taking on the job of clerical officer. A job for an eighteen-year-old kid or a stolid steady retired P.C. Marrasey could have gone out and earned four times what he was getting now as a security officer with a public company.

'You're a civil servant . . . Mr Marrasey,' he felt obliged to give him the same respect as the typists. 'Apart from anything else, I couldn't authorize the overtime involved.'

'That wouldn't arise, sir, I never approved of overtime payment for C.I.D. officers when they brought it in. I never claimed it then, and I wouldn't do so now.'

'That's just the point. You're no longer a C.I.D. officer, no longer a D.I. Things have changed, you can't opt out of overtime or anything else. You'd have your union on your back, and on mine.'

'I am not a member of the union. The civil service isn't a closed shop, at least the clerical side of it. I wouldn't be here now if I had to be a member of a union. But what I should point out, sir, is that apart from Mr O'Brien and Chief Inspector Lomax, who is dealing with a very involved complaint against police, the rest of your staff are not very experienced. We've had the usual crop of domestic murders and the odd spontaneous street killings over the past few years, but nothing involved, nothing complex. Nothing that needed the build-up of a good System. Nothing that would give any of them the experience.'

'And you have it? The experience?'

'The towpath killings, the nude murders, the Templeford torso, the Selby kidnapping – you remember, sir, they sent her fingers to the husband, one by one?' Smith remembered, remembered them all, classic cases, the sort you only get on the outer districts. Like the one he had now? Another classic for the district?

'I ran the System on the last two. Got a Commissioner's commendation on both of them.' No boastful claim from Marrasey, just a simple statement of fact.

Smith got to his feet. 'You can keep it going; for the time being at least. Then I'll have to think about it. In the meantime, I want actions in the book for a uniform and C.I.D. operation on the roads around the scene tomorrow morning from two hours before the shooting until two hours afterwards. Everything and everybody to be stopped and questioned as to whether –'

Marrasey was turning over the pages in the Action Book. 'I have that in, sir. Action number 16.' He showed Smith the neat copperplate. 'I'm just waiting for the names of the uniform officers to be deputed from downstairs. I'll get a detailed briefing typed up for each of them.'

I bet you will, you cunning sod. You're at your old indispensable best, aren't you? But Smith contained the words in his head and uttered others sharply. 'I want a sight of the draft briefing before distribution. Understood?'

'Yes, of course, sir.' Respectful submission in tones of approval. Smith acknowledged them with a friendly, firm, 'Keep it going then, I'll be at the mortuary.'

He did not go direct to the mortuary as there was still some time before Simonson was due at one o'clock. Instead he took a tour round the residential area near the Common, needing to know the lie of the land. When the statements started coming in, it would be important to know the references and locations mentioned by witnesses. Witnesses! At five in the morning in an area like this? He should be so lucky. Not even the milkman or the paper boy would be about that early. The houses, in their one and two acres of ground, lay well back from the tree-lined unmade private roads. Roads rutted and potholed; the defensive terrain of the upper middle class. Houses with burglar-alarm boxes hanging under the eaves, as threatening as wasps' nests. Stockbroker-belted in gravel drives, Company-perquisited in pantiles and double glazing; large open garages one-upping in the two-car game with B.M.W. *and* Alfa Romeo.

He saw a young woman emerge from a wrought-iron-gated

driveway, stuffing familiar statement forms into her document case, and guessed her to be O'Brien's statutory woman detective engaged on the house-to-house. Leaving the car he went up and told her who he was. She eyed him with some hostility, obviously sussing a Press ploy, and demanded sight of his warrant card. Even after he had produced it, some hostility remained. She introduced herself with clear deliberation as Detective Sergeant Elstow. No mention of her first name, omitting the usual prefix of 'Woman' Detective Sergeant. Well, that was obvious; or was it? He took in the shining but cropped hair, a white unadorned blouse, the severe skirt and jacket, the sensible shoes and thought it was a pity because she had a nice open face despite the frown. And good legs holding up a trim body.

'Have you come up with anything, Miss Elstow?' He did it deliberately, idly provocative, interested in her reaction.

'Sergeant Elstow, if you don't mind, sir.' He expected icy reproof, and was prepared to laugh it off, but again he was given the condescending, ignorant-child treatment. Who the hell did they think they were out here?

'Have you come up with anything, Elstow?' The gravel in his voice abraded her cheeks to a vivid scarlet. She battled with conflicting disciplines and subdued the personal one.

'I've got seven witnesses who heard shots. Only one of them is in any way specific. The one who phoned up in the first place, a retired colonel. He describes them, the shots . . .' She searched in her document case for the statement; the crimson was receding quickly, her face paler than before, her eyes bright. He thought maybe he had got her wrong but waited for her to continue. She scanned the pages, eyelids blinking rapidly. He had definitely got her wrong.

'The witness is Colonel Rees-Fraser, he has a D.S.O. and M.C.'

'All colonels have them, my dear.' It was his turn to be condescending. She failed to bite.

'He states that at 0502 hours he was in bed when he heard, to use his term, a single volley of controlled musketry.'

'Was he awake or asleep when he heard the shots?'

'He was awake. He suffers from arthritis. He got up and looked out towards the Common – he is certain the shots came from there. He phoned police using an extension by the bedroom window. He sat down by the window until 0600 hours.' She gave a quick upward glance at his face, saw its impassivity and went hurriedly on. 'The colonel saw the police cars arriving, but no other vehicles or persons on foot passed during the time he was at the window. Of the other witnesses, all were asleep or lightly dozing. Their descriptions of the shots run from car backfires to penetrating cracks and bangs. Three of them went to their windows for a look, saw nothing and returned to bed. Of those who remained awake for any period, none heard any vehicles passing or people walking about.' She was quite composed now, her face set, the reiteration of her report a tuneless monotone.

'You've got some good negative information in the statements, Elstow.' He was not prepared to let her off the hook just yet, but he allowed a hint of praise to enter his voice. 'Even though most of these houses lie fifty or sixty feet back from the road, you can't drive along here other than in low gear with the suspension thumping into the potholes. Somebody should have heard something, even through double glazing. If it comes up like this on the other roads round the Common it could be interesting.'

'You will appreciate, sir, I haven't seen all the occupants; most of the male members left for business before the house-to-house commenced. I'll pick them up on return visits this evening.'

He resisted a strong temptation to ask how many male members she had to pick up. Instead he simply said, 'I do appreciate that, Elstow.' As if to prove his earlier point, a white open-topped Mercedes sports came down the road weaving from side to side as the woman driver tried to avoid the deeper depressions. A grizzling three-year-old child was strapped in beside her. She, young, with a face of porcelain, had a swan neck swathed in green silk and her blonde hair armoured like a brass helmet. A Great Dane occupying the rear seat slavered at them with dull-eyed interest as it passed. A shrill voice, 'Oh dooooo be quiet, Peetikins. Mummy is doing her best to avoid the nasty bumpity bumpity bits.' The appeal seemed to have succeeded but only because a front wheel had lurched into a deeper rut, the impact depriving the child of breath. The crying started again with greater vigour than before, diminishing only with distance.

'What did your mummy call you when you were that kid's age, Elstow?' He tried to make it quizzically friendly, but it didn't work. The unpainted lips tightened for a moment, then words clattered out of them, clear and rounded, like balls of ice from a freezer. 'My mother called me Marion, sir. But it is not a form of address I wish to be known by in my professional capacity. I appreciate, in your position, you may deprive me of the dignity of addressing me by my rank but I will not be addressed in familiar terms by you or anyone else . . . sir.'

He took it quietly, with a nod of reluctant acceptance. There was nothing else he could do. He moved towards his car, then turned. 'That's fine, Elstow. When you become the first female Chief Constable in the world, just remember one thing.' She displayed some femininity by asking coldly, 'What would that be, sir?'

'When they dish out all your stars and crowns and laurel leaves and silver braid, they don't say "and here is a larger-than-ever dollop of dignity," Dignity and rank don't necessarily go together, Elstow. Either you've got it or you haven't. A good honest P.C. has a damn sight more dignity than a bad . . . Chief Superintendent?'

He watched her in the rear-view mirror as he bumped down the road; she was staring at the back of his car. Her face appeared to have reddened again.

Four

He got to the mortuary a little before one. O'Brien was there and the body was there still in its chair, with O'Brien and another detective unlashing two lengths of timber studding from the sides.

'You got his fingerprints on way?' He jerked a thumb at the corpse. O'Brien was still downcast. 'Yeh,' he said. 'We had to untie his hands, you know. There'll be hell to pay when . . .'

The door of the dissecting-room swung open, held speared on the rapier of Professor Simonson's furled umbrella. He stood for a moment to permit appreciation of his immaculate form, then entered, allowing the umbrella tip to slide from the door. It closed on its spring behind him.

'Ah, Smith, O'Brien, and?' He looked with spurious geniality on the third officer.

O'Brien supplied an answer. 'D.S. Blake, sir. He'll be Exhibits Officer.'

'Your photographer?'

'He's waiting in the office, sir. No, just coming through now, sir.' The photographer tried to emulate Simonson's performance with his tripod but out of necessity because he was additionally laden with a box of cameras. The varnish on the door was unkind to him; the metal legs slid on the smooth surface and the door banged into the photographer's face. The long thin scar that was Simonson's mouth curved in satisfaction.

'You people do realize, I am missing luncheon on your behalf?'

He spoke complainingly as if to expiate his pleasure in the photo-grapher's bruised nose.

'I'm told there is a pleasant little pub around the corner where they do an excellent Shepherds Pie. Would you care to join us afterwards, Professor?'

Simonson returned it with a cold eye. 'The prospect of sharing your plebian pabulum, Mr Smith, may in itself serve to assuage my hunger. Thank you, but no thank you.'

He turned his attention to the only disinterested man in the room, himself the now inanimate cause of all their interest and motivation. He walked round the seated body, bending to examine entry and exit wounds, pulling gently on the stiffened chin to determine the degree of rigor. Moving the arms, uttering thin little cries of 'Hmnnn' and 'Ahhh' to indicate interest and significance . . . Then, as if distracted by a loose tread in the progression of ascending logic, the cries changed to querulous and suspicious repetitions. 'Ehhh?' 'Ehhh?' 'Ehhh?' He began to sniff the air, porcine snout weaving about, sorting phenol from turpentine, formaldehyde from alcohol, until with a cry of triumph, he swooped down and heaved upwards on a rigid arm. Holding it by the wrist he took a long deliberate sniff at the fingers like a sommelier over a rancid cork. His head swung slowly towards Smith. 'You have contaminated my cadaver,' he snarled balefully. 'You've been taking fingerprints prior to my autopsy. This is unforgivable. The hands are awash in surgical spirit where you've cleaned off the finger-print ink. Did you imagine for one moment you could deceive me?'

'I'm sorry, Professor,' said Smith. 'You see, we have no ident on the body, and I wanted a good set before he stiffened up. If we get him identified quickly, if we can get him housed, we might get right on top of the job.' He knew he had explained the validity of his actions with less than justice and failed to dispel Simonson's outrage.

'And what about the fingernails?' asked Simonson, still affronted.

'One of the lab team got the scrapings beforehand . . . before we took the prints.' It was not uncommon, but generally done under the pathologist's supervision.

Simonson proffered his scalpel. 'Perhaps you would care to complete the autopsy?'

Smith held up placatory, fawning hands, tried obsequious words. 'I requested specifically, sir, that you perform the P.M. I knew at the outset, sir, that without your professional skill, my chances of clearing up this case would be remote. I just don't know in which direction to go until I have your findings.'

Simonson trained the double barrels of his twelve-bore nostrils on Smith, sniffed the sincerity of his words and grimaced at the pungent hypocrisy.

'The direction in which you go at this moment, Smith, is out of this mortuary – and take your corpulent colleague with you. Go to your pub round the corner and devour your bucolic pie. But get out of my sight.'

O'Brien attacked his pint glass with desperation, sighed in relief, and gave Smith a reproachful glance. 'Didn't work, did it?'

'What didn't work?'

'The B.B.B. formula you tried on Simonson.'

'What's the B.B.B. formula?' Smith sipped absently at his beer.

'Bullshit baffles brains.' O'Brien showed signs of exasperation. 'Come on, Guv, get on with it. Where's that old tact and diplomacy? You upset Mr Hessen this morning and now Simonson this afternoon.'

'In between I twisted the knickers off your Woman Detective Sergeant.'

'Oh, Christ, you ran into the Elstow?'

Smith nodded and took another slow pull on his glass. O'Brien finished his pint in gloomy silence.

'You should have warned me, George.'

'About the Elstow?'

'About the smell.'

'What smell?'

'The odour of sanctity. About Hessen being a bible-puncher. I asked you for the S.P. on him. You didn't mention he was a bible-puncher.'

O'Brien was indignant. 'But they all are! I thought you knew the way the job was going. If you're looking for the top, you don't join the knuckle-crunchers anymore; you join the Christian Police Association.' He waved for another pint. 'Haven't you seen the minutes on some of the files lately? You get a docket back these days and you're likely to read, "The reporting officer should remember Timothy 6,10." Nice and polite, as though anyone just might have overlooked the significance of Timothy 6,10.' He pushed his glass to one side to make space for a supporting elbow on the bar before he went on. 'I put up a report last week on a minor complaint against police. A right load of rubbish. I recommended no action against the three officers. You know what Mr Hessen said in his minute?'

'I can't wait to hear.'

'He wrote, "I disagree. Action as in Daniel 3,20 would be more appropriate." '

'And what did it say? Daniel 3,20?'

'Something about commanding the mighty men in the army to tie up three heathens and heave them into a fiery furnace.'

'Shadrach, Meshach and Abed-nego.'

O'Brien looked at Smith admiringly. 'I should have known you were well in touch, Guv.'

Smith shook his head in rebuttal. 'No, it's just that I got an O-level in religious studies. It keeps coming back like a song . . . a song of Solomon.'

He went over and savoured the Shepherds Pie simmering on the lunch counter, then returned to O'Brien.

'It smells good. Now what does one drink with Shepherds Pie?'

O'Brien looked at his beer, puzzled. 'What have you got in mind, Guv?'

'The road to a pathologist's heart is straight up through the gut.' Smith went back to the landlord's wife. She listened, smiled, and returned to the kitchen.

Simonson examined the bottle of Nuits Saint Georges with care. 'It's a good year,' he admitted reluctantly. 'And the shipper fairly reputable . . . What on earth is that fellow up to?' At the far end of the mortuary, O'Brien was covering a table with a white cloth on which he placed glasses, plates and cutlery. With something of a flourish, he lifted the tinfoil from a dish of steaming Shepherds Pie. 'Luncheon is served,' he announced proudly.

'Would you care to join us, Professor?' asked Smith politely.

Wiping the last vestige of meat from his plate with a piece of French bread, Simonson said, 'I must admit, Smith,' he held the morsel between finger and thumb for a moment, before delicately placing it in his mouth, 'that your timing was a matter of psychological perfection, catching me as you did, after completion of my work, in a rare moment of indecision about where to lunch at this late hour. Producing as you did, an excellent wine . . . An act of contrition?' The enquiry was benign. Smith lowered his head in submissive acknowledgement. 'And introducing me to such a delicious concoction as Shepherds Pie. A dish, I must confess, I thought synonymous with soggy cabbage, incinerated beef and all the other abominations of *la cuisine anglaise*.'

'Like a good wine, its origins have to be chosen with care,' warned Smith.

'Or like a good forensic pathologist, eh?'

Smith assumed that the muffled sound escaping from Simonson's lips was laughter, and offered his own in token agreement. O'Brien, endeavouring to enhance the convivial atmosphere, offered Simonson a cigar. Sight of the band was sufficient to justify refusal, but the rejection was courteous enough. Smith took full advantage. 'Am I right in thinking what we have here is a sort of firing-squad execution?'

Simonson seized upon his careless use of words. 'What we have here, is some sort of firing-squad *murder*. To describe it as an execution implies a degree of legality. However, I will subscribe to the general modus and agree that the shots were fired by more than one person, as the paths of two of the shots entered the back from opposing angles. As if from the flanks of a firing squad. Five shots struck and went out through the chest. I found none inside the victim. Three bullets had penetrated the heart and death was instantaneous.' Simonson helped himself to the last of the wine, pouring carefully. 'It was most efficiently done. Perhaps someone read my paper.' Simonson placed his ego on casual display.

Smith nurtured the incipient growth. 'May I ask what your paper dealt with, Professor?'

Simonson hesitated, as if considering the lustre of his pearls before casting them. 'I fail to see any harm in it, after all it was a purely gratuitous gesture on my part, nothing subject to the Act. A public service.' He lifted his glass to a gaping codlike mouth and threw the contents into the back of his throat.

'You see,' he went on, 'during the last debate on the restoration of capital punishment, I saw that what fogged the issue was the emotive question of hanging, as being the recognized and traditional means of dispatch. It was the barbaric ritual attached to a hanging that our parliamentary masters could not stomach. That, and the method. Trussing someone up, putting a rope round their neck and dropping them into a void. Too many people involved . . . too personal, they felt, the politicians, their own collective hands grasping the lever, heaving it over. It was this that had previously turned them against capital punishment, not a question of the justice of a death sentence *per se*, and certainly not the practicality of it. So I, in the rôle of a detached and objective observer, put up a paper to Home Office suggesting a means by which a death sentence could be carried out in an expeditious manner with no human presence or involvement at the time and place of execution . . . Other than the condemned, of course.'

Simonson's ego was now in full bloom, needing no stimulus other than a closely attentive nod of Smith's head.

'It merely required the condemned person to be strapped to a specially designed chair,' continued Simonson. 'Similar to the way in which we found our chappie on the table.' He gave a careless gesture over his shoulder to where the remains of the remains lay shrouded.

'He, or she, would have to be secured in a much more rigid posture, of course, but the only human contact would be in affixing the straps. The rest would be a button-pushing operation carrying the chair along rails to an adjoining execution chamber where it would come to rest completing a circuit and effecting the immediate discharge of, say, four to six rounds of heavy-calibre shot from electrically triggered firearms; previously adjusted and aimed according to the earlier ascertained organic placement of the vic . . . the condemned person's heart. There would be total destruction of the heart, death would be instantaneous and certified by electrodes within the frame of the chair and the readings remotely recorded. The charge used need not be heavy to avoid complete penetration of the chest cavity and could be adequately silenced to prevent any disturbing noise. There would be little haemorrhaging, and that could be contained by fitting an absorbent pad. Afterwards the body could be conveyed hydraulically or electrically to a lower or upper level and cremated. In all, simple, humane and efficient. But execution, my dear Smith. Not murder.'

The thoughtful ensuing silence was broken by O'Brien. 'By rights, the cremation should be carried out on a lower level,' he said. Simonson looked to Smith for more mature comment. 'Not only simple, humane and efficient, but also very hygienic,' he said without a trace of irony. 'Tell me, Professor. what response did you get from Home Office?'

'Oh, they couldn't fault the mechanics of my proposals. However, the civil servants objected on the grounds of cost; mainly the cost of policing demonstrations against capital punishment outside the prisons. Carefully omitting to mention the hundreds of thousands it costs to keep one lifer incarcerated. The political side, although they didn't say so in as many words, hadn't the guts to put my scheme forward for debate. Politicians are quite prepared to discuss capital punishment in the abstract; as a consequence of law, but horrified to say openly how it should properly be done. I said as much to the Home Secretary. He was quite miffed. Became rather offensive – or tried to be, within the exceedingly limited parameters of his powers of expression.'

'The road to hell is paved with good intentions.' Smith endeavoured to give genuine sympathy.

Simonson accepted it dubiously, but bitter memories with higher priority prevailed. 'I should have known better than attempt to perform a public service without payment. Politicians always suspect the motives of one endeavouring to serve the commonweal simply as a matter of duty.'

Smith recklessly extended further condolences. 'Knighthoods have been given for less noble work.' When the only response from Simonson was a modest, deprecating shrug, he offered a silent grace to Bacchus for the mellowing effect of good wine.

Smith, realizing he had been impetuous enough – and lucky to get away with it – took the matter no further. Simonson's discourse on justifiable homicide had little relevance to his own problems. Simonson himself seemed to realize he had made a descent into a level of almost friendly familiarity with the unqualified and the scientifically illiterate . . . And was possibly corrupted by them? No, that was impossible.

He got to his feet, extended his hand, and with it the benefits of his doubts, to Smith. 'Thank you for the lunch. Most enjoyable. Now, a few points from my examination you might find helpful.'

He was again coldly professional. 'As to the victim's age? Without further tests one cannot be precise, but not less than sixty or more than seventy-five. I will supply a more exact figure in three or four days. I closed his jaw against the rigor, by severing the temporo-mandibular joints from inside, and this with a few drops of glycerine in the eyes will give your photographer a reasonably lifelike picture of the face. No doubt it will smile upon the nation on tomorrow's newscast, and prove a more practical means of identification than your trespass on his fingers.' Simonson sharply reopened the old wound and Smith responded with a suitably pained expression. Satisfied, Simonson continued. 'He has worn glasses for some years. You saw the bridge marks on his nose, I presume? No matter, did you find his glasses?'

'No.'

'Then without the formula, enquiry of opticians will not help you.' Don't state the obvious, Professor, Smith spoke with his eyes. Simonson was too preoccupied to observe the frown.

'In late youth or early in adult life, he underwent surgery for a depressed fracture of the skull. I recognize the trephine work: Dobson-Pringle. Before my time but I know his plate. He died in 1942, predeceasing most of his patients. Dobson-Pringle was quite good – for a brain surgeon.' From Simonson, such grudging praise was the supreme accolade.

'What hospital did he work for?' asked Smith.

Simonson almost reeled at his appalling ignorance. 'Dobson-Pringle was a Consultant Surgeon. He demonstrated his skills in those theatres that suited his convenience, provided they had adequate facilities. Your victim may have been operated on in any major teaching hospital in Europe.'

Simonson moved on to other things.

'Dentures. He had partial dentures, top and bottom. Good expensive work, none of your ill-fitting National Health rubbish. Probably foreign in origin, but I will get my dental people to give you a fuller picture. As to aspects physiological; he has lived in the tropics for some years. Apart from progressive reduction of melanin – skin pigment; the stuff stupid idiots destroy by exposing their bodies to the sun, and wind up with skin cancer – there are indications in the spleen and liver of malaria. And not just ordinary malaria, M.T. malaria. Malignant tertiary malaria. Until I do some histology on the tissue samples I cannot commit myself, but it looks that way. The thing about it is, that although M.T. malaria is found in South America and Asia, it is commonest in Africa. My bet would be Africa. I suppose I'm influenced by the dentistry, lot of gold fillings, typically South African. But he didn't catch his malaria in the south, must have been further north. Any one of the dozen or so African states ten degrees north and south of the equator.'

Simonson paused to ensure his words had sunk home. 'Now assuming his fingerprints are not on record and nobody identifies his picture, where does that leave you, Mr Smith?'

'Up the well-known creek without a paddle,' said Smith sadly.

Simonson relished Smith's despair. 'Little I can add to raise your hopes.' He spoke in what, for him, were tones of gay banter. 'There is what I first thought to be a small bruise under his upper arm. Turned out to be a very old and faded tattoo. Some sort of linear motif, barely distinguishable. I've sliced it off. Let you know if I can make anything out of it under the microscope.'

Five

✦✦✦✦✦✦✦

By late afternoon, the Scenes of Crime Section in the Fingerprint Department had completed their searches and a teleprinter message reached Smith. 'Main collection and Scenes of Crime collection examined. No trace. No record of your victim.'

He had expected a negative result. For although he was investigating the gravest crime in the calendar, he could not avoid the feeling that this was a crime not involving criminals. That is so in nearly all murders. Yet this one involved a gang, a team. A firm. At least five-handed. It involved a squad; a firing squad. Reluctantly he turned his mind to the I.R.A. and phoned Paddy Donnelly, the Royal Ulster Constabulary's liaison officer with the Anti-Terrorist Squad at the Yard. He put a couple of questions to him.

'Well now, yes, it definitely does not sound like an I.R.A. job in my eyes,' said Donnelly in his Irish fashion. 'In the first place, they wouldn't go to all that trouble and palaver unless they were going to claim responsibility. Now, they haven't claimed responsibility so I would say they were not responsible.'

'What have you got in the second place?' asked Smith.

'Ah, well now. In the second place, the gombeens couldn't have found their way to your remote outpost of the metropolis without getting lost half a dozen times.'

'Maybe that's what happened, Paddy. Maybe that's how they came to wind up here.' He replaced the phone, leaving Donnelly to think about it.

At nine-thirty in the evening Marrasey, still as neat and dapper as he had been in the morning, reported that all immediate actions had been allocated and formally asked permission to go home. Smith thanked him and agreed. The question of whether or not Marrasey would continue to run the System was not raised.

At 9.43 p.m., Woman Detective Sergeant Elstow came in. She took out her quota of statements, marked up the appropriate entries in the Action Book 'Statements Obtained', clipped the forms neatly together and placed them in the numerators tray. Then she went to the blackboard and made note of the action numbers she had been allocated for later completion. Next she opened the Duty Book, glanced at her watch and wrote herself off duty at 9.50 p.m.

Smith had watched her deliberate precise performance through the half-open door of his office. As she closed the Duty Book he called out, 'Sergeant Elstow!'

She turned, her face set, and spoke with polite but defiant inflection. 'Yes, sir?' Indirect apology not accepted. She came into his office. He did not invite her to sit.

'Any of your witnesses see or hear anything in the way of a vehicle? People on foot?'

'No, sir. At least not immediately after the shots. The earliest vehicle seen and heard was a green Rover at 7.30 a.m. I've traced the owner, he was local and leaves for business at that time every morning. In addition, I've seen each person who went to work by car. The movement of people and vehicles going out in the morning follows a fairly consistent pattern. The people know each other, at least in the sense that they see one another regularly. Nobody saw any strange vehicles or pedestrians. I've also seen the milkman, and the paper-boy. They say the same. No strangers. No unknown vehicles.'

'The rest of the house-to-house on the other side of the Common produced much the same results. What should we deduce from that, Elstow?' He withdrew his apology.

'That they concealed themselves on the edge of the Common and waited until there were quite a few people about then casually slipped away. The usual burglar's trick, sir.'

'But there were at least five of them, Sergeant, and by six a.m. the Common was crawling with coppers. We'll have to do better than that.'

She blushed slightly, a delightfully suffused pink. Nothing angry about it, Smith was pleased to note. Totally feminine. 'I really don't see what else I can suggest, sir. I have been as thorough as I know how.' There was something of a plea in her voice and that increased his pleasure.

'Were any of your houses unoccupied, up for sale, occupants on holiday? Particularly those backing on to the Common.'

'There is Green Briars. It has been up for sale for some time.' She saw the possibility and said defensively, 'I walked round the outside. Admittedly only to see if it had been vandalized. The ground-floor windows are boarded up. The place was intact, solid. I'm certain of that. No sign of a break-in.'

'A good set of twirls and they're in. Are they not?' He posed the question firmly.

She reached down and fiddled with the clasp of the handbag primly held against her thighs, brought out a handkerchief and touched her nostrils, delicately, thoughtfully.

'Do you want me to get hold of some men and break in? Check the inside?' She uttered a cold challenge.

Smith raised horrified brows. 'Sergeant Elstow, are you suggesting I incite you to commit criminal damage and trespass? In this day and age?'

'There is power under Section 2, Sub-Section 6, Criminal Law Act 1967. Reasonable cause to suspect persons who have committed an arrestable offence may be inside. That should cover us.' She answered as if it was a question on a promotion examination.

'Reasonable cause to suspect? It's a possibility, no more. No, Elstow, the prospect of a pension doth make cowards of us all. At least of me, at this particular time. I have been exiled to the green and pleasant land of Outer District, to re-learn the book and proceed according to its holy word. You know the estate agent handling the sale, Sergeant Elstow?' He re-offered his apology.

She nodded, half-smiling. In triumph?

'Then be on his doorstep, first thing in the morning. Request him – implore him – to send a representative to Green Briars with the keys in order that we may lawfully examine the interior in furtherance of our enquiries. Also arrange for a lab team to be waiting outside the gates. Got that? Then goodnight, Sergeant Elstow, and may chaste dreams enhance your slumber.'

She almost grinned. An overture of friendship? Or was it an incipient sneer of contempt? 'Goodnight, sir.' Then, tartly, 'You are a better detective than you are a poet.'

At 10.20 p.m. O'Brien came back from interviewing a caller at the counter, who had come to say he could solve the case. He threw the statement into the tray with exaggerated disgust. 'The first nutter. Says it's down to the same people who are controlling him by cosmic rays. I had to blast him into earth orbit. Come on, Guv. Just time for a quick pint at the pub across the road.' Idly, Smith waved him away and grumpily O'Brien departed.

At 10.35 p.m. a voice echoed round the empty outside office. 'Anyone about?' Smith opened his door. A stooped figure in an old gaberdine raincoat was perusing the Duty Book. Long shaggy grey hair sprouted from the back of an otherwise bald head, like a halo. 'Oh, hullo, Owen,' the man said, 'I was beginning to wonder if the enforced eight-hour day also applied to murder enquiries. That the day of the nine-to-five detective had arrived.'

Smith waved Tom Palmer into his office, got out the scotch bottle and two glasses. Palmer sat down, gathering his voluminous coat across his knees.

'The same amount again,' he said, as Smith held the water jug poised over his glass. 'From what I hear you're back in murder exotica again. A sticker?'

Smith spread his palms. 'Looks that way. No ident on the body yet.' He reached into the desk drawer and produced five little plastic bags.

Palmer presented one to the light bulb and said, 'Huh huh.' Then taking the bullet from the bag, and holding it between finger and thumb, he said, 'Huh huh' again and went on, 'I haven't seen one of these for a long time.'

'What are they?'

'Point three-o-three ball. Standard British army calibre from the eighteen-eighties until 1957. This could have been manufactured any time between, say, 1918 and 1956.'

'That narrows the field considerably, Tom. Thanks a lot,' said Smith sourly, and took his whisky neat.

Palmer ignored the sarcasm. Emptying out the other bullets on the desk, he stood them in a neat line, then bent down to align them before his eyes. 'Oh, your horizons are going to be widened to an even greater extent, Owen.' His right hand fumbled deep in the pocket of his coat and came out with a small magnifier. The finger and thumb of his left hand produced a pair of rubber-tipped tweezers from his waistcoat pocket. Each bullet came under the glass, and was returned to its precise position. Taking a slow sip of whisky between examination of each bullet, he said 'Huh huh' and returned the magnifying glass to the depths of his pocket and his empty whisky glass to the vicinity of Smith's bottle.

'Well now, Owen,' he raised his recharged glass in salute, 'I can, with reasonable certainty, eliminate all the hundreds of thousands of Vickers machine guns and Bren guns, all of which were chambered to take this calibre bullet. For each bullet was fired from a rifle, the same make of rifle, but five different rifles. Once I get these to the Lab and under a proper microscope, I can probably eliminate the odd million or so Lee Metfords, American Springfields, Canadian Ross and P.14s, which were chambered for .303 and have varying land and groove characteristics, which will – or will not – take them out of the picture. That leaves us with the great and magnificent Short Magazine Lee Enfield rifle. The real Angel of Mons. An angel of death, but it saved the B.E.F. in 1914.' He took another drink to endorse his sentiments.

'We can discount the earlier Marks before the Rifle No. 1 – Mark III of 1907, as used in the First and to a large extent in the Second World War. The rifle was developed through various Marks up to Mark VI, when it was simplified for ease of production in 1939 and became Rifle No. 4, Marks I and II. There were various other adaptations, Owen. I won't confuse you with them. But in brief, all you've got to do is to find five S.M.L.E.s out of around ten million manufactured . . . Give or take a couple of million,' he added encouragingly.

'But they're all museum pieces by now,' Smith protested.

'By no means.' Palmer winced at the thought of such disregard. 'A lot are still in operational use in Africa. At least, in the few African states the Russians and Chinese haven't Kalashnikoved. India, Pakistan . . . Quite a few kicking about there. Back in the late fifties and early sixties, we sold a million or so to dealers in the States. You could buy a good S.M.L.E. for ten dollars.' Another wince, this time at the thought of such waste.

'Try and confine it at least to the U.K., Tom,' pleaded Smith.

'Well, I imagine the Army have retained quite a few for emergencies. In case of need for another Home Guard. Arms dealers, rifle clubs and the like, have probably got quite a few. That should be easy to check. God knows how many ex-squaddies from the War have an illegal souvenir under the bed . . . Soldier's best friend, his rifle.' The afterthought provided a sad pause for reflection. Palmer took another drink. 'Want some advice, Owen? Don't bother your backside trying to get them by chasing rifles. It's a waste of time. Find the people first. Then you'll find the rifles . . . if they still exist.'

'What about ammunition?'

'Same applies. Plenty of it about. Even though they stopped U.K. manufacture in the sixties. If you had found a cartridge case it would have been stamped with the year of manufacture. Not that it would have helped much.'

Smith poured more whisky and sank back in his chair. Respecting his reverie, Palmer allowed his interest to dwell on the scene-of-crime photographs lying on Smith's desk. Taking them up he flicked idly through them until, on reaching those taken in the mortuary, he stopped, peered closely, fumbled again for his magnifier, and took it, and his eye, down almost to the surface of the print. Raising his head, he pursed his lips and began cooing like an outraged wood pigeon. 'You know what you've got here, Owen?'

'It's an old tattoo. Simonson took the skin off to see if he could make out the design.'

'I *know* the design, Owen.' Palmer scratched two jagged parallel lines on Smith's blotter. Smith levered himself halfway out of the chair, then sank back slowly.

'I've seen that in military histories. The S.S. You sure?'

'I've seen it in the flesh, Owen.' Palmer was smiling, almost youthful, his eyes sparkling as they raced back through decades of time. '*Das Schutzstaffel*.' He licked anticipatory lips. 'One of the *Blut und Boden* boys. Oh, he must have been long overdue, Owen.'

'What's this *Blut und Boden* stuff? Does it help to identify him?'

Palmer sank back in his chair, dismissing his resurgent prime in a short burst of sardonic laughter. '*Blut und Boden*. Blood and Soil. The . . . what? . . . the atheistic Nazi version of *Gott mit Uns* . . . the deification of Aryan purity. Identify him? Well, it cuts the odds. But it's going to be difficult to find out how many S.S. men are still around.'

'Well, at least it gives me his nationality.' Smith began formulating in his mind a message to Interpol, Wiesbaden.

'Not necessarily.' Palmer cut him sharply adrift. 'He need not necessarily be German.'

'How come? And how come you know so much about them, Tom?'

The spark rekindled in Palmer's eyes and he drank deeply of the Scotch. There was a hint of expansive loquacity to come. 'Are you ignorant of the military career and derring doings of Thomas Palmer, Warrant Officer Class II, in the great I am Corps?' He pointed a forefinger at an invisible rank badge on his forearm, and in a rich regimental voice said, 'What do you think this is, laddie? The top off a Fry's cocoa-tin?'

Smith played along by standing stiffly to attention and saying, 'Yes, sir. No, sir. Three bags full, sir. And kiss me goodnight, Sergeant Major.'

They laughed it off, sliding into embarrassed grins at their own childish behaviour. Smith waited for Palmer to continue. Eventually he did. 'Towards the end of the War, I was in the Intelligence Corps with the War Crimes Commission. We had a lot to do with the S.S. Dear me, dear me, a *lot* to do with the S.S.' His mild imprecations held the poignancy of a forgotten pain, slowly remembered. Uttering a short analgesic grunt, he gathered his coat around him as if preparing for his long journey back through time.

'The S.S., the *Schutzstaffel*, was formed in the early days of Nazi rule to counter the growing power of the S.A. The *Sturmabteilung*, the Brown Shirts, the original Nazi bully-boys. The S.S. did their first slaughterhouse job on the S.A. just to show what they really could do, given a war, a few conquered countries and their indigenous Jewish population. They became the Führer's personal bodyguard, then expanded this rôle to control internal security throughout Germany. They formed their own Intelligence Bureau, the S.D., the *Sicherheitsdienst*. One object was to keep tabs on the *Abwehr*, the military intelligence service.

'Long before the war started, they had already liquidated quite a few German generals and other Staff officers who were beginning to think Hitler was a boil on Germany's arsehole that had to be lanced. They ran the concentration camps. They formed S.S. divisions that were *of* the German army but not *in* the German army. Incidentally, you must distinguish the Waffen S.S. from the general S.S. When the war came along the Waffen S.S. Divisions fought like tigers. Fanatical tigers, perhaps, but tigers. And some of the S.S. regiments acted quite honourably towards the conquered peoples. Provided they weren't Jewish, of course.' He lingered quietly for a time, in a sombre grey past, then returned with a start as if from a nightmare. 'So,' he barked the word, sundering his dream, 'given the overt and covert fascists existing in non-German Europe before the war, all these and more, imbued by the *Blut und Boden* ideal, came to the surface after the conquest of Europe. From Spitzbergen to Marseille, from Brest to Kharkov, the *Blut und Boden* beast came out in various national forms. We had one of our own, The British Free Corps . . .

Recruited from P.O.W.s . . . Didn't amount to much. But they were all controlled by the S.S. All in the general S.S. The S.S. wasn't just an élite organization within the Nazi party. It became the Nazi party. It became Germany.' Palmer's craggy but fleshy face folded back into melancholy corroded canyons.

'Were they all tattooed like this?' Smith asked. 'Everybody in the S.S.?'

'Christ, no. Only senior ranks. *Sturmbahnnführer* and above. Even then, not with the double flash. Only their blood group. The others? Well, a few had the double flash put on. Exhibitionists in the lower echelons. Like soldiers in any army. Like your victim! But the practice was frowned on as non-German. Non-Aryan.' He looked again at the photographs of the corpse. 'I doubt if the bastard is entitled to be called a victim.'

'So the odds are he is German?'

'The odds are,' said Palmer, helping himself to the bottle. 'But you'd better cover the outside chance by sending his prints and picture throughout the Interpol networks, which, of course, cuts your chances on the most likely ident source east of the Curtain because as you know they ain't in Interpol. And most of the non-German S.S. were recruited there – Estonia, Latvia and the Ukraine. And another thing, I'd keep the S.S. angle well under your hat. There are very few Germans who will admit to knowing an S.S. man, let along being one.'

'What about records? The Germans were great ones for keeping personnel records.'

'The S.D. records went up in smoke. Those that didn't the Russians got hold of . . . and hung on to.'

At 11.20 pm, Commander Hessen bounded into the office like an avalanche. 'Hallo, Owen. Still about? Good show. Any developments? . . . Why Tom, haven't seen you in a coon's age.' Palmer blinked rapidly to Smith for assistance over his vigorously shaken shoulder.

'You know Carey Hessen of course, Tom, the District Commander? He's a great admirer of your work.'

'Ah, yes, of course,' said Palmer vaguely. 'The Saudi Embassy shooting, wasn't it?' A tentative and erroneous assumption. Smith made another rescue attempt. Holding up the remains of the bottle, he asked, 'Would you care for a drink, sir?'

Sight of the bottle chilled the bonhomie. 'No, thank you, Owen.' Hessen pulled himself upwards into Commander form.

'You chaps go ahead if you must.' The condescension verged on pity. 'I always believe in doing one's job without alcoholic inspiration. Crutches are for cripples, Owen.' He made for the door. 'Just wanted you to know I'm still about if you need anything.' The door quivered in lingering condemnation.

'One for the road, Tom?' said Smith as if there had been no interruption.

Six

♦♦♦♦♦

Apart from Mr Marrasey, the office was empty when Smith arrived at 8.30 a.m. on the second day of the investigation. 'Nobody in yet?' he barked, disturbing the dull ache behind his eyes, causing it to pulsate and swell.

'They have been in and gone out, sir. Some to the road blocks . . . others to the scene of this action you instigated last night after I left. At Green Briars, the unoccupied house.' He seemed mildly put out by initiative taken in his absence.

'I thought Sergeant Elstow was taking care of that on her own? With the Lab team.'

'Mr O'Brien anticipated the possibility of the people we're after being still in there. He took the rest of the squad down there . . . Armed, sir.' Another hint of disapproval in Marrasey's voice when he said 'armed'.

Smith was not altogether displeased. It was a possibility. Maybe O'Brien was right. He should have thought of it himself. Had his head not been full of millions of Lee Enfield rifles and thousands of uniformed S.S. men, goose-stepping inside his skull, he would have thought of it himself. Or would he? No alcoholic inspiration there. 'Crutches are for cripples?'

Marrasey offered coffee. He refused it, assuaging his guilt like a masochistic sinner, saying, 'I'm going down there. To Green Briars. Won't be long.'

The house was a Victorian monstrosity. A roofline heaving with cupolas, domes, castellations, fretted balconies, brown peeling paintwork and ornate chimney-pots. Below, curved bays clad in decaying stucco supported the upper windows, uncurtained yet blind. At ground level the windows were protectively coffined in plywood, buried in walls drowning in a sea of ivy. The limestone portico struggled to keep a few inches of its dark grey Gothic columns above the clutching growth.

Under the portico, O'Brien was in argument with a young man encased in a waist-hugging suit, trouser-bottoms flaring aggressively over high-heeled boots. Both stopped talking to turn enquiring faces towards Smith's approaching car.

'What's the trouble?' asked Smith.

'This is Mr Victor from the estate agents.' O'Brien provided a huffy introduction. 'He wants to come in with us. I've told him it might be wiser to let us go in and have a look round first.'

'I am responsible to my principals for the house and contents. My principals would be most annoyed if anything was broken. This is a very valuable property.'

'You could have fooled me,' said O'Brien casting a jaundiced eye round the desolate weed-choked grounds.

Smith raised a placating hand to smother Mr Victor's protests. 'No doubt my colleague, quite rightly, did not inform you why we think it wiser for the police to go in first.'

'No, he certainly did not,' replied Mr Victor indignantly, shaking a coiffeured head, ruffling the crest of a heat-blown wave.

'That is because he did not have my authority to do so,' explained Smith gently. 'But accepting you as a responsible person in a position of trust, I can tell you the reason is that there might be people inside who would shoot the first man across the threshold.'

Mr Victor wavered. 'Oh, I see,' he said.

'So while you are quite at liberty to come with us, I must tell you we cannot accept responsibility for your safety.' Smith placed a hand on Mr Victor's shoulder as though in farewell to a dear friend.

'In that case I withdraw my objections.' Mr Victor handed over the keys and formally closed the conversation by buttoning his tight-fitting jacket with precise dignity.

Smith took the keys, and with O'Brien went up to the massive oak door.

'Where are the others?'

'Back and sides.'

'You tooled up?' O'Brien opened his jacket showing the holstered Smith & Wesson. He withdrew it as Smith inserted the key.

'Will there be any shooting? Any damage?' A hesitant afterthought had struck a confused Mr Victor, calling from some distance down the drive.

'Don't worry,' O'Brien called back, 'we're trained to only shoot people.'

Smith pushed the door open into a dark hallway. The daylight penetrated to the foot of a wide staircase.

'Do you know when the house was last visited?' Smith stood recklessly framed in the doorway.

'They had a potential buyer looking around three weeks ago.' O'Brien joined him, gun in hand.

Smith was now inside the hall, running his fingers along a moulded shelf waist-high above oak panelling. He showed his fingertips to O'Brien. 'Clean as a whistle.'

'The bastards have been here all right. Question is, are they still here.' O'Brien edged towards a door in the panelling. 'According to Victor, the mains switches are in here. Let's have some light on the subject.'

Smith came in behind him and pulled his hand away from the main switch.

'They just might have forgotten about that.' The handle had a ribbed flange around its edge. He forced the switch up with the blade of a penknife. A shadowy brownish light came dimly from lamps set in the oak panelling.

'Get another couple of guns in here. Tell them to start at the top of the house and work down. We'll cover the hall.' He went over to a heavy straight-backed chair and sat down wearily.

Gone were the high spirits of the previous morning. He had allowed himself to be panicked by the fears of less experienced junior officers. If the riflemen had been here – and they had – they were not going to sit around waiting for him to find them. They had gone. Quietly, unobtrusively, merging with the commuter rat-race like good burglars would. But they were murderers!

The house was clean. At least, the ground-floor area was clean, as was the basement area. Kitchens, cellars, storerooms and boilerhouse had been systematically cleaned.

Mr Victor was pleased and surprised. Three weeks before, when he had brought in the potential buyer, it had been raining heavily and they had left muddy footmarks over the hall carpets.

He had intended coming back at a later date to vacuum them. 'But I've been simply rushed off my feet.'

'You haven't hoovered then?'

'No, definitely not.'

'Was there a Hoover in the house?' asked the leader of the Lab support group eagerly. Mr Victor obligingly produced the vacuum-cleaner from a cupboard. The Lab man fell on it, unzipped the cover, uttered a refined hiss of 'Oh, Sssherbet,' to express his chagrin at finding the dustbag missing. It was not in any of the dustbins at the back of the house, and no ash littered any of the fireplaces or the boiler to indicate that it had been burned. The downstairs area of the house had been cleaned. Not only the obvious upper surfaces, but the undersides of tables, chairs, fixtures and furnishings where the unwary tend to leave forgotten fingerprints: like on mains switches. But nothing, not even a useful glove mark was found.

Upstairs, the dust was undisturbed. Upstairs had been declared out of bounds by whoever had taken temporary occupancy of the house. The leader of the Lab team complained bitterly. 'It's all those confounded police documentaries on T.V. Clever-dick policemen showing how they did it. When what was done was done by others, who don't even get a mention.' For the leader of the Lab team was a civilian scientist, a back-room boy, whose day in court never received credit comparable with the value of his evidence. He resented that fact, but more deeply he resented the ease with which the lay criminal had learned to forestall his efforts.

Smith accepted the failure of science more philosophically. For him as a detective there was a positive side to the negation of science. Indications of local knowledge were beginning to emerge. From the sandpit hidden in the middle of the Common, to this empty and isolated house. Those responsible for the killing had either taken a lot of trouble to find a suitable site for the execution . . . The execution? The murder! . . . Or knew of its existence. And that of the house? All right, an examination of the display boards in the estate agent's window could provide knowledge of the house. But why the house? Why was it necessary? Not merely as a place to hole up after the killing. Why indulge in such a thorough cleaning operation? The riflemen had been there before and after the killing. So had the victim . . . at least beforehand.

S.S. man? Old Tom Palmer, 'I doubt if the bastard is entitled to be called a victim.' He should have seen it before. The possibility had entered his gut when he drove round the area yesterday. Why hadn't it got through to his brain? Elstow! The intervention of rank-conscious, sex-proud Elstow. Sexually aware Elstow. At least he was sexually aware of her. Bitch. Get out of my mind and let me think.

The firing squad and the condemned man had all assembled at the old house, then, just before dawn, made their way through the grounds at the rear of the house, out to the Common, down into the sandpit. Ready – Aim – Fire. Afterwards back to the house to wait for a couple of hours. Not waiting idly, busily cleaning and polishing. Then out into the road to join the thickening traffic down to the throughway. Why had they come to his manor to carry out an execution? Damn it, a murder! Military-style reconnaissance to find a suitable site? Or local knowledge of its existence? Priority for the Action Book. 'Obtain details from estate agents of all persons who for any reason have shown interest in Green Briars.'

An agitated Mr Victor, waving inventory sheets, came upon Smith down in the cellar. 'There is something missing,' he said.

'I know,' replied Smith. 'One heavy oak kitchen chair. Victorian, I imagine. Not all that valuable, I would say.'

'It is in the inventory at forty-five pounds.' Mr Victor gave the impression that forty-five pounds was forty-five pounds.

'We'll give it back to you in due course. It's been damaged a bit, but by then it will have a history and should make three times the price at auction.' He gently led a confused Mr Victor back up the cellar steps and returned to where he had seen the faint but fresh scratch-marks on the stone floor. Something had been there. What? An old sideboard? A long packing-case? Something. Three sets of parallel marks. Overall length six feet. About two and a half feet wide. A bed? A camp bed? Possible. Probable. The penultimate resting-place of the condemned man? Did he eat a hearty breakfast? How long would it take the Lab to analyse the stomach contents? Not that it made much difference at this stage. Like five Lee Enfield rifles out of ten million, it was another card for the System. Later on it might be useful. But first, as old Tom had said, 'You'll have to find the people first. Then you'll find the rifles.' Yet as a prerequisite to finding the people, to finding the rifles, he had to find an identity for a dead man. A dead S.S. man?

He left the cellar and found Elstow sharing Mr Victor's dilemma over a sudden threefold increase in the value of damaged Victorian kitchen chairs. Telling Elstow to get in a pair of tracker dogs and supervise the handlers in a search of the grounds, he left to go back to the office. If she wanted equality, let her get her feet wet and her clothes messed up. Let her get her hands dirty and her face smeared. He had more important things to do. The media were coming in at eleven for a Press conference. How to play it? He wanted good coverage of the dead man's photograph. It had come out reasonably well. The eyes glittering, madly alive in a film of glycerine; lids held open with thin strips of touched-out Sellotape. Full, petulant, half-gaping lips closed by the same means. They had not succeeded so well with the mouth. The slack jaw hung against the invisible tapes as though caught in a moment before an insane scream. A hundred and fifty copies had been run off for circulation. Give them a little bit of drama. 'It is vitally important we ascertain the identity of this man.' Hold the picture up to the camera. 'Do you think you recognize him? If so, please telephone this number or get in touch with your local police. Any help we receive will be treated in confidence.' Give them a brief description of the corpse. Mention the skull operation. That should do it. Then would come the awkward questions. How was he shot? How many times? What kind of weapon? Any dangers in revealing these facts? Allowing the killers to know what he knew? They knew anyway. Allowing the nutters to embellish false confessions? A possibility. But he had never known a false confession that couldn't be broken. Or a genuine one that couldn't be corroborated.

He decided to give them the lot, the full firing-squad theory, including the chair. That would ensure front-page treatment in all the nationals. They would keep it alive on speculation and conjecture for at least three days. But not the S.S. tattoo. Definitely not the S.S. tattoo. An ace in the hole, only to be played when the stakes were high enough.

In any case, why had no one claimed responsibility? This was a boastful killing. An act of vengeance demanding recognition. An endeavour to dignify murder! By whom? For whose benefit? For the benefit of the murderers . . . The executioners? A killing to the soundless accompaniment of 'Pomp and Circumstance'? 'Deutschland Uber Alles'? 'The Wearing of the Green'? A selfish vengeance shared by five men armed with obsolete rifles who wanted the world to know that retribution had been taken for a grievous crime. Content enough, or careful enough, to deny the world knowledge of the crime and the criminal. Denying him that knowledge because to do so would identify his executioners . . . his murderers, damn it. Proud men who would not kill in a secret sordid way. No back-alley bludgeoning. No anonymous stab in the back. They wanted their victim to know he was going to die, and why he was going to die . . . Even how he was going to die. But shrewd, cautious men, careful to leave only the vestigial signs of their pride, in the form of a dead man and five old bullets. Taking away the five old rifles. Hanging up their weapons among ten million obsolete guns. Leaving five old bullets . . . and a faded tattoo. Did they realize they had left him the tattoo? The ghost of an S.S. man beckoning him back to a nebulous war? A war in which no doubt the S.S. also had pride.

In which, of all the atrocities committed in that war, lay the crime of the dead man? History never itemized the individual parts of atrocities. Atrocities had to be heaped and shovelled together. Atrocities only came in mounds. Compacted. Concealing identifiable, individual anguish. He had seen it on film. Atrocity was a pile that could only be comprehended in mass, assimilated in bulk; and thus neatly labelled atrocity. Preserving the mind from madness in considering each shard of individual suffering.

Was there, in the structure of those dead mounds, some molecule that survived in vengeful memories? A particular part confined to some select group of survivors?

Smith shook himself loose from maudlin introspection and returned to reality. For God's sake get a grip on your brains! Just because you've got a potful of nothing, don't try and fill it with fantasies. Thirty years ago your victim, your imaginary war-criminal S.S. man, could have been one of those original ageing idiots of the fifties riding around on high-powered motorcycles seeking a lost youth. Doing 'a ton' along the Western Avenue or North Circular Road. Embryonic Hell's Angels, tattooing swastikas and other Nazi emblems on their arms and backsides, wearing HATE on their knuckles like a declaration of war. There's pride for you. The sort you know. Stupid, selfish and malicious. No Pomp. No Circumstance. Just Rock Around the Clock.

Have to have words with Simonson, in case he has tumbled the tattoo. Sincerely courteous and respectful words. And the same with the coroner. Very nosy people, coroners.

He called for the Action Book as soon as he returned to the

office. Marrasey reluctantly postponed making a batch of entries and brought it to his desk. 'There are sixty-eight actions listed. Thirty-nine outstanding, most of these supplementaries arising out of the house-to-house. A list of all registered Lee Enfield rifle owners should be on the teleprinter from Firearms Branch within an hour and I've been on to adjoining provincial forces to supply similar details. Also I've actioned enquiries at car parks and other likely parking places, the railway station, pubs, the library and so on, on the off-chance somebody took notice of a strange car parked up for a considerable time.'

'Yes. That's a reasonable line. I'll O.K. that. Any chance of some coffee now?' Smith looked up from the pages.

'Yes, sir. Shortly, sir.' Marrasey sounded like a busy waiter. 'We are going to be hard-pushed to maintain a viable completion flow on outstanding actions, sir. Is there any chance of assistance on loan from other districts?'

'No. They've got their own troubles. Allocate according to the main priorities. No need to tell you what they are. We can clutch at straws when we've eaten the loaf.'

'It's still a very large loaf, sir.'

'Then use yours and get me some coffee . . . please.' He had not meant to reduce his angry order to a growled request, but that smooth shell of compact dignity in which the man lived seemed to demand reciprocal respect.

Give the fellow his due, he was entitled to respect. Without chivvying or bullying, using only patient guidance and demonstration, he had the three young police cadets and two women police officers indexing, filing and cross-referencing with great accuracy. The System was being given a solid foundation of minute detail. It was too early to test it fully. In another three or four days when it had meat on its bones he would ask for some obscure statement relating to a vehicle seen, a possible suspect loitering, a cry heard, then see if the correct reference was found in less than a minute. In three or four weeks, when the System had really grown, he would still expect the same result. Yes, he would continue to let Marrasey run the System. The man was right. No one else could do it better.

The phone intruded annoyingly. Commander Hessen. 'Ah, Owen. I am told you have arranged to hold a Press Conference at eleven. Why was I not informed?'

'It seems you have been.'

'But not by you, Owen.'

'I did not think you would wish to be troubled by such a minor matter.'

'Appearances before the media are not minor matters, Owen. The public projection of the police image is a matter of great importance. That is why officers of my rank and above are given courses on how to handle themselves on T.V. It is no reflection on you, Owen, but you have not had the advantage of that course. So I will take responsibility for the Press Conference. Clear?'

'As crystal.'

'Good show. Now I have been in touch with Mr Smallbone in Press Liaison. For a start, the venue will be changed to my office; it being a more quietly restrained and an altogether more suitable setting than your cluttered and untidy Incident Room. Remember that, Owen. Whenever possible, choose your own setting. Now we haven't much time, so just toddle over to District H Q pronto and fill me in on the salient points. You can sit at my right hand during the interview. I will cast the odd full-toss in your direction to let you get your eye in. Oh, and change your shirt. Light blue is a good colour. Now is there anything I should be concentrating my mind on pending your arrival?'

'Yes, sir. Book of Samuel, chapter one, verse twenty.' Smith replaced the phone.

In his office at District H.Q., Hessen reflected for a few moments but, receiving no inspiration, reached for the leather-bound Bible in his desk drawer. Turning the pages, he read:

'Tell it not in Gath, publish it not in the streets of Askelon; lest the daughters of the Philistines rejoice, lest the daughters of the uncircumcised triumph.'

Closing the book gently, he replaced it in his drawer, thinking to himself, 'Typical C.I.D. officer. Has only read the filthy bits.'

Then another thought struck him. Withdrawing the Bible, he inserted it amongst the few weighty law books on his desk stand, turning the stand round so that the gold lettering would face the T.V. cameras. He went to the front of his desk and peering through boxed fingers he viewed the picture from a distance of ten feet. It was very clear.

Watching the newscast that evening while dining on a bacon sandwich, Smith had to admit that Hessen handled it well. The large open face, the grim but friendly smile, exuded confidence and determination. The firm nod of comprehension, halfway through a question, displayed alertness and intelligence. The words he uttered were articulate and sincere. But he put his own bat to the friendly full-tosses, the yorkers went to Smith's end.

'How many men involved?'

'Mr Smith. What are our estimations on that?'

'At least five.' He, reticent and taciturn.

'How did the murderers manage to escape the police cordon thrown up round the Common as soon as the shots were heard?'

'Have you any thoughts on that, Mr Smith?'

He, hesitant, because it was a 'when did you last beat your wife' question. Seemingly evasive, because he had no thoughts. Because there was no cordon. Just the gradual accumulation of police that occurred at all major incidents. Finally saying, 'It seems probable they went to ground in an unoccupied house at the back of the Common.'

None of the journalists actually asked the killer question, but it would be in all their reports. 'One wonders why the police did not consider this possibility at the time?'

But the photograph of the victim was prominently displayed, and particular reference was made to his early skull fracture and his contracting M.T. malaria. This latter aspect led to speculative questions about revenge killers from Zimbabwe, Uganda, Zaïre, Angola, or simply the all-embracing Third World. Headlines sought conjectural terrorists, reaching out to settle scores with a white exploiter of their wealth and freedom, deep in the jungle of an English suburban Common. This was a racial issue and Commander Hessen was strong on racial issues. 'Ah, gentlemen. These are possibilities, and in such a sensitive area we shall and will approach them with an open mind. But I must point out there is no evidence to lead us in that direction. And in the absence of evidence, we would never apportion blame for this crime to any racial or national group. That would not be in the least helpful.'

Smith disentangled a string of bacon rind from his teeth and spoke to Hessen's fading image. 'Yea verily, old son. It is hard for thee to kick against the pricks.'

'You should just give chapter and verse.' O'Brien had entered and stood behind him.

'I've told you before about barging in without knocking.' Smith switched off the set.

'I did. It was drowned by the voice of our lord,' O'Brien protested strongly. Then subdued by a glare, went on, 'There is a member of the aristocracy on the blower. A Lady Constance Lowderton.'

'Wanting?'

'The person in charge. I'll have her put through.'

He expected the voice to be imperious and haughty; found instead that the tones were gentle, almost frail, yet tinkling with a thin remote steeliness.

'Are you the police gentleman who was on television a moment ago talking about the body of an unidentified man?'

'Yes, ma'am. My name is Smith.'

'You are not the one who was wearing uniform?' Doubt and disappointment intermingled with her question.

'No. I was the one in plain clothes.'

'Oh.' The disappointment was now obvious. 'I wished to speak to the person in charge. The gentleman in uniform.'

He explained patiently that the gentleman in uniform was in charge of a great many things but that he, Smith, was specifically in charge of enquiries concerning the body of the unidentified man.

'I see . . . very well,' his status was accepted reluctantly. 'Then I would be obliged if you would call on me tomorrow, to discuss the matter. Shall we say at eleven?' She gave him an address, a house named 'Beaucourt', near Cinder Hill at Horsted Keynes, Sussex.

'Lady Lowderton, can you identify the photograph of the man shown on television?' Smith came bluntly to the point. Hesitancy on the end of the line . . . A gathering of thoughts. Another nosy nutter?

But when the voice returned, steel predominated. 'Mr Smith, I will only say this. Sight of the photograph brought memories of someone I once knew, that were so strong I acted on immediate impulse and telephoned your number. I rarely act impulsively, and I regret doing so now without giving the matter more mature consideration. However, I have no wish to avoid my responsibilities and you may call on me – or not – just as you see fit. Goodnight.'

Smith found himself saying, 'Hullo . . . hullo . . . Lady Lowderton,' to a series of unresponsive buzzes. He dialled out to the exchange supervisor, and after some hassle obtained Lady Constance Lowderton's ex-directory number. The first three digits had completed their orbits when recent words sounded a warning in his ears. 'I rarely act impulsively.' As he was now doing. Lady Lowderton was no nutter and her title was twenty-two carat, of that he was sure. A mental picture of her took shape, words formed on her lips, 'I never discuss personal matters on the telephone. Please bother me no further with this nonsense.' No, leave it. If there were golden eggs to come from this goose they would be all the fresher in the morning. Tugging his forelock to the phone he said, 'As ye wish, m'lady.' Then he went into the main office to beckon Woman Detective Sergeant Elstow into his.

Seven

✦✦✦✦✦✦✦✦

'Bim Bam' Bailey threw two quick lefts into the phantom face of
his manager, but withering scorn still poured from Alfie's lips.
'You bleedin' berk. You've got scrambled eggs for brains.' He
tried a right cross; the diatribe continued. 'Changin' the roadwork routine. Goin' down along the river. Why diddencha jump
in? Think the filth won't notice?'

He got Alfie Joss on the ropes and went for the body. Short
solid punches into the gut. Still the words came as thudding
counterpunches to his head. 'You leave the thinkin' to them as has
the equipment to think wiv. You get back along the road you've
always worked. The law gives you a pull? . . . Fine . . . Yeh, you did
maybe hear a bang. You fort it was a backfire. But otherwise
nuffink. You saw nobody. You saw nuffink. Schtoom, that's the
policy. *Total* schtoom.'

He blew Alfie out of his mind with a looping right of such
ferocity his body swung with the impetus like a discus-thrower;
and as he circled cat-like to regain his balance he saw the lights of a
car coming up behind him. 'No I diddent,' he called mockingly to
the reappearing face of Alfie Joss. 'I don't see nuffink. I don't see
no car. I don't see nobody. I don't see my full whack of the
purse-money neither, you fievin' fuck-pig.' He jogged along,
waving on the fast-approaching car. If it was the law, he'd act
nonchalant, like, wave them past; if they stopped, he'd give them
the big surprised, 'Who me?'

The offside bumper took him at the back of the knees and the chrome grille around the radiator slammed into his pelvis throwing him into the air. He had a momentary vision of branches; leaves etched against the dawn sky, the unwinking eyes of an owl ... All before crashing down on the roof of the car above the windscreen, before his spine broke. Before he was ejected over the rear of the car, and before his brain ruptured on impact with the road.

The house, plain four-square Georgian, sat in a sward of meticulous lawn, with only fluted columns supporting a modest pediment above the front door giving it a hint of refined grandeur. Although of reasonable size, it was not a large house, and its proportions were of such angular perfection as to make it, at first sight, unobtrusively modest. There was a round ivory bell-push in the middle of a highly polished brass surround. Smith gestured to Elstow that the honour was hers. A low double dong resulted, followed shortly by the approach of staid unhurried footsteps.

It was a lawyer who opened the door, and although it had been many years since Smith had seen such a lawyer, he knew immediately that he was one. One who wore trousers of subdued bronze striped in grey, a black single-breasted jacket over a double-breasted waistcoat adorned with a thick gold watch-chain looped across the gentle slopes of a swelling stomach. A florid, almost Bohemian, bow tie counterpointed the ensemble, as if the wearer wished to indicate that while he might be fuddy, he was not duddy.

Responding to Smith's introductions with discreet wobbles from several chins, he said, 'How do you do. I am Sam Jones. Lady Lowderton's solicitor.' Smith was mildly disappointed. Such an archaic figure demanded something Dickensian. A Brass, a Heep, a Buzzfuzz. Something less plebeian than Sam Jones. But the voice was right. Rich, redolent of Madeira wine and cherry cake. His presence was a certain sign that Lady Lowderton had given the matter more mature consideration.

'Lady Lowderton is in the conservatory at the rear, Chief Super, this way.' An unsubtle hint from Sam Jones that, despite appearances, he was not only the dignified family solicitor solely concerned with investment advice, wills and conveyancing, but a man of wider experience of policemen, villains, and the magistrates courts. Smith wondered if Sam Jones dressed according to client and occasion.

The quizzical frown that passed across Lady Lowderton's brow on cognizance of Elstow's gender changed to an approving curve of her lips at closer appraisal of the severely cut dark-green costume and demure pink blouse.

'Won't you both sit down.' A gracious hand indicated two contorted cast-iron chairs whose only concession towards comfort was a coat of white paint. Lady Lowderton occupied a couch of similar construction, but one well provided with cushions. She smoothed wispy frills and flounces on a long white high-necked dress, then nestled in her chair amongst ferns and potted palms, like a reclining stork.

'It was kind of you to come.' Blue eyes, diluted by age but still sharp, dwelt beadily on Smith. He tried to assess her years. Old; amplified to elderly; but alert. Very alert. So much that was old was coming into his life of late. Old, alert, and still dangerous.

'Lady Lowderton . . .' he began. Only to be stopped by her head turning reprovingly to one side, the raising of a delicate finger.

'Mr Jones. If you would be so kind.' Jones took his lapels in each hand and addressed the assembled company. 'Lady Lowderton, Mr Smith,' the chins wobbled in deference to his client. 'Lady Lowderton has informed me of the circumstances that bring us together this morning.' Flesh oozed over his stiff collar into the folds of his tie as he rested the onerous burden placed upon his head down on his chest. 'She has asked me to act for her in this matter, and indeed has apprised me of the reasons for her call to you. And accordingly authorizes me to speak on her behalf. Now, sir –' the head lifted, skin draped from his neck in reptilian folds. 'Your spokesman last night said that any information would be treated with the utmost confidentiality.' The right hand shot from his lapel to end in a spearing forefinger. The leading question was fired. 'That is an absolutely binding guarantee. Is it not?'

Smith ignored both face and finger. He looked at Lady Lowderton. 'Only as tight as the law allows.'

'And how tight is that, Mr Smith?' She displayed quiet interest. Smith shifted uncomfortably on the hard ridged iron, wondering if Sam Jones' legal mind had devised the seating arrangements.

'It depends on what you have to tell me. It depends if what you say is material and relevant to a prosecution. It depends on lawyers.' He gave Sam Jones the full benefit of an icy glare. 'You see, if what you have to tell me is evidence that cannot be found from another source, then possibly, probably, you would be subpoenaed to give that evidence, if you were unwilling to give it voluntarily. If what you have to tell me would be helpful to the defence of an accused person, then, at the very least, we would be severely criticised were we to conceal such facts from his lawyers. Even if it doesn't come to a prosecution, I could not conceal the source of evidence of identification from the coroner. I presume that's mainly what you have in mind. Identification?'

Lady Lowderton got to her feet with difficulty and the aid of a gold-topped cane. Smith made no move to assist. Elstow was half-way there only to be waved aside by the cane. Bent-backed, Lady Lowderton looked across at Smith. 'Well, at least you're frank, young man.' Then turning to her solicitor she said, 'You were right, Sam. But you were wrong in saying the police would lie to maintain their guarantee.' The rubber ferrule waved under Smith's nose. 'He's given the same reasons for not maintaining it that you did.'

'I hope you don't think I'm so stupid I would not realize that fact, Lady Lowderton.'

She swung round on Smith with surprising alacrity.

'So! Had my solicitor not been present you would have maintained this false promise?' Gone were all traces of gentility and frailty, the voice rasping, demanding. She returned to her couch and awaited an answer, hands poised lightly across the top of her cane.

'No. I would have told you what I have already told you. I will do my best to see what you may say is treated in confidence; within those limits. After all, such circumstances may not arise. The probability is they won't.'

She rocked back and forth in petulant annoyance. 'Well, at least you're an honest man, Mr Smith. But in the circumstances I think I'll keep my skeletons in the cupboard.' Sam Jones coughed loudly in an endeavour to conceal the indiscretion. She acknowledged the warning by clutching her cane close to her bosom.

'Good day to you, Mr Smith. Sorry you have had a wasted journey. What I had to say was just an old woman's fancy in any case. Not relevant, as you would say.'

'I would still like to hear it, Lady Lowderton.' Smith tried a pompous, heavy-handed appeal. 'I need hardly remind you it is your public duty to assist me to . . .'

She was on her feet in a flash, ramrod stiff in her fury. Abuse falling on his head like molten lead. 'Assist you to what? To solicit bribes? To fail to protect the elderly and infirm? To fail to protect people being shot down in cold blood?' From a reclining stork she had changed into a hovering hawk. 'To protect the public, eh.

That's what you were going to say? A mess of yahoos and hob-bledehoys, who scurry in and out of factories like sheep; at the behest of people with the morals of gangsters and the methods of protection racketeers. Then you enter my home and tell me I'm failing in my public duty.' A final searing potful: 'How *dare* you!'

Smith looked up at her and said coolly, 'At least I've cured your lumbago, or was it sciatica?' Then in firmer tones he went on, 'Now kindly listen to me for a few moments, Lady Lowderton.' He rose to his feet and met the approaching form and opening mouth of the solicitor with a stiff arm, shoving him back on his heels. 'And you listen as well, Mr Jones. Listen carefully.' His words bludgeoned Lady Lowderton back into her nest. Jones retreated, brushing fat fingers up and down his waistcoat as if removing some deadly virus.

Smith turned to her ladyship, dropping his voice to a reason-able and reasoning level. 'It matters little to me whether you say another word, or tell me anything. The moment you picked up that phone last night and told me who you were was enough. Even if I never came here this morning, all I have to do is sort out who your servants are or were; your butcher, your baker and your candlestick-maker. I talk to them and I dig into their minds and their memories. I find out who your friends and relatives are, or were. I dig them up, Lady Lowderton, I excavate, and I let the dirt fall where it may. Need I go on?'

She had listened carefully and took it calmly. Turning to Jones she asked, 'Well, Sam?'

The solicitor clutched at his lapels, his face as florid as his tie. In a voice dripping with torts, malfeasance and embracery, he said, 'We will take out a writ, an injunction.' Fingers caressed the front of his waistcoat. 'A summons for assault.' His eyes sentenced Smith to six months.

'Oh, shut up, Sam! The bloody man has me over a barrel.' The rubber ferrule made a series of quick dull plopping sounds on the tiled floor as she vented her annoyance. The sound eased to a steady deliberate beat as, grimly pensive, she studied Smith's impassive face.

Slowly the wrinkled features softened. Gradually, a tranquil serenity smoothed and emulsified the arid skin. 'Last night I told you I acted impulsively. I also acted emotionally.' Her voice was soft, toneless. She turned to her solicitor. 'Show him the photo-graphs, Sam.'

Obediently the solicitor went to a black japanned deed box and delivered an open album of photographs into Smith's hands. On one side was a full-length studio portrait of a middle-aged man in morning dress. The face bore a resemblance, but no more than that, to the face of the unidentified corpse. On the opposite side, the head-and-shoulders representation in half profile of a young man wearing a high-peaked Army officer's cap, the three pips of a captain visible on his shoulders. The photographer had skilfully touched out any blemishes, leaving only the contours of a youthful unlined face. But nothing could be done for eyes that stared myopically into space, as though the subject had defective vision and, in his vanity, removed normally worn spectacles to enhance his military bearing. Smith concentrated on the one visible ear, the deep lobe, the flaring helix, the curve of the auricle, feeling with growing certainty he was seeing the face of his corpse when it once was young. It would be a question of later measurement against some known standard, the size of, say, a button on the uniform, then photographic superimposition. But this he was sure was the man, the dead man, and the last of the line: her line.

Elstow's earlier searches at the Cobb Common library had found Lady Lowderton listed under 'Widows of Knight: Daughter of Augustus Pyrnford (*dec*. 1938). Bro. Antony (*dec*. 1940). Married 1939 Sir Rufus Lowderton (*dec*. 1963). No issue . . .' He wondered why she had surrendered to his threat. There was no one left to dig up. Pride? Hope? The possibility of a surviving child?

He looked from the photographs to Lady Lowderton. She answered his unspoken question. 'My father, Augustus Pyrnford, on the left. My brother, Antony, my younger brother, Captain Antony Pyrnford, on the right. He was reported missing, believed killed, France 1940.'

'Did your brother have an operation on his skull before he was reported missing?'

'Two years before.'

'The surgeon. Can you possibly remember the name of the surgeon who carried out the operation?'

She kept him waiting for an answer, but only to conceal displeasure and replace it with a feigned wound at his assumption of a failing memory. 'Of course I do. Sir Henry Dobson-Pringle,' she said wearily.

He did not allow elation to break the façade of solemnity he had imposed upon visage and voice.

'Lady Lowderton, I can tell you with almost absolute certainty that your brother's body is now lying in the mortuary at Cobb Common.'

She made no attempt to conceal her emotion. 'Oh, hell and damnation!' she exclaimed angrily. 'As soon as I saw those mad eyes I knew it was him.' She leaned forward in the chair, casting about in quick darting movements of her head, as though seeking a means of escape. Plop, plop, plop, went the rubber ferrule on the tiled floor. Smith realized for the first time it was not sisterly affection that had prompted her interest. No desire for continuance of her paternal name. It was a greater emotive force than blood tie. It was curiosity. A compulsive curiosity, now bitterly regretted.

Sam Jones came over, washing unctuous hands. 'May I offer my sincere condolences, Lady Lowderton.' He disengaged the left hand and tried to lay a sympathetic palm on her shoulder. She jerked away in sharp disgust, turned to Sergeant Elstow, saying, 'Well, young lady, you have kept a very proper rein on your tongue since you've been here. What would you do in my predicament, as one woman to another?'

'I don't know what your predicament is, Lady Lowderton,' she replied.

Another thudding exasperated plop on the floor. 'Damned if I do either. But I fear the worst. That foolish boy. I fear the worst.' Then with a false fond smile, she added, 'Such a glorious fool.' She settled back in her cushioned nest, a dreamy, age-absent smile on her lips. Smith gave her a few moments then signalled with his eyes for Elstow to go in again. She too waited awhile, then began, 'Your worst fears, whatever they are, Lady Lowderton, may be justified, and indeed may be publicized. But if you tell us all you know about your brother's past, we can probably contain the information to the limits of its relevance to our enquiries.'

Fascinated, Smith watched the old woman, functioning as she did in brief outbursts of spasmodic energy, sinking back as now, as if to assimilate further power from an inner source. She had listened to Elstow, head nodding gently, fingers stroking a strand of maidenhair fern that fell across her shoulder from a nearby urn. Absently, half-sighing, half-singing, she began a weird but placid litany. 'Possibly. Probably. Presumable postulation. Within limits, and subject to circumstances beyond our control, we promise and guarantee absolutely. In and out. Up and down. Round and round the mulberry bush.'

The top of her cane rotated under a bejewelled claw. Winding herself up, Smith thought, waiting for the storm. It came, not wildly, but with controlled ferocity, straight into the face of Sergeant Elstow. 'My brother's past? That's all dead men have, isn't it? A past. No future. Antony had no future after that foppish idiot fractured his skull . . . After . . . his father was destroyed by . . .' Smith saw Elstow recoil at the sight of viperish lips drawing back to spit in her face, 'the Jews!'

The old woman retreated into her nest, drawing her feathers about her, muttering, more to herself than those present. 'Poor Antony. How they used to snigger. Pater broke. Pate broken. Oh, what swines they were. One dud cheque and the regiment threw him out. Killed Papa.' Suddenly savage again, 'The Jews killed Papa. Took the business. Took his life. No future for poor Antony.'

Sam Jones came forward. 'Lady Lowderton . . .' She looked up at him, sullen and suspicious. 'What do you want, Sam?'

'I think we should call it a day.'

The cane waved at Smith and Elstow. 'What are we going to do about *them*?'

The solicitor allowed the weight of the problem to draw down head and shoulders. Smith eased his burden. 'Mr Jones is not in a position to do anything, Lady Lowderton. Neither are you. Unless it is to tell us what you can about your brother.'

Sam Jones came through as Gladstone to Victoria. 'The position is, ma'am, that having invited these persons in we cannot, as it were, slam the door in their faces. To do so, would, as the officer implies, invite unrestrained burrowing by the police into the very foundations of the family. Lady Lowderton, in seeking to ascertain if, after all these years of sorrow, your brother still lived – at least until a few days ago – I am afraid you have opened the floodgates.' Jones, like any good solicitor, knew when to accept the inevitable, knew when to advise the client to plead guilty. 'Leaves my hands free for a powerful plea in mitigation. Probably get you off with a bind-over.' Across the top of Lady Lowderton's head, he gave Smith the knowing smile of a conspirator offering mute compromise to a participant. Smith raised his head slightly in acceptance. Jones began his address.

'My advice, ma'am, is to be frank. I am sure we can rely on our police friends here to appreciate the strain and suffering you have endured these many years, and hope they will act with understanding and compassion. We must put ourselves in their most competent hands, trusting in their honour and discretion to

70

maintain the good name of your late brother. Confident that nothing can besmirch the reputation of such a gallant officer and gentleman. One who obviously suffered such grievous wounds in his country's cause that all memory was lost to him. One who wandered alone, knowing nothing of those by whom he was cherished, and who, sadly, thought he had perished many years ago.' Sam Jones bowed to the Bench where Smith and Elstow sat in uncomfortable silent judgement. Smith leaned forward in his seat and, smiling benignly, whispered in a tender voice, 'Tell us everything you can about your gallant brother, Lady Lowderton.'

When Smith got back to the Murder Room with Elstow, the first thing he noticed was a change in Mr Marrasey's appearance. The normally composed, expressionless features had a hard rigidity as if clamped on inner anger. The usually firmly buttoned waist-coat hung limply open; a tight grey curl drooped untidily from the side of his head. By his standards, he was almost dishevelled. The old-fashioned fountain pen was poised motionless over a blank index card on which a globule of ink had dripped unregarded. Mr Marrasey's mind was not on his work. Smith passed to his own office unnoticed.

O'Brien scrambled out of Smith's chair as he entered. 'Got a bit of a problem, Guv.'

'What kind of problem?' Smith thumbed through the internal directory, seeking Tom Palmer's extension at the laboratory.

'We had a hit-and-run near the Common this morning. A fatal.'

'So what's the problem? That's down to the uniforms.'

'He was in the Action Book. The victim was in the Action Book. A boxer, "Bim Bam" Bailey.'

Smith replaced the phone without making the call. O'Brien gave him the Action Book. 'Number 163,' he said. Smith examined the entry. It had gone in the previous day. The source read: 'Statements 24–36–37 from Action No. 9 mention man in tracksuit; pugilistic appearance, seen boarding first train out of Cobb Common Station. May be identical with boxer Joe "Bim Bam" Bailey, known to exercise on roads around Common during early mornings.'

In Marrasey's neat hand, the action was allocated to Det. Sgt. McCrae. 'Arrange for interview and obtain statement from Bailey in due course.' The result column was blank. No statement had been obtained.

'Bit of bad luck,' said O'Brien. 'Ours – and his. Still,' he added consolingly, 'I doubt if he would have seen anything. He was a nice fighter to watch. But thick – thick as two planks. Walked into everything head-down. Bound to finish arse-up sooner or later.'

'Not in my Action Book,' said Smith grimly. 'At least, not as an incomplete entry. What hit him?'

'A Daimler Jag. Dark blue.'

'Contact bruises? Paint traces?'

'Yeah. The ridged rad grille was imprinted right across his backside. Paint adhesion on the shoulders of his tracksuit. No debris at the scene, though. No lamp glass, no fragments. Nothing broken on impact. Except poor old "Bim Bam".'

'Accident or deliberate?' Smith laid the ball at O'Brien's feet. He tapped it tentatively into the air, seeing no way through to the goal. 'It's a narrow road, dead straight, overhung with trees, just getting on dawn. Worst kind of light. Dull red tracksuit. Anyone belting along could have lost him against the trees. Someone who has been on the piss all night. It's happened along that stretch before. That's what Marrasey thinks. He knows the ground. Upset him, though. Mr Marrasey doesn't like hit-and-runners.'

'Does anyone – ' Smith was cut short by a loud tearful voice in the outer office.

'You tell Mr Smiff I want to see him. Mr Smiff knows me. You tell Mr Smiff, Alfie Joss wants to see him.'

O'Brien gave Smith a puzzled frown. 'The uniforms had him down at the mortuary to identify the body. You know him? Joss, Bailey's manager?'

'I might when I see him. Wheel him in.'

Alfie Joss shambled into the office, a sodden handkerchief clasped to his face. He promptly collapsed into the chair by Smith's desk and threw his head into folded arms. From under rearing shoulders a muffled howl emerged. 'They killed my boy, Mr Smiff. The dirty bleedin' bastards killed my boy.' Smith waited patiently for the sobbing to cease but finding it apparently unending, he rose, crossed in front of his desk and pulled Joss sharply upright by the shoulder. Red eyes, wallowing in a sea of tears gazed up at him. Pitiably.

'You've known me before?'

Joss spread the damp handkerchief, seeking a dry corner to wipe a dripping nose. Smith tossed a box of tissues in front of him. Pulling out several, Joss buried his face in them, voiding his nostrils in long oleaginous eruptions.

'You've known me before?' repeated Smith.

Joss completed the mopping-up operation with a quick swirl of tissue round his face.

'Doncha remember, Mr Smiff? Eight or more years ago, you was Detective Chief Inspector at West End Central. Me boy, Joe, had bovvers over some aggravation in a club. He was a minder an . . .'

'And he fractured some poor bastard's jaw,' Smith finished it for him in a power surge of recollection, 'and you came in and tried to bung me a ton to square it up.'

'There was no need to kick me down the apples,' Joss stifled a reproachful sniff. 'I got the screws in me back as a result.'

'So who do you think killed your boy?' Smith switched him from one painful subject to another. Joss's courage seemed to evaporate with his grief and tears. He sat in downcast silence, shredding tissue paper between his fingers, then kneading the pieces into a tight ball, picking it to shreds again.

'Well?' The word fell ominously from Smith's lips. Joss sniffed again, defensively.

'Maybe I was a bit hasty, Mr Smiff. Maybe it was an accident after all.'

'And maybe it wasn't,' Smith came round his desk again, stood threateningly over the huddled manager and jerked his head round on the end of a handful of shirt front. 'Now you listen to me, pigshit. I've already had a long hard day, being pecked to pieces by an old crow. I'm no sooner back than I've got you slobbering all over my desk. So just you open your mouth and tell me what's on your mind.' He pulled Joss closer. 'The stairs here are just as hard as the ones at West End Central. And there are just as many. I promise you, you'll hit every one of them on the way down.'

Joss found some courage and struggled against the restraint. 'Now look 'ere, Mr Smiff. Don't come the old acid. This ain't eight years ago. You ain't dealing with no toe-rag. I got friends. I got people higher than you – ' The words ended in a high-pitched squeal as, front and back, Smith's open hand whipped across his cheeks. O'Brien studied the light fitment in the ceiling.

Smith threw Joss back into his chair, and returning to his desk, got out the scotch and poured two glasses. Pushing one across to the whimpering manager, he said, 'Now you know me even better than before, Alfie. So let's be friends. Let's be sensible, and talk sense.'

Joss smiled weakly and took up his glass. 'Sorry, Mr Smiff.

Didn't mean to bottle out. But there's nasty people involved. Animals.'

'Name the species.'

'Wot? Oh!' Hesitant comprehension. 'The Twoomeys, Mr Smiff. They wanted the boy to eat canvas last time out. Put up some heavy bunce.' Bravado straightened him against the back of his chair. 'I told them to stuff it. "Bugger off," I says to Mick, "I puts me boy in straight. Stuff it up your arse," I says.'

Smith sighed. 'You're a liar, Alfie. King Kong wouldn't tell Mick Twoomey to bugger off. You're a bleeding monkey, Alfie, but you're no gorilla. Take another drink and think again – harder.'

'Swelp me, Mr Smiff . . . '

'Alfie, listen to me.' Smith leaned across the desk and placed a firm friendly hand on the manager's forearm. 'The Twoomeys wouldn't have wasted your boy like that. They would have knee-capped him. Or gone in with iron bars on the ankles and elbows. They wouldn't waste him, Alfie. They would leave enough to crawl around. The Twoomeys are free-enterprise people, Alfie. They are progressive, they believe in incentives and motivation. Besides they wouldn't run the risk of denting a nice Daimler Jag on you, or your boy.' Smith shook the manager's forearm confidingly. 'You get my drift, Alfie.' He felt the arm tremble under his hand. Joss withdrew it and nursed it tenderly against his chest as though it had already suffered multiple fractures. His head moved from side to side, as he considered the odds, the risks . . . and the consequences.

'You won't grass me, Mr Smiff? You won't blow it around? Total schtoom?'

Smith placed a reverent hand over his heart. 'On my mother's grave, Alfie.' Joss cast anxious eyes at O'Brien. 'He's Mutt and Jeff,' said Smith reassuringly.

Joss spoke from under a bowed head. 'That geezer they shot up on the Common. The boy saw them.'

'What did he see, Alfie? Tell me what he saw.'

Joss opened helpless hands. 'Well, he diddent achally see them blow the geezer away. He was taking a breever near the pit, when he hears the bang. He was a game boy . . . ' Fresh tears welled in his eyes. Smith pushed over the box of tissues.

'I know he was a game boy, Alfie, I saw him do Kid Sheridan.'

A wan smile, appreciation for the memory, and another whisk of tissues to dispel the tears. 'You gotta give the boy credit, Mr

Smiff. He was all guts. No brains, but all guts. Anyhow, he dwells where he is for a bit, then he creeps to the edge, sees the geezer in the chair and them five or six other geezers just climbing out of the pit. Wiv rifles, Mr Smiff. They was carrying rifles. Then they slide into the trees. After that, nuffink. The boy comes on to me at home; an' that's the story, just as he tole me. I swear to you, Mr Smiff. Nuffink else.'

'Nothing at all, Alfie? . . . '

'Well, he kept on about the geezers climbing out of the pit. He fort they was old geezers, took 'em a time to climb out . . . Said they was moving all stiff, like they was old geezers. I wouldn't pay much heed to that, Mr Smiff. The boy's minces wasn't all that clever.'

O'Brien returned from seeing Alfie Joss to the front door, with a worried frown on his face.

'Y'know where he'll make his next stop?' O'Brien didn't wait for an answer. 'Straight to the Yard. Complaints Investigation Bureau. You shouldn't have belted him, Guv. That one's trouble.'

'There will be no Yard problems, George,' said Smith calmly. 'Alfie's cow-fodder, a natural grass. But he'll only talk to coppers for bunce or a belting. A little of either will loosen his tongue and justify his conscience. Besides if he does complain I'll shop him to Micky Twoomey. Or at least he thinks I will.'

'What about Twoomey? He runs a Daimler Jag.'

'He and his firm run three or four. But what I said to Joss was straight. This one isn't down to Twoomey. This one is down to my Action Book, and I don't like that, George.'

'Nobody pays better than Twoomey for sight of an Action Book or anything else.' O'Brien hung in doggedly.

Smith punished him with fierce searing eyes. O'Brien absorbed the heat in defiant silence. Smith pointed to the outer office. 'They're your people out there. From your Division. If any of them are bent it's down to you.'

He turned to stare through the window in moody contemplation. Down in a corner of the yard, a lost dog was whining in miserable solitude behind the wire mesh of its pound. The dog looked up, their eyes met and the whining changed to a fierce defiant bark. It was as if the dog recognized him as an enemy, one of those responsible for its confinement. The dog reared on its hind legs, forepaws scratching at the wire. The bark changed to a series of short appealing yelps. He turned away from the window.

O'Brien was still standing, watching him. 'Maybe you haven't got anything better to do than stand there looking miserable, but I have, so piss off and let me get on with some work.'

'I see, sir,' said O'Brien huffily. 'Is there anything you particularly want me to do?'

'Yes. Get me another bottle of Teacher's.'

Smith rapped the desk-top in frustration, searching for thoughts scattered by the arrival of Alfie Joss. Muddled by O'Brien's inference of a bent copper. He had always found bent coppers muddling. Confusing. Sight of the internal directory brought him back. Tom Palmer! He wanted words with Tom Palmer. And the Press Liaison officer. He would feed the media with the identity of his victim, as an emetic; see if it sickened in someone's stomach.

Eight

✦✦✦✦✦✦✦

'Good of you to look in, Tom.' Smith left the bottle on the desk. Palmer gathered his coat tails about him and reached for his glass. 'It's no problem, Owen. I live on the ground, and I always visit a watering hole on the way home. This one's the cheapest I know. Cheers.' Palmer took a slow drink, then said, 'Nothing I can do for you, Owen, until you find the five rifles. Find the rifles and I'll put the bullets up the spouts.'

'No. It's not that. I just want to talk to you as an old soldier.'

'You know what they say about old soldiers, Owen.'

'They never die?'

'No. Not that one, Owen. They do. Just like everyone else. Never mind. What's on your mind?'

Smith told him about Captain Antony Pyrnford.

'Served in the R.A.S.C., eh? Not what one would call a fashionable regiment. Busy lads, they were. Into everything. But militarily outré for the Pyrnfords of this . . . of that world.'

'He was originally in the cavalry. They bounced him. Like his cheques.'

'Yes, that must have been a bad tumble. Eighteen faults. Eliminated from show jumping. Transferred to the brush-and-bucket brigade.'

'While the sister didn't say so directly, I got the impression he thought the Nazis were the greatest thing since sliced bread. She certainly did . . . and still does. Dear Antony spent quite a bit of leave time in Germany before he was thrown from the saddle.

Language courses, so she said. She took him to a couple of parties at Joachim's house at Northwood in Middlesex when he was over here on diplomatic visits.'

'Joachim?'

'Joachim von Ribbentrop. The German Foreign Minister.'

'The champagne salesman.'

'Lady Lowderton didn't quite approve of him either.'

'What about it?'

'Antony got on famously with the Military Attaché. The German one.'

'So did a lot of others at the time. We 18 B'd quite a few of them when war broke out.'

'18 B?'

'Stuck them inside for the duration. Potential traitors. Some got the benefit of the doubt though. Or had influence.'

Palmer abruptly finished his drink and lurched to his feet. 'I know the way you're going, Owen. You're on a road to nowhere.' He buttoned his coat. 'I've been there. I don't want to go back, and I'll tell you why. Your victim was last heard of by his one solitary living relative during the phoney war in Beaucourt, France. Then the real shooting starts and he disappears into the blood and shit. It was a long war, Owen. Thirty million people died in it. When you get to that many millions, the hundreds of thousands either side don't count. They're not going to change the total just because you suddenly find one extra. Forget the war, Owen. A killing hate doesn't stay on the boil that long. Even if it did, what have you got? Out of that thirty million, a solitary sordid act of revenge. Five old bullets and a delayed death.'

When Palmer had entered the office, Smith saw for the first time that the years had suddenly eaten deeper into his flesh, like a wasting disease. Palmer could not maintain his initial burst of age-defiant banter. There was now a despondency about him, a sagging weariness, evident in the heavy blue-black pouches hanging under his eyes. Palmer had been drinking even before he had arrived. And he had not been sleeping for some time either.

'I've also got five old men and a contemporary killing.' Smith tried to resurrect his interest. He went on to tell Palmer about 'Bim Bam' Bailey. Palmer saw no reason to undo his coat buttons. He stayed long enough to say, with considerable effort, 'I'm sorry, Owen. You may be right. You probably are. But row me out of it. I thought I could do it the old soldier's way, deodorized like a fairy tale. But the stench is coming back, Owen. I thought I had forgotten the stench.'

Palmer spurned Smith's offer of a car to run him the half mile or so to his home. Smith knew he wouldn't be going home in any case but to a corner table in the saloon bar of the Cock and Hen to sit in moody silence. To seek a memory-deodorant in the aroma of whisky. Later Smith would try and get along there. Try and cheer him up, the miserable old bastard. The phone shrivelled his intentions. It was Simonson. A stiff, almost apologetic Simonson.

'Smith?'

'Yes.'

'Ah, Smith. I may have inadvertently misled you when I offered a speculative suggestion about the victim's past years being spent in Africa. My dental people tell me the fillings and bridgework are South American in origin. Brazil, to be precise. Sao Paolo, to be particular. You will receive an international dental identification chart in tomorrow's post. Now a note of warning. All that means is the fellow was wealthy enough to go to Sao Paolo for dental treatment. Not that he was necessarily resident in the city. Certainly not when he caught his malaria. He would have to be more up country, deeper in the interior, and not necessarily the interior of Brazil. Are you with me, Smith?'

'I'm slightly ahead of you, Professor.' He told him about Lady Lowderton and the S.S. tattoo, securing Simonson's qualified agreement not to mention the tattoo in his report.

'Provided the Coroner has no objections, Smith. And, Smith, in the circumstances, you will forgive me if I do not wish you good hunting.'

At times, thought Smith, you sit on it selfishly, waiting for the right moment: the Little Jack Horner syndrome; other times – most times – you sit on it to distinguish between the knowing and the nutters. And still other times when you don't know what the hell is the best thing to do with it. This tattoo, this S.S. man's stain, had elements of all three; and would be sat upon heavily.

Three days passed and the number of outstanding actions dwindled, at least those with any possible substance. Details of firearm certificate holders on .303 Lee Enfields had spewed out of the computer in surprisingly large numbers. The owners were mostly rifle clubs, but there were quite a few in the hands of private individuals. These locally had been checked and cleared, but there were so many others, a pro forma had to be duplicated and sent out to other Districts and Provincial Forces asking for similar action.

The Vehicle Licensing Centre got a heavy request for details of ownership on all Daimler Jaguars of dark blue colour. That would be forthcoming – just as soon as a computer malfunction had been sorted out. Special Branch records had been searched for any trace of Antony Pyrnford. Negative. Nothing. Questions to and answers from Willie Woolover, Commander S.B. (Ops). 'What about pre-War records? Sir Oswald Mosley's British Union of Fascists? Members of – Associates of – Supporters of – Overt? Covert? Hangers on?' 'Sorry, old boy. Dead. Defunct. Weeded. Had to cut back on out-of-date stuff in programming the nice new computer. Still got a few living prominents though. Nothing there identical with the subject of your enquiry.' 'Can you have a word with the funny people? See if they've got anything?' 'Can but try, old chap.' Later. 'Sorry, old boy. Nothing doing re your enquiry of our friends.' 'Does that mean nothing known – or nothing doing?' 'You can take it either way, old chap.'

Nine

✦✦✦✦✦✦✦

Two breaks came in quick succession; out of the blue. And as in the way of most major investigations, they were not products of hard slogging routine already completed. They came unexpectedly, without warning. Although, as Smith subsequently said, in sternly correcting O'Brien, they should never be described as lucky breaks, they were the opposite. They were connections, manufactured outside the System. But nevertheless a linking of known factors, temporarily separated by time and space They would have come in due course.

The first connection came in the form of a large and robust man, clad in coarse tweeds of great durability, who appeared on a Friday afternoon at the front desk.

He identified himself proudly. 'Ex-Detective Sergeant Horace Slawthorpe, Scarborough Police. Could Ah have a word with one o' t'lads on't murder of yourn?'

Smith, passing through from the Communications Room where he had been studying a list of stolen Daimler Jaguars on the V.D.U., stopped and said with a smile, 'I'm one o' t'lads ont' murder.' Ex-Detective Sergeant Slawthorpe turned his head to one side and dryly spat his disdain at Smith's imitation of a Northern accent. 'Aye, owd lad. Talk lik' that and tha might get thissen inside a Yorkshire pub, but tha'd never get thissen owt. Not alive anyhow!'

Smith offered a mollifying hand and asked, 'What can I do for you, Sarge?'

'Ave ye tied oop your killing wi' an identical one we had in Scarborough back in 1945?'

The big Yorkshireman's voice carried strong implications of a serious neglect of duty on the part of the Metropolitan Police.

'Tell me more,' replied Smith indicating the way through to the stairs. 'Tell me a lot more.'

'Now then. Ah hope this isn't going to take all day.' Slawthorpe heaved himself ponderously up the stairs. 'Ah'm down wi' a few lads for Rugby League Cup Final tomorrow. Thought Ah'd pass an hour or so till opening time. See how tha' was getting on wi' it. See if it were same as our case. See if there was a chance of clearing ours oop.'

The fact that more than thirty-five years had passed seemed no reason for Slawthorpe to lose interest in his unsolved murder. As he pointed out. 'Ah'm probably only bugger left alive who worked on t'job.'

They had found their body on 6 August, 1945, on the foreshore, out at North Bay. 'Tied to a chair he wor, just like yourn. Shot back to front he wor, just like yourn. But shot nine times by nine different rifles! Army captain he wor. Name of . . . Boswell. That wor it . . . Captain Derek Boswell. Not that he wor much of a so'djer mind. Medically unfit for active service. Nervous debility or some such. Shell shock, most like. Had been in France in 1940. Came out at Dunkirk. Area Entertainments officer he wor when they shot him. Putting on shows for the troops. They must have been terrible shows, lad, if that wor outcome. Suspects? Did we have any suspects? Oh, aye. About a hundred and fifty bloody thousand. Every bloody so'djer, sailor and airman in Yorkshire. It wor a shambles, lad. Troops on leave. Troops being demobbed. Others being called-up. Some being sent home all over bloody country. Others being sent overseas. It wor hopeless, lad. Couldn't even get decent coverage int' papers, wi' them dropping atom bomb on Japs, same day like. Papers only had four pages in them days y'know, lad. Nae bloody room for our murder, int' face of that atom bomb. What wor that, lad? A tattoo? Nay lad, never noticed any tattoos on him. Mind you, wi' nine three-o-three bullets coming out of his chest, he could hiv had Royal Navy review at Spithead tattooed on't and t'lot would've sunk without trace. Under his arm? Nay, lad. Only hair, and not a deal of that as I remember. Did we find any bullets? Ah tell thee, lad, we found bullets by the bucketful. There wor a war on, lad. So'djers wor practising wi' rifles, machine guns and God knows what along that coastline for bloody years. Bullets wor as common as whelks in those days. No cartridge cases though. Army wor very canny ower cartridge cases. Brass, tha' knows. Regiment? That wor another thing. He worn't in no regiment. He wor int' R.A.S.C. Half bloody army wor int' R.A.S.C. But this lad Boswell he wor attached to an Area H.Q. Nearly all old men or medical cases. Did administrative jobs like liaison with civil power. Requisitioning buildings and the like. Seeing to Home Guards and such. Putting on shows for so'djers! A more harmless collection of nice old fellahs at that Area H.Q. ye couldn't wish to meet. Couldn't see the reason for killing this one at all, lad. Though Boswell worn't all that old. Twenty-five or so. Around that mark. A Captain Pyrnford? Nay, lad. Name don't ring a bell at all. The enquiry report? God knows if that still exists. They amalgamated Scarborough force into North Riding around 1948. That's when Ah got owt, lad. Took a half pension and ran, before they made me sheep dip sheriff on't middle of Egton High Moor.'

Slawthorpe waved a reproachful hand at the sight of Smith's whisky bottle. 'Nay, lad. Not for me. Ah've been a beer man all my life. Provided it's Yorkshire bitter.' A fervent plea for help. 'Does tha' know where we can get a drop of Yorkshire bitter in London?' Smith gave him the location of a couple of free houses where there was a chance, and Slawthorpe took reluctant leave. Like a work stallion transported back from idle pastures to the heavy furrows of his prime and strength, he wandered around the Murder Room, recreating his manhood in the piled statements, the registers, indices, the incessant telephones and the Action allocation board. 'Aye, lad,' he said fondly. 'Murder investigation don't change much. All them damned moty cars, wireless sets and computer gadgets they 'ave these days, it's nae wonder the villains 'ave it all their own way. Nae policemen about, only bloody electrical engineers riding round in moty cars.' Ponderously, he lifted a large, shining, brown leather boot; resting it on the seat of a chair, as a circus elephant might place its foot on a pedestal. Leaning on the raised knee, he said, 'Nae substitute for a pair of big boots, broad shoulders and a strong arm. That, and a deal of commonsense.' A thick forefinger tapped the side of his head. 'It's nae what others put in there that's important, lad. It's what tha puts in thissen.' The finger moved down to prod his chest above the heart. 'And in here as well. Compassion. Tha needs a good sized chunk of compassion.'

The foot was lifted from the chair, the hand from the heart extending to enfold Smith's. 'Ah'll see thee, lad. You've got my address; any time you're Scarborough way, look in. Ah've nae phone, can't abide them in the 'ouse. If it's anything urgent; just ring station. All t'lads at Scarborough know ex-Detective Sergeant Horace Slawthorpe.'

'I'm sure they do,' said Smith in farewell, 'I'm sure they do.'

Old men were intruding upon him again. Old men – alive and dead. And of the latter, there was yet another to come: the second break . . . or as Smith preferred to call it, the second connection.

It came the day after Slawthorpe's visit. 'Cheeky old sod,' O'Brien had complained. 'A pensioned-off detective sergeant from the sticks, and he comes stalking about the office like an Inspector of Constabulary. Didn't even call you sir, let alone me.' 'Aye, owd lad,' Smith had replied, with great lack of concern.

It came after Commander Claude Rissington, in charge of the Fingerprint Branch at New Scotland Yard, walked into Smith's office, shortly after Slawthorpe's departure.

'Hullo, Claude,' said Smith reaching for his bottle. 'What brings you out here? Apart from my scotch, that is.'

'The attraction of green fields and country air, Smithie, old son. How are you settling down in this rustic paradise? All these chicken thieves and cattle rustlers keeping you busy?'

'That, and the odd murder.'

'Ah, yes. I knew there was something besides the dubious pleasure of seeing your ugly mug again. Your murder victim, Pyrnford. Did you know he died a fairly rich man?'

'No, but I'm sure you're going to tell me, Claude.'

'I am, old son. After you have recharged my glass.' Smith did so, saying, 'What's wrong with the phones these days, Claude? It's a lot cheaper, at least for me.'

'Any excuse to fly the confines of the coop, Smithie. They are hard to come by lately.'

'So what's yours? Your excuse, I mean?'

Rissington made large round eyes and held his mouth open dramatically, before speaking. 'Gold, Owen. In the form of Kruger Rands, lots of them. All nicely parcelled up and sent to the Commissioner as an anonymous donation to the Police Widows and Orphans Fund.'

'So?'

'Well, as you know, all contributions to Police charities are gratefully received, but the Commissioner is a bit leary about anonymous ones. Especially large ones in the form of Kruger Rands. Never know where they have been. Never do for the Commissioner to be a receiver of stolen property. So the parcel came down to us for examination: at least after the bomb experts had a look at it, in case it was something really nasty. On one of the gold pieces we found a partial print, ten points of similarity with the right thumb of your dead 'un, Pyrnford. Not enough for a court, but enough for us to say it's him.'

'How were they delivered, and when? The Kruger Rands?'

'By parcel post. Postmarked Trafalgar Square office, the day after your laddo was stiffed. And must have been posted by them that stiffed him. Wouldn't you say?'

'It's possible.'

'It's likely. Queer though. What do you make of it, Owen?'

'Pride.'

'What?'

'Pride. There's been a lot of it about lately.'

Rissington did not choose to pursue Smith's cryptic statement. He went on. 'Nothing on the wrappings. Address typewritten. Same with the note inside. Simply said, "For Police Widows and Orphans." It was typed on an old Remington, well out of production. Find it and you're close, if not home and dry.'

'How many did they make, Claude? Ten million?'

Once again, Rissington ignored Smith's oblique sarcasm. 'There's more for your System. Everything went across to the lab. Whoever licked the back of the stamps was a secretor. Group O.'

'More millions. Group O take in forty seven per cent of the population.'

'You always were an ungrateful bastard, Owen.'

'That's why you're knocking such a hole in my scotch.'

'A small price to pay for the gems of wisdom I bring.' Unabashed, Rissington helped himself. 'The coins were in a soft leather belt. Goatskin. The biologists found some spores on it. Fungi spores. Fungi of three different species, only found in the tropical and semi-tropical regions of Central and South America. The belt, and probably your victim, could only have come from South America.'

'Just like his choppers. His false choppers.'

Rissington took it with great equanimity and forbearance. 'I'll pass on all your previous ambiguities, Owen. But I can't let the last one go by. What choppers?'

Smith told him about the origins of Pyrnford's dentistry, finishing with a solemn warning. 'If you say it's something to get my teeth into, Claude, I'll hit you over the head with my bottle.' And holding the bottle in his hand, he looked at it and added. 'With my empty bottle.'

Ten

••••••

The revelations of Commander Claude Rissington were grist to the mill of the System, avenues of further investigative exploration that had to be trodden according to the will and energy of South and Central American policemen at the behest of the Interpol network, accompanied by photographs and reports full of polite, diplomatically worded requests and suggestions but not implicit demands. It was a search for historical fact that might explain a present circumstance. But it was not a current connection.

The third current connection came because the name of the suicide and the company he owned was in the System. Even though the body was found forty miles away at Farnham in the police area of the Surrey Constabulary. It came because the details in every Crime and Incident Summary circulated by forces surrounding the capital were searched against the System's indices. And in the Business section was the Cobb Common branch of A.H. Loach and Sons Ltd, on whose books was the house Green Briars, and whose Chairman, Albert Henry Loach, had been found dead inside his parked car with a length of rubber tubing running from the exhaust pipe into the front compartment. The fact that his car was a dark blue Daimler Jaguar made similar and obvious connection in the Vehicle Index.

After a brief phone conversation with the police at Farnham, Smith immediately ordered Elstow to drive him there. Taking umbrage at being left out, O'Brien unwisely asked why.

'Because you've got work to do,' Smith hammered his words at him. 'Get your fat behind out to this fellow Loach's house at Oxshott. See his family. I want his antecedent history back to his year of birth. To the moment of conception, if necessary. And particularly, I want details of any military service. And turn the drum over while you're there. You're looking for a .303 Lee Enfield rifle, or better still, five of them.'

'So there is nothing personal in it, taking the Elstow with you?' O'Brien allowed his feeling of insecurity to show. Smith was not prepared to be merciful. 'Yes, there is something personal in it; she's a better driver than you are, she's a damn sight better-looking than you are, and she knows what Loach looks like.'

'As long as it's not a question of her powers of perception being considered superior, that's all right,' said O'Brien, happily mollified. Smith shouldered him aside, muttering, 'Powers of perception. My God. What three months working among the intellectual middle class will do to a man.'

Elstow did not drive a feminine car. It was a souped-up manual Escort that she handled like a rally driver. Heel-and-toe braking, the gear lever slammed through the box, a steady five thousand revs on the counter, she tooled the car through traffic without hesitation, but with precise judgement. They zoomed along the Guildford by-pass, until, beyond the modern cathedral that looks like a power station, she made a crisp swerve on to the Hog's Back where the Farnham Road rides a ridge far above the rolling beauty of the Surrey countryside. Smith took his eyes from the attractions of the view to the attraction of Elstow's left leg as it thrust hard on the clutch pedal. Admiring its firmness as she made the gear change, admiring the relaxed curve of its calf after it was achieved. The action of her left leg had brought her skirt far above the knee, the lower thigh in its nylon sheath lay under his gaze. He feasted on the sight.

'You fancy me, don't you?' The sound of Elstow's voice jerked his head guiltily upwards, snatching him out of a lascivious reverie. He expected to meet cold angry eyes, a face contemptuous of his masculine weakness, but her eyes were firmly on the road ahead, her face loosely relaxed, lips slightly open, a glimpse of small pearl-button teeth. He reached across and placed his hand on the exposed thigh. 'Yes, Elstow. I fancy you,' he admitted.

'You bastard,' the intensity of her words was heightened by the softness with which she spoke. 'I fancy you as well.'

He moved his hand further along her thigh, fingers gripping at her flesh. The car slewed into a lay-by and stopped. She came at him fiercely, awkwardly lunging across the transmission tunnel, her lips wet, her hands reaching for him. He held her tightly, frustratingly distracted by the large mirror on a truck parked ahead, the driver's leering face. Pushing her gently back, he said, 'Later, Elstow, my lovely Detective Sergeant Elstow. Later.'

The Detective Inspector from Farnham met them at the mortuary and led them inside. The body lay naked on the autopsy table, plump flesh, inert and flaccid as soft clay, hung limpet-like against the zinc, awaiting the pathologist's probing knife. Flesh, tinged with a faint mottled pink colouration, displayed the inevitable brush strokes of carbon monoxide absorbed in the blood.

'Is that him?' Smith asked Elstow. 'Is that Albert Henry Loach?'

The Farnham D.I. intervened. 'He has already been identified by his son.'

'I've known relatives to stick up ringers before now.' Smith still looked to Elstow for confirmation.

'It is him, I've seen him often enough at his Cobb Common branch.' Elstow confirmed it and the Farnham D.I. smirked an unspoken 'told you so'. But Smith's attention was now on a three-inch wide diagonal pressure mark, running white across the dead man's pink torso. Another such mark was visible at the side of the hips. Smith looked to the Farnham D.I. for comment.

'Seat belt,' he said. 'When we found him, he was still wearing his seat belt. A lap and body combination.'

Smith did not conceal his dubiety. 'So we are to assume he drove the car to the quiet country lane where he was found. Fixed up the gubbins to the exhaust, got back in the car, switched on the engine and strapped on his seat belt. Why? He wasn't going anywhere. At least, nowhere that required a seat belt.'

The Farnham D.I. considered the point carefully before answering. 'You didn't know Mr Loach, did you, sir? Mr Loach was a self-made man; started up in a front-room estate office in Guildford after the war, with just his service gratuity. Now he has offices all over two counties. Made himself a million in twenty years. A well-respected man was Mr Loach, bit of a rough diamond, maybe not averse to a tax fiddle or a sharp deal on the property market, but a well-respected man. A proud man.' The

Farnham D.I. offered his last words directly to the corpse and went on with a final tribute.

'Bert Loach wouldn't want to be found lolling about slumped all over the place. He would want to be found upright. Straight up. That was his first slogan, "You get a straight-up deal with Albert Loach." '

Smith nodded, apparently receptive. 'That sounds logical,' he said appreciatively. 'Yes, that sounds good.' He paused, then asked sharply. 'Did he leave a note?'

'Not as such,' replied the Farnham D.I. 'But on the condensation inside the windscreen he had written with his finger, "Sorry it was an accident." It was still there when we found him, must have done it while waiting for the gas to kill him. Had us going as to what he meant by it, until you told us about your hit-and-run.'

'That, and the car, should be enough to tie him in with Bailey.' Elstow sounded disappointed. 'It looks as if Bailey died in an accident after all.'

Smith let it pass without debate. 'Let's have a look at the car.' He pushed other conflicting thoughts to the back of his mind to get the basic routine sorted out. 'And his personal property. I want a look at his personal property.'

They walked round to the police station where the Farnham D.I. tipped out the contents of the property bag. The wallet was thick with notes, the cheque book had few recent stubs, none of any great significance. An assortment of business cards, credit cards and the usual documentary trivia of every businessman. A thin gold watch, a thick gold signet ring . . . but no diary, no address book. Smith asked for an itemized list and photocopies of the documents to be forwarded to him later . . . 'Just for the System, you understand.'

Then through to the yard at the rear of the station where the Daimler Jaguar was parked. Although the tyres were rimmed in mud where it had been run off the road and the personalized number plate at the front pushed back, the bodywork was polished and resplendent. Smith spent a lot of time inside the car. The general layout was unfamiliar, he was not in the Daimler Jag league. But the seat-belt rig was fairly standard, with the securing clip sliding into a flexible stalk between the seat and a padded console. On the console were mounted the control switches for the electronically-operated door locks and windows. And how highly polished was the wood veneer, the leather and glass, covering facia, fittings and instruments, reminding him of the ground-floor rooms at Green Briars – Spacious, late Victorian manor house in its own grounds. Requires slight renovation, £96,000 for quick sale. Apply A.H. Loach & Sons Ltd, Estate Agents.

Smith mentally placed Albert Loach in the driver's seat, saw him strapped there, upright and proud. He reached for him with friendly ruminative thoughts. 'I'm not buying it, Albert, not your manor house or the manner of your death. Push over, Albert, let me drive.' He slid into the driver's seat, drawing the seat belt across and clipping it home. There were marks on the housing! Two closely parallel scratches, no, deeper than that, indentations. On the top and bottom edges. Something hard, metallic, had crunched tightly over the release button.

'You're stuck in the driver's seat, Albert, and all your friend – your killer – has to do is throw a loop over your protesting left arm and lash it to the steering wheel. Something strong, yet soft, that won't leave a mark, like a silk scarf. Then the same with your right. You're stuck, Albert, you can't get at the window switches or the ignition. You're about to die, Albert. And all you went out for, was a discreet little trip with your friend. A ride in the country, somewhere nice and quiet, for a chat, a confidential chat. What about, Albert? Subject for discussion: "Why did you kill 'Bim Bam' Bailey?" Why did you Albert? He was no danger to you or your friend. Or should it be friends? The five old riflemen.

'Why did you kill Bailey, Albert? And why were you killed? Answer to both questions. Panic? Is that it, Albert, you panicked and they panicked because you panicked? But did they all come to see you die like a goldfish in a bowl? I don't think so. One would have been enough to take you, Albert. They can't all be as old as you. With the throttle set on a rich mixture you would be comatose in ninety seconds at your age. Dead in two or three minutes. He, or they, gave you a lot longer than that, long enough for the condensation to form, and provide a pad for a note of apology on your behalf for the death of Bailey. Not that anyone figured that out beforehand, Albert, it was the inspiration of the moment. I'm sure you appreciated it, I'll bet you were no mug when it came to taking advantage of a situation. So your hands were untied and whatever it was that locked your seat-belt was removed, then the door was shut and you were left behind, Albert. Straight up and stone dead!'

The Farnham D.I. was leaning in at the car door offering a penny for his thoughts. 'Well, I'll make it a fiver, sir, seeing you're a Detective Chief Superintendent.'

He let it go over the top; everybody was a smart-arse these days. Only they were described in words like 'confident' and 'self-assured' on their annual fitness reports. Instead, he stated simply, 'Albert's corpse may be genuine, but his car is a ringer.' Then slammed the flat of his hand on the bonnet to emphasize the point. 'This motor hasn't been in contact with anything heavier than a wash leather.' A kick delivered to the muddy tyre did little for his pent-up anger. He had indulged in reckless speculation and was now committed to it; he was just as much a smart-arse as the Farnham D.I. but he went on, 'And that is the conclusion Mr Straight-up Loach wanted us to arrive at when we got round to inspecting it. Get your Car Squad to check out engine and chassis numbers against his current registration and you'll find out.'

Over his departing shoulder he called out, 'And you can have those thoughts for nothing.'

As the Farnham D.I. subsequently reported to his own Chief, 'Loach's car was a ringer, sir, but I still think conscience caught up with him and he committed suicide.' He was quite put out when his Chief, who was having severe problems with mortgage and subsidence in his newly built house, snarled at him, 'Show me an estate agent with a conscience and you show me Paradise.'

Eleven

◆◆◆◆◆◆◆◆◆

The inside of Elstow's Escort seemed cramped and uncomfortable after the luxury of the Daimler Jag. Smith sat waiting for her to move, fingers probing his temples, moodily attempting to tie up loose ends inside his head. After a while he said to her, 'What are we waiting for?'

'I'm waiting for you to make a decision,' she replied.

'What decision?'

'My place or yours?'

'Yours is nearest.'

He was thrown backwards by the sudden acceleration, then jerked forward as she braked for the main road, his head thudding painfully against the facia. Rounding the corner, Elstow held up the loose end of his seat belt. 'Didn't you learn anything from the fate of Mr Loach? Like the TV jingle, "Clunk click every trip." '

Elstow watched as Smith sat up in the restricting confines of her single bed. Catching her eye he smiled down at her and caressed her face. Reluctantly, he said, 'I guess we'd better get back to the factory, my darling, in case O'Brien has come up with something.'

'Not so much of the *my* darling. You have no proprietorial rights in here. I took you because I wanted you. Remember that . . . darling.' But she spoke softly, without rancour.

He moved his hand to an exposed breast, bent to kiss the tiny nipple and slid his hand down over her flat belly. She writhed under his probing fingers. 'Bastard,' she said as he pressed himself on her. 'Bastard.'

'Clunk click every trip,' he whispered in reply.

It was spontaneous and quick for both of them. No lingering aftermath. She called to him from the shower, 'How often have you exercised the *droit de seigneur* of a detective chief superintendent over your female sergeants?' Reluctantly, overt jealousy overcoming her independence.

'If you're an example, Elstow, not often enough.'

'In my case, it didn't happen like that. I was merely curious,' she was lightly offhand.

'In your case, so was I. But let it go at that. Here's to the next time.'

She came back at him. 'Next time, if there is a next time, it will be at your place. And I will tell you when. I've still got my pride, you know.' She emerged clad in a bath robe. 'Your turn and don't forget to clean the cubicle when you've finished.' A towel hit him in the face.

Suddenly overwhelmed by an uncertain modesty, he wrapped the towel around his body before emerging from the sheets. 'Y'know Elstow, you've just said it, if there is one thing that runs through this case like a silk thread, it's pride. Everybody is stuffed full of pride; the killers, the victims and . . .'

'And me!' She was dogmatic on the point.

'And especially you, Elstow, darling Elstow. But somehow their pride is different, indefinable. It's the sort of pride you feel at a Trooping of the Colour ceremony. A historic pride, a one-day-in-the-year pride. Once the day is over, you forget it until the next time round. Someone amongst these five or six men is keeping that sort of pride alive, once a year. But that particular one, nobody needs to keep his pride alive, it's permanently present. Fuelled by hatred.'

'Then why don't you destroy it, darling. You're good at that.' She had made a discovery and it saddened her.

O'Brien looked at Smith's still damp hair with speculative interest. Smith returned it with a casual lie. 'We stopped at Guildford on the way back and had a swim in the pool.' O'Brien feigned envy. 'Oh, yes sir. Lucky you. Water warm enough, was it?' From Smith a sharp edge carved into a more immediate topic. 'What did you find at Loach's drum?'

'A German helmet, two Nazi daggers, and an unregistered

Luger pistol; rusty, no ammo. No Lee Enfield rifles, no .303 bullets. Shoes and clothing all polished, all cleaned. No sand. No vegetable matter. Anything at Farnham, sir?'

'Nothing, at least nothing positive, except his car is a ringer. They had taken his clothes and shoes to the lab. I expect the result will be the same. If he was a member of the firing squad, we know they're a very clean firm.' He spoke irritably, as though distracted by unimportant side issues. 'These war trophies. Was he in the army? What outfit?'

O'Brien kept him waiting, licking provocative lips, relishing his role as a keeper of secrets, until his neck nearly snapped as Smith jerked him forward by the end of his tie. 'R.A.S.C. He was in the R.A.S.C., wasn't he?'

Indignantly, O'Brien fought to free himself. 'They don't call it the R.A.S.C. any more, they changed the title over ten years ago,' he said loftily. 'It is now the R.C.T., the Royal Corps of Transport.' Smith waited menacingly until O'Brien had straightened his collar.

'And you have checked army records?'

'And I have checked with the record office of the R.C.T., which now incorporates the former record office of the R.A.S.C.' O'Brien was not disposed to relinquish his role lightly, but Smith merely relaxed on the edge of his desk and said patiently, 'With what result?'

The strain was too much for O'Brien, the words gushed out in strident sycophancy. 'You will be pleased to know, sir, there is a definite connection. Pyrnford and Boswell were respectively C.O. and second-in-command of the 1404th Independent Ammunition Platoon, R.A.S.C. The unit was in France until the Dunkirk evacuation in June 1940. The high and mighty Mr A.H. Loach, Esq., was only a Driver, another name for a Private, in the same unit. Boswell got out of France O.K. But Pyrnford, as Lady Lowderton said, was listed "Missing believed killed." That still stands. I didn't get involved in explanations about it being more than forty years premature. As to Loach, he was taken prisoner of war, released in April 1945. Spent the . . .' O'Brien could not resist a pause for effect, 'the rest of his service stationed at Filey, Yorkshire, less than fifteen miles from Scarborough.'

Smith let him get away with it, smiling indulgently. He asked, 'When was he finally discharged?'

'March 1946. Took his war gratuity, came south and set himself up . . .'

Smith raised a restraining hand. 'I know what followed. What about the others, this 1404th whatever it was, did you get the names of the rest of them in the unit?'

O'Brien tried not to sound disappointed. 'Ah, well sir, it's not as simple as that. You see, personnel are not listed by unit title. Only by name and army number. On the names alone they had a job sorting out our three from others of the same name. There were more than a quarter of a million men in the R.A.S.C. during the war.'

'Anything less than a million in this job does us a favour. Never mind, go on.'

'To get the unit title we would have to examine every record card manually; the war-time records aren't in the computer. And I do mean we would have to do it, no way are they going to do it, on our behalf. Even then, they will only let us in if the Ministry of Defence agree.'

'We'll do it if we have to, but let me try and find an easier way out.'

Once again, O'Brien had his questions waved aside. 'Keep all this out of the System for the time being,' ordered Smith. 'Type it up when the office is empty, then file it in my safe.' To O'Brien, Smith sounded remote and desperate. 'What have you got in mind, Guv?' he persisted.

'Pride,' replied Smith, still far away. 'Pride and hate.'

'Another motto for the Force?' But Smith was already on the phone, speaking firmly now, vigorously in control.

'Mr Smallbone? I want another conference set up. Press, T.V., all you can manage. As soon as possible. I want it out tonight. Important new developments, fresh appeal to the public for information, all that shit. What's that, Mr Smallbone? No, there will be no need to inform Commander Hessen, he's at Bramshill Police College, a guest night, he is the principal speaker.'

He replaced the phone, shushing O'Brien's protests and gesticulations at Hessen's listed engagements pinned on the wall, dialling out again.

'Hello Andy. Power to the Press. How are you? Good. Myself? Not too bad, Andy, could be better. Listen, I am calling a press conference in a couple of hours . . . Like hell you'll send the local stringer. I'm calling in past favours. I want your finger on the trigger of a few loaded questions.'

For the second time in a fortnight Smith watched himself on T.V.

This time against a carefully posed background of subdued activity in the Murder Room.

Mr Marrasey had politely but firmly refused to participate in the charade, saying, 'I do not wish to appear unhelpful, but it may be wiser if my Civil Service masters do not see me actively engaged in the investigation.' Smith was only too pleased to agree; the last thing he wanted was aggravation from some Civil Service supervisor. Bit players he had in plenty, but Marrasey had the System running like a Swiss watch and was now irreplaceable. The camera panned around the Murder Room; Elstow, cool and efficient, mouthing silently into a telephone. Behind her, two handsome young detectives, endeavouring to look serious and wise as they pored over an inconsequential statement. His own head filled the screen. He fielded the preliminaries with ease. Andy Yuelle fired the bullets he had prepared and he answered as though painfully wounded.

'I can only say there is a strong possibility that "Bim Bam" Bailey witnessed the shooting. We know the car in which Mr Loach was found dead, although identical in colour and model to the one that killed Bailey, was not identical with the car he owned at the time Bailey was killed. You must draw your own conclusions as to why Mr Loach hurriedly and secretly changed his car. Until we trace the original, it will not be possible for us to say if that was the vehicle that killed "Bim Bam" Bailey.'

'Are the police suggesting Mr Loach was responsible for Bailey's death and was himself killed as a consequence?'

'That may be so,' he said surlily as though loth to concede the point. Then, as if furious at having to endure the chains of official restraint, threw them aside and snapped into the microphones, 'I personally believe all three deaths are linked, that all three men were the victims of vicious, sordid murderers. A gang of cowardly wanton killers motivated by a desire to preserve their own filthy hides.'

That said, he had stalked out of camera, ignoring the clamour of further questions, to seek refuge in his office and fasten trembling fingers on the neck of his whisky bottle.

It took Commander Hessen twenty-four minutes from the conclusion of the newscast to reach Smith's office. He found Smith still grasping his alcoholic crutch.

'Hullo, sir,' said Smith, surprise showing on his face. 'I thought you were dining at Bramshill tonight.'

'No, I am dining there tomorrow night, as you well know.'

There was a fine white rime around Hessen's mouth as though his lungs held liquid oxygen under pressure. 'You were supplied with a copy of my listed engagements, were you not?' The words hissed icily at Smith.

'I'm sorry, sir, I must have misread the date.'

In the following silence, Hessen's face called him a thousand-fold liar. He held on, waiting for Hessen to renew the assault. 'Your act of gross discourtesy, not to say indiscipline, by holding this press conference without reference to me is bad enough. But when the first my wife and I learn of Albert Loach's death is when you make the disgraceful suggestion, in public, that he was some-how involved in murder . . . Well!' Inner grief quelled outward rage. Hessen continued in lamentation, 'You have defamed a fine old man. Albert Loach was a good friend of ours, Smith. My wife and I. Godfather to our youngest son. I have left my wife completely distraught.'

Smith gave a token apology. 'I'm sorry, I didn't know you were acquainted.'

Hessen brushed it aside. 'I said he was a friend, Smith. It may be that you have mere acquaintances. I have friends. Albert was a former Mayor of this Borough, a supporter of many charities, and President of the Cobb Common Rotary, to which he intended to propose my membership. He was a Churchwarden –'

'He was a crook!' Smith brought the eulogy to an abrupt end, leaving Hessen open-mouthed, disconcerted by Smith's virulent composure.

'Preposterous.' Hessen failed to endow his ridicule with the certainty of faith.

Smith heaved a bundle of tattered old files onto the desk. 'You should always have a C.R.O. and registry search on prospective godfathers. Their sins may be weeded from the main collection but the roots are always left behind in the indices and the plant recoverable from the archives. Withered old nettles they may be, only alive as long as he was alive, but still capable of stinging his friends.' Hessen watched, fascinated, as he untied the dusty tapes holding the files together.

'Like the one in 1932 when he was eighteen. Indecent assault on a fifteen-year-old girl. Placed on probation for three years on condition he joins the army. Or like the one in 1949. Fraudulent conversion of £160 paid to him as deposits. Seems he took sixteen different £10 deposits on one house, and when it came on top he didn't have the money to repay the other depositors. Got it from somewhere though before the trial, robbed Peter, no doubt. Anyway, the fifteen Pauls got their money back before the trial and Loach got away with a fifty-quid fine. These were his only convictions but there were a couple of heavy Fraud Squad enquiries into some of his property deals in the sixties that came to nothing because they couldn't prove an intent to defraud. The old maxim, promises as to future conduct are not of themselves fraudulent. He was good at making promises as to future conduct.'

'The offences are well out of date. They cannot be cited as convictions.' Hessen sought refuge in the Rehabilitation of Offenders Act. 'And much that goes on in the day-to-day conduct of large and reputable businesses finishes up in Fraud Squad files, without being necessarily evil.'

'Oh indeed,' Smith agreed, 'but we keep it all on file, don't we, for our own . . . guidance? Not exactly a suitable godfather for a police Commander's son.' Smith saw the dawning realization in Hessen's eyes and followed through with two blind, brutal stabs at the belly. 'Got your house through him, did you? Priced a bit below the odds, was it? Made out a covenant to pay for your son's education, has he?' Hessen winced under the thrusts; mercilessly, Smith twisted the blade. 'Could be misinterpreted, that sort of thing, if it came to "A" Department cars. Gives some smart-arse the opportunity to minute the papers with, say, "A clear failure to observe the wisdom found in Ecclesiasticus, 2,1." '

'My faith is not founded on the shifting sands of Apocrypha,' said Hessen fretfully, but cast an enquiring glance at his persecutor, nevertheless.

' "My son, if thou come to serve the Lord, prepare thy soul for temptation." Here endeth the first and only lesson.' The words rolled from Smith's mouth with sanctimonious cadence.

'I was not tempted,' cried Hessen, drawing a moment of defiant dignity to add strength to his rebuttal, only to lose it before Smith's hard, implacable face. 'Naïve, perhaps,' he offered a defensive compromise. 'I honestly never gave it much thought. It is a common enough gesture among people . . .' An instant of arrogance, 'You would never understand.'

'Wouldn't I?' Smith saw the sweat on Hessen's forehead and licked hungrily at the salt. 'Lowlier than thou, am I? Incapable of understanding the mutual middle-class corruption that passes as a comedy of manners. The reciprocal unspoken understanding. The natural acceptance of the natural generous gesture without obligation; that is more binding than a ball and chain. It took your old family friend thirty years to learn the secret. But you always knew it; and were wined and dined out of your morals and your mind as a result. Think clear, Mr Hessen. Think clear.' He withdrew the blade, but only to stab again at his weakened victim. 'When did you last see Loach?'

'About a week ago.' Immersed in troubled thoughts about his future, Hessen answered in a vague compliant way. 'Just over a week ago, eight or nine days, over lunch.'

'You discussed the murder, Pyrnford's murder? Kept him abreast of developments, like the possibility of "Bim Bam" Bailey being a witness. Saw it in the Action Book on one of your early-morning visits, did you?'

'We certainly discussed the murder. Bert Loach is – was – a responsible local councillor, entitled to be kept informed about matters affecting the community.' A bovine wariness settled, with some difficulty, on Hessen's frank, open face; then fled, broken by anguished alarm. 'Oh God. You don't think he killed Bailey as a result, do you? You don't think he was in the firing squad?'

Smith made no attempt to staunch his wounds, instead he enlarged them, ripping them open with the switched car, Green Briars, the R.A.S.C. coincidence, that became certainty within the long-disbanded ranks of the 1404th Independent Ammunition Platoon. And with each torment Hessen stiffened, finding a martyr's strength.

'I shall resign, of course. The only honourable thing I can do.' His voice as firm and steady as his out-thrust chin. Only a minute twitching of his right eyelid betrayed his emotions.

'For Christ's sake grow up.' Smith exchanged the knife for the whip. 'Atonement in the form of self-sacrifice is nothing more than the impotent coupling of self-indulgence and self-pity. Don't be a bloody idiot all your life. You've been thinking clean for so long you imagined you were equipped with a moral filter removing impurities automatically, without thought or consideration.' Smith felt suddenly sickened by his own callousness. Hessen was openly weeping.

'Go home, sir,' he said quietly. 'Get a good night's sleep. You've been overdoing it. Forget all this nonsense about resigning. It's strictly between ourselves. Down to Larkin. No one else will get to know . . .' He poured a tiny scotch for Hessen. Then, to give the man an opportunity to compose himself, pretended the water jug was empty and went to the washroom. Returning, he met Hessen striding down the corridor. He went past him, head held high, without a word of acknowledgement. Smith watched the broad shoulders disappear down the stairs. Back in his office, he found the glass containing the small whisky drained dry. He smiled and said, 'Yeh, schtoom on this. *Total* schtoom.'

For three days Smith waited for a reaction, a response. Reaction there had been from the Press and the Yard. Critical comment about intemperate and emotive language. A summons to the fifth floor at the Yard. Explanations demanded and given. Explanations examined and critically received. A rough, 'You're clutching at bloody straws, man.' And a smooth, 'On balance, I feel that anything gained, if anything is in fact gained, will not outweigh the damage done to our image.' And a threat, 'Any more of this nonsense and we will tie you to a desk in C.R.O.'

On the morning of the fourth day, he found it lying on his desk when he arrived at eight-thirty. He had had a sleepless night. Nothing to do with Elstow, who had shared his bed; or her amused contempt at his failure to respond. All to do with a fear that this cheap provocation had been ignored and that he had made a fool of himself for nothing. And no matter how deeply he ploughed the darkness, hoping to turn up a gleam of inspiration in the dark meadows of the night, finding only the empty dawn, bare and fallow.

Oh, the routine work was still going on, the System was fed, and in turn was providing substance. But only as a life-support, keeping heart beating and lungs pumping but bringing no spark to a moribund brain.

Now, in broad daylight, there it was; lying on his desk, post-marked Trafalgar Square. The typeface on the label the same as that on the Kruger Rand parcel. He had been addressed as 'Mr Owen Smith'; the 'M' of 'Mr' stood out blacker than the other letters, having been typed several times on top of another letter; a 'C' was it? For 'Chief'? A mistype? Or a mistake?

Gently, he pressed the large envelope between his fingers, the contents thick, but flexible. Records? Documents? The flap was unsealed, held in place with a split-pin staple. Opening it, he drew out a sheaf of paper, handwritten, but with a typed note pinned to the first page.

'Dear Sir,

With reference to incidents currently under your investigation which you have described as vicious and sordid murders, committed by a gang of wanton, cowardly killers, in order to preserve their filthy hides. Regrettably, the killing of Mr Bailey justified such a description, at least in a singular sense. I confirm your suspicions as to the murderer's identity and reveal that he has been punished accordingly. He acted without the authority or consent of his former comrades-in-arms, motivated by self-preservation and greed. Defects, alas, long present in his character.

Respecting the other matters under investigation, I must, in the name of my comrades, the few still alive and the many long dead, maintain their honour and repudiate your words. To this end, I enclose a copy of my wartime journal for your consideration, confident that this record will amply prove the justice of our actions to you and the world.

I am, sir,
Your obedient servant,

Michael Lugard.'

No formal signature accompanied the typewritten name of Michael Lugard. More care, more caution? The sixty pages of what he called his wartime journal were photocopies, but the original handwriting was there, tight, crabbed, and clearly legible once the eye adapted to the minute script. Smith slid the pages off the end of his thumb, signs of staining here and there, occasionally the letters faded. And although in the main the writing was firm and controlled, now and again, particularly towards the end, a tremor, a jerkiness, sometimes a tight compression of sentences with barely a space between the words.

He let the pages riffle through his fingers once again, catching glimpses of familiar names, Pyrnford, Boswell, Loach. Places – French towns – Doullens, Arras, Dunkirk. Repeated datelines in 1940. There was a lot of it, but then a lot had happened in 1940.

Smith hung a 'Do not Disturb' sign on the door of his office and ordered the switchboard to intercept his calls and divert them to O'Brien's desk. Then he took up the pages, and, as his victim had done before they took him down to the sandpit and shot him, he began to read the diary of Sergeant Michael Lugard.

PART TWO

Sergeant Lugard's Diary

The War Diary of Sergeant Michael Lugard,
Royal Army Service Corps, incorporating
the history of the 1404th Independent
Ammunition Platoon, R.A.S.C.

Preamble

I am cognizant of orders that to keep a personal diary without
authority, while on active service, is forbidden by Field Service
Regulations. I am also aware it is an order more honoured in the
breach than the observance. Particularly by officers. Nevertheless, I disobey this order reluctantly, having sought permission
from my Commanding Officer, Captain Pyrnford, to maintain a
record of the platoon's actions in the form of a regimental history.
I have read many such journals and found them of great interest,
even though it seems they mainly catalogue the victories of the
regiments concerned and ignore their defeats. At least the
inglorious ones. Or are all defeats glorious?

However, my request was refused as presumption and imper-
tinence on my part. I fear Captain Pyrnford thinks me too big for
my boots by displaying evidence of literacy and intelligence. As to
that latter aspect, I did at least matriculate from my grammar
school at the age of sixteen and a half and promptly joined the
Army by adding two years to my existing age. A fact that may
cause some, but not myself, to doubt my intelligence. Having
decided to disobey the order against personal diaries, I may as

well go the whole hog and include some autobiographical detail in the unlikely event of this journal coming under interested eyes in later years.

My parents are both dead. My mother, a suicide, largely due to the drunken bestiality of my father, a clerk with a firm of dubious solicitors. He died the day after I finished schooling, falling from the balcony of our fourth-floor flat whilst in a drunken rage. He had been rummaging amongst the empty whisky bottles deposited there, seeking one with a few drops still left. Finding none, he proceeded to throw the empties down into the court-yard, cursing at the top of his voice. Deliberately or accidentally, I do not know, he retained a grip on the last one – all the way down. The police told me afterwards the bottle was found still in his hand, unbroken. Not so his skull. His death caused me no regrets, but my intention of joining the Army was precipitated by the police saying as I was under the age of seventeen and without relatives to take me in, I would likely be placed in a home, being, as they quaintly put it, 'in need of care or protection.' The next day I enlisted, using my mother's maiden name of Lugard. She was Irish and Catholic, and may God give her rest even though she committed a mortal sin.

At first, perhaps in a fit of *folie de grandeur*, I thought of applying for a commission, having the required educational certificates, but soon realized enquiries into my background would be rather stringent and in any case with such plebeian origins and parentage, a commission in the peacetime British Army of 1936 would never be granted. However, I found it remarkably easy to join as a ranker by simply stating I was eighteen years of age and forging my dead mother's signature, (forgive me, mother, God grant you rest), on the parental consent. No birth certificate was required and obviously no enquiries were made. And on 17 August 1936 I became Rifleman Michael Lugard in the regiment of my choice, the Rifle Brigade. I wanted the Army, possibly as a substitute for my parents, a very immature reason. But I also wanted the Army for the certainty of its discipline, the inviolability of its rules and orders (one of which I am in the process of disobeying). I wanted the Army for the simplicity of its purpose, the cohesive masculinity of its regiments and formations. I wanted something to cherish beyond myself, and I found it in the Rifle Brigade.

By March 1939 I was a full corporal serving on the North-West Frontier in charge of a section on reconnaissance patrol, part of a small punitive force going into the tribal territories. I don't know exactly what happened, but probably some solitary Pathan saw the section labouring up the ridge and, setting the sights of an old Lee Metford on maximum elevation, fired a single shot in our general direction. It seems the bullet was almost spent when it whined down at the end of its trajectory to enter my chest just below the right clavicle. Had we been in a less remote area the consequences of the wound would not have been too severe but the bullet penetrated the upper lobe of my lung and by the time I got to base hospital in Peshawar, the lung had collapsed. I was told by an orderly; the senior surgeon was himself ill and the only other doctor incompetent to perform an operation of the nature required. But regimental spirit prevailed. The colonel secured a place for me aboard one of the latest Royal Air Force planes, a Bristol Bombay transport going back to the U.K. Thirty-six hours later I was operated on at the Military hospital in Shooters Hill, London . . . A Blighty one in the grandest style. Part of my lung had to be removed but I was discharged fit for service.

By then the war was clearly on its way. A war in which I desperately wished to participate. However, ignoring the opinion of the M.O. who said I was A.1., regimental élitism considered a man with only half a lung on one side could not withstand the rigours of war conditions in an infantry regiment whose endurance in marching and fighting was a matter of pride and legend. Despite firm but respectful protestations, I was posted to permanent duty at the training depot as drill and small-arms instructor and given a third stripe. I worked hard at the depot for the first three months after the declaration of war, during which time I made several applications to be returned to regimental duties. All of them refused.

I began to feel my only battles would be on the parade ground and rifle ranges. Then an A.C.I. (Army Council Instruction) came round seeking experienced N.C.O.s to serve in France with the R.A.S.C, a corps that apparently consisted of untrained territorials and recent conscripts.

The R.A.S.C., as I know from my studies of Army formations, has as its main role transportation for every military purpose. (They used to call them Waggoners.) Truck drivers carrying ammunition, petrol, oil and basic rations, taking troops to their jumping-off points. Manning tank transporters, staff cars and ambulances. They are not combat troops but have to be capable of combat in what seems the unlikely eventuality of their being called on to fight. For that reason, many are in its ranks from choice, and others, directed into its ranks, are happy to be there for the same reason. Not a particularly enticing posting for a regular like me to seek. But it will get me to France, and once the war really starts and casualties mount, I can wangle my way back to the Brigade easier than I could from the depot; where we were continually told a good instructor is worth a company in the field.

I put in an application to transfer to the Service Corps, which the C.O. viewed with extreme disapproval. 'My God, sergeant. Do you really want to join these fellows. They are nothing more than a collection of dry-grocers and garage hands!'

I replied, 'They are going to France, sir, where the war is, and that's where I want to be.'

'But they have no regimental tradition; an amorphous bunch of odds and sods. I tell you this, Lugard, I am most reluctant to forward your application. It could have an adverse reflection on the Brigade. You do realize that? These people simply do not soldier as we understand the term.'

'It seems the nearest I will ever get to active service, sir, unless you could reconsid –' I seized what seemed to be a last opportunity, but it didn't work.

'That is out of the question, Lugard. You are highly regarded here, capable and intelligent. With the Army build-up coming, in six months or so you could be depot R.S.M.'

To be an R.S.M.! My ultimate promotion aim. But not at the depot. That really would be permanent. I replied, 'Thank you, sir, but it is active service I seek, not promotion. I respectfully insist, sir, my application for transfer to be submitted in accordance with the A.C.I.'

That was as firm as I had ever been to an officer above the rank of lieutenant, and clearly the C.O. did not like it. Red blotches appeared on his face and his lips tightened. He looked at me for a long time in silence. Seeing me in a new light. As something subversive, dangerous, not conforming to the best traditions of the Brigade. At last he threw my application back in his tray and said, 'Very well, Lugard, you seem to know what's best for you.' I found it a cutting remark but I have long been accustomed to the iniquities and injustices of rank. Three days later my posting came through and I was on my way to join the 1404th Independent Ammunition Platoon, R.A.S.C. No one wished me luck or even a happy New Year.

I have been writing the foregoing preamble during the past six hours waiting for the troopship to get up steam and sail to somewhere in France. Now I can begin the diary proper with notes and recollections of the past three days with my new platoon – and it seems, despite the complement of a captain and a lieutenant, it will be *my* platoon.

Friday   29 December 1939
Arrived at Southampton by rail by 15.20 hrs. Ascertained from R.T.O. the 1404th were at Bassett Green School about three miles from the city centre. No prospect of W.D. transport so I marched there with full kit. Found the school was in use as a transit camp for small detachments awaiting embarkation. No guard mounted at the gates. Men sitting about on their beds and it looks as though they've been there all afternoon, if not all day.

Found the orderly room occupied by a short, tubby sergeant from Glasgow. A territorial Army man named William Menzies, or as he chose to pronounce it, 'Wullie Mingies.' I introduced myself and endeavoured to ascertain our respective seniority in rank. His amiable reply was, 'Hey, you're the regular, Mac. Dinnae bother, it's aw yours.' So the first thing I bothered about was to move him out of the headmaster's office he had quartered himself in and take it for myself. Back to the orderly room to find the platoon establishment.

O/C. Captain Antony PYRNFORD, Regular Army.
2nd i/c Lieutenant Derek BOSWELL, T.A.

Sergeants (2)	– Self and Menzies
Corporals (4)	– 2 Reservists. 2 T.A.
L/Corporals (6)	– 3 Reservists. 2 T.A.
	1 Conscript.
Other Ranks (37)	– 16 Army Reservists
	14 T.A.
	7 Conscripts
Total Strength	– 51 all ranks.

Vehicular	12 –	3-ton W.D. Bedford trucks.
strength:	2 –	30-cwt W.D. Bedford trucks.
	1 –	10 h.p. Hillman car – officers for the use of.
	2 –	open-bodied Morris 15-cwt trucks with A.A. Bren mountings.
	2 –	500 cc Triumph m/cycles. Civilian requisitioned.

Weapons:	2 – Brens for A.A. or field use.
	1 – Lewis gun for field use.
	1 – .55 Boyes A/T rifle.
Personal weapons:	
Officers, N.C.O.s	.303 S.M.L.E. rifles.
& other ranks –	.38 pistols –
	2 for officers' use
	2 for use by dispatch riders

As my former C.O. said, 'An amorphous bunch of odds and sods.'
All the T.A. men were from Glasgow. The usual motley crew of
employed, unemployed and unemployable that joined this part-
time self-styled army to play soldiers, or get a few bob and a free
holiday at the annual camp. Menzies tells me they've just been
paid a £3 bounty for being called in for war service. 'Jist in time
for a guid auld Ne'erday.'

'Where are the officers?' I asked him. He said he had not seen
them since Christmas Eve. I ordered him to get the platoon on
parade immediately in F.S.M.O. (Field Service Marching Order).
He protested saying, 'They wüll jist hiv finished their teas an' be
gettin' ready to go doon the toon.' I repeated my order slowly and
clearly.

With a few exceptions, their webbing is filthy, rifles dirty and
uniforms bedraggled. I select six exceptions and a corporal and
assign them to guard duties for the next twelve hours. A poor
reward for at least endeavouring to appear soldierly. But a sentry
must appear soldierly. The remainder I order to be back on
parade in two hours with kit and equipment blancoed and
polished, rifles cleaned and slightly oiled. There were some mut-
terings at this. I marched and double-marched the muttering out
of them for thirty minutes. Then told them to be back on parade
in one and a half hours. They dismissed quite smartly and in
silence.

Saturday   30 December 1939

I had the platoon on parade again at 0800. After last night's
spruce-up they now have an outward appearance of soldierly
discipline. I am concerned about the reservists. An experienced
but truculent lot. They have all done at least seven years with the
colours, then found themselves a comfortable niche in civvy
street, only to have their slippered feet hauled out from under the
table and thrust back into Army boots. But they were regulars

once and I will make them regulars again.

I had just completed rifle inspection when I saw a Hillman drive through the school gates. The sentry didn't even challenge it. Out got two officers. One, a captain, booted, spurred and breached, cavalry-style, carrying a thick blackthorn as a swagger-cane. The inner wire has been removed from his cap and it is pushed up at the front: also cavalry-style. Worn at what novelists call a rakish angle. The cross-belt of his Sam Browne in place, despite a recent A.C.I. stating the crossbelt must not be worn. Why? I don't know.

Obviously, this was the C.O., Captain Pyrnford, and his 2nd i/c., Lieutenant Boswell. Mr Boswell wore the usual officer's service dress, with cloth belt. Capt. Pyrnford seems to be one of those officers who ignore orders of which they do not personally approve; provided discovery of the breach does not lead to more than a few words of recrimination from above. Not necessarily a sign of a bad officer. I have found some of the more flamboyant officers quite good with the men. By that, I don't mean easygoing. I called the parade to attention and saluted. Saw him eye my brigade cap badge and dark green chevrons. A somewhat petulant twist of the lips and a slight frown from behind gold-rimmed glasses. But he said nothing and inspected the parade. Finding the usual pin-pricking faults officers must find on every inspection. I then brought the parade to port arms. The arms drill was terrible. Nothing I could do about that. It will take at least another week to get their timing to my satisfaction.

However, instead of inspecting weapons, Captain Pyrnford had me stand the men at ease whilst he addressed them. His voice, a loud but languid drawl. 'Yoah peepul,' he said, head in the air, legs wide apart, the blackthorn across his buttocks. 'Yoah peepul knowah as much about sol'jing as myah backside knowahs about steam nahvigation on the lowah reaches of the Zambezi river.' He paused for effect. And the effect was one isolated snigger from a conscript; quickly silenced by the end of the captain's stick being whipped round and pointed at his face. He swung the stick to and fro, encompassing the entire platoon. 'At this moment yoah can neither fuck, fight nor follah a band.' The stick swung threateningly to and fro. 'But you will lahn to sol'jer . . . and lahn quickly. Or else . . .' Here the captain twisted the handle of his stick and drew out a sword blade . . . 'Or else Iah will castrate each and every one of yoah.' He slashed the blade in upward and downward cross-cuts and it thrummed the air in a most impressive

111

manner. The men looked on in stolid silence. Completing his little exhibition of swordmanship, the captain reverted to sweeping the naked blade slowly along the ranks. 'Tomorrow at 0700 we mawch to meet the Hun!' Having exploded that damp and expected squib, the C.O. sheathed his sword, ordered me to dismiss the men to their duties and report to him in the office.

Captain Pyrnford is not much older than I. The glasses make him look older. And I'm glad to say his normal speech is not so exaggerated as in the exhibition he made of himself in front of the men. I don't know what they thought of it; I wasn't greatly impressed. He went too far and it lacked dignity.

His first words to me showed resentment of my Rifle Brigade origins. Told me to get rid of my cap badge and dark chevrons and assume those of the Corps. Then he asked, 'Now what on earth made you jump into this particular latrine bucket?'

I explained about the wound and the reasons for my transfer. The captain has a shallow depression on his right temple that he fingers gently when one is speaking to him. After I had explained he said, 'Yes, jolly good. Need a chap like you; regular soldier.' But as if to remind me of my place, he went on, 'I'm regular army too, you know.' More fingering of his dented skull. 'They also shunted me into this shit brigade. My particular Pathan was an idiot Gunner subaltern. Got me on the downswing with his mallet during the third chukka of an inter-garrison match. An accident; or so he said. The cretin damaged an optic nerve. That's why I'm here. Got to wear these now.' He adjusted the frame of his glasses. 'But I am regular army and I know the game, so don't try to put anything over on me.' Another adjustment of his specs. 'I can see through wool, you know, so don't try to pull it over my eyes.' I resented both the implication and the threat but said nothing.

He went on to give me his orders, such as they were, for tomorrow's embarkation. I found him completely obdurate to, or totally uninterested in, various alternatives and suggestions I proposed in respect of the order of march and about keeping a war diary. I begin to feel it was not only defective eyesight that caused his former regiment to rid themselves of Captain Pyrnford.

Sunday   31 December 1939
We marched, if it could be called marching, to the docks this morning, having run the vehicles down yesterday for loading aboard ship. I suggested to the C.O. the heavy packs and kitbags

should be stowed in one of the vehicles, to ease the weight carried by the men. He refused, saying it would do the blighters good. It may, but it did nothing to enhance the soldierly bearing of the 1404th Independent Ammunition Platoon, trying to march with full pack, kitbag, rifle and respirator. I do not yet know what precedence the R.A.S.C. have on an order of march, or indeed if any thought was given to the subject, but my platoon was fortunately well to the rear, with a battalion of Argyll and Sutherland Highlanders ahead. The Jocks, carrying only their small packs went along in grand style, marching at ease to the steady beat of a song:

It's an Argyll furr me
It's an Argyll furr me
If he's no an Argyll, he's nae use tae me.
Oh your Cam'rons are braw
And yurr Seaforths an 'aw
But the cocky wee Argyll's the pride o' them aw.

All Jocks claim this song, changing it according to regiment. I've heard it as 'a Gordon furr me', or 'a Cam'ron', or 'a Seaforth', and many the fight I've seen between them in disputes as to rightful ownership. It carried the 1404th along in its wake for a mile or so but the weight of about seventy pounds of equipment straggled them out.

Skiller, one of the conscripts, despite his youth, has no youthful form. A potato-shaped body from which limbs protrude like crudely jointed matchsticks. He has spasmodic failures of coordination, his left arm going forward with his left leg and the right doing the same. Most difficult for a normal person. Thankfully this didn't happen on the march with both arms holding his kitbag on top of his backpack, his rifle dangling from his neck by the sling, and bumping painfully against his hip with each step.

The rest of them were in much the same predicament. The Wee McQuish, one of the Glasgow territorials, was cheerful enough, but only because his mate, a raw-boned giant he calls Big Sanny, carried his kitbag for him, with his own balanced on his shoulders. Don't quite know what to make of Sanny, surname Bruce. He soldiers effectively and willingly but with an ill-concealed insolence. One of the older T.A. men, around twenty-four. Superior in speech and intelligence, when it suits him. They say he has a degree from Glasgow University. Nothing in his sheet to substantiate that fact, if it is a fact. Sanny, I presume, is a diminutive of his first name, Alexander.

A slithering sound from the rear brought my attention to Turnbull. Another conscript; reduced to pulling his kitbag along the ground like a sack of coal. I ordered him to get it back on his shoulders. He staggered along, lower lip quivering, eyes tearful. Turnbull was married just before Christmas. Stupid man. No, stupid boy. Far too young. He approached me the day I arrived, to ask timidly if he would be getting embarkation leave. I strongly banished any such notion from his mind. My first sight of his welling tears and protruding lower lip.

The corpulent Sergeant Menzies was chivvying other stragglers along, unencumbered himself by pack or kitbag. Both had been smuggled into the boot of Captain Pyrnford's car, in collusion with his driver. One of Menzies' 'terriers' as he calls them. The officers went ahead. Capt. Pyrnford had told me to take charge of the march, turned to Mr Boswell and said, 'Come along, Derek, old lad. First objective, a decent cabin on the trooper.'

An old soldier of the first war – Pip, Squeak and Wilfred medals ablaze on his breast – was firmly at attention as the Argylls marched past. His shoulders dropped, his chest sagged and his head turned in shame as the 1404th Independent Ammunition Platoon shambled along. For the first time I have doubts about leaving the depot.

2316 hrs. At last the ship is under way. We have been on board since 0950. All the men have had to eat is a tin of bully and a packet of biscuits. And that is our ration for the trip.

Some enterprising deckhands have made buckets of tea and sell it at a penny a cup. No sugar. I can't drink tea without sugar. The territorials are all right with their bounty but most of the others are broke. The C.O. failed to draw pay because of his prolonged and, I am sure, unauthorized Christmas leave. The territorials are buying tea for their comrades. Shows a good spirit. I can make something out of this lot yet. But Menzies and his Glaswegians are going to spend a dry Hogmanay on the high seas.

Have just been up on deck, pitch black, an intense darkness that almost has substance. I sense the presence of other ships around us. Gripped by the excitement of it all. Can't sleep. Returned to the warm corner I found against the funnel and carry on writing.

The sailors are uncommunicative about when or where we will disembark; but over there, in the dark, is the fecund belly of Europe. Oh dear, Mr Gilbert who taught me English wouldn't like that. 'You are too fond of the orotund analogy, boy. Avoid the orotund analogy at all times.' To hell with you, Mr Gilbert. It's a war that, apart from an occasional sea spew, has so far given no sign of viable birth but I can feel its being for the first time tonight. Those who hope the blood-starved foetus will die in the womb, had better run whilst they have the chance, they are cowards and traitors, without honour. All I have is my honour, my country and . . . my regiment? My platoon! Suddenly I am very tired.

Monday   1 January 1940

Crossed the Channel in the night without incident to greet the dawn of a New Year, a new decade, at Cherbourg. Held the platoon at ease on the dockside waiting for the C.O. and Mr Boswell to disembark. When they eventually did, both were hungover. Apparently they managed some sort of New Year celebration in the officers' saloon. Nothing in the way of coherent orders. 'You're a sergeant, aren't you? Get on with it.' I got on with it. First secured breakfast for the platoon. Then back to the docks. Transport off-loaded and moved to vehicle park. First sight of French army who guard the place. Not impressed. A poilu in worn blue uniform, unshaven, boots dirty, rifle slung, wandering about with hands in pockets, a cigarette hanging from his lips. Got a surly stare in reply to my tentative 'Bon jour' then he turned his back and ambled away. He is a man in his late twenties; another recalled reservist, I suppose.

Marched the men back to the Gare Maritime where we are billeted pending Movement Orders. The wind off the sea cuts like a knife, the sky clear and bright as a diamond. Some French seaplanes droning around all day, just beyond the harbour. Taking off, circling, landing, again and again. A flight training base, I suppose. Spotted a battery of French seventy-fives mounted for ack-ack defence. The guns unmanned, except for a couple of soldiers standing with their backsides to an open brazier. Well, I don't suppose the arrival of the 1404th justifies a start to this war that isn't a war.

The Gare Maritime is a huge concrete beehive, although the activity is not so productive. Until recently this was the arrival and departure point for the great transatlantic liners. The rich and famous slipped out of the trains and along the galleries into the ships. Now the building resounds to the clatter of hobnailed army boots. We, and hundreds of other newly arrived British soldiers, are billeted in the place awaiting movement orders. The many levels within the monstrous structure are lined with rough wooden double bunks. The men just milling around. Nothing laid on to occupy them. Discipline is lax, but no one lies on their bunks by day. The cold is too intense. The great arched roof throws down a rolling thunder of stamping feet and thrashing arms. A primitive soldier's dance against his greatest enemies; cold, hunger and boredom.

On the platform at the open end of the terminal where the railway tracks enter, half a dozen blackened cauldrons, known in the Army as Soyer stoves, spew thick smoke from tall thin chimneys. Cooks, in filthy once-white overalls, idly stir the glutinous contents inside the boilers. Groups of soldiers huddle round the stoves, not so much impelled by hunger for the contents, but simply to be close to a source of heat. Three times a day the men are offered food from the Soyers by the simple and continuous expedient of opening can after can of M. & V. and emptying the contents into the boiling pots. M. & V. (meat and vegetables) is notorious for having ill-fed the British Army as a stand-by ration since the Boer War. Tin-tainted, foul-smelling and inedible to all but the strongest stomachs. In the morning and evening they serve a smoky, dung-coloured, unsweetened fluid they call tea. Meals are looked at with dismay, tentatively tasted and discarded in disgust. The privilege of rank affords me better food in the transit Sergeants Mess.

Tuesday   2 January 1940

Still stuck in the Gare Maritime. Possibility of Movement Orders tomorrow. Last night was interesting. Around 1800 a number of French soldiers came in, and as if by established practice allocated themselves to various levels offering to buy clasp knives, underwear and shirts from the British. They did not lack customers. Most of the men, still soft from civilian life cannot stomach the khana from the Soyer stoves and need the money to buy food in the town. Have concluded the first words of the French language learnt by the British soldier are not 'Voulez vous jiggy-jig avec moi, mam'selle' but 'Deux oeufs, pommes de terre frites avec pain et beurre.' That being said, and in the absence of action by any other N.C.O., I took it upon myself to clear these rapacious Frenchmen from the building. Used soldier Pushtu in preference to my limited school boy French. The sharp staccato phrases puzzle and confuse the Frenchmen . . . They retreated, offering only the violence of Gallic gestures and curses in reply.

During the latter part of the evening, Driver Quarrie came to my cubicle at the end of the landing. Driver Quarrie was in serious trouble.

One of the Menzies 'terriers' and one of the few smart men I had sorted out for guard duty on my first parade of the platoon. The silly fool has ruined his rifle. For a soldier, a cardinal sin, worthy of six months in a military detention centre. Yet his honesty in admitting it and the manner of its commission softened my heart. Quarrie, a lad of eighteen, tells me he is from a village, Carmunock, just outside Glasgow, where he worked on a farm. Apparently for that reason, he is fresh-faced, pleasant-featured and well-proportioned as opposed to the coarse, wizened wiriness with which many of those brought up inside that scabrous city seem accursed. Foolish Quarrie had been cleaning his rifle barrel, a process I suppose I should explain in case this document reaches the eyes of a non-military reader. (Delusions of literary grandeur, Lugard?)

In the butt plate of every Army rifle is an aperture, holding an oil bottle and a pull-through. The pull-through is a length of strong cord with three loops at one end and a cylindrical brass weight at the other. For cleaning the barrel, a piece of soft flannel is used. This cloth, 4 inches × 2 inches in size, is always referred to as four by two. Because of demand it is in short supply and has to be cherished. Quarrie's own portion, good soldier that he is, or should become, had been used and reused, washed again and again until it had finally disintegrated.

Fearing his rifle barrel would be contaminated by the salt air on the crossing, Quarrie had unwisely cut a piece from the tail of his army shirt and attempted to use this wodge of flannel to clean the barrel. Needless to say, it had jammed tight just beyond the breech. In desperation, the silly lad had tied the free end of the pull-through to a steel rail and heaved on the greater leverage of the rifle stock. He thus succeeded in ramming the cloth even further up the barrel and eventually snapping the cord. I am not an entirely humourless person and I suppose it was the sad, yet comic incongruity of the situation that prevented me from taking disciplinary action against the 'good soldier' Quarrie. Here he was, newly arrived in the theatre of war, anxious and keen to face the enemy – with a jammed and useless rifle.

Now I should mention that, in his wisdom, the designer of the pull-through had foreseen the crass stupidity of men like Quarrie. The four by two should always be placed in the middle of the pull-through's three loops, the purpose of the bottom loop being to resolve the problem Quarrie had created. A hooked rod can be inserted from the breech and the jam pulled out backwards. Unfortunately, during the so-called training he was given in three months of peacetime territorial soldiering and such as he has received in the four months since the declaration of war, no one had explained the proper way to use a pull-through. The silly lad had placed his shirt tail through the bottom loop! The obstruction, therefore, impossible to shift.

I became very angry at the sending of such ill-trained men to France. The fact he could drive a truck seemed his only qualification. He and half the platoon have never even fired ball ammunition. Quarrie distressed by my anger which was not really directed at him. The poor lad is fearful of both detection and disgrace. I console and reassure him. He responds. I gave him some 'old soldier's' advice on how to get round the problem of his rifle.

Wednesday   3 January 1940
0800. Reported to Captain Pyrnford at officers' hotel. First time I have seen him since disembarkation. No Movement Orders forthcoming after all. Possibly tomorrow. His only orders to me, 'Keep the men busy with something or other.' Returned to the Gare Maritime to find the entire complement of troops lined up on the railway platform with rifle numbers being checked. The parade organized by an irate C.S.M. and four sergeants of the Royal Engineers. A company of Sappers occupy the landing below ours. At 0300 Quarrie had crept down to the Sapper lines and substituted his useless rifle for one of theirs. Well, Sappers being mechanically minded people should have no great problem in clearing the gun. But their C.S.M. is very irate indeed. He has already inspected the serial numbers on the rifles of my platoon without success. I had anticipated trouble and lent Quarrie my rifle. His substituted one is under the boards of my bunk. I didn't serve on the N.W. Frontier without learning to preserve my rifle from the *budmashi*. The C.S.M. of the Sappers was engaged in a ferociously restrained argument with an outraged R.S.M. of the Argylls, for daring to call his men on parade without prior permission and consultation. The Sapper C.S.M. was outranked, and his protests of little avail in face of the gross affront he had placed upon the dignity of the Argylls. The rifles of the Argylls were not inspected, at least not by the C.S.M. of the Royal Engineers.

Afterwards marched my platoon down to the vehicles lines. Vehicles inspected by Sgt. Menzies, who knows much more about the mechanical side of things than I. He is worried about radiators freezing up. Despite a clear blue sky, the sun is a distant blood-red ball, pulsating with cold. It can be looked at with unshaded eyes. No frost, yet every pool of open water is ice, solid. Anti-freeze was supposed to have been put in the engines prior to embarkation but supplies had temporarily run out. Six men were posted to keep the engines running for ten minutes in every hour, day and night. Menzies finds some batteries flat, and rightly curses the men for their laziness in using starter motors when his instructions had been that the engines be turned by hand.

An obvious division of responsibility will be for Menzies to look after the mechanical side. I will take care of training and administration. To that end I will see that Driver Quarrie gets a lance-corporal's stripe and is made orderly room clerk. Not a role for which he is best suited but he seems to have a tidy mind and I can guide him until he gets the hang of things.

I allowed town passes for off-duty personnel from 1700 until military curfew at 2230, and made a point of inconspicuously watching the landing before expiry of curfew to be sure there was no trouble as far as the 1404th were concerned. Trouble there had been in the town, but only between Sappers and insulted Argylls. Most of my platoon were back, disgruntled but intact before 2230. They had found notices up in all the bars and cafés prohibiting the sale of spirits and fortified wines to other ranks. All they could get was what they called 'gnat's piss' French beer. I had seen the notices before and fully approve.

Last in were the Wee McQuish, his oppo, Big Sanny, and surprisingly the timid Driver Turnbull. McQuish began relating their experiences with all the relish of a traveller returned from an unexplored land; his voice as strident as a kettledrum. 'Ah'm tellin' ye,' he said, still wide-eyed at the wonder of his discovery. 'Kip shops, brothels, mair kip shops in this wan road than there are pubs in Argyle Street. An' ye jist walk in. Nae bother. An' ye shid see them, the hooers, ye shid see them. Tits aw hingin' oot. In't that right, Sanny? In't that right?' His appeal for corroboration was quite pathetic. Bruce supported him with the tranquil knowing smile of one relishing the enlightenment of the ignorant. McQuish returned to his tale with renewed vigour. 'An' ye shid hiv seen this yin, wan o' the hooers, somebiddy pit a franc piece on the corner o' a table an' she cocked a leg ower it an' it jist disappeart. Ah'm tellin' ye, it jist disappeart.' He eyed his audience for signs of disbelief. Finding none, he went on, 'An who dae ya think wiz the only yin tae go up the stairs? This yin.' He slapped a blushing Turnbull on the back. 'Could nae haud him back.'

All this was taking place in front of Loach's bunk. One of the more truculent recalled reservists, who has done his seven years with the colours. Six of them overseas. Loach sat up on his bunk and spoke with a harsh sneer of experience. 'Why don't you shut up, you Glasgow git, and get some service in. When you've fucked fifteen shit bints along the banks of the Sweetwater Canal in Egypt, and turked all the two-rupee *ramjanis* in the Bombay cages, you can come back and talk about your "hooers". But until you do, get back to your pit and let us get some sleep.' Loach was quite effective. It quietened them. All except Sanny Bruce.

'Och, now now, ye canny blame the wee fellah.' (What a deadly smile the man has.) 'We, ignorant, peace-loving, Glesga' keelies, imprisoned by poverty to the limits of the city trams, haven't had the opportunities to travel about the colonies and dominions in the service of the King Emperor. We even find the English peculiar. But then the English *are* peculiar.' All the Scots laugh in agreement. 'You canny blame the wee lad for getting a bit excited at his first experience of sexual frankness and liberality. We are in the land of Baudelaire, who said sexuality is the lyricism of the masses. You mustn't be too harsh on this wee laddie who has just discovered that fact after four hundred years of Calvinist repression. We haven't enjoyed, if that's the right word, Loach, your wide-ranging adventures in carnality.' With one hand, Bruce tipped Loach's bunk up on end. Loach was in the top section and it left him clinging to the sides. 'So you'll be a little more understanding, won't you, Loach?' All Loach could do is say, 'All right. I'm sorry. I just want to get some sleep.'

The incident ends peacefully. I'll have to watch Bruce. Mark him for promotion? Get him on my side.

Sunday   7 January 1940
Movement Orders received 4 January. Now well en route to field position as yet unknown to me. I have to rendezvous with Captain Pyrnford near Doullens 1430 tomorrow, 8 Jan. I note the time is conveniently after lunch, at least for him.

The move began in dramatic fashion. At 0330 on 4 Jan. I was awakened by shouting and bawling on the platoon landing. Investigated to find Captain Pyrnford, booted, breeched and spurred, striding about waving his naked swordstick and yelling for the men to get on parade in F.S.M.O. in five minutes. 'Come on. Come on. We're off to fight the Hun.' He was half-drunk.

I got the platoon on parade on the railway platform below. Pyrnford came swaggering down. 'Righta now, yoah peepul. We'll be in the operational theatah of waah in a fewah days. Let's see if yoah can fwighten the Hun as much as yoah fwighten me. Sar'nt Lugard, ma'ch 'em up and down. Airc'aft action, front, rear and both flanks.'

My hesitation in carrying out the order was not due to any lack of alertness on my part. Just the sheer stupidity of it at such a time and place. The drill was devised for troops on the march under enemy aircraft attack. Dependent upon the direction of attack the order is given, as for instance, 'Aircraft action – Right! Five rounds rapid – Fire!' Whereupon the men would come to the halt, swing right and blaze away. It had been introduced as a drill manoeuvre just before the outbreak of war and assiduously prac-tised by the regular army as though it were the total answer to ground-strafing enemy planes. I imagine that whoever devised it thought in First-War terms of a wood-and-canvas biplane oblig-ingly sailing in about ninety miles an hour and around one hundred feet altitude. Such action may have been effective then. But to assume it would deter or even damage modern planes attacking at 300 mph as we have seen in Spain and Poland is about as intelligent as marching men across open ground into the Ger-man machine guns on the Somme.

Why have I become so rancorous and complaining of late? Before the war I could carry out the most idiotic orders without thought or question; as a good N.C.O. should. I have been read-ing too much, writing too much. I have been thinking too much. A dangerous practice in the army. Only private soldiers and G.O.C.s can afford the luxury of thought, and then only the former can do so with impunity.

Captain Pyrnford calls out, 'Wake up, Sar'nt Lugard, I'm await-ing.' I begin the ludicrous performance. At least the conscripts, and a few territorials, have had some training in the drill. Most of the reservists missed it, but have the old soldier's astuteness to follow the movements, although a second or so behind the others. The remainder dither and whirl in confusion. Bolts clatter and triggers click in the semi-darkness of dim lights. Pyrnford thrashes about with his sword stick. 'Terrible, terrible. Theah is no fire control. Make 'em shout. Bang, two three; Bang, two three; Bang, two three.' I do as I am told and so do the men. Other units are awakened by the row and faces appear on the landings above as we indulge in this ludicrous pantomime. Abuse and cat-calls shower down from above. Pyrnford oblivious. I am inwardly disgusted. We kept it up for over an hour. Only fear of the consequences – and my own power of command – kept the men from mutiny. Just before 0500 Pyrnford called a halt, as though bored with it all, or had regained his sobriety. Probably both. After I stood the men at ease he handed me the Movement Order, maps and a map reference. I naturally thought he would lead the convoy. Not so. 'Dammit, you don't suppose I'm going to chug along at convoy speed all the way across France, do you? I've got more important things to do. You can read a map, can't you? Then get on with it, sergeant.'

I asked about billeting for the night halts. He is astonished by my lack of initiative. 'The men have the backs of the vehicles. You and Menzies can requisition a room in a pension. Sign a chitty.' He is quite right. I've had some difficulty in adjusting to the 'comforts' of fully motorized movement. However, temperatures well below zero destroy any illusion that one can sleep, let alone sleep comfortably in the back of a truck. I ignore the C.O.'s suggestion to sleep in a pension and spend the first night with Driver Quarrie in his vehicle. Sat up most of the night huddled in blankets talking with him. He is limited, but interesting in his tales of Scottish country life. Mustn't allow this association with self and Quarrie to develop too openly.

At the second nights' stop, endeavour to find warmer accommodation and discover that straw-filled barns have been allocated for use by troops in transit, although not mentioned in the Movement Order.

Our allotted route has confined us to mainly secondary roads and is by no means the shortest way to the rendezvous. South-east to Vire, and Alençon. North to Evreux. North-east towards Rouen and Amiens, but always skirting the towns as though the presence of British troops would be a provocation. To whom, I don't know. The local population; or the Germans? There is a sinister unreality about this war that is not a war. We are in a sort of limbo. The differences, not only of language, between us and the French are wide. And the barrier widened by their response to our friendly overtures, not only of disinterest, but on occasion of truculence and hostility. We have now reached the village of Pierregot, north of Amiens, where we are spending the night.

Tomorrow by a complex zig-zag of secondary roads, a fairly short run up to our rendezvous with the C.O. near Doullens.

Monday 8 January 1940

I had timed the arrival at the rendezvous for precisely 1430. The map reference indicating a crossroads about ten kilometres north of Doullens by the village of Bouquemaison. For the first time I have the two Bren guns placed and manned on their A.A. mountings on the back of the open 15-cwt trucks. Ahead of the convoy I deployed a section with rifles and the Lewis, another with the Boyes A/T at the rear. The vehicles are spaced at one-hundred-yard intervals with other sections picketing the flanks. We are now inside the B.E.F. theatre of operations and I have adopted as warlike a posture as the limitations of the 1404th Ammunition Platoon permit. Despite the nature of the journey I have seen to it that the men maintain a high standard of cleanliness in both person and equipment. I await the arrival of Captain Pyrnford, or the enemy, with reasonable confidence.

He arrived with Mr Boswell, shortly after 1000, abusive and again half-drunk, as was Boswell, although he remained soporific in the car. Pyrnford said he had been searching for us for hours and that I had rendezvoused at the wrong reference point. I got out the map to show I was correct and he slashed it from my hands with his stick. 'Don't argue with me, Lugard, if you want to keep your stripes.' Needless to say, no praise for my tactical disposition of the men.

Friday 12 January 1940

After Pyrnford's disgusting behaviour as previously described, he returned to his car yelling, 'Follow me.' I had to recall the pickets, a delay adding to his impatience and abuse. Eventually he set off at high speed with only our two dispatch riders capable of maintaining contact. But they knew their job and stopped at the road junctions to await and direct the convoy. Fortunately we had only a few kilometres to travel and reached the village of Beaucourt without losing contact. Captain Pyrnford was waiting by his car with unabated impatience and bad temper. Beaucourt is to be our permanent base. No billets or quarters had been requisitioned. I had assumed Pyrnford's main purpose in going on ahead from Cherbourg was, despite his apparent disregard for the morale of his men, to ensure they were at least reasonably quartered. But, as I learned later from unguarded words dropped by Mr Boswell, they had made a completely unauthorized and highly illegal diversion to stay for two days with friends of the Captain's in Paris where 'they had an awfully jolly time.'

So it was another freezing night in the back of the vehicles for the men and myself. Captain Pyrnford and Mr Boswell, however, got themselves established outside the village in a fair-sized house which is now the Officers Mess.

Next morning, before we could organize ourselves, orders came in to collect ammunition from the railhead at l'Arbret and establish dumps in a corner of Lucheux Forest. Sgt. Menzies, with Mr Boswell in charge, got on with moving the ammunition, whilst I, with the ten remaining N.C.O.s and men, set about organizing quarters, a platoon H.Q. and, above all, a cookhouse.

For two weeks we have been living on M. & V., sometimes hot, more often cold, alleviated, if that is the right word, by bully beef and biscuits. The nearest thing we have to a cook is Corporal Reeves, a reservist, who on discharge married a girl whose father owns a fish-and-chip shop in Lambeth. He had served behind the counter and done a bit of frying before the war started, ruining, at least for the duration, his potential inheritance. Anyway Cpl. Reeves 'volunteered' to be platoon cook and with two helpers unpacked the pots, pans and stores, and got himself organized in an empty and now requisitioned stable, at the rear of the village café. There is a large, if somewhat tumbledown, barn adjacent, that will do for a mess room. For our main billets, we have requisitioned the village hall and three dilapidated but unoccupied houses, the smaller of which I reserved for Menzies and myself as a Sergeants Mess. I have also changed my mind about Driver Quarrie's intended post as Platoon Clerk. His arithmetic is very poor. He will serve as orderly in the Sergeants Mess. Driver Chivers, a weedy, bespectacled but serious and studious type with previous experience clerking in a town-hall office, is better qualified.

By the end of the first day at our permanent base, Menzies and his men have moved nearly one hundred tons of ammunition to the dump in Lucheux Forest, returning late in the evening to a hot meal of bully beef fritters, chips and tea, provided by the now enthusiastic Corporal Reeves. Probably he sees opportunities for fiddling the rations; but I will see he doesn't. Anyway, his meal was a great success and for the first time in over a week, the men bedded down reasonably well fed.

The next day continued with more ammunition shifting from

railhead to dump. At the southern end of the forest, a huge petrol point has been established by a R.A.S.C. company, who have been in France since October '39. I made a quick courtesy call at their Sergeants Mess to learn what I can. Most instructive were the uses to which empty army petrol tins and the wooden boxes in which they are packed can be put.

Petrol comes in oblong sheet metal cans, each holding four gallons, packed in wooden boxes for transit because the cans are so thin and fragile they puncture easily. When cut through the centre the cans make ideal washing bowls, filing trays and storage bins. With the top removed and a wooden handle nailed in place, they are excellent for carrying or boiling up water, or as coal scuttles. The wooden boxes make storage cupboards for almost everything, or, simply pushed together, make a bed that at least obviates the discomfort of lying on the ground. But I had to move fast to acquire the last remaining wooden boxes. Petrol is now being sent out with the tins packed in cardboard cartons, useless for anything, particularly petrol. If it was vulnerable in the wooden boxes, it is much more so now. The C.S.M. reckons fifteen to twenty per cent is lost through leakage.

Without consulting an officer, I diverted three ammunition trucks to pick up the last of the boxed petrol. Menzies says, 'Aye well, it's doon tae you if they tumble it.' But he, more than I, has been subjected to recent tirades from the C.O. about various minor matters, so don't anticipate being shopped by him. In any case, we had to renew our petrol stocks. All I have done is ensure it is delivered in the most advantageous form.

In four days we have established a considerable ammunition dump in the forest, got an efficient platoon H.Q. working, the men quartered in reasonable comfort, fed as well as the limits of Cpl. Reeves' improving ability and imagination allow, and, for the first time in several weeks, paid! Consequently, there is tonight, jollification at Jacques' Café in the village on 'gnats' piss' French beer. The order against serving spirits to the troops is strictly enforced. Jacques' three sallow, fat and moustachioed daughters are busy preparing and serving the deux oeufs, frites and pain du beurre, at cinq francs a time. Jacques and his family very pleased and happy with the business. The rest of the village surly and uncommunicative. They don't want us or our war. As far as they are concerned the war doesn't exist. And it doesn't! The unreality persists. Time in limbo lengthening.

Saturday   13 January 1940

Two days of slight thaw have given me the chance to get some badly needed deep latrines dug. On the morning after our first day at Beaucourt, I found disgusting evidence of their lack, at the rear of the main billet. There are some filthy, lazy and stupid people in this platoon. Junior N.C.O.s lacking initiative. I ordered improvised surface latrines, using the ubiquitous petrol tins. Not very satisfactory. Today we can get picks and shovels through the frozen ground for the first time. And make a discovery, surprising, sobering and macabre.

Six inches down the diggers turn up cartridge clips, small-arms ammuntion, a rifle barrel, a Lewis magazine, bits of mess tins, a steel cigarette case . . . and bones. The whole area is a midden of the First War. The remnants are laid on one side, curious pathetic souvenirs. The metal items surprisingly bright, chillingly malevolent, as if saying, 'Remember what happened here last time?'

Tuesday   16 January 1940

The thaw was short-lived. Road surfaces again ice-bound and dangerous. One dispatch rider in field hospital at St. Pol with a broken arm. I inspected the morning sick parade. Only two men, one of whom was Driver Turnbull of the quivering lip and involuntary tears. Those conditions still present when I asked what his trouble was. He stammered and blushed, saying he had a sore throat, but went on to say he now felt better and could he withdraw from sick parade. He was in such an embarrassed and confused state I almost pitied him. But as he assured me he was now feeling all right, I dismissed him. I am not certain I did the right thing. Something is troubling the man – but it doesn't take much to trouble Driver Turnbull.

Later I went out to the ammo dump in the forest to inspect another use to which the empty petrol cans have been put. With one side opened up and the interior filled with earth, they make fine construction blocks and the four walls of a badly needed guard room for the dump guard was erected in no time. With the tins opened out and flattened, a tight roof was put on over cut-down branches. A stove and chimney, all out of petrol tins, also fitted. This should improve the lot of the guard who had previously shivered in a tent when off watch.

Returned to the Mess for supper to find Sgt. Menzies preparing to go into Arras, where Gracie Fields was putting on a concert for the troops. Six tickets had come in for the platoon. Capt. Pyrnford, Mr Boswell, Menzies, Reeves, Greig (Pyrnford's batman/driver) and Chivers, the platoon clerk, had secured them. I thought the distribution could have been fairer but said nothing.

Sunday   21 January 1940
At 0400 Driver Turnbull fired his rifle for the first and last time. And blew his brains out. He was billeted in one of the houses with McQuish, Bruce, Loach, L/Cpl. Verney and two others.

At least he had the goodness to do it outside. The shot woke up the billet and they went out and found him. I was sent for to take charge. He had done it in the usual way, muzzle in the mouth and reaching down for the trigger. I had seen it often enough in India, where the Deolali tappers ended the heat and misery of cantonment life with a bullet. Odd how they all do it the same way. Especially Turnbull, who could have known nothing of the method. Unless Loach . . .?

I sent for Lieutenant Boswell. He arrives, looks, utters a 'Eaugh' and walks away at a light-infantry pace. An hour later Capt. Pyrnford appeared. In the meantime I had questioned the others in the billet in an effort to find a reason. Nothing helpful materialized. I assume that like all the others who have done the same thing, Turnbull just couldn't soldier. From what I've seen of the poor sod there is every reason to think so. But Loach is morose and evasive. Hiding something?

Contrary to my expectations, Pyrnford did not become angry at the inconvenience caused by Driver Turnbull's death; there will have to be a Court of Enquiry. He examined the body with great interest then said quite jovially, 'Our first fatal casualty eh? I suppose it won't be the last. Gets rid of the cowards and weaklings before the battle begins.' Am half inclined to agree with him. So much for Driver Turnbull! I wonder what his newly married, freshly widowed, and no doubt pregnant wife will make of the telegram 'died whilst on active service.' She will not know the difference between that and 'killed in action' and assume he died heroically. If, as I think he will, Pyrnford leaves it to Mr Boswell to write to Turnbull's wife, I can influence him to maintain the illusion – despite the lack of any action with which to sustain this fallacy.

Tuesday   23 January 1940
Discovered the reason for Driver Turnbull's suicide!

Loach appeared on sick parade this morning clutching his ribs and displaying a badly bruised face. He told me that whilst unloading at the dump last night he had slipped from the tail-board of his truck and fallen heavily amongst the ammo boxes. An obvious lie. I marched him into the Platoon office, where the pressure of my rank, against the inbred fear of his seven years regular service as a private, produced something akin to the truth. He had suffered his injuries at the dump all right, but at the hands of Driver Bruce, who blamed him for causing Turnbull's death. I asked why, and was told by Loach that Turnbull had approached him and sought advice because he, Turnbull, discovering an ominous discharge from his sex organ after his visit to the Cherbourg brothel, thought he had a dose.

According to Loach, he had assured him there was nothing to it. He had caught a dose twice in his service. He said he told Turnbull just to go sick and let the quacks have a look at it. I told Loach to get back on sick parade and stick to his original story. I then got hold of Bruce, who had a slightly different tale to tell. Without equivocation Bruce admitted 'duffing up' Loach. It seems Loach was coming the 'old soldier' in the billet with the younger men like Turnbull – getting them to clean his kit and cadging money. He was also the barrack-room raconteur with hoary tales of the Frontier Province, hot weather suicides, and shit-bint-shagging down in the Canal zone. Of how he gained his V.D. medal and bars, and of the performing donkey in the Port Said exhibition.

The night before Turnbull shot himself, just as everyone was hitting the pit for the night, Loach came in with Turnbull. They had been beering it up together in Jacques' Café. Then as everyone was sitting about on their beds Loach announced, 'And who do you think has got himself a right dose? Our blushing violet here.' Turnbull protested, crying, 'You said you wouldn't tell anyone.' Loach imitated him, then went on, 'Don't be a bloody cissie, a few scrapes of the hockey stick will make a man of you.' He continued to regale the billet with all the grisly details of the 'hockey-stick' treatment for V.D. The 'hockey-stick' is a surgical implement inserted in the pipe of the male organ, then opened up, umbrella-fashion, and withdrawn. Those who have been treated in this way, and I've known a few, seem to take a delight in regaling the innocent with details of the pain and suffering this oft-repeated operation causes. Whether they indulge in this storytelling to justify their carnal behaviour or to enhance their masculinity, I do not know, but they do it *ad nauseam*. I can understand, even if I cannot sympathize with, the fear, the guilt and the shame that caused Driver Turnbull to take to his rifle.

I have no doubt that Bruce, in that casual offhand way of his, told the truth. My anger was more simulated than real when I said in future, if there was any sorting out to be done in the platoon I would deal with it . . . and left it at that as far as he was concerned.

Loach came back from Field Hospital with a handful of aspirin and marked up M. & D. (Medicine and Duty). I have taken him off driving and appointed him latrine orderly and general dogs-body for every dirty job going.

Friday   26 January 1940

The artillery regiments we serve are in Divisional reserve and spread out between Lille and Armentières, seventy-six kilometres from our present base. We have begun to establish an advanced dump in their rear. Why we cannot push the whole unit forward, I don't know. Pointless to ask Pyrnford, who will regard such enquiry as insolence on my part. Mr Boswell says it is because the French refuse to allow the military (ours and theirs) access to railheads in the towns, in case it encourages German bombing. We are obliged to use isolated sidings as a result.

What with this, and paper pamphlets being dropped over Germany instead of bombs, we seem to be running the war on a policy of doing absolutely nothing to upset the Germans lest it provoke their anger and retaliation. The unreality of this war that is not a war persists. Must be ruinous to the morale of front-line troops, sitting about waiting for something to happen. Well, I know they won't be sitting around, they will be building defensive positions, but is that any better? All we hear from official communiqués is 'patrol activity along the Maginot Line.' The Germans have been supreme in everything they have tackled so far. I thought when they encountered armed resistance for the first time in Poland their weaknesses might show but instead we have learned a grim lesson at the expense of the Poles. Or have we? Rumour has it, the politicians have plans for another Munich. Surely not!

Monday   29 January 1940

Heavy snow puts the kybosh on road movement. Made good use of the lull to get in some small-arms training; well, instruction rather than training. I have no access to ranges for live-ammunition firing, but I manage to get most of the platoon drill-practised with the Bren L.M.G. and our solitary Boyes A/T rifle. L/Cpl. Rushton, a reservist, only eight months out of the colours, is still familiar with the complexities of the Lewis gun and training a two-man team. Our small-arms ammunition stock is unsatisfactory. Whilst we have plenty of .303 ball, we have no tracer for the Brens for A.A. purposes; the only way we are likely to use them. The gun itself is an excellent infantry L.M.G. but I cannot see it being an effective A.A. weapon. Having only the aperture infantry battle-sight fitted, the gun cannot be trained quickly enough to sight on low-flying fast-moving enemy aircraft. Without tracer, fast along-the-barrel sighting is hopeless, when the gunner cannot see where his shots are going. And accurate deflection shooting is impossible. I am told the absence of tracer is due to a Geneva Convention ruling prohibiting the use of tracer in infantry weapons. I trust the Germans will be equally scrupulous. We have but five rounds of .55 armour piercing for the Boyes A/T and because of shortages, this is all a line of communication unit such as ours is likely to get. No one in the unit, myself included, has ever fired this weapon in practice. I can only hope we are not called upon to fire it in anger at more than five tanks. That being said, the men have taken to weapon training with enthusiasm and given time I'll fulfil a promise to myself to make real soldiers out of this 'collection of drygrocers and garage-hands.'

Friday   2 February 1940
The C.O. has gone off for what he calls a three-day course. On what I do not know. No orders came through Platoon H.Q. placing him on a course. His driver returns saying he dropped him at Calais where he is to pick him up next Monday. As Calais is now being used for cross-Channel troop transit, I suspect a highly unauthorized week-end in London. Only too pleased to be rid of him. He slides away most week-ends in any case. Paris, probably. He acts as though it were still the peacetime army. In his absence, Mr Boswell pliable and amenable to reason.

More tickets come in for a troop concert in Arras, with George Formby, a popular Lancashire comedian. I have a draw made excluding those who went to the Gracie Fields' show. I drew a ticket to cries of 'fiddle'.

The theatre in Arras was jam-packed. Red tabbed colonels and above occupying the boxes with senior French officers in gold-braided Képis and capes lined with red silk.

I watch the French with interest as they sit blank-faced listening to songs about lamp-posts, window cleaners and Chinese laundrymen. Formby tells a joke that began with him pulling his trousers out from the waist and looking down inside. He laughs and says with astonishment, 'Eeee, Ah never knew that.' These actions and the phrase are repeated several times with greater emphasis and innuendo. Eventually Formby looks up and explains . . . 'Ah can see me shoes down through me trowsis.' Loud laughter from the troops. The French display tight, polite smiles of incomprehension. The senior British officers, aloof disdain; some, frowning disapproval. Seated next to me was another sergeant R.A.S.C., who said, 'It's a pity. A joke the French staff would appreciate is not understood. Whilst the British staff understand, they do not appreciate. That typifies the Allied position.'

I take to this chap and we leave at the interval to find supper. He knows Arras well, being a sergeant clerk at B.E.F.-G.H.Q. located near the town. He led me to a small café where we had an excellent meal. En route we passed a brothel queue where I saw two of my men. Lust overriding the humour of George Formby and the fate of Driver Turnbull.

Sergeant Chatham-Howard is more than a hyphenated name. Like me, in his early twenties. But not a regular, a volunteer at the outbreak of War. I assess him as public school and interrupted Oxford. Promoted to Senior N.C.O. rank pending a War commission. He happily discusses G.H.Q. plans and intentions. We stay where we are along the Belgian frontier and wait for the Germans to attack through Belgium and possibly Holland, then the B.E.F. and the French rush into Belgium and meet the Germans along the River Dyle; the far right being held by the French along the Maginot Line. I appreciate the intelligence but chide him for giving it to me. He said, 'My dear man, a five-year-old boy playing with toy soldiers could assess our intentions just by looking at our dispositions. And I can assure you the Germans have a battalion of people along the Belgian frontier doing just that.'

'Germans?' I asked in astonishment.

'Of course not. French and Belgian sympathizers. And probably two or three of our own. Baillie-Stewart wasn't the only Sieg Heiler in the British Army, you know.'

I asked him why we don't attack first. He feigns shock. 'The French would never permit a silly thing like that. Somebody might get hurt.'

I sat in front of the truck as we drove back to Beaucourt, hearing above the engine the mournful bawling of the men in the back, 'South of the border down Mexico way . . .' Then to a more cheerful, 'She'll be coming round the mountain when she comes . . .'

It does little for my morale.

Sunday   4 February 1940

I have begun to realize just what 'Independent' in the platoon title really means. We have virtually no worries about inspection from higher formations so long as we do our job. Capt. Pyrnford appreciated this much earlier than I, and takes full advantage. He uses the army for his own personal convenience. A car supplied, good quarters, a French cook, Paris-London weekends, visits from civilian friends.

At 0100 I went up to the forest to check the dump guard was doing its job. In the dead of night, the forest is a dark, mysterious place, full of sudden hidden rustlings and sharp unexplained cracks that make sentries nervous. I took care to make my approach fairly obvious lest it bring a bullet without prior benefit of a challenge. However, as I tramped between the banks of ammo boxes stacked on either side of the forest road, I got a very satisfactory, 'Halt. Who goes there?' from Dvr. Uckfield. He was even glad of my company . . . Until I found he had one up the spout and his safety catch forward. And no doubt the first pressure was fully taken up on the trigger of the rifle he pointed at me. I verbally thrashed him for such undisciplined weapon-handling, then turned out the off-duty guard from their slumbers. Found three rifles loaded and cocked. But at least they had their safety catches applied.

Whilst in the process of sorting out Cpl. Sinclair, guard commander, for failing to display the qualities of a good N.C.O., Bruce came to his rescue by offering me a mug of tea laced with rum. The rum was legitimate issue, a pint being given to the six-man guard to ward off the cold. I took it and allowed my wrath to subside. I even made something of a joke of it. 'If you must shoot a sergeant, wait until a German one comes along. Then you'll get a medal instead of a bollocking.'

Bruce points to the red-hot fire in the guardroom and, using the

Glasgow argot of his friend McQuish, said, 'Wull ye no come in fur a bit, an hae a wee crack?' An invitation to casual conversation without rank or rancour. Well, it doesn't do any harm for a senior N.C.O. to fraternize with the men, so long as it's not done too often. So I sat down with them around the stove prepared for a few minutes of give and take. The Wee McQuish was first to speak. (I wonder how he and Bruce manage to arrange to get together even on guard? I wonder, indeed, why I trouble to record this story. No matter.) McQuish was urging his unlikely comrade, 'Hey, Sanny, tell the sarjint aboot the first night at the terrier camp last summer, jist afore the War. Go on, Sanny, tell him.' Bruce demurred, but I supported McQuish's urgings, hoping for a deeper insight into the man.

'Well,' Bruce began, 'in common with thousands of others I joined the T.A. last April to avoid conscription. Better four years of one-night-a-week soldiering than eighteen months of full-time square-bashing. Or so we thought. It was a delusion that affected the oddest assortment of men. From Glasgow razor-slashers to half-educated dafties like masel'. Most of the razor-slashers opted for the Cameronians though; or the H.L.I. if their legs were good enough for the kilt. And it gave them a free bayonet for the occasional street fight. But by the time the fortnight camp came round in July, we were still without uniforms or equipment, and had just got round to mastering the intricacies of the "about turn" at the weekly drill.

'A week before camp, they issued us with a set of First-War webbing, a rifle, and tunics and trousers of the old brass-buttoned service dress. We were ordered to get the lot cleaned and prepared; ready to entrain for Camp the following Saturday. It took so long to issue kit to the two hundred or so new recruits, nobody had time to show us how to fit it together, and if you think we were a bit of a sight marching through Southampton, it was nothing to the crowd that assembled in Queen Street Station, Glasgow, that Saturday morning. Ammunition pouches upside down and wrong way round, water bottles hanging round some necks instead of at the side. Backpacks dangled from waist-belts and a few just carrying their sidepacks because they couldn't see where to fit them. Five-foot-six men had trousers for six-foot men concertinaed round their ankles, and six-foot men had theirs halfway up their calves. It was a sight to strike terror into the hearts of the stoutest men, sergeant. I think even you would have turned tail. As it was, there was only room for two-thirds of the men on the train, so the remainder, including the wee fellah here and masel', were designated rear guard and told to come back at six when they hoped to have another train.

'We eventually arrived at the camp about nine-thirty; were sectioned off and allocated a bell tent. Twelve men to a tent. Then they told us we would find a palliasse down there, some straw to fill it with up there, and two blankets each from the truck over there. And above all, it was impressed upon us ... Standing Orders must be read and strictly complied with! Well, by the time we got down there, up there and over there, it was getting a bit dark, but still enough light for us to read the all-important Standing Orders. They mainly concerned the way we had to lay out our kit each morning. Outside the tent if dry; inside if raining. And underlined was the statement Reveille 0600 – Lights Out 2200. Apart from me, the others were ignorant of Army terms. The Wee McQuish, here, asked what it meant; "This Reveille and Lights Out business." As he said, "Ah mean, there's nae electricity laid on." Before I could explain, a lad named Jackie Kerrigan jumped in. His father was a barber at Maryhill Barracks, and in consequence of that heritage, a self-appointed military expert. "Uch," said the erudite Kerrigan, "it's just the Army way o' sayin' at six in the morning the sun rises and at ten o'clock at night it goes doon." Well far be it for me, sergeant, to destroy such perfect logic. We returned to our tents.

'Have you noticed, sergeant, that however raw the recruit might be, the first thing he does is instinctively demonstrate primordial territoriality and lay claim to a bed-space? The Territorial Army was well named. All of us put down our blankets, heads to the outer walls, feet into the centre pole. Most discarded their uniforms down to shirts, by which time it was around ten-thirty. Can you imagine twelve young Glaswegians going to bed at ten-thirty on a Saturday night, sergeant? No, you're not that daft. Somebody foraged candles from the wet canteen. Somebody else produced a pack of cards and in nae time attaw we had a lively pontoon school going.

'It must have been around one in the morning. I was holding the bank and dealt the cards. The bets were laid, tuppences, thruppences; one wealthy bastard even laid a tanner. I dealt the second cards. A few stuck on what they had, others twisted once and stuck. If I went down I would be out nearly three bob. A large hole in my meagre purse. I turned up my blind card; an ace, to a three. I twisted a deuce. I twisted again; another three. I had only to turn another card for an unbeatable five-card trick, when there was such a battering of swagger canes on the tent walls and a voice bellowing "Orderly Officer". As my card-playing comrades looked in amazement at each other, the tent flap was pulled aside and the disembodied head of a young boy second lieutenant poked in. Above that head appeared another head, an older head with a face like an old boot. The eyes in the young head widened in horror, then lifting to the head above, uttered tremulous words from rosebud lips. "Not only lights on after lights out, Orderly Sergeant . . . but, but, but . . ." The innocent lips had great difficulty in formulating words to describe the sordid scene before his baby blue eyes. And when words eventually escaped, they came in a suppressed shriek. "They're gambling, Orderly Sergeant! Look – Look. They're gambling with money . . . and, and, and . . ." The shriek descended to a horrified whisper. "With cards . . . They are gambling with *cards*." Above, the experienced head of the Orderly Sergeant nodded in solemn agreement. The tent flap was pulled aside and the boy lieutenant stood revealed in full dress blues complete with sword. "What in the name of heaven are you playing at?" A demand for enlightenment.

'Seated round the guttering candles we exchanged pitying glances at such appalling ignorance. "Pontoon, sir," said the Wee McQuish in a polite endeavour to fill an empty mind.

'But it was beyond the officer's comprehension. "What the devil do you mean . . . Pontoon?" The poor boy was screaming again.

'I tried to soothe him with an explanation. "It's from the French, sir, *vingt et un*. Twenty-one. You deal each player a card . . ." I stopped, because it looked as though the boy lieutenant was choking against the tightly clipped collar of his tunic. His face went quite purple, the breath spluttered out of him and he stotted jerkily to and fro like a punctured balloon. Eventually he fell over his sword and had to be helped to his feet by the Orderly Sergeant. It took him a time to gather sword, uniform and himself together. But once reassembled, he attacked gallantly.

' "Stand to attention when an officer speaks to you. How dare you . . . you low guttersnipes. Stand to attention. D'you hear?"

'As you can imagine, twelve men crammed inside a canvas cone that is itself only twelve feet in diameter, can only stand if they lean forward at an angle of forty-five degrees. We had earlier discarded our trousers for the sake of comfort and thus stood leaning forward in our shirt tails, whilst this silly pompous boy went on and on about our heinous and execrable crimes. Now I should point out that to the Glasgow poor from which most of the tent's occupants came, underpants were a sybaritic luxury far beyond their means. I should also point out the law of motion, which dictates that suspended objects will swing out to the centre of the earth. And the centre of our earth, immediately below the objects in suspension, was seven or eight brightly burning candles. As we stood listening to our long catalogue of military crimes, the unpleasant smell of smouldering pubic hair began to fill the tent.

'The Wee McQuish, being so short, suffered most and was the first to break. "Please, sur," he gasped, "Ah'm burnin'."'

' "Are you indeed," said the boy soldier, whose wrath appeared to make him oblivious to all else but nevertheless was slightly appeased by McQuish's admission. "And so you should be. I'm glad that at least I have made clear the burning shame of the disgrace you have brought on yourself and the Corps."

' "Please, sur," squeaked the Wee McQuish, "It's nae wae shame Ah'm burnin'. Ah've got ma balls hingin' right ower these bluidy candles."

'The boy soldier went into his stottin' dance again, until the Orderly Sergeant stepped in to save the situation. "Outside, the lot of you," he cried. So there we were, standing in our shirt-tails in the cold night air, as barebummed as the march-past of the 42nd Highlanders. He took our names and numbers. And explained that in the Army gambling was a great sin, with the solitary exception of Tombola, and even that nonsense could only be played under supervision in the wet canteen.

'Next morning we were marched in before the Company Commander. The boy soldier, still in a state of mild shock, described our vile crimes. The Company Commander, being an older and more experienced man, was not so much shocked as saddened by it all. He lectured us at great length about our low and evil ways, hoping, as he put it, that having lifted ourselves out of the gutter into the Territorial Army, we would emerge not only as upright soldiers of the Army but also of the good Lord. Thus reprimanded, we were dismissed.

'For me the matter did not end there. An hour later, I was on parade again before the Company Commander with about fifty others. As you can imagine, the sudden influx of several hundred men into the unit brought about a need for N.C.O.s. Having been a corporal in the Cadet Corps at school, I was considered potential N.C.O. material. So also were those who had been in the Boys'

Brigade or the Boy Scouts. Even service in the Life Boys or the Cubs was worthy of consideration. So there was I, amongst this assortment, standing stiffly to attention as the Company Commander passed in inspection. He took one look at me and I was ordered one pace forward, right turn and marched away from all possibility of rank and glory. Thus was ruined what might have been a distinguished military career. Much more terrible, I never got my winnings on the five-card trick.'

Bruce ended his tale with that very deadly smile of his, McQuish gazing at him in admiration. 'Jeez, yer a great wan wae the words, Sanny. That's jist the way it wuz.'

I went out with Bruce as he left to relieve the duty sentry. I said to him, 'That reprimand is out of time. You can still get your stripes. You could even get a commission.' He laughed loudly. 'Sergeant, I will participate willingly in this piece of monumental stupidity, but I won't accept responsibility for it.'

I wonder why I waste so much time recording his story? Because there is nothing much else to do, I suppose. How I long to achieve something positive.

Thursday   14 March 1940

I see I have not made an entry in the diary for over a month. Although I have maintained a firm and resolute face by day, night finds me overcome with lassitude and low spirits. Quarrie tries to cheer me up in his naïve and innocent Scottish way, but I have little time for him. Sgt. Menzies becoming too personally involved with the men in Jacques' Café. At least three times a week he comes back to the Mess 'stottin' drunk' as he puts it. 'Jeez, we hid a rare auld rammy doon in Jacques's Café last night. Ye shid hiv been there. Ah gote stottin' drunk.'

Only he and the full corporals can afford to get 'stottin' drunk' three nights a week. The others have a pay-night binge only. Some evidence that Jacques is dispensing the occasional Calvados or Cointreau. If I can substantiate this, I'll do Jacques all the way.

Much has been done and our rear and forward dumps are growing. The work is wet and dismal, for a thaw has set in. The cold is preferable to mud. Met Sgt. Chatham-Howard in Arras last night; he tells me that a platoon from the Duke of Cornwall's Light Infantry was caught with their trousers down and wiped out. It seems the occasional British battalion has been allocated a sector in front of the Maginot Line somewhere in the Saar Valley, alternating in and out for a week at a time.

According to C-H, there is no greater purpose to this than to let the French troops know that not all the British are sitting on their botties up in the Pas du Nord and Pas de Calais and going round shagging their women. Nobody was really supposed to start anything but some of the D.C.L.I.'s predecessors did a little aggressive patrolling. This apparently upset the Germans and the unfortunate D.C.L.I. had no sooner arrived in position when they were bombarded by artillery and scragged by a German fighting patrol.

C-H says it has created a 'bit of a fuss' at G.H.Q. and questions are likely to be asked in the House. The D.C.L.I. suffered at least twelve casualties. At least twelve! I've known of heavier casualties in a skirmish with the Pathans, or in Palestine with the Arabs. Nobody asked questions in the House then and there wasn't even a war on. I suppose it's all because of those sacred vote-holding civilians coming into the Army.

Well, at least there seems to be something of a war going on somewhere. But as C-H says, 'We're going to put a stop to that sort of thing.'

Some Sappers arrived a couple of days ago and began putting up Nissen huts. I look beyond the fact that we are reasonably comfortable in our now well-laid-out billets, and view the permanency of Nissen huts as an indication of military thought being directed towards static trench warfare. Four years in Beaucourt trolling ammunition up to Lille and back? I wish I was back at the Rifle Brigade depot.

Sunday   24 March 1940
A visiting padre comes round and in spring sunshine we had an open air church parade. Pyrnford breeched and spurred for the occasion, leading the hymn singing at the top of his voice, 'All peepul that on eth dooo dwell . . .'

This, despite his annoyance at hearing of the Padre's intention to visit and preach to the 1404th. I presume this put the kybosh on plans for another illicit weekend; lest his absence cause ecumenical affront and ecclesiastic complaint at Corps H.Q. C. of E. Padres are easily upset by lack of protocol. And now by other things, as they find themselves outnumbered in Catholic and licentious France. 'Seek ye the inspiration of Christ in the wilderness to quell the lustful carnal desires that flourish in sinful places. Yield not to temptations of the flesh.'

All this from thick wet lips flapping over an obese paunch.

Afterwards, I marched the men back to their dinner. We've had no fresh meat for five days and it was bully-beef stew again. Bruce came up to me with his mess tin and asked in that insolent, mock serious way he has, 'Just when are we likely to be tempted by some real flesh, Sergeant? All this carnal beef is too easy to resist. Next time try and get hold of a Scots Presbyterian minister to give us a sermon. He wouldn't even know the meaning of carnal and would only go as far as the dangers of strong drink. And the Army has already solved that problem.'

This raises a laugh at my expense, so I put Bruce on cookhouse fatigues to keep him (and the others) in place.

Tuesday   26 March 1940
Since the beginning of February, I have been learning to ride one of the Triumph Speed Twin motor cycles, and am now reasonably proficient. I can take over from Menzies on some of the convoy runs to the forward dump, and when Lieut. Boswell is not in attendance, I take the opportunity to have a run round our 'front-line' positions along the Belgian frontier.

Much hard work has been done in preparing defensive positions and a lot still going on. I wonder how they manage to carry out any training programmes with all the digging and wiring they have had to do? Some concrete pill-boxes being built; and although this is no Maginot Line, it is quite impressive. Can C-H be right in saying we are to abandon this front when the balloon goes up and push forward sixty miles to a river line in Belgium? If the Belgians haven't the guts to get into the war now, why should we abandon prepared positions to rush in and help them? And why spend all this time and effort in preparing the positions when it would be better spent training and preparing the troops for war? What war? Is it yet another demonstration of the army's negative thinking? If there is nothing positive for the men to do, get them to dig a hole. Then fill it in again. Must read my Liddell Hart again and try and make some sense out of what is happening. What is not happening?

Thursday   4 April 1940
The troops now quartered in the Nissen huts, although the officers and sergeants have retained their respective messes. According to C-H, the main reason for putting up the Nissens is because the French are upset at the requisitioning by the British of houses, village halls and the like.

From a 'Comforts for the Troops' fund we've been given a wireless set that works on batteries, and although the programmes from home are faint, we can hear them by huddling round. Mr Chamberlain says 'Herr Hitler has missed the bus.' Why does he still call him 'Herr' Hitler? Is he still hoping for another bit of paper to wave about? Even Pyrnford, for all his 'Hun' and 'Boche' talk, refers to 'Herr' Hitler in a peculiarly admiring manner.

They have a wireless set in the Officers Mess. I had gone there to get the nominal roll signed as Pyrnford and Boswell were listening to the news. Speaking directly to the wireless set, as if replying to the Prime Minister himself, Pyrnford asserted in his parade ground voice, 'Yoah silly man. Herr Hitler has his own bus and he will ring the bell to start it when it jolly well suits him.'

I am more than a little worried now about what I've been putting in my diary. I only write when Menzies and Quarrie are out of the way. Keeping it in the bottom of my kit bag is risky. If I have an accident on the motor bike and someone goes through my kit, I'll lose my stripes and spend the war doubling round the Aldershot glasshouse in full marching order. I wonder why I take such a risk in keeping the diary? At first I was convinced my motives were honourable. Now they seem egocentric, disloyal, schoolboyish at best. Yet the diary has a use as a dustbin for my thoughts, and putting them on paper at least clears my mind for a time. I am beginning to question so much I previously admired and respected. It is all Pyrnford's fault, and Boswell's too. They are not officers; Pyrnford's nothing more than a West End play-boy making a personal convenience out of the army. (I notice I haven't referred to him by rank for some time?) The trouble is there appear to be quite a few Pyrnfords about. Active service largely destroys the remoteness officers enjoyed in peacetime.

Many of them don't realize this and arrogantly display their vices and weaknesses for the troops to see. I hope when, and if, the war really begins their virtues will be equally apparent. In the meantime, I will hide the diary under a loose flagstone beneath my bed.

Thursday   11 April 1940

'Herr' Hitler boarded his bus on 8 April and drove it into Norway and Denmark. According to the wireless, troops landed by parachute and aeroplane to capture Oslo. There was little resistance! Norwegian ports as far north as Narvik have been invaded by sea and occupied! Where was the Royal Navy? Although the wireless speaks of sea battles and the sinking of German ships, our reaction seems that of a fat, elderly gentleman struggling to get out of a deep comfortable armchair when suddenly awakened and told his house is on fire. Met C-H last night in Arras. A lot of the officers at G.H.Q. speak as though carrying troops by aeroplane is unfair, like submarine warfare. Yet I know back in India from '36 onwards, we moved troops by air at company strength on several occasions. C-H tells me a brigade has been ordered to stand-by to go to Norway, with the possibility of it being increased to a division. Apart from that nothing has altered. U.K. leave for troops who have been over here six months is still going ahead!

I can hear Menzies and a couple of his 'terriers' mournfully and half drunkenly 'South of the Border-ing' at the top of their voices. I wish they could find a new song. In the meantime, back under the flagstone for the diary.

Monday   22 April 1940
Pyrnford has been quite pleased with himself and almost civil to me these past few days. He has even turned out fully accoutred to inspect guard mounting on two occasions during the past week. A task usually left to myself, Menzies, and, occasionally, Mr Boswell. Afterwards he complimented me on the turnout and standard of drill.

I get the impression his pleasure lies in being right about 'Herr' Hitler providing 'his own bus'. Our succession of retreats in Norway make me ashamed. I console myself with the thought that we cannot be so blind and stupid. That a plan exists for the French and ourselves to deliver a smashing blow straight into Germany and it cannot be altered or diverted by what is happening in Norway. I have seen French tanks on the newsreels. They are massive and impregnable. Tracked fortresses. Nothing the Germans have could stand against them. And the French have them in large numbers.

Taking advantage of Pyrnford's mellow moods, I raised this with him, quoting Col. Martell and Maj.-Gen. Fuller on the use of armour. But, as usual, this annoyed him as a presumption on my part. He sneered and said, 'The fucking froggies are all wind and piss. They are bloody Bolsheviks. It's the bloody Bolsheviks we should be fighting. Not the Hun.' Why does the man assume that anyone without a commission is incapable of intelligent discussion, understanding only the obscenity of barrack-room language? I conclude that he himself is merely a highly polished version of an ignorant foul-mouthed hooligan. No wonder the cavalry got rid of him. Maybe they fixed it for that Gunner subaltern to belt him over the head with his polo mallet. And despite his disparaging remarks about the French (with which I'm inclined to agree) he frequently entertains in the Mess some of his French friends from Paris. Sleek men and slinky, well-dressed women, driving big expensive motor cars.

Although I have great pride and satisfaction in the way I have created something approaching a military formation out of the rag-tag-and-bobtail I had to begin with, the continuous arrogance and ignorance of Pyrnford, the obsequious and ineffectual scur-ryings of Boswell, all combine to make me sick of it and them.

One means of escape is in recent A.C.I.s. Suitably qualified N.C.O.s who hold 1st class certificates of education may put in for commissions. I will give it another two or three weeks to get the men trained to my satisfaction, then apply. Perhaps I can get myself back into a line regiment. '2nd Lieutenant . . . Michael LUGARD?' Damned if I don't finish the war as Lieutenant-Colonel, then God help Captain Pyrnford if I come across him.

Wednesday   8 May 1940
Our gunners went away three weeks ago for training somewhere in the south. We didn't go with them. I suppose they will use ammunition from existing supplies in the training area. Our base and forward dumps have been fully stocked for some time, so ample opportunity for training of our own. I have had a com-pletely unauthorized rifle range constructed and all the men have fired thirty rounds of rifle. Bren and Lewis sections the same. As shots, the reservists aren't too bad, but with a few notable excep-tions, the conscripts and territorials are pretty poor. One of the exceptions is Driver Quarrie, who made some good short-burst groupings with the Bren. I never allow him to escape training because of his duties in the Sergeants Mess, despite Menzies' complaints about lack of hot meals.

No additional ammo for the Boyes A/T, so we cannot fire that. Not that anyone wants to. All we have heard are stories of its back-breaking recoil. Even I have never seen it fired. When we first got them back in the R.B. depot, the small-arms instructor who drilled us in it (without ammo) said the shot would penetrate up to three inches of armour and then ricochet round the inside of the tank, killing the crew. And although it looks a deadly and efficient weapon, I take his statement with a great deal of salt.

To my gratification, for I never sought his permission, Pyrnford commends my initiative over the rifle range. He and Boswell come up frequently and bang away with their pistols at empty bottles. Most of the bottles are intact. The .38 ammo nearly expended. At the end of the week I will prepare my application for a commission.

Saturday   11 May 1940

The balloon has gone up; the War has started. It began Thurs. night. Enemy planes came over and dropped a few bombs near Arras. We could hear the crump of bombs and see the sparkle of A.A. shells in the sky. Without waiting for orders, I put half the platoon out on picket in case of parachutists. They went out in great spirit and those that I held in reserve were disappointed not to be chosen.

Pyrnford came back from Arras with tales of great destruction which do not seem justified by the small number of bombs dropped. He says a R.A.F. base at Reims was bombed and completely wiped out in another raid the same night. He goes about flourishing his sword-stick with a wolfish grin on his face, refusing to wear a steel helmet or carry his respirator anti-gas. Clearly enjoying himself. Well, so am I.

The Germans have gone into Holland and Belgium. A great battle going on for a Belgian fort. Eben something or other. Parachutists used. I've strengthened our pickets. Suggested to Pyrnford we should move everybody and everything under cover in the Lucheux Forest. For once he agrees, but it will not apply to him or Boswell. 'Be damned if I'll give up the mess.' He quite sensibly adds, 'Besides we have to maintain our location for receipt of orders.' So leave platoon H.Q. and a Bren section in Beaucourt. All else to the woods.

Sunday   12 May 1940

More bombing around Arras last night. Could see the glow of fires. We are pretty secure in the forest, plenty of good cover. Advance columns of the B.E.F. are in Belgium. We are stuck here with our gunners making their way back from the training area. Went for a wide recce on the motorbike. An ominous sight on the St. Pol–Doullens road. Several civilian cars packed to capacity, mattresses tied on the roofs, all heading west. Some of them tearing along like madmen on the wrong side of the road. I had not expected this.

Tuesday   14 May 1940

Have been feeling apprehensive all day. Holland seems finished, and the Belgians are obviously in retreat. The wireless tells of a flight of Fairey Battle bombers that went out to try and destroy bridges over the river Meuse. None of them got back; some damage caused to the bridges! Troops of the B.E.F. have been in action according to Pyrnford. 'The 12th Lancers are in amongst the Hun, Sar'nt Lugard.' A triumphant flourish of his sword-stick. 'Knocked the shit out of 'em.' Then spoiled it by adding, 'All the rest in retreat.' The 12th Lancers are mechanized cavalry and that is the only remote connection between them and Pyrnford. So good luck to the 12th Lancers. Long lines of civilian cars on the St. Pol–Doullens road now, horns blaring at the slightest delay. Some of the men in them of military age. Are they running away?

I look at it from their point of view. No doubt they are getting their families to safety and will return to join their regiments.

Thursday   16 May 1940

We are still hibernating in the Lucheux forest whilst presumably ahead of us the war goes on. The batteries for our wireless set have packed up and little in the way of reliable information reaches us . . . Nonsensical rumours abound. The French have collapsed at Sedan and German tanks are in Reims. This is coun-terbalanced by word that German bodies lie twenty deep along the Albert Canal and they have lost sixty thousand men. I con-vince myself that the first story is false and the second true. But I don't like what is happening on all the roads around us. The cars of the rich have gone. Replaced by the cart-pulling, perambulator-pushing poor. Thousands upon thousands of them – men, women and children, trudging along . . . in silence. It is a disquieting silence. These usually voluble people do not speak or even look at you. Only the children look at you. Mute appeal. To what, in God's name? They should have stayed where they were. I had not expected this.

Pyrnford has taken to dashing about on his own. Sometimes in his car, sometimes on one of the motor-cycles. To what end and for what purpose I do not know. Nothing falls from his lips but curses at 'Those damned frogs clogging the roads.'

Our first sight of the enemy! But only in aeroplanes flying high to the east. A large formation of Heinkel 111's sailing unper-turbed through the puff balls of A.A. shells. Then follows the crump of bombs. The men watch with interest. It is a distant spectacle, interesting, without personal danger. No one seems to think it could just as easily be them beneath the bombs. Another skill I acquired during the dull months is recognition of various types of aircraft from pictures and drawings in magazines. I also wanted to be able to identify German tanks and armoured cars. A few weeks ago, I asked C-H if there was an instruction manual available for this purpose. If one exists he has not seen it. 'Besides, old chap, if you have the misfortune to run into a Jerry tank, I'm sure you'll know.'

Sunday   19 May 1940

We have moved forward at last and did so yesterday. Not so much a forward move but a sideways and backwards move to the north of Albert. A town that has nothing to do with the Albert Canal in Belgium where sixty thousand Germans were supposed to be slaughtered. They weren't. It has everything to do with the supposed German break-through at Sedan. They did – and are now deep in our rear! A confused, hectic and sleepless twenty-four hours, but I am not in the least tired. A few of our guns are in action along the Somme, near Cléry, and we moved up twenty tons of ammo last night. Some enemy tracer and Very lights visible across the river. Gunners say they, and the Royal West Kents, beat back a German tank attack last night.

After dropping our load it was back to Lucheux to replenish. Not an easy job. Panic and chaos on the roads. Roads jammed with refugees. Some we unavoidably ran into in the dark and we must have killed and injured many. Never stopped to find out. Saw several French and a few British soldiers interspersed with the refugees. Can they be running away? No, they must be posted there to try and control the refugees. Someone fired shots at us as we came back through Doullens. No one hit, but two windscreens holed and three side cab panels punctured. A few jumpy drivers as a result. Who fired the shots? More rumours of German parachutists dropping behind our lines. Whispers about 'fifth columnists'. I remember C-H and his talk of French and Belgians working for the Germans.

At seven this morning the 1404th fired its first shots in anger. At least, Driver Quarrie did so on behalf of the platoon. Three low-flying Dornier 17s came right over our convoy outside Marmetz. The crew inside clearly visible. Quarrie managed to fire a few rounds at them from the Bren truck before they disappeared behind the trees. Then Boswell came along, greatly agitated, and stormed at poor Quarrie 'for giving away our position'. Quarrie answers stoutly saying, 'I thocht that wiz whit ah wiz here furr, sir. Tae kill the bastards.' Boswell threatens him for answering back and while he is going on, another formation fly over. This time we get a short burst of M.G. fire from one of them and everybody scatters. It is over in seconds. No casualties. Some of the men watch the sky for more. Boswell runs up and down screaming. 'Don't look up. Don't look up. They can see the white of your faces from ten thousand feet. You'll give away our position.' The man is an imbecile, and a frightened imbecile at that.

No sign of Pyrnford, he is out tearing around as usual. But he is enjoying it. I'll give him that.

Tuesday   21 May 1940
Now outside Arras.

Confusion piles on chaos, and out of it, defeat. Unknown to us at the time, we got out of Albert in the early hours yesterday just ahead of the Germans. The Royal West Kents weren't so lucky. Their leading companies drove all unsuspecting into the town's main square. No sooner had they arrived than a horde of Stukas dive-bombed them. Then large numbers of German tanks moved in along every road. They were bottled up and slaughtered after putting up a brave fight. Only a few escaped. I get all this from a surprisingly communicative Pyrnford. He tears about everywhere and is absolutely fearless. Oddly enough, Driver Quarrie mentioned seeing him from the back of the A.A. Bren truck as he came through Louvencourt where the R.W.K. were in position prior to their fateful move into Albert. Said Pyrnford was wearing a red and white armband. A staff officer's brassard! Quarrie must have been mistaken.

Now keep my diary on me at all times. It fits neatly in the large map pocket on the front of my battledress trousers.

Heavy fighting all around us. Yesterday the platoon was detailed to bring fighting troops forward to Vimy Ridge; although it is difficult to define where is forward. To the south is forward, as is to west and east. A strong British counter-attack went in this afternoon around Arras. Rumour has it going well with great slaughter of Germans. Yet rumour also has it that Abbeville fell to a panic retreat in the face of light reconnaissance by German motor-cyclists. A voluble and excited Pyrnford says the Abbeville report is perfectly true. The man is at his best in defeat. His flamboyant cursing and sword-waving at attacking

German aircraft seems magnificently appropriate. Except to Boswell, who sees every Bren and rifle shot at enemy aircraft as a certain invitation to bring down their wrath personally on his head. Pyrnford's shining blade must seem like a flashing beacon to him. During every air attack he sits cowering in the womb of the Hillman.

So far no casualties from several air attacks. But two three-tonners destroyed. We have dug in for the night. More pathetic debris from our predecessors of '14-'18 comes to the surface to mock us. Just to the north, great carved figures on the Canadian War Memorial at Vimy Ridge frown in dismay. Bullets whine through serried headstones above their graves. Shells delve among their bones.

I am torn by guilt and anger at our betrayal of them. At our failure to defend their memory, their sacrifice.

Wednesday   22 May 1940
The great Arras counter-attack has ended in defeat. Today we picked up a number of various administrative personnel, officers and men, out of Arras and ferried them to Dunkirk, dropping them near the docks. They seem to think they are going home. They call themselves 'useless mouths.' Being got rid of because they are simply in the way. Another rumour?

Thursday   23 May 1940
Been working ammo out of the Dunkirk docks to dumps in the Forest of Nieppe. Two moderately heavy air raids. Platoon H.Q. set up in a sunken road by the village of Steenwerck, near Armentières.

Our first casualty – Driver Skiller – he of the uncoordinated arms and legs. Another formation of low-flying Dorniers, a casual burst of M.G. fire as they went over (obviously they had no great interest in us) but Driver Skiller got the bullets in his chest and fell in his tracks. We buried him in a corner of a field.

Where are the R.A.F.?

We hear our guns are lost. Some at Arras, others elsewhere; we know not. The batteries were split up piecemeal and sent hither and yon. So it seems we really are a collection of odds and sods, available at anyone's beck and call. But for the past twenty-four hours no one has beckoned. Apart from the occasional fruitless sortie to fight rumoured parachutists and rumoured tanks in our vicinity, we have slept and rested. Another rumour. Jacques, the café proprietor from Beaucourt, has been seen spying again in his black Citroën. Everywhere we go, someone says Jacques was seen nearby. But when I question the men, it is always someone else who saw him. Jacques is always 'seen' in the vicinity of some disaster. At Albert. At Arras. Just before the air attack that killed Skiller. Armentières was heavily bombed an hour after we drove through. Jacques was definitely seen in Armentières just beforehand, by somebody who told somebody else. I am convinced it's nonsense. In the vacuum of fact, rumour rushes in. 'The G.O.C., Lord Gort, was killed at Doullens.' 'Hitler's plane crashed yesterday. He, together with Goebbels and Goering are dead. That's why it's so quiet today. The Germans want an Armistice.' An illusion dispelled by another heavy air attack on Armentières this evening.

Cpl. Reeves fed us on stolen chickens boiled up in the Soyer. A welcome relief from the eternal cold bully and biscuits we have lived on for the past two weeks. Has all this happened in just two weeks? The Germans are at the Channel having taken Boulogne! Truth or rumour? We are cut off. Fact!

Friday   24 May 1940
Last evening we went to Bergues, near Dunkirk, and parked alongside the canal with a view to loading up at the docks first thing in the morning. We awoke to find water up to our axles, and only managed to get the vehicles out with difficulty. In the night someone decided to flood the low-lying countryside in an effort to hold up the Germans.

Bergues is a sleepy, picturesque town with an ancient walled fortress. In spite of everything, many citizens, and quite a few French soldiers, take full advantage of the glorious weather to fish the canal with great long rods. A peaceful, almost idyllic scene in the early-morning sunlight. We eventually got our vehicles dried out and moved into the docks. Cratered, badly damaged, but still a viable port, dominated by a great spreading cloud of black smoke drifting above us like a shroud. Source; burning oil tanks.

The masts and superstructures of three half-sunken ships sit like skeletons in the sea-way. Twisted railway lines, poised snakelike. Dying flames lick the wall of a burned-out warehouse. French soldiers, marching a column of German prisoners, hands in the air. Reassuring. We must have beaten them somewhere. Marching them to what? To where? Firm shouted commands from ship and shore. There is an inspiring air of grim determination about the place.

At midday, the indomitable French ack-ack on top of the citadel opened up with their seventy-fives. We looked for cover but this time the Germans were not interested in Dunkirk. It was Bergues that got it.

Bergues was a sleepy, picturesque town —

Saturday   25 May 1940
A bad day. Two men killed by enemy action. Driver Quarrie was murdered by Captain Antony Pyrnford!

We got to the docks at Dunkirk at 1115 hrs for another load of ammunition. Half an hour later, the inevitable German planes appeared. A larger formation than I had previously seen. At least forty aircraft in the first wave, majestically sailing across blue skies at about 1200 feet. Contemptuous of the futile dandelion clocks of ack-ack flowering around them. Bombs dropped from this height are preceded by a screaming pressure wave, more unnerving than the blast of the subsequent explosion. When one can see the source of death, the impression that its dry fingers are reaching for you, personally, is very strong.

When the planes first appeared I stood on the quayside, the railway trucks behind me. Prepared to watch, to command, to act when necessary. But the fearful sound of falling bombs, closer to me than ever before, drove me back step by hesitant step, until I stood with my back against a railway truck, stiffening my shoulders against its side, my feet dancing under the juddering, thudding explosions. I saw heavy cobbles erupt and crash against vehicles, trucks and men. At the end of the quay, a crane rose slowly in the air and, silently it seemed, slid across the dock. Incendiary bombs hissed and smouldered on the ground, somehow innocuous and comforting. And as the first wave turned away, others approached, inexorable, pitiless. Below, in the blast-filled cauldron, I was useless, helpless, hiding myself in a detached numbness. I saw Driver Quarrie dazed and exposed on the Bren mounting, his useless little pop-gun swinging wildly, as successive blasts rocked the truck. I was fixed in a paradox of despair and euphoria. Muscles like water, but mind omniscient. Somehow, I saw myself walking across to Quarrie, motioning to him through the heaving thunder to take cover. For seconds that were hours, I considered taking over the gun, watching the German planes so high in the sky. Feeling that the effort of climbing into the truck was too much, and in any case – pointless.

I patrolled our line of vehicles. One was burning; its load of ammunition boxes exploding singly, in regular rhythmic sequence. An incendiary burned close to another vehicle. I drove it clear and was returning, when I saw Pyrnford standing over Driver Quarrie who was crouching under the A.A. truck. The captain had both fists clenched above his head, one holding his sheathed swordstick. He was castigating Quarrie over something or other. Suddenly, as if to match his rage against the storm around us, he dashed his stick at Quarrie's face. It bounced harmlessly from the tyre behind which Quarrie ducked. Thwarted, Pyrnford stepped back, drew his pistol and shot the boy twice in the body. And all the time I was trudging in a slow-footed trance towards them, screaming at Pyrnford, but not hearing my own voice. Pyrnford picked up his stick and came towards me, eyes demonic behind his glasses, face a livid, sweating mask.

'Abandoned his gun. Cowardice in the face of the enemy,' he waved his pistol at Quarrie's exposed boots. 'Punishable by death. Cowardice in the face of the enemy!' As if to prove he was incapable of such a crime, he lifted his pistol and emptied it at the departing planes. 'I will not have cowardice in the face of the enemy.' He stalked away shouting, 'Come along, yoah peepul. Get off yoah bellies and get on with yoah work.'

The men began to appear from under the railway trucks where most had sought cover. Five were missing, including Boswell. Two we found in the rubble, their heads crushed by flying pavé. Two more are simply missing. I doubt if they have been killed. They are probably trying to squeeze themselves in amongst the gathering throng of 'useless mouths'. Boswell we found cowering in the iron bucket of a dockside crane, quite near the still-exploding truck. Each successive blast sent him tighter in to a corner. The inside of the bucket smelled strongly of excrement.

I have said nothing to anyone about Driver Quarrie's death. The others assume he was killed by enemy action. But Bruce knows. He came up and asked me, 'What are you going to do about that murdering bastard Pyrnford?'

Sunday   26 May 1940
We are in 'laager' as Pyrnford calls it, near the village of Houthuist, along a shallow sunken road with cover on one side from

overhanging trees. A fairly quiet day so far (1800 hrs), with no calls on our services and only the occasional swarm of enemy aircraft overhead. They pay us no heed. (Where is the R.A.F.?)

There is great anger smouldering in me over the death of Quarrie. I am determined to do something about it. The trouble is, what? How, in the midst of death, destruction and defeat, can I do anything? Who will I go to? Who will listen, or care about the puny killing of one man when so many others are dead in greater glory?

I made a reconnaissance on the motorbike this morning and, in the maze of narrow lanes and tracks, lost direction. By an abandoned farmhouse I came across a Brigadier sitting alone on a grassy bank eating a can of bully. His bullet-riddled car was in the ditch, the driver's body still inside. I went up to him, intending to report the murder of Quarrie, but his eyes were as dull as those of a dead horse. His face gaunt with weariness. Dried blood caked the outside of one ear. He asked, kindly enough, what I wanted. God, how could I mention such comparative trivia. Lamely, I said that I seemed to have lost my platoon. He raised his head and smiled at me. It was a very tender smile. 'Then we are both in trouble, sergeant. I've lost my entire Brigade.'

I offered to take him on the pillion anywhere he wished. He declined, shaking his head absently. Then, apropos of nothing, said, 'I expect Calais has fallen by now. The Rifle Brigade have held it for the past week, to the last bullet, to the last man. But I fear the last bullet has been fired and the last man is dead. I have a son there.' He spoke without pride or even sadness, quietly, as though describing a sunset so sombre and magnificent that other words would be an intrusion. It's the first I have heard of the defence of Calais by the Rifle Brigade. And I was not there! I longed to ask him more about it. Was there, is there still a chance they may hold out? But I could not bring myself to intrude further upon a grief that screamed the louder because it had no voice or expression. I wanted to ask his son's name in case I knew him. He would be an officer, of course. A gallant gentleman like his father. I wanted to tell him I once served in the Rifle Brigade, that I should rightly be with his son in Calais. But the Brigadier's eyes were far beyond my presence. All I could do was salute him and say that I had to find my platoon. However, he was conscious of me, for he stood to return my salute and wished me luck. My last sight of him was sitting on the high bank, arms grasping a bent knee, chin resting on top, eyes gazing towards where only the Germans can come. I have a feeling he will rest there for a long long time.

A grey dismal rainy dawn. Calais has been overwhelmed and the Rifle Brigade have, as the Brigadier said, fought to defend the town to the last bullet and the last man. Who was it that said, 'When I am opened you will find Calais lying in my heart'? One of the Tudor queens. I've forgotten which. It is not a claim I will ever be able to make. Damn Pyrnford. (Why do I blame him?) Rumour has it the Belgians have surrendered?

We are now reduced to water-carriers, picking it up in cans from Dunkirk and dumping it at various water points along the coast road between Bray Dunes, La Panne and out nearly as far as Nieuport. The roads are full of marching men heading for Dunkirk and the coast. Useless mouths? Surely there can't be as many as that? Roads also clogged by great lumbering French army trucks, going God knows where. From the fields around us a heaving stench of rotting flesh. Dead cows lie bloated, legs in the air. Dead horses adopt a more natural recumbent position, but still stink. Here and there, dead men just lie and rot. Sight now and again of occasional British tanks and armoured cars, west of Nieuport. They display large British flags, presumably so they won't be shot at by our own troops. Our airmen are not so fortunate. Yes, we have had intermittent sight of the R.A.F. during the past two days. Occasional dog-fights high above. German planes shot down and presumably some of our own. But when the parachutes float down everyone assumes them to be German and opens up on them without thought as to whether it is friend or enemy floating in the sky.

It is now 2340 hrs. We are in laager at Uxem, south east of Dunkirk. Over there, the black night is tinged with red, and riven by bomb blasts. The road beyond the barn in which I sit with candle and diary is full of marching men. Went down to the end of the track to join Sgt. Menzies, Cpl. Reeves and others watching them go past. They march quite jauntily, some of them; others can barely drag themselves along. We ask them where they are going. All we get in reply is, 'Christ only knows.' Yet there is good heart in them – and us.

Pyrnford ordered me to take four men in a three-tonner to La Panne early this morning to obtain field rations. The man has changed since he shot Quarrie. The flamboyant stick-waving and exaggerated cursing has ceased. He is now snappish, edgy and restless. There is an air of uncertain expectancy about him, as though he is awaiting some anticipated event and is unsure of the form it will take. Conscience? Fear of the consequences? Boswell only emerges from the Hillman at night, and then only to relieve himself. No one, including Pyrnford, even acknowledges his presence.

Arrived at La Panne, 0700. After a strong argument with an M.P. on the outskirts, who said the vehicle was to be run off the road and destroyed. I indignantly protested that we were not 'useless mouths' wanting to be evacuated. He in turn said to my astonishment, 'The whole fucking B.E.F. is being evacuated, sarge.' I gave him a good dressing down for calling me 'sarge'. I will not be called 'sarge' by anyone. When I explained that the 1404th were still operational in the field and all I wanted were rations, he let us through.

An amazing sight. The place is a beach resort, relatively undamaged. Large imposing houses overlook the sea. The streets full of troops wandering about uncaring, uncontrolled and disorganized. Some drunk. A café behind the beach with tables out on the pavement incongruously selling beer. Overhead, a couple of Messerschmitts were machine-gunning a beach we could not then see; a single Bofors gun spat-spat-spatting at them to no effect.

Stopped again just short of the beach where the M.P. said ration boxes had been dumped. This time it was a C.S.M. of the Welsh Guards who had a Bren-gun post set up on the street corner. Again I explained all I wanted was to pick up rations. The Welsh Guards are from the G.H.Q. defence company. Lord Gort's H.Q. has been set up in one of the large houses. The C.S.M. reluctantly let us through with the vehicle, but we cannot take it on the beach because it will be bogged down in the soft sand. He directed us to open ground behind the dunes. We will have to manhandle the rations to the truck.

The dunes packed with soldiers, sitting in small tight groups along numerous depressions and hollows in the sand. Sight of a smooth wide beach, the tide going out. A paddle steamer beached high and dry, with several other small ships also stranded. The paddle steamer named *Gracie Fields*. I missed her concert, now I was going to miss her boat. Out in the seaway, a dozen or so other ships, together with a couple of destroyers, steam slowly up and down. Overhead three Spitfires flew in, to patrol at low altitude.

Long lines of men tail away from the beached ships, waiting to be allowed on board. Presumably when the tide comes in they hope to float away to safety. Other serpentine lines form to the water's edge. There are no ships before them, and at first I could not understand their lemming-like behaviour. Then I saw a ship's boat manned by sailors pulling into the beach to pick up ten or so of the waiting soldiers, turning to row them out to larger vessels offshore. So many men, so few at a time.

McQuish expressing wonder, 'Did ye ever see anythin' like it in your life, Sanny? The Broomielaw wiz never like this. No' even on the first Saturday mornin' of the Glesga Fair, wae hauf the toon goin' doon the watter tae Rothesay.' I don't quite know what he meant, but before Bruce could reply Lord Gort, V.C., himself appeared, striding along the beach with an aide. Bluff and hearty, stopping occasionally to stare out to sea. We watched him, and everyone else watched him with awe and respect. Tall, broad-shouldered, barrel-chested, every inch a soldier. McQuish asked anxiously, 'Whit's he daein', Sanny, eh? Whit d'ye think he's daein'?'

Bruce replied, 'He is considering the possibility of striking the sea thrice with his cane, parting the waters, and marching his men back to England dry-shod.' I sorted Bruce out for showing such disrespect and ordered him and the others to get the ration boxes loaded into the truck.

Hard hot work under a blazing sun, carrying the heavy cases of bully and biscuits across soft sand and over the dunes. After a couple of hours, I granted a break for a smoke. The men had only just lit up when the single Bofors went into action. Further along the beach towards Bray Dunes, a small battery of 3.7s whip-cracked at the sky. Guns on the destroyers boomed across the sea. The long lines of waiting men begin to undulate, like strands of seaweed before a storm, then for a moment stiffen, only to dis-integrate into separate fleeing particles like ants made mad. Overhead, a clear blue sky, riven by German arrowheads driving unerringly through a thin screen of protesting puffballs. The Spitfires have gone, the Heinkels have arrived. Bombs come down; sea, sand and sky torn and lacerated. 'Cry Havoc and let slip the dogs of war.'

This time I absorb it, relish it, revel in it; the insane magnificence of righteous war. War in all the elements. Even when Messerschmitts came in at low level, rattlesnaking along the beaches, machine guns ripping and tearing, I stood before them hip-firing the unmounted Bren in something akin to ecstasy. Sand erupted, and showered about me from bomb and bullet. I was blown over twice but got up unharmed and continued firing until the gun seized; the action clogged by sand. At sea a Stuka fal's screaming upon a destroyer, only to be broken on the wing. Others followed. Then the destroyer, with flames erupting from her stern, came slowly to a stop, still afloat, red-black smoke spewing from her, in distinct resonant belches like spume from a dying whale. She recovers, staggers forward, turns, gains speed during a respite, then more come down on her and she is devoured in a convulsion of sea and flame. Suddenly the planes are gone, one by one the guns cease firing, and miraculously a thick carpet of seeming corpses rise from the sand, and slowly, as iron filings drawn to a magnet, the lines reassemble and the patient waiting begins again. The destroyer is afloat, head down, the sea licking her wounds. Other ships smouldering. Distant black dots bobbing on the sun-dappled water, small boats rowing amongst them. A quiet. Still as a Remembrance parade. Scarcely audible under its weight, McQuish squealing and moaning over by the ration dump. 'Oh ma God, Sanny. Ah'm bad hit. Ah've got an incendiary bullet in ma back.' Bruce and the others rush to where McQuish lay squirming face down in the sand. They burst out laughing! McQuish howls, 'Sanny, Sanny, Ah'm no kiddin'. Get me hame, Sanny. I want tae see ma mammy!'

'You silly wee bugger,' Bruce says. 'You are definitely going to burn in hell fire, but not yet. This is just your second initiation.' He lifted a burning cigarette from the middle of McQuish's back. Someone, in their anxiety for cover, had thrown a cigarette down on the quickly recumbent McQuish. It had eaten through his shirt and burned on his flesh throughout the duration of the raid. Everyone thought it a huge joke – except McQuish. Apart from a large blister across his spine he is unharmed.

We were continuing to load rations when a gunner captain approached, the side of his face swathed in a dripping field dressing, even his one visible eye swam in a bloody pool. 'You chaps coming or going? I'm the beachmaster on this section. Got to get you fellows organized, y'know.' He forced a gay nonchalance into his voice, but only succeeded in making himself more anguished than his appearance already indicated. I was not clear to which direction his 'coming or going' referred, so I explained we were taking rations back to the perimeter.

'Oh good,' he said. 'Just hold off the jolly old Boche for another couple of days till I get rid of this lot. I'll still be here. Keep a place for you on the *Saucy Sal.* Carry on. Cheerio. Good luck.' He sauntered back to the foreshore, staggering now and then, straightening up, pulling himself forward. Reminded me of the destroyer. God, how I admire that officer.

We got out of La Panne by 1500, fully laden with rations plus six Bren guns, two Boyes A/T guns, ammunition and three cases of 36 grenades. All abandoned among the dunes. British soldiers abandoning their weapons! It is appalling.

Before we left the beach a beehive buzzing began. Someone had definitely heard a news broadcast that the Americans and Russians had issued a joint ultimatum to Germany, demanding they pull back from all occupied territory. Otherwise the Americans will send a thousand bombers to destroy Berlin and the Russians will invade with ten thousand tanks and ten million men. Five kilometres out of La Panne we saw another huge air attack going in on the beach. So much for ultimatums.

Thursday   30 May 1940
Sgt. Menzies took two trucks into La Panne last night and got further ration supplies which we have dumped at designated points around our section of the perimeter. Before he left, I was worried about the possibility of desertion by some of the ten men going with him, bearing in mind the darkness and availability of evacuation. I paraded them before departure, held a formal inspection of arms, choked two off for being unshaven, and the others for dirty rifles, although, in fact, most were clean and lightly oiled. Told them I would inspect them again one hour after their return. 'If you are late on parade . . .' I loosed five rounds rapid into the bank of the sunken road. They all got back safely.

We sit inactive along our sunken road. In the distance, the rattle of M.G. fire. It is possible to distinguish between German automatic weapons and our own. Theirs have a higher rate of fire. *Natürlich!*

Why are we sitting here on our rumps doing nothing? They must need men up in front. I have seen the exhaustion on the faces of men coming out of the line. Yet we spend hours doing nothing. Odds and sods. Drygrocers and garage-hands. Open all hours. Your custom greatly appreciated. Prompt deliveries made.

Pyrnford edgier than ever. Apprehensive? Yes, you murdering rat. I'll have you court-martialled if it's the last thing I do. Bruce saw it all, as well as me. And Loach! He kept his mouth shut until Bruce got it out of him. Also learned that Loach has been selling rations and petrol to refugees during the past two weeks. Another matter to be dealt with later.

I can see Pyrnford from where I sit. He's down by the main road staring to where I have the Boyes A/Ts posted. The road along which the German armour will eventually come. 'Don't forget. Aim for the sprockets,' I told that daft Glaswegian, L/Cpl. McDermott. 'Excuse me, sergeant. Whit urr the sprockets?' Ye Gods! Was I so engrossed in getting them properly drilled in the mechanics of siting and firing the weapon that I forgot to outline the vulnerable areas?

Dusk. Pyrnford stands on the top of the bank watching the German Very lights through his binoculars.

2320 hrs. Pyrnford has just come roaring up on the Triumph he always rides now. Still the cavalryman. Gives him an excuse to wear his boots and breeches. Never wears a steel helmet. Said he is going to Div. H.Q. to see if there are any orders for tomorrow. Might be our turn to head for the beach at La Panne. 'How does that strike you, sergeant? Running off to Blighty by tomorrow night?' Sneering at me. I replied, 'Yes, sir. Sounds fine, sir.' And away he goes. Will tomorrow find us huddled and cowering among the dunes, waiting like shivering sheep for some kind sailor to row us away from defeat and disgrace? Back to our mammies. (Mother, forgive me, I have not thought of you this many a long day. God give you rest. God give us all rest.)

Friday   31 May 1940
The 1404th Independent Ammunition Platoon, R.A.S.C. are in the front line and await the enemy in good heart and with determination!

At 0200 Pyrnford came tearing back through the darkness and aroused those asleep (myself included) with stentorian cries and wild hulloos. It took but a few seconds to assemble the men, for we slept, as we had slept for the past two weeks, fully dressed and equipped. Pyrnford has most emphatically regained his old form. The sword blade was out and held aloft.

'We peepul have been given the great honah of holding a section of the line against the might of the Hun army. There are peepul in England now abed . . .' He intended to give us a bit of Henry V but lost it and had to weakly improvise. 'Who will curse themselves for ever, because they do not share our great uh . . . privilege this day. We will stand to the last bullet and the last man.' I knew the 'last bullet last man' bit would come in. And whilst I endorse the sentiment, I deplore the expression as indicative of defeat. Within an hour we had destroyed our vehicles, with the exception of the motor-cycles and two three-tonners needed to carry us to our intended positions. By dawn we had occupied a few close-gathered houses and a small barn on the north bank of the Bergues–Furnes Canal. Despite intermittent shell-fire, we have modestly fortified them with such material as is immediately to hand. Platoon H.Q. is a few hundred yards to the rear.

We have rid ourselves of Boswell. He came stumbling out of the Hillman to Pyrnford's reveille, disgustingly unwashed and unshaven, as he has been for several days. After addressing us, Pyrnford took him to one side. The outcome was an obsequious slobbering, and a grabbing of Pyrnford's hand by Boswell; a backward march of several paces, saluting all the time, until he reached the Hillman wherein he jumped and roared away. A useless mouth if ever there was one. No doubt he has gone to join his kin. It was a shrewd move on Pyrnford's part. We do not want a coward in our midst for what we have to do.

1215 hrs. Went to Platoon H.Q. with a plan of the defensive positions I established; and to ascertain location of troops Pyrnford said were on our flanks. I have been out over a kilometre on both sides without making contact. If that is the case, we are too tightly concentrated and should be covering a wider front. But there is no time to readjust our positions. Driver Chivers, the platoon clerk, says Pyrnford rode east an hour ago without giving reasons. What's he up to now?

Artillery fire persistent, but shells falling well beyond us. Some mortaring coming in close by. No sign as yet of enemy troops or armour. Machine-gunning from long-range but indirect. We must wait.

1443 hrs. No sign of Pyrnford. Has he been killed – wounded? Or has he deserted us, left us to die? In that case there will be a last bullet, and a last man to fire that last bullet into Captain Antony PYRNFORD!

*   *   *

Smith put the last few pages aside, closed his eyes and gently massaged an aching forehead. Maybe it was about time he got his eyes tested. Maybe then he could see the shape of this man who had come so tantalizingly close, this Sergeant Lugard: quickly responsive to the cheap jibe. But still careful, still cautious, still thinking ahead. Of what? Much as he would like to, he could not sit on this, forget Little Jack Horner, this was mandatory fifth-floor fodder. Copies to A.C.C., D.A.C. (Ops), D.A.C. (S.B.) through District Commander Hessen. The Xerox was going to be busy, the Police National Computer was going to be busy. Everybody was going to be busy. Fresh meat for the System – new indices – new headings; Served in Army, Rifle Brigade, R.A.S.C., Cavalry Regiments. Places served. India, Egypt, Palestine, U.K., France. Possibly more to come. New sub-indices and cross-references to everything: Glaswegian origins. Studies Military Strategy. Job Status: truck driver. Local Government official. Fish and Chip fryer. And don't forget Plays Pontoon. Don't they call it Blackjack now?

First he had to finish it, this diary. And start over again; re-read it until he got himself into the guts of this Sergeant Lugard – unknown soldier. He swallowed some Aspirin and reached for the last few pages.

Postscript
++++++++++++++++

Written 18–21 December 1945

The dates are irrelevant, Pyrnford. The only relevant day will be when those of us who are left have found you. The only relevant time; the time you come to read this part of my journal. Are the last words of the last entry still clear in your mind? We held out for three days, Pyrnford. You would have been proud of us (or would you?). How we slaughtered your Hun as they tried to cross the canal. Yes, Pyrnford, *your Hun.* The forward Brens massacred at least eighty of them. Sgt. Menzies and I accounted for another twenty or so with grenades. Brave Menzies. He died trying to put grenades into the turret of a German tank that came up behind us. You will be displeased to know I put it out of action with the Boyes.

By the second day we were surrounded and down to twenty-eight men, with four of those badly wounded. Then help came in the form of ten men from the French 12th Division, who had fought their way out of Bray Dunes through the German advance, in an attempt to make their way south-west to link up with the main French army. They had heard our firing and linked up with us. How they fought, these gallant, gallant Frenchmen. How badly I misjudged them. By the night of the third day only two of them were left alive, and we were down to nineteen. Our ammunition nearly finished. I said nearly finished Pyrnford. I buried the last fifty rounds (the last bullets, Pyrnford) in the cellar of the now-ruined house which was our fortress. *My*

Calais. I also buried our well-oiled weapons and my diary. All securely wrapped in waterproof gas capes. Remember in what astonishingly good condition those First War relics were when we dug them up? We swore an oath; that those of us who survived would return and exhume the guns and the last bullets and use them on you. One of us will find you, Pyrnford.

We broke out that night intending, with our two brave Frenchmen, to make our way south-west to the Somme, where we felt *your Hun* must be held. Broke out is wrong, suggesting a fight. We sneaked out, slithering through their lines. For five days we scurried and scuttled through fields, through woods, nipping across roads in the intervals between German convoys. Swimming canals, fording rivers, hiding up in the green wheat and barley, so near encamped Germans we could smell their coffee, almost taste their pork. All we had were mouldy apples and raw cabbage. We nearly made it. Covering one hundred and sixty kilometres to Bouchon, east of Abbeville, where we heard the sound of far-away guns calling, like drums, to a distant parade. Seeing the beckoning white specks of A.A. bursts to the south.

An isolated cottage provided a resting place, in which to gather our strength for the swim across the Somme. I had reconnoitred the river bank and it seemed deserted. The river was wide and deep; maybe not all would make it but we all intended to try.

It was not to be, Pyrnford. We were awakened by jack-boots in our ribs. Someone had seen us in the cottage. It was quite a small detachment that got hold of us. Smart-looking lads, so they were probably in reserve with nothing much to do. But they were brutes, Pyrnford. I did not then know the significance of the silver flash on black collar patches. In fact, the first thing I saw when I awoke was the skull and bones of a cap badge, and for an elated moment thought we had been miraculously found by the 17/21st Lancers, the old 'Death or Glory' boys. You remember, Pyrnford? But the weight of their boots dispelled that illusion.

They were, of course, from the SS Totenkopf Division, with whom I am sure you are even more familiar. By sun-up, an officer had arrived on the scene. A grim-faced fellow, whose massive depth of jaw in no way matched his shallow beetle-browed forehead. As he listened to the tale of our capture from an N.C.O., there was much Ach So-ing from his lips and evil glances cast in our direction. He came over to where we were lined up. He wore fine leather gloves, very shiny. I'll always remember those shiny, black leather gloves (amongst other things, Pyrnford).

He took hold of the Wee McQuish by the front of his coat and pulled him out to one side. Then he came back for L/Cpl. Nelligan and placed him beside McQuish. Then again for Jean Offoy, one of the French soldiers. By the time I realized all three wore civilian coats, looted days before to replace ripped and sodden tunics, his pistol was out and he calmly shot them; saying before each shot, 'Spion.' 'Spion.' 'Spion.'

They died before fear could replace bewilderment. McQuish, who was last, managed a dry-throated 'Maaa' before he fell. You would have been proud of *your Hun*, Pyrnford, he went two better than you. And did a neater job, one bullet for each of them straight into the heart. He must have had a lot of practise.

I moved to Bruce, fearing his reaction, but he was quite calm, white-faced but quite calm. I could feel every muscle in his frame, rigid as marble. 'I'm all right, Sergeant. I won't do anything stupid. I want to live, for I have many things to do.'

They let us bury our three comrades – rather, they made us bury them. For three days we were held under guard and interrogated. No need to go into detail for you, Pyrnford? We were put in a truck and driven to Rouen, the town still smoking from recent battle. We were handed over to the normal Wehrmacht. (Is normal the right word, Pyrnford?) They certainly treated us with a respect due to fellow soldiers. I was emboldened enough to complain to an English-speaking officer about the shooting of the three men. He listened sympathetically and indeed offered a disturbed frown, but only said, 'At least they did not shoot all of you. Be grateful for that, sergeant.'

We were taken to a field outside Rouen, soon to be crowded with hundreds of other captured British soldiers. Many coming in from the 51st Highland Division taken at St. Valéry, many others like ourselves from the Dunkirk perimeter, who tried to get through south-west. And oh, what tales they had to tell. Of gallant officers and brave men, of desperate marches and glorious stands. It may have been a shambles, Pyrnford, but it was a splendid shambles, as imperishable as Corunna. It was all you left me, Pyrnford; all that followed for me and the others were years of degradation. You deprived me of my war. You robbed me of my victory.

They spoke of other things, Pyrnford, of strange staff officers, ordering guns to be abandoned; supply convoys to destinations in the hands of the enemy; of troops told to pull back from good defensive strongpoints, or to advance against strongly held enemy positions. What were you doing swanning around on the motor-cycle, Pyrnford? Was it you that Quarrie saw at battalion H.Q. of the Royal West Kents? Was that why you shot him? Did you send these brave men to their death in Albert? Officially they say not, the orders were genuine. Oh yes, I am in a position to find out, Pyrnford, but more of that later.

After a week at Rouen we were given into the tender mercies of Sudeten auxiliaries, the Volksdeutsch, whose answer to everything was the boot, the rifle butt and occasionally the bullet. To supplement these, they had whips and dogs. They marched us the five hundred-odd kilometres to Trier in the heat of July, feeding us once daily on a mug of ersatz coffee and a quarter-kilo of black bread. Occasionally, very occasionally, they would give us half a litre of tepid water garnished with a few sodden cabbage leaves. They call it *Suppe*. Sometimes, if you were very lucky and the ladle was lifted from the right spot, a greasy dollop of fat landed in your bowl.

I dreamed of food, Pyrnford, I crammed rich pieces of nutritious bully beef into my mouth, I thrust stomach-filling spoonfuls of M. & V. between my lips; but they melted on my tongue like summer snowflakes, before I could devour a single morsel. I could have escaped a dozen times on that march had I the strength to convulse the ever-present thought into action.

During the heat of the march my mind took my body on escape after escape. Running like a gazelle with loping never-tiring strides, leaping rivers, effortlessly clearing high walls. Seeing the slow flight of bullets fired by my pursuers, swerving from their path, laughing as they harmlessly slid past. But the only escape was in the dream. For in reality I had no intention of escaping, not whilst I had responsibility for what was left of *my* platoon. *My* platoon, Pyrnford. It was my duty to hold them together. Whatever happened.

Many died on that march, Pyrnford, but none of *my* platoon perished. We scrounged, we bartered, we shared equally. But I was still the platoon sergeant. I was in command of *my* platoon.

Along the route of march, the once anglophobic French were magnificent. A surreptitious bag of potatoes passed to us here, a few apples there, a loaf of bread, a flask of wine somewhere else. We were even grateful for water. But once across the border into Germany, it was different. In the streets of Trier, it was different. A mob hissing and spitting its malevolent hatred, its contempt. It was difficult to endure their contempt, Pyrnford. Did we perhaps feel we deserved it?

But I got the Platoon to Stalag V III B at Lamsdorf. We built the fucking bastard place. Recollection brings an angry spasm, Pyrnford. Such coarseness creeps from my lips as a result of the past five years. Why should I bother to explain to such a naturally foul-mouthed lout as you?

On arrival at V III B we were deloused, scalped and addressed by the S.B.O. A fussy little R.S.M. who must have been there some time and captured with full kit. His uniform was immaculate and his behaviour was all an R.S.M.'s should be, with a standard of discipline appropriate to a recruit training depot. Very right and proper in a recruit training depot. But in a P.O.W. camp? To obey the Germans so religiously?

The food we received was little more than what we had on the march. The same ersatz coffee, the same bread, the same *Suppe*. Sometimes a spoonful of jam or a sliver of sausage. We worked and starved there month after month.

More rumours, Pyrnford. But only rumours about when the Red Cross parcels would arrive. They'll be here tomorrow! Nothing. But definitely next Tuesday! Nothing. But one of the guards saw a Red Cross van only fifty kilos south and coming this way! It never arrived. But it's near Christmas! The S.B.O. says they'll certainly be here a week before Christmas. Did you have a Merry Christmas in 1940, Pyrnford? *Frohe Weihnachten, ja?* We froze and starved.

It was a year before the parcels actually arrived. A year in which three went for the wire. Not because they were trying to escape. At least not in the literal sense. Remember the hot-weather suicides, Pyrnford? They left the last one hanging on the wire for two days. But nobody from the 1404th tried it, Pyrnford. We had something to finish.

V III B grew into compound after compound – Merchant Navy compound – Royal Navy compound – R.A.F. compound. By August 1941, a Russian compound. A bullet for any British P.O.W. who went near the Russian compound. Poor bastards. We thought we were hard done by. No Red Cross parcels for the Russian compound.

After more than two years of captivity, working parties, and saluting every German officer for as long as he was visible, I got a bit bolshie, Pyrnford. Had a row with a German officer about the food and another with the S.B.O. Was listed for a shunt. The entire 1404th volunteered for the same draft. Know where we finished up, Pyrnford? We became *gorniks* in a *kopalnia wegla*. You know what that means, Pyrnford? We became miners in a Polish coal mine, you traitorous bastard. Oh, how the Stygies loved us. A Stygy? A *Sztygar*, a foreman, you pig-ignorant piece of excrement. A *Volksdeutsch* Pole with a big stick for laying about us when he thinks we aren't working hard enough. Then there was the Ober-Stygy. A big fat German supervisor, a jolly laughing fellow. 'You tommies kein stomach zur arbeit,' and to prove it would punch us playfully in the gut. 'Arbeit Macht Frei,' Pyrnford? Our *kopalnia* was about ten kilometres from a place called Auschwitz. We've just heard about Auschwitz, Pyrnford. Did you visit Auschwitz by any chance, when you came to the mine P.O.W. compound in May, 1944? Very smart you looked in your British Free Corps uniform. And what a good job for us you were too vain to wear your glasses and couldn't see us at the back of the *appel* parade. Had you done so, I am sure we would not have gone to the coal face next day but to slag-heap clearance. Many Russian P.O.W.s went to the slag heaps. They never came back. A change of appearance was it? Probably you knew by then you had picked the wrong side and feared future retribution. How right you were. The bushy moustache and the dyed black hair didn't fool us for a moment; we recognized you before you even opened your mouth.

'Yoah peepul must realize, the true friend of Britain is the great German nation; united and victorious under its magnificent leaduh, Adolph Hitler. The great leaduh, the Führer, had hoped that after the invincible German Army had conquered France, and spared Britain the agony of invasion, our country would see reason and join him in the great crusade, still being victoriously carried on against the Bolshevik horde. Unfortunately, the arch-communist and tyrant, Churchill, has our poor country in his grip, aided as he is by that evil Jew communist in America, the swinish Roosevelt. As a result London is in ruins, a desert of rubble extending five miles in every direction from Piccadilly Circus, and growing wider every day under a hail of high explosive from the new German V-weapon which cannot be stopped.'

How sincere and patriotic you were when you went on to say, 'I am here to give you the opportunity of fighting for our dear country, in the ranks of the British Free Corps, to prevent the further destruction of our towns and cities. Together with our comrades in the German army we will smash and destroy the evil of Jewish Bolshevik communism for ever. No one will be asked to take up arms against our poor misguided countrymen; only against the slimy Russian. For, once we have smashed him, you can rest assured the communist Jewish alliance of Churchill and Roosevelt will fall apart and we can return home to a newer and greater Britain. Where, I can assure you, all who play their part in the British Free Corps will have an even greater part to play. Not only in our own land, but in the establishment of a great new order throughout the world. Now then, what do yo' say? Who is for Britain and the British Free Corps?'

Who wrote your speech? Goebbels? Not at all your style, Pyrnford. Not a single obscenity; still your diction had somewhat improved. Elocution lessons? So thorough, the Germans.

You didn't have the swordstick to wave about either. Didn't they trust you with it? Maybe Goering was envious. They only had room for one Siegfried, Pyrnford. You stood up well to the boos and jeers. I suppose you had done it all before and were used to it. And we didn't disclose your identity to the other P.O.W.s. Oh, no. You are strictly our responsibility. I haven't seen you since, but some day you will read this. Some day.

By the way, you will be pleased to know that as a result of our behaviour, they cut our rations and refused us Red Cross parcels for six months.

In January 1945 they marched us out of the coal mine. The Russian horde wasn't defeated after all. They were less than a hundred kilometres away. I suppose by now, German P.O.W.s are down the mine in our place.

Anyway, we marched away, Pyrnford, out of Poland, through Czechoslovakia, freezing and starving. Back on the turnip diet. Sometimes a rotten potato or two, between every ten of us. But no bread, no *Suppe*. And we were back in the war. The Russians strafed us, then the Americans bombed us. I lost four of the platoon. One . . . just died. Two went in a Russian air attack. One was shot by the guards when he tried to sneak out of the barn they were holding us in overnight, to get some food. They were the 1404th's only casualties. Dozens of others from different regiments and formations died on that march.

You nearly did for us, Pyrnford. How long was it we were on the march? Six weeks, eight? I don't know. To say we were swept along by the tide of war gives too strong an impetus to our progress. German soldiers, civilians, slave workers and we P.O.W.s crawled through burning towns and a devastated countryside like slag on a river of lava. And from the lava came flames that devoured yet gave no warmth. Fumes that stifled without the complete mercy of suffocation. By Regensburg we would go no further. By Regensburg we could go no further. All that had taken us to Regensburg was a faint scent of deliverance. Our thoughts and plans for you, Pyrnford, so long nurtured and prepared in Stalag and *kopalnia*, so grimly resolved and promised in the ears of our dying comrades, were discarded and forgotten, as with raw pinched nostrils we sniffed the burning air for an elusive whiff of freedom. But all we found was the odour of our own enteric excrement and incontinent urine. The blood of endurance can only course in the breath of hope. No word passed between us, we were far beyond collective action. At Regensburg, we knew we would just lie down and wait for death.

One hundred and eighty-six British P.O.W.s marched from the Polish *kopalnia*. Seventy-three wasted men crawled into the ruins of Regensburg in Bavaria. And there it was, no dream, no mirage, the thing the guards promised we would find in Ostrava, in Brno, in Trebič, in České Budějovice, in Wolfstein and Deggendorf, as they drove, kicked and wheedled us across the Polish border and the width of Czechoslovakia: a Red Cross van laden with parcels. Life itself. How pathetically pleased the guards were afterwards. 'Nice for you, eh, Tommy. We Rotekreuze packet bringen. Sehr gut. Ja?'

'No, nicht verstehen, Erik. Nicht verstehen, Carl. Fuck off, Hans.'

How deliciously slowly we ate the tinned pilchards, drank the hot chocolate, smoked the rich Virginia tobacco. How carefully we hoarded the generous remainder, as we lolled in the tepid sunshine of early spring, like a pack of starving wolves who have gorged themselves on a fat caribou on whose carcase much meat remains. No. After eight months I give way to an illusion. There was nothing lupine about us. We were more like rats, each jealously guarding its hoard against predators. Still, with food in our bellies we were strangely unconcerned by the trembling earth beneath us as great fleets of American bombers pounded the German nation to dust. Memories of France and Dunkirk? Insignificant in the face of this!

Then one morning we awoke and the guards were gone. Not that they had been guarding us with any great vigour for the past few days. But now they had vanished in the night, leaving us strangely alone. Elated, for deliverance was at hand. Yet fearful because of its promise. Fearful of the means by which it would be accomplished. Air bombardment? A rolling barrage from massed artillery? Mortars? We could not die now. Not again. We scraped cover for ourselves with bare hands and tree branches. But when deliverance came, it came casually, in anticlimax. Sight of a strange little vehicle stopping by the roadside, a man in a green-grey denim blouse, wearing a helmet we thought at first to be German, opening his trousers to urinate on a back wheel. I called out recklessly, 'Are you Americans?' The urinating man dived to the ground, a heavy machine gun swung round. I called again, 'No, No. We're British. British P.O.W.s. Don't shoot!'

A nasal voice replied. 'Right. Come out slow with your hands on top of your heads.' We all obey. As senior N.C.O. I went forward to explain, taking my hands from my head as I approached. 'Keep 'em up there,' said the man behind the gun. Very battlewise, very professional. I was humbled by these Americans, feeling foolish and incompetent. (You robbed me of my war, Pyrnford.)

The man whose call of nature we had interrupted wore silver insignia on his shoulder and painted stripes on his helmet. This I took to indicate commissioned rank. I saluted and explained our position.

He showed little interest, saying they had come across the likes of us before in the past few days. We should wait where we were. The rest of the American Third Corps were coming up fast. We had better stay right out in the open with our hands on our heads for 'They are sons of bitches – mean and twitchy.' It was all rather humiliating, Pyrnford. But after years of degradation, mere humiliation is easily accepted. They roared away in their jeep, followed at intervals by more jeeps, half-tracks, and heavy trucks, the occupants of which stared at us with cold suspicion. It is surprising how humiliation melts in the heat of liberty and after a time I was no longer prepared to sustain the indignity of placing my hands on my head every time an American vehicle appeared. Most of the others followed suit. By then, the passing troops must have been satisfied sufficient of their number had already passed, for us to be considered harmless. None of the sons of bitches got mean or twitchy.

We spent two more days on the road between Regensburg and Landshut watching the victorious Yanks drive on. Eventually some American M.P.s came along and we were placed in billets just outside Landshut, and briefly 'processed' as they call record-ing our individual particulars. We were left to roam around much as we pleased, but I ensured some semblance of smartness and discipline was re-introduced insofar as our worn and tattered uniforms permitted.

Late one afternoon I went for a stroll with Bruce (we discussed our plans for you, Pyrnford) and as we passed near a temporary cage full of German prisoners, I felt Bruce stiffen and grasp my arm. Behind the wire, leaning against a cowshed, was the heavy jaw and low forehead of the black-gloved S.S. Totenkopf officer who had shot McQuish and the others all those years ago. He had been wounded in the hand and leg, for one hand hung by his side in a thick pad of dirty bandages and one leg of his breeches had been ripped away and the lower thigh similarly encased. He had lost his gloves, his face was much thinner, his eyes dull, but there was no mistaking that massive jaw.

We saw the American sergeant in charge of the compound. He listened to our story, nodded sympathetically, went to the window and called to a guard, 'The big Kraut with one leg in his pants, bring him over to the gate.' He handed me a Thompson gun from the rack. 'You take the motherfuckin' son of a bitch for a walk into the trees. Bring the gun back afterwards.' Lend Lease? Or is it Lease Lend?

We pushed the hobbling prisoner through the gate, the sergeant shouting, 'Be sure and get his name. I've got to cross him off the record.'

His name was Klimpt, Heinrich. Heinrich Klimpt. Obediently he limped in the direction of the trees, massive chin ponderously thumping down against his chest. Grunting in pain with each step. He realized our intentions. They meant nothing to him, for he, like us a few days ago, had cut adrift from life, was floating, waiting to sink. We told him of his crimes five years ago. Nothing. No reaction beyond an inclination of his head to one side, a protruding lower lip, a momentary opening of half-closed eyes, thick dismissive flesh creasing a narrow brow. No words, but saying, 'So long ago, so many since. How can I remember? What do I care?'

I had given the gun to Bruce. McQuish was his friend. He turned to me. 'He is not the man we want. Is he? Why should we dissipate our hatred on him? By killing him we might lose some of our hate. I don't want to waste it on this empty hulk. I'd get scunnered.'

I fully agreed with him, Pyrnford. Klimpt was a soldier . . . of sorts. He had some slender claim to battlefield justice for his actions of June 1940. What he may have done since was not our concern. Whatever he had done, he had done in the name of his own country. That defence is not open to you, Pyrnford. What we would do – *will* do – we will do for ourselves and in the name of our dead comrades.

When we brought Klimpt back, the American sergeant was not surprised. 'I guess five years behind the wire has knocked the guts out of you.' He was not being malicious, only endeavouring to show some sympathy. 'I suppose before long we'll start pitying the bastards,' he said.

'It's not pity,' replied Bruce. 'Only magnanimity.'

'That's a big word.'

'It's a selfish trait peculiar to the British. They only use it to serve a purpose,' said Bruce.

They flew us home from Landshut, low across the face of Germany, raddled, scarred, pock-marked. The face of a leper. I took forty-eight other ranks to France in January 1940. I brought thirteen out of Germany in April 1945. All things considered, not a bad average. A survival of the fittest?

Back in Blighty they debriefed us at length. We told them about Klimpt. They have probably hanged him by now. A healthier better-fed Klimpt. A more fearfully aware Klimpt? Just an idle thought. None of Bruce's magnanimity towards Klimpt now. They asked us about British Free Corps recruiters, and we told them about the visit of an officer to the *kopalnia* compound. No, we didn't know his name. Describe him! Build? Medium. Height? Average. Hair? Medium brown. Eyes? Too far away to say. Voice? Talked posh just like an officer.

They asked us what happened to our C.O. In discussing this eventuality, Loach suggested we say our last sight was of you running towards a German tank waving your swordstick. It had the attraction of credibility. Consistent with your malignant stupidity, Pyrnford. But we didn't want them awarding you a posthumous V.C. So we simply said we didn't know; nor did we know what happened to Boswell. You belong to the survivors of the 1404th Independent Ammunition Platoon, Pyrnford. To no one else.

They gave us a month's leave, most of which I spent reading about the war. Oh Pyrnford, the battles I have missed, the glories you robbed me of!

I am back in Germany now. Commissioned! A lieutenant in the Field Security Police . . . Antony! Rounding up collaborators and war criminals. Glaring coldly at our Russian allies. Does that please you, Antony? I have access to records and files. You Antony, are listed Missing in Action – believed killed. In due course your name will desecrate a Roll of Honour.

My F.S.P. training was given near Brussels, and it was easy to get from there to the scene of our stand on the Bergues–Furnes Canal. Our weapons and my diary were still there. The rifles are back in England now and have been used once again . . . on Boswell. I defended him at his Court Martial to the best of my ability but a majority found him guilty of Cowardice and Desertion. Reverting to my responsibility towards the Platoon, I took command of the firing squad that administered our justice. Three Platoon survivors could not participate, being in hospital; one of them, in Netley, completely mad. The weapons have been cleaned and put away. They will be brought out once again, for although the 1404th no longer exists, its spirit lives in those who survive. Few soldiers have a peace-time purpose, Antony. We have! Some day you will read these words. And remember. For they are written for you, as was written for us . . . and our dead:

'At the going down of the sun, and in the morning –
WE will remember them.'

Part Three

Tribulation and Trial

Twelve

++++++++++

'Sergeant Michael Lugard is dead!' A woebegone O'Brien, lumpily dejected, trailed into Smith's office and made his sad pronouncement. The contents of Lugard's diary had been inserted into the System like white-hot metal into cold water, producing a stream of hissing bubbling Actions. Search all names against R.C.T./R.A.S.C. and other regimental records. Ditto war casualty lists, ditto War Graves Commission, ditto Criminal Records, Registry and all Road Traffic offender indices. Ditto Central Registers of Births, Deaths and Marriages in England and Scot land. Enquiries to be made at last known addresses of all established survivors of the 1404th Independent Ammunition Platoon. Follow up as necessary. When traced, premises of survivors to be searched for weapons. Any survivors traced to be detained.

The tasks would not be finished tomorrow – or by next week or even by next month. Names, without further identifying details such as a date of birth, were just names. The best they had to go on was information from the Defence department that soldiers were not sent to France in 1939 under the age of nineteen. 'At least as far as possible, y'know.' So they looked for their survivors amongst those born during or before the year 1920. But it was going to be a long job. And the first result brought O'Brien into the office bewailing Lugard's death.

'Under what circumstances?' asked Smith tightly.

'During an American air attack on Regensburg, 30 March 1945,' replied O'Brien.

'Then he couldn't have written the postscript to his diary.'

'No.'

'But he did write it, you idiot, the handwriting is identical throughout.' The diary had taken the enquiry into another dimension. One he could not yet control. But control it, he must. He snarled at Tom Palmer who, relaxing in the one comfortable armchair, had just finished reading the diary. 'Now we've got another one working a ringer on us.'

'Looksh that way,' said Palmer, thick-tongued. He took out his upper plate and cleaned it on one of Smith's tissues. Replacing it, he pressed it carefully into the roof of his mouth before speaking again. 'Being the senior N.C.O. and dedicated lad that he was, he would have collected all the I.D. from casualties sustained on the march. It would be easy for him to swap his identity with another suitable orphan. This guy was thinking a long way ahead.'

'But why?' For O'Brien it was not good enough, somehow Lugard had got under his skin.

Smith kicked his desk in exasperation at O'Brien. 'That brewer's goitre round your belly must have reached your brain. It's obvious. Come the time he found Pyrnford and Boswell and stiffed them, the platoon connection between these two would turn the enquiry towards any survivors. But he didn't reckon on it taking nearly forty years to find Pyrnford. He must have transferred to Field Security Police in his new name. Where did he go from there, he couldn't soldier in the F.S.P. for ever?' The panel in the side of the desk cracked under another kick. 'I know the bastard is alive, I can almost feel his breath on the nape of my neck, I can almost hear him saying, "You must be in agony lad, I'm standing on your back hair. Get it cut." ' And in a nervous reflex movement Smith patted the generous growth hanging over his collar. He really did need a haircut.

'Well, I've already done a check on F.S.P. records,' said O'Brien, grimly defending his I.Q. 'And there is no Lugard listed as serving in any rank.' Lifted by inspiration he went on, 'Maybe it's Lugard that's the stumer name. Maybe he didn't want to show out in his real name in case the diary came a tumble. He was worried about that possibility.'

'It's definitely gone to your nut. From now on, no more than two pints a night for you. Go on, get back to your desk. Come back when you've lost at least forty pounds.' O'Brien waddled from the office under the threat of Smith's raised foot.

'I admire your faith in him, Owen; Lugard, I mean.' Palmer

stirred restlessly in his chair, licking his dry lips. Smith gave an indeterminate shrug, afraid to admit to the mental difficulties he was encountering in relating past events in the diary to his present problems. Events, mundane and momentous, trivial and tremendous, petty spite vying with great treachery, puerile comedy with casual tragedy. It was the transition in time that bothered him. How did you keep such a quest for vengeance in being over long decades? The answer was in the diary, but did it really explain how the flames of hatred had been kept burning for so long?

He had not expected the diary in reply to his public diatribe. All he had expected was some form of contact, a threatening, abusive phone call, an anonymous letter, something fresh to get his teeth into; well, he had a mouthful now. And what the hell did Lugard mean at the end of his letter when he said, '. . . prove the justice of our actions to you . . . and the world'?

He made his mind up firmly and faced the challenge of Palmer's question. 'I have faith in his diary, Tom. It's factually true, I'm sure of that. Whether it's objectively true is another question, and an unimportant question as far as I am concerned.'

Hunching down in the folds of his raincoat as though still winter-cold in the warmth of approaching summer, Palmer received Smith's declaration of faith with a sceptical leer. 'The diary could be a big con. You've only got photocopies, the whole thing could have been written in the past week with the intention of making you put all your investigative eggs in one basket. You've blown so much of the background to the media, any nut could have invented this tale.'

'Not any nut who wasn't there, who wasn't in the B.E.F. Who wasn't a P.O.W.'

'All right then, a nut who was. There seem to be plenty of them about.' Palmer grinned into the folds of his raincoat as if sharing an introspective secret with himself.

'No. Fucking well, no!' Smith adamantly and violently rejected Palmer's logic. Adamantly, because he instinctively felt Lugard's existence. Violently, because he was running a risk by doing so. He talked himself along the path he had chosen to tread. 'He probably got a lead from his F.S.P. enquiries as to where Pyrnford had bolted. To South America with the other Nazi cowboys. He couldn't go after him alone; it was a matter for the platoon, what was left of them. And once out of the army, I doubt if they fancied a tour of jungle service at their own expense. Even if they had the money. Loach was skint for years after the war before he made his pile. So they just sat back and waited for Pyrnford to come home to roost. They probably held a reunion once a year like any other bunch of old soldiers. But somebody kept tabs on Pyrnford over the years and, what is important, somebody was in a position to keep tabs on Pyrnford. Who managed it? How did he manage it? He got himself into some international organization; Secret Service? The executive side of the diplomatic service, embassy security, cypher clerk? Queen's messenger? Travelling bloody salesman?' He swung round on Palmer. 'Tom, for Christ's sake stop sitting there like a sheikh in a shithouse and imagine Lugard in Germany all those years ago. You were in Intelligence, you may have spoken to the man.'

'I spoke to many. The F.S.P. were as thick as fleas on a mangy dog, and worked hand-in-glove with the "I" Corps. But you're asking too much of human memory, at least of mine. I cannot sort out a Lugard-like character from a thousand forgotten faces.' No grin from Palmer this time, only a haunted emptiness in his eyes. 'Would you mind giving me a drink.' A plea coupled with a command. Smith heard the desperation in it and apologized lamely for his inhospitality, afterwards saying, 'I only want your picture of the man, Tom, you both belong to the same era.'

Palmer watched the generous measure resting on the desk before him, made to withdraw a hand from his pocket then thrust it back. Meditatively and mildly amused, he asked, 'Are you trying to find Lugard in me, Owen? Is that why you had me read this anachronistic nonsense? You think I might be Lugard?'

'I checked you out in that direction some time ago,' Smith admitted with a rueful smile. 'The job reeked of soldier like a Grenadier's barrack-room with strong overtones from the inside of a copper's boot. Now we know Lugard had experience of both. Sorry, Tom, but before I had the diary, you looked good for the part.'

'Oh, don't apologize. I'm proud you should think me capable of once being that proud leader of men, Sergeant Michael Lugard.'

'What's your opinion of the guy? As a soldier, as a man?'

As if deciding defeat was inevitable, Palmer reached out a relaxed arm, took up the glass of whisky and drank with slow deliberation. Clutching the glass tightly against his chest with both hands he spoke down into the remaining contents. 'Opinion of Lugard? A professional hero, self-conceived. A gun fetishist. Guns are necessary to battlefield heroes. Take away his tactile talisman and he is just your average coward. Remove . . .'

'Tom, I've seen that old movie many times.' Smith cut in on him cruelly; regretting he had brought this old sot into his confidence, there were more reliable sources. Trouble was, you couldn't help feeling sorry for drunks who still retained a measure of lonely independent dignity. If Palmer had heard him, it did not reflect in his ravaged face, he was now loose and loquacious.

'He was a frustrated imitation Lawrence. T.E. not D.H. A repressed homosexual right down to the motor-cycle syndrome. After the Rifle Brigade rejected him, he used the R.A.S.C. the same way Lawrence used the lowest ranks of the R.A.F. and the Tank Corps, even if he did hang on to his stripes. I wouldn't be surprised if he didn't secretly enjoy his time in the P.O.W. camp and the Polish coal-mine. The man was a moral flagellant. And probably a physical one as well, maybe that was why he got so upset about Quarrie.'

'The man *is*!' Smith reminded him. Palmer yawned disdainfully into his glass before emptying it.

'Is? I doubt it. What has he got left now Pyrnford's gone? Now Loach has gone? Now his hate has gone? He's too old to generate new hatreds, Owen. Believe me, I know.'

There was a knock on the office door and O'Brien came back in, his face once again in mourning. 'That Scottish comedian, Alexander "Sanny" Bruce? He's also listed "killed in action." The same air attack on Regensburg. I thought the Yanks were on our side.'

'Ringer number two, Owen?' said Palmer mockingly.

'Number three, if you include Loach's car,' replied Smith. 'I wonder how many more there are to come?'

It was the names not mentioned in Lugard's diary that worried Smith. The unfolding history of the 1404th, as recorded by Lugard, had only compelled him to mention comparatively few names amongst the total strength. The deaths of some of the named had been stated, others were unnamed. He gave the diary to Marrasey and asked him to prepare a breakdown. In less than two hours, Marrasey returned with the figures listed under appropriate headings. It was neatly done. Nineteen had been named in the diary, leaving thirty-two unnamed. The named casualties listed, the unnamed postulated. The deserters shown. Four? Wasn't it just two that supposedly skipped away from the docks at Dunkirk?

He put the analysis in his tray. Later, when it was quiet, he would study it, see if there was anything to be learned. So many names, even more shadowy soldiers without names, still alive, still present. He could feel them as he felt Lugard, out there in the streets, five, maybe six of them, the hate draining out of them into the sand on the Common with Pyrnford's blood. No, not five or six, only four or five. Loach was on the casualty list now. His casualty list. Mr Marrasey was waiting patiently for further instructions.

'What do you make of this Sergeant Lugard, Mr Marrasey?' Smith asked idly. 'Old Tom Palmer sees him as some sort of grammar-school imitation Lawrence of Arabia, right down to the masochistic homosexuality bit.'

Marrasey smiled indulgently, 'Mr Palmer's pseudo-Freudian utterances have entertained the saloon bar of the Cock and Hen for the past ten years, sir. I'm afraid the origins of his philosophy are to be found more in the bottle than the book.' Marrasey had quickly resumed his former neatness after a brief period of dishevelment following the callous killing of 'Bim Bam' Bailey. His condemnation of Palmer became coldly efficient. 'I would say there is more of the disillusioned Lawrence in Mr Palmer than in Sergeant Lugard. Lugard was a professional soldier, unlike Lawrence, who was little more than an exhibitionist with a flair for highly literate banditry, and I do not distinguish between either area of opportunism. Lugard may have been an idealist, but not at the expense of his own country.'

'I don't see much idealism in a man who harbours a personal hatred for more than forty years, and gratifies it in an act of murder,' countered Smith scornfully.

Marrasey gave ground reluctantly. 'He may have been personally motivated, sir, but his purpose may have been beyond personal vengeance. Perhaps he sought, not only to avenge his dead comrades, but to expiate what he considered the greatest shame to befall the British army. Its defeat in France. A defeat brought about by Pyrnford and his counterparts, civil and military. Time cannot erode such guilt . . . at least to his way of thinking.'

Smith looked at him dubiously for a moment, then laughed deprecatingly. 'Maybe I'm too young to appreciate the weight of your argument, Mr Marrasey. I only know what I have read about Dunkirk. Stirring stuff.'

'Like the vodka martini of James Bond, sir,' said Marrasey with an enigmatic smile. 'Maybe it is time for it to be served thoroughly shaken. Even though it may be a bit bruised as a result.'

'Did you serve with the B.E.F., John?' Smith had had enough of responding to Marrasey's formal stiffness. As soon as this case was finished he would take him out with the others and get him, neatly, pie-eyed pissed.

Marrasey refused to unbend. 'Everyone served in those days, sir. Yes –.' The phone shrilled its summons for attention. Commander Hessen was on the line from District H.Q.

'Owen, I must see you right away.' It was the first time Hessen had spoken to him since the exchange of words after his unauthorized news conference. 'Are you alone?' Hessen sounded anxious. Smith put a hand over the mouthpiece and asked Marrasey to leave. 'I am now.'

'Come over and see me right away. I can't say more on the phone but it affects us both.' A dull resonance of lonely anguish and capitulation caused Hessen's voice to vibrate like a low organ chord in an empty church.

Smith found him hauling one foot after the other across his office carpet as though ploughing through deep snow. 'I am lost, Owen.' Hessen spread his arms in dramatic appeal. 'Lost in a web of deceit. I should have put my papers in, honourably, as I intended.'

'What's up now?' Smith was succinctly unsympathetic. Hessen's call had excised a tumour of painful thought growing in his brain and he was upset at himself for accepting the relief so readily. The Commander was flinging a despairing hand at the telephone. 'First, the Deputy Commissioner, right out of the blue, a plague of solicitors . . .' He began incoherently, realized it and tightened his lips and his mind. He began again, slowly. 'The Deputy Commissioner has been on to say that this diary of yours, or rather of your mysterious Sergeant Lugard, has been offered for serialization to one of the weightier Sunday papers. Some solicitor in Bedford Square got on to the Yard saying he has been authorized to act for Lugard over publication rights. Proceeds to be donated to the International Red Cross.'

'Not the Widows and Orphans, this time?' Smith's curiosity was aroused. And he remembered Lugard's words, '. . . prove the justice of our actions to you . . . and the world.'

'And that's another thing the Deputy mentioned.' Hessen went sighing back to the burden of his original cross. 'Oh, how I've been plagued by solicitors, Owen.'

'The other thing the Deputy mentioned?' Impatiently, Smith

steered him back on course.

'Yet another solicitor, down in Sussex this time, Jones, Samuel Jones, has written to the Commissioner claiming the Kruger Rands, presented to the Widows and Orphans, as the estate of the late Captain Antony Pyrnford and as such, the property of his next-of-kin, Constance, Lady Lowderton.'

'We'll have to let the Widows and Orphans worry about that one. Have you any more solicitors?'

'Loach's solicitor.' The words tolled from Hessen's lips in a knell of impending doom. 'Will going to probate. Contains a passage, "after all lawful debts are paid and all covenants entered into by me have been funded, the residue etc. etc." He just wanted me to know the covenant would be fulfilled. Congratulations old boy, nudge nudge, wink wink.'

'What did you reply?'

'I didn't. Just mumbled something and hung up. What do I do, Owen? What do I say?'

'I presume you didn't go cap in hand to Loach and ask him to fund the covenant?' Hessen was shocked into sensibility by the suggestion. 'Certainly not. The first I knew of it was when he came up to me at a council reception and told me of its existence.'

'Then you write to his solicitor using what he would call a form of words. First renouncing the covenant, then saying, "The covenant was made without my knowledge or consent before I was aware of its existence." No need to explain that Loach told you about it before the solicitor did and that you had accepted.'

Hessen struggled with his conscience. 'A lie that isn't a lie, a truth that isn't a truth. Half truth that is half lie.'

'Truth avoidance, like tax avoidance, isn't a crime, at least outside the witness box.' Smith pointed to the blank T.V. screen in the corner. 'It's a modern art form, recognized and respected by politicians, trade-union leaders, and the giants of industry. The new language of the carefully chosen word. Having no known form of interpretation, T.V. interviewers are reduced to attempting it as if translating Chinese. "So what you are saying is" then they try to put their own words in the guy's mouth only to have them twisted back into even obscurer and more carefully chosen words. I wouldn't worry about it, Commander Hessen, sir, nobody searches for truth nowadays, only for controversy.'

Smith repeated his gesture at the television set. 'You can watch the consequences six times a night. The longest-running panel game ever. Don't miss the great Innuendo, Speculation and Conjecture Show. Anybody with a controversial allegation to make can play. No formal proof needed. Can your allegation beat the carefully chosen word defence? If you make the controversy bell ring you win the star prize. Don't worry, Commander Hessen, sir, stick to your form of words. Nobody can prove a damn thing.'

Almost appalled by the sadistic pleasure he was gaining from witnessing Hessen's maimed morality, Smith waited for a response. Damn it, he genuinely wanted to help the man, not abuse him. But as he waited, there was a growing awareness that, as with Palmer, his words had no impact. In Hessen's case it was because they had been muffled in a cloud of concern, surrounding him like a blanket. Concern for his name, his family, his future, but above all for his reputation.

'When the diary comes out in the papers, I'm finished, Owen. Even if I do resign, the reporters will come after me like hounds from hell. All that about Loach in the diary.' The first fine clawmarks of worry were beginning to mark Hessen's young face. A screw of revulsion deepened them. 'Boasting about the number of times he had contracted venereal disease. Sickening. The man has eaten food from my dishes, Owen; used my toilet.' The desk quivered under Hessen's arms as an enormous shudder racked his frame. Smith ignored it, reaching for the only thing that mattered to him.

'What's the name of this solicitor who's pushing Lugard's diary?' Hessen searched amongst a mass of scribbled notes cluttering his usually immaculate desk.

'The firm is Garvey, Remson, Joyce and Partners. I don't know who is actually dealing.'

Smith made a note. 'I wouldn't do anything about resigning, sir. I don't think you've much to worry about. Not for the present, at least.'

'They're in Bedford Square,' Hessen shouted after him in hopeful relief from the door of his office. 'But I haven't a note of the number.'

'Don't worry, I'll find it,' Smith shouted back. 'In the Yellow Pages.'

Thirteen

◆◆◆◆◆◆◆◆◆◆◆◆

The office was elegantly furnished, a little ostentatiously so for the simple dignified façade of the building. So also, was Mr Justin Kepple a little too elegantly attired for Smith's taste, even though his bottle-green velvet suit owed more to Marks & Spencer than it did to Savile Row. And even though he wore it with an easy grace, enhanced by a delicate tripping step on small feet lightly shod in thin imitation lizard-skin slippers, not quite by Gucci.

Mr Kepple was one of the young partners and had greeted Smith effusively. 'My dear sir, do come in. Anything we can do to help the jolly old hard-pressed forces of law and order, will be done. Within reason, of course . . . Sherry?'

He presented the crystal goblet to Smith on a silver salver. 'I do believe you are the first policeman I have met in a professional way. We don't do crime here, nothing so nasty. Contracts, copyright, companies floated, that's our thingie. Nothing nasty; spiteful perhaps, occasionally horrid, but nothing nasty. We just arrange . . . thingies.' And compulsively he centred an onyx ash-tray on a small reproduction Regency table. Perching beside Smith on the overstuffed leather couch, he thrust clasped and complaisant hands down between his legs and said, 'Now do tell. How can we help you?'

'How were you instructed in the matter of the diary?' Smith began with a direct thrust and to his surprise it was not resisted.

'By letter,' replied Mr Kepple. 'Through the post in the usual way. Unregistered, I might add. Original diary with handwritten letter of instruction enclosed.'

'May I see it?'

Mr Kepple withdrew a warm hand to raise his sherry glass for the parry and, waving the tulip-shaped vessel by its base, he said, apologetically, 'My dear sir, sincere regrets. No can do. Client confidentiality, you do understand.'

Smith saluted with his own glass in acknowledgement, then tried again. 'Where was it postmarked?'

Mr Kepple considered his position, then said, 'I think I can concede that. London-Heathrow: the airport, you know.' Smith knew. Cautious, careful, shrewd. Twice to the busy Trafalgar Square office would still preserve anonymity, thrice might provoke a memory. Time for a change to the equally busy office at the airport.

'How can you be sure the sender owns the copyright?' A probing lunge. Mr Kepple awarded him the raised eyebrows of approval. 'Oh, good point,' he said, and repeated it, 'Jolly good point. Do let me explain. We rely entirely on the handwriting, our letter of instruction conforms ab-so-lutely with the writing in the diary. Expert opinion. Ab-so-lutely solid.' Mr Kepple stretched his 'absolutelys' to their syllabic limits to indicate his strength, and contented, returned his hands to their sheath between his legs. Smith applied some corrosive acid.

'You realize it will not be possible to publish the names in the diary? At least not Pyrnford's, Boswell's or Loach's. Probably not even Turnbull's.' The hands were sharply withdrawn and fluttered wildly in the air. 'Oh, I say. You're not going to arrest the client, are you? You're not going to pull that sub-judice thingy on us?'

'Oh, I'll arrest him, Mr Kepple,' said Smith with a confidence he could not substantiate. 'But when, I don't know. I'm not talking about arrest, I'm referring to libel.'

Mr Kepple brought his hands together gleefully. 'Ah, but you cannot libel the dead.'

'Oh, yes you can.' Smith withheld a childish impulse to add 'Yah boo,' but went on to explain. 'A libel on a person dead, tending to injure or provoke their family, is a criminal libel and can get you two years. I'm quite sure Pyrnford's sister, Lady Lowderton, would be provoked, and Loach's two very large sons would seriously breach your peace.'

'Truth is a complete defence.' Mr Kepple boldly went *en garde*. 'We would fight. Our publishers are fearless. Ab-so-lutely fearless.'

'Truth is no defence to criminal libel. It might get you a reduced sentence but then you would have to prove it and to do that you would have to call your client.'

'Oh dear.' A crestfallen Mr Kepple dropped his blade and wrapped himself in his own arms, wandering disconsolately round the room. 'All those blank spaces where the names should be. Toothless. It simply wouldn't have any bite, particularly minus the aristocratic thingy, Lady Lowderton, the thirties thingy. And the nostalgia market is pos-i-tively brist-ling for any old thirties tat.

'Still,' Mr Kepple unravelled himself from his comforting arms, brightening considerably in the process. 'It won't apply to the foreign rights. Our agents say the Americans are simply ah-gog. The French and Germans too. So, not to worry.' He was stricken by a sudden horrible thought and turned anxiously on Smith.

'You aren't going to do anything nasty like nicking dear old thingy Lugard and letting the world in on the diary for absolutely nix, nothing and niente?' Anxiety made Mr Kepple forget to accentuate his adjective. Smith rewarded him with a consoling smile.

'No prospect of an early arrest. Even if I nicked him tomorrow, it would be at least six months before he came to trial. So your little bit of vanity publishing should be quite safe.'

'Vanity publishing be blowed, old son,' said an outraged Mr Kepple. 'There is at least thirty thou in this.'

'It's still vanity, nevertheless,' replied Smith.

He had not expected much from the visit to Garvey, Remson, Joyce and Partners. But it had to be done, and not only for Hessen's sake. Ninety per cent of investigative enquiry was a waste of time, straw clutching, but there was no way of telling beforehand. Kepple had given him a nice polite little run-around which is always better than a kick up the backside. And he had had his moments with Kepple. A hollow victory; the newspaper's lawyers would have spotted the criminal libel angle in any case. They would probably go ahead on publication with anonymous initials where the names should be. The names, what were the bloody names now? What were Lugard and his men up to, in offering the diary for publication? An eye to the future? Thinking of their old age? He laughed inwardly. Was it really vanity? This pride that had always been present. No longer were they content it should be only vaguely apparent. Now they wanted it to be flaunted.

Elstow had dropped him at Bedford Square and he had told her not to hang around, but to go to his flat in Kennington and wait for him. A flashing eye had compelled him to place a submissive hand on her shoulder and add, 'please'. He walked into Tottenham Court Road and had reached St Giles Circus before he found a cab to take him home.

She had found one of his shirts, and was sitting by the flickering gas logs, otherwise naked, drinking tea. On her crossed legs lay his copy of the Sonnets. Without taking her eyes from the pages she said, 'Your phone's been ringing on and off for the past thirty minutes.'

'You didn't answer, did you?' This time she did look at him, contemptuously, for his concern and for thinking she would be so stupid. He rang through to O'Brien.

'We're just leaving Bedford Square. Anything doing?'

'I rang there, they said you left half an hour ago,' accused O'Brien.

'We had ignition trouble. Do you want Detective Chief Superintendent trouble? I asked if there was anything doing?' Rasping at O'Brien, having to lie always angered him.

'Yes, there is something doing,' O'Brien responded archly. 'The Creeping Greek in the Interpol office has been trying to get hold of you all afternoon. Why? He wouldn't say.' He heard the receiver slammed huffily into its rest.

'Something important?' Elstow asked him.

'Before thy beauty, form and grace, all circumstance must lose the race.'

'I haven't come to that bit.' Elstow turned a page.

'You won't. Courtesy of the extemporaneous Owen Smith.' He took off jacket, tie and shirt, kicked away his shoes and sat beside her on the sheepskin rug. 'Is there any tea left in the pot?' he asked.

Fourteen

++++++++++++++

The parents of Nicolas Kyriacou had brought him to England from Cyprus when he was three years old. At the age of twenty, he had walked out of his father's barber shop in Islington and on the intended bride arranged for him. He joined the Metropolitan Police and became a keen constable, entering the C.I.D. after four years to become a zealous detective. Particularly, in regard to the activities of his compatriots, in the vice and porn rackets of Soho. And with even greater zeal, against the Turkish Cypriots operating the drug rings of North London. Unfortunately, and unnoticed by the medical examiner when he joined the force, his early years as a soap-boy in the shop had weakened his arches, and four years on the beat, followed by long periods of pedestrian surveillance as a detective, brought about their collapse.

They gave him a chair in the Interpol office where his unabated dedication, and a Levantine ability to master the rudiments of many languages, brought him regular promotion and eventual full responsibility for the administrative end of Interpol U.K. and the rank of Detective Superintendent. A tendency to assuage his ailing extremities in wide-fitting, soft suede shoes, soled with thick crepe rubber, in which he shuffled round the corridors of the Yard, brought him the nickname of the Creeping Greek. Despite its implications, he bore the sobriquet good-humouredly, knowing that at the Yard, the more pejorative the title, the more respected the holder.

There was some discomposure behind Nicolas Kyriacou's

flashing smile as he greeted Smith and Elstow. 'What's the problem, Nick?' queried Smith over an extended handclasp.

Kyriacou's face contorted in apologetic disgust. 'A right bleedin' cock-up, that's the problem.' The cockney accent was wildly at odds with his darkly handsome features. With a 'begging your pardon, miss,' to a stoically resigned Elstow, he went on, 'I take the mum and dad back to Paphos for a month, and when I gets back, the office is in a right state of choss. A right boss-eyed state of choss.'

Smith glanced through the glass panel to the outer office. Kyriacou ran the tightest administrative section at the Yard and there was nothing in the orderly progression of work to indicate anything approaching a state of 'choss'. Kyriacou opened his safe and threw a well-stuffed docket on the table. Then he pulled out a teleprinter message from the drawer. 'I gets this from the Interpol General Secretariat this morning.' He read the message to Smith.

' "Re PYRNFORD Antony, alias Meir, alias Roeder, alias Tompkins, etc. Subject mentioned your ref/1873/49 et seq. Is he identical with PYRNFORD Antony mentioned in press reports as found murdered UK 27 April? If so, please cancel forthwith." ' He looked across at Smith. 'Is he identical, Owen?'

'You will have to tell me more, Nick. A lot more.'

Thumbing through an uneven assortment of reports, messages and radiograms, Kyriacou went back to the first faded sheets. Smith interrupted him, 'I searched Registry as soon as I had Pyrnford's name, and got no trace. How come you're holding all this paper?'

'It's an unregistered docket, Owen, S.B. originated. It began back in 1949, long before my time.'

'But I've also searched S.B. They say nothing known.'

'Owen, that's my problem. I've been on to them as well. I've been upstairs personally to the section concerned, and all I get is the puzzled frown, the pregnant pause, the pathetic perplexity. And it's genuine, Owen, they really know nothing from nothing.'

'What is the section concerned?'

'It used to be Frazer's. You know Dougal Frazer.' It was not a rhetorical question, more an assumption of shared respect for Frazer. As though mention of Frazer's involvement explained everything. It would be more accurate to say Smith knew of Dougal Frazer, Chief Superintendent, Special Branch, retired. For years Frazer had been with, and towards the latter years of his service, ran, the liaison section working with the funny people across the river, in the Secret Intelligence Service. A man only sighted on rare occasions at the Yard itself, when his large loose-limbed frame might be seen slouched over the C11 indices in Criminal Intelligence, concealing the object of his interest, or heading for the security checks of the limited-access Sensitive Records Room. A man who wore a permanent quizzical half-smile like a facial affliction, who acknowledged a friendly greeting with a penetrating, inquisitorial glare, a cold nod; and then went past you without a word. A man who only addressed you to require, never to request. And who was invariably called 'sir' even before he held a rank demanding that courtesy.

'Frazer opened the docket when he was a Detective Constable S.B. working under Moncrieff. That was back in 1949 when the Scottish Mafia ran the job.' Kyriacou continued, 'The report was signed by him on behalf of Moncrieff.'

'Moncrieff's been dead for five years, so there is no way of checking if he really authorized it.'

'I don't like the way your mind's working, Owen.'

'Never mind. How does it read?'

Kyriacou was reluctantly undecided. 'It's got a "Secret" stamp on it, the whole docket.'

'Nick, you're left holding the baby. I'm left holding the body. Come on, it's time we shifted the load.'

'Well, nobody up in S.B. wants to know, so here goes, bombs away.' Kyriacou yielded, then tried a delaying digression. 'Fancy a drop of ouzo? I brought four bottles back from Cyprus, lovely stuff.' Smith declined firmly. 'What about you, miss?' Kyriacou tried Elstow. Smith refused on her behalf. Pointing to the docket, he said, 'Get on with it, Nick.'

'A right pair of miserable schnorrers I've got here,' complained Kyriacou, and followed up with his worst insult, 'A couple of bleedin' Turks I've let in.' Smith reached across the table for the docket. Kyriacou snatched it to his chest. 'All right, all right,' he said. 'Business first.' He wet a finger to disentangle the early dog-eared papers.

'There is nothing really startling. Only unusual thing is the time it's been kept alive. Frazer began it with a circulation to all West European and South American agencies, those that were Interpol members, asking for passive trace and movement reports on subject Pyrnford--Antony. He gives a nicely detailed description right down, or should it be up, to a dent in his nut. States he was then holding a Netherlands passport in the name of Kerke–Arie. Alleged crime . . . Murder. But this is the twist! Frazer concludes – " The crime has political implications, therefore arrest is not, repeat not, demanded, and extradition will not be sought." '

Kyriacou repeated his offer of ouzo and even went as far as producing the bottle. He met with another joint refusal. 'Bleedin' racial prejudice,' he moaned. 'You're influenced by that myth about Greeks bearing gifts.'

'Get back to the docket or your skull will be as flat as your feet,' said Smith.

Kyriacou cursed him fluently in Greek, Turkish and Arabic as he replaced the bottle in the cupboard. Gratified by that, he returned to his story. 'As you know, political crime is right out as far as the Interpol Charter Nations are concerned. So he was right to specify no arrest, no extradition. But why not? For murder it's always arguable that no murder is politically justifiable. Well, unless he's a Turk.' Smith held back an impulse to say 'Or unless he was British, back in the fifties.' Instead he asked, 'Does Frazer identify the victim?'

'Not a hint. He winds up the report by saying, "Chief Inspector Moncrieff directs all sighting reports be passed only to Detective Constable Frazer and no other person, including Mr Moncrieff." All that bit is heavily underlined in red ink.' Kyriacou went on, musingly, 'Chief Inspectors were real big wheels back in those days. Not like now. Ten a penny Chief Inspectors are, nowadays. My deputy, Wharton, nine years' service he's got. Hasn't nicked anything heavier than a drunk in charge.' He responded to Smith's threatening fist with, 'Okay, okay, back to the docket. From then on in, every time Frazer went on leave or away on assignment, he gives a contact number. First sighting report we get on Pyrnford is in 1951, arrives Montevideo, Uruguay on SS *Moyhana*, Liberian registered cargo-passenger vessel out of Leopoldville, Belgian Congo, as it then was. Uses the Kerke passport. Intended destination Paraguay. Purpose of visit, business and commercial. We get nothing from Paraguay because Paraguay ain't an Interpol member nation, then or now. Next Pyrnford turns up in Lisbon, October 1953, off a Panamanian ship, ex Buenos Aires. The Argentinians must have missed him on the way out but the Portuguese clocked him on arrival. Paraguayan passport this time, in the name of Meir–Stefan. He dwells in Lisbon for three days, then goes out on a P & O boat for Cape Town. For some reason the South Africans lose him. Maybe the bung went in, maybe it was political. Anyway, he is back in Montevideo by August 1954, en route to Paraguay.'

Kyriacou tried to divert Smith once more. 'Sure you wouldn't like some ouzo?' Smith repelled him with a forefinger straight to the docket. Kyriacou said 'shit' under his breath, then flashed a brilliant smile of apology at Elstow. Returning to the papers he went on. 'Subject went scuttling around South America over the next few years; Buenos Aires, Rio, Montevideo, Sao Paulo, Caracas. By then he had been pretty firmly housed in Rosario, and connected with an import-export firm; Roeder, Bergman & Santos. By 1973 he has joined the jet set and was in Madrid for four days, then he was off to Johannesburg. We lose him, because by then South Africa has been outed from Interpol. Anyhow, a month later, he is back in Rio making tracks for Rosario. All this goes to Frazer, but all we get back is a "seen and noted" and orders to maintain movement notification. Now everything is being centralized through Interpol, Paris, who get a bit browned off, from time to time, about the duration and continued necessity for these negative vibes. They raise the occasional squawk. Equally so, by then Frazer is the big wheel with the funny people, and obviously convinces Paris to keep the screws on. Not through me, you understand. A direct Section One job, under the Old Pals Act.' Here Kyriacou broke off to take fiery issue with Smith's abstemiousness.

'You still don't want no ouzo?' He transferred his ire to Elstow. 'And you still want no ouzo?' Both still wanted no ouzo. 'Well, sod you, I'm going to have some ouzo.' He poured himself some ouzo, adding just enough water to pearlize the spirit. Before drinking he threatened them again. 'I warn you, in Cyprus where I come from, to let a man drink alone and reject his hospitality is an insult that can only be settled by death.'

'You come from Islington, you cockney slob,' said Smith.

'All right, in Islington where I come from, the same applies.' Smith and Elstow both took a glass of ouzo, and a calmer Kyriacou returned once more to the docket.

'Two years ago Frazer retires. Almost his last official act is to come down to me with another report saying he is taking a job with the funnies, and as the Pyrnford docket is really their baby, existing arrangements will continue and all reports passed to him immediately by phone to his home which is now, St Andrews, Scotland. The report has a minute on it from the Assistant Commissioner Crime saying, "Action at (A) above to be strictly com-

plied with, and total confidentiality to be rigorously observed." '
Kyriacou reflected on the final pages of the docket, saying, 'I
always sussed them Yank golfers for C.I.A. men. Every year when
they come over and take that cup back, I'll bet it's stuffed with
secret microfilms.'

'Is that the end of the saga, Nick?' Smith was quietly patient.

'Christ, no! The bing bang-walloper that is going to grind yours
truly, Nicolas Kyriacou, Detective Superintendent of this parish,
into the dust is yet to come.' Large, sympathy-seeking chestnut
eyes traversed the space between Smith and Elstow several times.
And as if to enhance the funereal solemnity of the occasion,
Kyriacou corked his ouzo bottle and returned it to the cupboard.

'My heart can only bleed for you, Nick, when I know what
happened.' Finding no solace, a tempestuous rage suffused
Kyriacou's fine Grecian features, making them momentarily,
coarse, sinister and ugly. 'What happened!' he shouted, 'I'll tell
you what happened. Uncle Tomas died, that's what bleedin'
happened.' He allowed his rage to expend itself by the process of
unlocking his cupboard and pouring another glass of ouzo. This
time he was so morbidly engrossed with his problems, he offered
none to Smith or Elstow, whose glasses were still more than half
full in any case. Calmer now, he seated himself at the table. 'Two
days before I take me Mum and Dad to Paphos because Uncle
Tomas has died, and the family have to decide who gets the
taverna he owned. Uncle Tomas had no children, and Aunt
Katya has died six years previous,' He began to simmer gently,
but kept the lid down against the pressure. 'Relatives, you should
see my bleedin' relatives! From Nicosia they come, from Episkopi
and Limassol, even from bleedin' Famagusta they come, where
the bleedin' Turks are supposed to have them behind barbed
wire. Like vultures, from –'

'From bleedin' Islington they come!' Smith slammed a closed
fist on the table top. 'Forget the gathering of the Kyriacou clan
and get back to the time before it happened.'

'Yeh, yeh,' sighed Kyriacou bitterly. 'Why should I burden you
with my personal problems. I got enough professional ones.' He
fingered, almost fondled, the last pages of the docket. 'Okay, here
we go. The day before the day before I go to Cyprus. Two days
before, right? I get a call from Madrid. Pyrnford has arrived on
passport Tompkins. Now because they got all this E.T.A. trouble
with the Basques, the Spaniards are running close tabs on
everyone who is a bit sussy. They say they are going to keep

Pyrnford ready-eyed. So I ring Frazer at St Andrews. He gets a bit terse about the close surveillance the Dons are putting on his man, but he had to swallow it. Next day I get a call from the Dons in Malaga. Pyrnford is nearly an hour out of Malaga airport having rowed himself aboard a charter flight to Gatwick. Straight away I rings Frazer again. "Okay," he says, "I'll deal," he says. "Fine," I says, "Let me know when I can cancel this historic document." "Will do," he says. So I tell my deputy about the docket and to cancel when he gets Frazer's call, and off I goes to Cyprus rejoicing. When I resume duty this morning, knowing damn all about your job, I've got this squawk from Paris on my desk. Frazer never cancelled.'

Kyriacou closed the docket, making little jerky, patting gestures on the cover with the tips of his fingers, and all the time smiling hopefully, appealingly, at Smith.

'Now, tell me, Frazer's Pyrnford ain't identical with your Pyrnford, is he, Owen?'

'He is, Nick. Right down to the dent in his skull.' Smith was unmerciful. 'Frazer cancelled him all right. Him and a few others. He has taken you and Interpol for a ride all these years. It's a pound to a penny every signature endorsing his action reports is a forgery.' Two hands flew to Kyriacou's face to cover it in a dolorous mask. Slowly he withdrew his head and howled at the ceiling. 'Uncle Tomas, you stupid old git. Why couldn't you hang on another week!' He pushed himself to his feet and went for a slithering slow-footed walk to the door, opened it and pensively looked up and down the corridor as if seeking some casual passer-by to provide a solution. But it was well after six in the evening and there was no chance of finding anyone in that corridor at that time. He shuffled around and closed the door. He came over to the table, picked up the Pyrnford docket and hurled it at the wall. Yellowing old pages scattered across the floor.

'Forget it, Nick.' Smith said. 'It wouldn't have made much difference. You've cracked the job for me and I'm grateful as hell.' The significance of Smith's earlier words came through Kyriacou's preoccupation with his own fate.

'Frazer? You putting it down to Frazer?' Incredulity stretched his already wide mouth. 'How? No way he could get down from St Andrews in time. The Malaga flight was on the tarmac at Gatwick just over an hour after I phoned him.'

'He didn't have to get down to Gatwick, he had the other survivors of the gallant 1404th on hand to make the pick-up. But he was there in time to get on parade with the firing squad.'

'You're losing me, Owen. I've been out of touch for the past month. I only know you've got the man in my docket shot full of holes.'

Smith ignored him, he was too busy dialling the St Andrews number shown on the papers. He listened to the harsh purr of the ringing tone for longer than was necessary. Not that he would have had anything to say had there been an answer, he simply wanted to know if Frazer was there – in St Andrews. Well maybe he was, but he wasn't in the house, or again, maybe he was, and was just not answering the phone. 'Idiot,' he said, deriding his own reckless stupidity. He might as well have sent Frazer an open warning he was on to him. He replaced the phone and turned to Kyriacou. 'You can open another docket, Nick. This time on Frazer. I want an All Ports warning out on him in case he tries to leave the country. We are probably too late but do it anyway. Then get your radio room to put him out on the Interpol network. And this time you can say, "Arrest is demanded; extradition will be sought."'

'God, I hope you know what you're doing, Owen. Troubles I got already.' But Smith was again at the phone. Marrasey's clipped voice answered. O'Brien was out. He glanced at the clock, nearly seven, the bugger would be on his first pint of the night. He told Marrasey to book him aboard the early flight to Edinburgh in the morning, then get in touch with the Edinburgh Regional Crime Squad and request a car with two men to meet him at the airport and assist him with an enquiry in St Andrews . . . and they had better be armed.

'You did say St Andrews, sir?' enquired Marrasey. Smith confirmed it. There was a pause before Marrasey replied. 'Very good, sir, that will be done. Oh, by the way, sir, you may be interested to know, I've just had a gentleman call in at the station a few minutes ago to say he had found a cartridge-case in the sandpit. He has left it where he found it, marking the place with a stick. There is no one else in the office. Shall I send a uniformed officer . . .' Smith cut him short. 'No, I'll pick it up on the way back. About forty minutes.' A pensive, anxious, Smith replaced the phone. Kyriacou shuffled to his side and laid a troubled hand on his shoulder. 'I'll have to get authority for these circulations you require. I mean, putting out a "wanted" on somebody like Frazer. I'll have to get a senior officer's authority.'

'What the hell do you think I am. A fucking Boy Scout?'

Kyriacou winced at the profanity in Elstow's presence, giving her a surrogate 'begging your pardon, miss' smile. He came back to Smith. 'Okay, Owen, it's done. Down to you. Down to me. But just one thing before you go.' Grasping Smith's elbow and ushering him towards the door, he said, 'After we both get the sack, you fancy coming in with me on a nice little taverna in Paphos? I can get it for us cheap!

Fifteen

++++++++++

The tail-end of the rush-hour was well ahead of them as Elstow
thrust her powerful little car out of the underground car park at
the Yard and into the thinning traffic. Bursting out of Storey's
Gate into Birdcage Walk, zooming past the Palace and the Royal
Mews, a snappy gear change right turn at Eccleston Street, then a
booming left into Eaton Square. Another sharp right past Bel-
grave Place, through the amber into Pont Street and a wriggle
along the narrow double-parked confines of Beauchamp Place,
where the young trendies had overflowed out of the pubs onto
the pavements clutching and quaffing their pints of 'cooking'. A
nicely judged timing of the traffic-light sequence took them
briskly along the Cromwell Road and across the refurbished
elegance of Hammersmith Bridge on their way west to Cobb
Common. The undemanding driving along the throughway gave
Elstow a chance to ask her questions.

'I've only had an opportunity to skim through the diary. Are
you saying Frazer was Sergeant Lugard? Smith shook his head.

'No. Frazer was Bruce. Only a Bruce could become a man like
Frazer.'

'But they say Frazer was a particularly humourless person. The
Bruce character seemed to see the funny side of life.'

'Maybe his sense of humour was crushed in a Polish coal mine.
Maybe he lost it earlier to an S.S. officer, or it died on the march to
Regensburg. Whichever way it went, it was replaced by hatred.
Bruce supplied the hatred, Lugard the pride. Both long-lasting

197

Scots and Irish characteristics. Between the two of them, they kept an emotional pot boiling for over forty years, with enough gas left over to keep the other surviving platoon members nicely simmering.'

'I would have thought that in Loach's case, self-interest would have kept him out of it.'

'They had the Boswell execution to keep Loach in line. Not much doubt in my mind that Loach spotted him when he was stationed at Filey after the survivors were split up. He would know where the others were stationed and put out a call for the 1404th to reassemble. They would probably still have been in the U.K. so it wouldn't have been difficult. And at the same time, hate would still be red-hot in all of them. Boswell was available, Pyrnford wasn't, so Boswell got the seat with the sea view and a backful of bullets. It's possible the shrewder heads of Lugard and Bruce considered Boswell unworthy of the effort and only went along to avoid dissension in the ranks. And, being the great forward planners that they are, it would help keep them all together for the day they found Pyrnford.'

'But why have they waited all this time? Frazer had him traced years ago. One would think Frazer at least was in a position to go out and kill him.'

'That was not what Lugard wanted. It had to be done formally, with pride, and it had to be done by all the 1404th who were still alive. Above all, Pyrnford had to know it was going to be done, and why.'

Elstow, narrow-eyed, assessed Smith's reasoning, frowning slightly. He told her to relax, she would get wrinkles. She jerked the gear stick into second and scudded alongside a freightliner occupying half the outside lane. Smith had a close-up of huge spinning wheels and edged away from the door. Fearlessly, Elstow forced her way through the narrow gap. Above him, Smith saw the truck driver's lips form the words, 'Fucking cow.'

'Why wasn't Pyrnford pulled on his fake passports at all these ports he went through?' She probed as though nothing untoward had happened.

'It's speculative, but the way I read it is that Pyrnford was used as a courier by the expatriate Nazis in South America. A financial errand-boy transferring funds. Topping up accounts here, placing investment income there. He got through on the fake passports because of two possibilities. One being the bung went in on his behalf, and two that Frazer was using Section One influence outside Interpol to keep him on the loose.'

Smith pointed to the road junction ahead. 'Do a left here, I want to pick up that cartridge-case from the Common.'

Elstow lost her frown and smiled. 'It's the first time I've been asked up to the Common to find a cartridge-case,' she said.

With Elstow at his side, Smith looked down into the sandpit. The air was redolent with the lonely evening sounds of early suburban summer. A distant lawn mower putt-putting over a hidden lawn, faint laughter from a far-off tennis court, a clip-clopping of hooves on the bridle path beyond the trees, where a string of novice riders, suddenly ten feet tall, trotted along, still too rigidly tense to sneer down in supercilious rectitude at lower mortals. Below in the sandpit, a straying collie snuffled excitedly at the ground into which Pyrnford's blood had poured a month earlier. The dog dug in an exploratory paw to scrape away the surface, sniffed again at the fresh sand, but finding nothing of substance cocked a disdainful leg and peed over his excavation. Bounding away up the opposite slope, he stopped briefly to deposit further proof of his presence against a stout stick thrust into the sand.

The position of the marker was not where Smith had expected it to be. He had thought any ejection of cartridge-cases would have been at the estimated position of the firing squad. Indeed, that one had been found at all surprised him, the search had been thorough. Still as the marker was right at the base of the far slope it could have been overlooked; and it was possible one of the squad had unconsciously cleared his bolt action on the way up.

'Wait for me,' he said to Elstow. 'I'll go down and have a look.'

'No!' Her shrill refusal astonished him. He saw she was shivering. 'I'm not staying up here alone, the bats are out. I can't stand bats.' Laughing at her fears, he offered her a hand to help her down the slope, then changed his mind and gallantly swept her into his arms. Holding her close, he went charging down through the loose sand, both of them now laughing aloud at the innocent incongruity of it all. Still carrying her, he struggled over the uneven pot-holed surface to the marker and there, kissing her, he placed her on her feet. 'Elstow, my beautiful bitch,' he said, 'when this one is over, maybe we will buy into that taverna at Paphos.'

She pushed him away gently. 'You and the Creeping Greek can have it all to yourselves. I've got other plans.' He saw the determination behind the soft smile.

'Still intent on being the first woman Chief Constable, that it?'

'Why not the first woman Commissioner of Police of the Metropolis?'

He was about to reach for her angrily, his masculinity outraged, when he saw the sand spurt from the ground between them. And even as he heard the crack of the shot, two further gouts of sand sprayed over his shoes. He felt his heart jump under the unexpected impact of sound. Elstow had the knuckles of one hand jammed in her mouth, and was looking wild-eyed about her. Grabbing her under the arm he ran, not really knowing where, shots hitting the ground inches ahead of his feet. He changed direction, Elstow tripped and went over. He dragged her, stumbling, this way and that. Still the shots came, preceding his wavering legs with spiteful little eruptions. His eyes swept the rim of the pit as they ran, trees and bushes, nothing else. They were like beetles in a bucket being stoned by a sadistic child. Elstow fell again; this time he left her where she lay and walked, quite slowly, to the centre of the sandy basin, halting with his arms in the air. 'All right, Lugard,' he called out, turning round to encompass the seemingly deserted rim. 'Is this what you want? Would it do any good if I said Kamerad? You hear me, Lugard, Kamerad. Or should I –'

The bullet hit him and he spun round, knowing only he had been hit somewhere. At first he felt no pain, then a spreading, numbing ache, the blood came running, richly red, down his arm and with it a sickening agony that brought him to his knees. He knew he was screaming because Elstow was at his side with her arm drawn back and was about to slap him across the face.

'Don't you bloody well dare,' he shouted at her, but too late. Then she was smiling down at him, or was it that her face was melting, distorting. She had two heads, three heads merging and separating. A black curtain was being lowered in front of him. He tried to duck under it, to escape, to retain his vision, but it slid down faster. Blackness.

He pushed himself through into a confined space of noise and pain, knowing from the high-pitched blee blah that he was in an ambulance. Elstow was there with him, not smiling, white-faced, hair awry, blood on the sleeves of her white blouse, his blood from where she had held his wound. She was not looking at him. He tried to touch her knee but could not move his left arm. Reaching over with his right, she started at his touch. 'Marrasey,' he said. 'Get him in. Get him circulated wanted. All Ports warning. Get one out on him, right away.'

From her a placatory smile under worried eyes. 'Relax now, we'll be at the hospital in a couple of minutes.' Fumbling for a hold with his good arm, he tried to raise himself by the bracket above his head. She restrained him, soothing him. 'Come on now, don't be silly, relax.'

'Listen,' he said wildly. 'Marrasey is Lugard. Get a team round to his drum. Get him circulated.' Her face, puzzled and uncertain, wavered again and disappeared behind the curtain.

'When did you last have something to eat?' The voice was professionally sharp. He was stretched out naked, seeing the back of a white coat in front of tiled walls, a scalpel in a hand, the tapes of a surgical mask. Simonson? Got him at last, had he? 'Shepherds Pie,' he said, trying to stifle uncontrollable giggles.

'I didn't ask what, I asked when?' The voice was sharper, he saw the eyes above the mask, it wasn't Simonson.

'Tea,' he said cogently. 'Cup of tea just after four. Before that breakfast, seven a.m. I'm bloody starving,' he complained. And was ignored. The pain came back, sharply centred in the upper part of his left arm. But now he had it under control. Wishing to see the wound, he tried to raise his arm, then realized he was lying face downwards on the operating table.

'Is my arm going to be all right? I'm not going to lose it, am I?' The surface of the surgical mask stretched a little.

'Only eight or nine grammes, and most of that has gone already. Just going to tidy the ragged edges and sew you up. Get him on his side, sister. No, not that side, I prefer to work on top of the table, not through it. Right, Digby, you can put him to sleep.' He heard the voice saying faintly, 'Bye bye, now,' as he sucked greedily at the anaesthetic for he had had a long hard day.

He was ravenous when he recovered his senses. Hessen was at his bedside, *The Times* on his knees, folded to the crossword. But the blank spaces were still blank. Hessen's mind was not on the crossword and, from the faraway look on his face, not on Smith either.

'I suppose I've missed supper?' he said.

Hessen jerked guiltily. 'Oh, Owen. You're awake. How do you feel, old chap?'

'Hungry. And my arm hurts like hell. Did they get Lugard?'
'Lugard?'

'Marrasey then. Lugard is Marrasey.'

'Er, no. We thought you were raving, well delirious. You weren't?'

Smith nursed his arm under the thick pad of bandages. 'Not this time.'

'That's what Elstow thought. She eventually persuaded O'Brien to check his home. He wasn't there. But only because he went on leave last evening.' Hessen became consolingly assuring. 'He always takes this period for his annual holiday. He goes touring.'

'On his motor-cycle?' Smith posed the question, sourly facetious, but Hessen reacted with curiosity.

'Yes, he rides a monstrous old Norton. How did you know?'

Smith groaned in reply. 'God, I've got to get out of here.' Throwing aside the bedclothes, he had one leg out of the bed before Hessen came at him. 'Now, I'll have none of this nonsense,' he chided, powerful arms forcing Smith back on the pillows. 'You stay where you are,' said Hessen firmly. 'Shock, you know.' Going on learnedly as though an M.D. figured among his diplomas. 'You can never tell about shock. A fair old chunk of flesh has been shot out of your arm. Big as a golf ball,' and to show the full gravity of the wound, he added, 'competition size.'

'St Andrews,' Smith gripped Hessen with his good arm. 'You've got to get the police at St Andrews to pick up Frazer. Ex-Special Branch man, address in my notebook.'

'Not to worry, old chap. Elstow has been on to them. Seems Frazer also left for his holiday shortly after you were playing clay pigeon down in the sandpit. But nothing necessarily suspicious in that, Owen, a Friday evening, early start before the weekend. Lots of retired people take their holidays at the end of May. Cheaper, you know.'

'And Frazer also goes touring at this time of year?'

'I suppose you could call it that. A walking holiday on the continent. His wife says he likes to get away for a week or so on his own.'

'Old habits die hard. Frazer got used to doing a lot of walking on the continent. And Loach, did he take a continental holiday as well at this time of year?'

Mention of the name brought a grey cloud to Hessen's face. He lifted his hands from Smith's unresisting shoulders. 'He didn't live in my pocket, you know,' an aggrieved sniff indicated injury and offence. A small silence stood between them, broken by a whining call somewhere beyond the screens surrounding them, 'Nurse, Nurse! Me tube's come out.' A chair was pushed back, the firm slap of competent, confident feet on wooden boards, brisk female tones. 'You must sleep on your back, Mr Parry. No more of this rolling about.' Shortly, another whine. 'Ow, that 'urt.'

They listened to footsteps retreating, then hesitantly, Hessen asked, 'By the way, how did you get on with Garvey, Remson, Joyce and Partners?'

'The first instalment will probably be out this Sunday.' The cloud deepened and the weight of it pulled Hessen's mouth down at the corners.

'But I don't think they will mention any actual names,' Smith said, adding drily, 'to protect the innocent.' Hessen managed a wan smile to indicate his appreciation. Still hungry, but now colossally tired, Smith turned on his unwounded side and went to sleep.

He discharged himself after breakfast next morning, despite a medical warning that he should have further bed rest for at least twenty-four hours. Promising he would do just that at home, he met Elstow and a solicitous but subdued O'Brien outside the entrance. He carried his left arm suspended in a low wrist sling. The wound still hurt like hell, and although he had been given a number of pain-killing capsules, he rejected their brain-deadening comfort. Shaking off O'Brien's attempt to ease him into the front seat of Elstow's car, he asked him, 'Have you turned over Marrasey's drum yet?'

'No, sir.' O'Brien was sullenly defiant. 'I don't think words from a semi-conscious man who has just been shot justifies me going in that strong.' He tried to ameliorate his deficiency. 'I've had the place under observation, though. Nothing moving.' He met Smith's cold stony glare with snivelling protest. 'Well, you can't blame me for bottling out. Just look at Marrasey's handwriting, it don't bear any resemblance to the Lugard diary, you must understand that.'

Smith took out the small phial of pain-killers and held them under O'Brien's nose. 'That's about how much bottle you've got, mister. And it's just about the size of your brain. When Lugard joined this job as P.C. Marrasey and started putting in reports in his cramped writing to those half-blind old sergeants and inspectors they had after the war, he would get his pocket-book thrown in his face, and told to write something they could see. Nobody writes the way Marrasey does naturally, and being Lugard he took lessons in calligraphy. Not because he thought the day would come when it would fool some idiot of a Detective Chief Inspector, but only because he wanted to get on in the job.' O'Brien took it between tightly clenched teeth and said nothing. Smith understood his position all right. He understood a lot of things now. A few months ago when O'Brien seemed destined to be a no-hope D.I. for the rest of his service, he would have crashed straight in. But now he was, unexpectedly, a D.C.I. he had an eye to the future. Like others he knew. He told Elstow to drive to Marrasey's home.

He lived on the top floor of a small block of flats, less than ten minutes' walk from Cobb Common police station, which, to Smith, explained why he had never seen him on a motor-cycle. Smith pressed the bell a couple of times as a formality, waited for the strident ring to die away, then said to O'Brien, 'Got any 'loid on you?' Without a word O'Brien produced a five-inch strip of mica from his inside pocket. Smith slid it between the jamb and opened the door. The living room was furnished with the bare essentials, all very clean, and very neat. There was a bookcase, and Smith studied the contents with envy. The illustrated military histories, the biographies of the great commanders, the works of the tactitians and strategists. And Marrasey had not neglected his police studies either. The familiar books were present, Archbold, Stone, Blackwood, and even the didactic Hans Gross. On top of the bookcase was a framed photograph, amateurishly taken and slightly over-exposed. Ten soldiers stood in an awkward, self-conscious group, thin men, gaunt, unsmiling, but erect. Their battledress uniforms were ill-fitting and obviously brand new, still creased in the wrong places. In the centre was a young, but not young-looking, Marrasey with the three chevrons of Sergeant Lugard on his arms. Yes, thought Smith, Lugard would only be satisfied with a dead sergeant with whom to swap identity. He wondered if the late Sergeant Marrasey compared, not only with Lugard's rank, but with his exacting soldierly qualities. And there was Bruce, taller than the rest, tight lips slanting sardonically towards the incipient quizzical half-smile of Detective Chief Superintendent Dougal Frazer. It was Elstow who recognized Loach. Smith found it impossible to ascertain which of the remaining haggard faces had become that of the elderly flabby corpse he had viewed in Farnham mortuary. Working awkwardly with one hand, Smith removed the picture from the frame and found written on the back, 'R.A.S.C. Holding and Posting Depot, Woking, Surrey, 23 April 1945.' No names had been allocated to the men depicted. He replaced the photograph in the frame, resting it back on the bookcase, stepping back a pace to ensure it was neatly centred.

Smith turned his attention to a long shallow cabinet screwed firmly into the opposite wall. Made of stout oak, it had been well carpentered and finely waxed, close-fitting doors were held securely shut by a strong padlock. Rooting round the kitchen until he found a heavy hammer, Smith attacked the cabinet ruthlessly with his good arm. O'Brien reluctantly offered to take over, but was brusquely shouldered aside. Breathing heavily, Smith battered the doors wide. Inside the cabinet, neatly in a slotted rack, five Lee Enfield rifles were mutely and menacingly arrayed. All were clean and lightly oiled, even the slings had been freshly blancoed, the brass fittings polished. Eight other slots in the rack were empty. In all, space had been provided for thirteen rifles.

'So there were only five of them,' said Elstow.

'No. There were six. "Bim Bam" Bailey was right the second time,' muttered O'Brien. Smith cocked an enquiring head in his direction.

'Loach's son, Alan, came into the nick last night, all worried. He had a Lee Enfield rifle with him. It had been dumped on the doorstep a few days ago with a note tied to the trigger guard. The note read, "Even though he died in dishonour, his rifle should accompany him to the grave. As it was with his comrades, so let it be with him." It was signed, "Sergeant Michael Lugard".'

'This was a few days ago, when the rifle was dumped?'

O'Brien shrugged. 'Three, to be exact. The son sussed it connected the old man with the Pyrnford killing and intended to comply with instructions when the body was released for burial. But when news of your shooting went out last night he got a touch of the seconds and brought it in.'

'But Pyrnford was only shot five times,' insisted Elstow.

Smith turned to the photograph. Ten pairs of sunken eyes were reproaching him for his earlier malice and vandalism. Bringing down the hammer he still held, until it touched the head of Sergeant Lugard, he said: 'This one. He gave the orders. The Ready, Aim, Fire, bit. A coup de grâce wasn't necessary, any more than it was necessary for Boswell. The only guy he has actually shot recently was me.' He softly caressed his wounded arm without taking his eyes from the photograph. Then he rounded on O'Brien, and spoke to him flatly, hurtfully formal. 'You know what this means, Detective Chief Inspector?' O'Brien drooped, downcast. 'It means, while you were taking the soft option of deciding I was off my head and raving, Marrasey came back here after using me for target practice. Cleaned his rifle, and put it neatly away, before departing on a leave which you presumably authorized without consulting me.'

'Marrasey is my clerical officer, my responsibility. It's up to me to authorize his leave and I did. The System was running smoothly, McCrae was on top of it. There was no reason why Marrasey shouldn't go on leave – it seems he books this period every year.'

'So I've heard. Do you think he'll send us a postcard?' Smith felt the pain easing in his arm, as though it were being transferred to O'Brien's misery-martyred face.

'You are being unfair, sir,' Elstow snapped at Smith's neck. 'More than two hours elapsed before I told Mr O'Brien what you had been on about in the ambulance. I thought you were in a bad way. You looked in a bad way. I only remembered after they told us you were in no danger.'

The dull ache returned to Smith's arm and spread into his breast. He turned to the photograph on the bookcase. It was so easy to pick out Marrasey. Whereas the others stared dispassionately at the camera, his Sergeant Lugard head was high, proud and defiant. He swung round to O'Brien and Elstow. 'Well, don't stand here feeling sorry for yourselves. Get the rest of this drum turned over and see if you can find a bloody typewriter.'

They did not find a typewriter, and Smith was not greatly surprised at their failure. Despite the photograph, despite the incriminating presence of the rifles, somebody was still being careful, cautious and shrewd. Somebody who played a grim little war-game with him; not wanting to kill him, only to kill time, to stop his clock for a couple of hours. Tactics: delaying tactics.

The knot of reporters waiting for him outside the police station were raucously persistent, despite his repeated bellowing of 'No comment' through the closed windows of the car. In the Murder Room, he found those inside peculiarly quiescent and totally absorbed in their work. Covert glances were directed at his wounded arm, and he assumed that this, together with the fact that Mr Marrasey had worked undiscovered in their midst, accounted for such assiduous attention to their duties. Only when he opened the door to his inner office did he discover the true reason. Cyril Fairchild, Assistant Commissioner (Crime) was sitting in his chair, eating black grapes.

'Want one?' Fairchild pushed the brown paper bag in Smith's direction, but not quite far enough to give his invitation genuine presentation. 'They were originally intended for you. After all, when one sets out to visit one's officer, supposedly lying sorely wounded in hospital, one can't go empty-handed, can one?' There was a hint of frost in the air of Fairchild's patient enquiry. He went on to make it explicit. 'Even though there are times when one would almost prefer to be taking flowers to that officer's funeral.' He shoved the chair back on its legs until he could loll comfortably against the wall and viewed the flush on Smith's face with clinical interest. 'You do have a penchant for creating problems, Owen. We go to great lengths to bury you in an area of urban tranquillity and you rise like a vampire from the grave to disturb our dreams and ruin our slumbers. You are heading for the stake through the heart, my lad. Or you could leave your body to science – the sooner the better.' Fairchild popped another grape into his mouth and asked, 'How's the arm, by the way?'

'Sore.'

'As is my head. Do you think you could enlighten me a little on all this? after all I am the A.C.C.' He slid forward. 'You have deigned to report the brief facts in progress reports from time to time,' Fairchild conceded, 'but it is the sudden unexplained emergence of the suspect personalities, both ex-police officers of distinction and repute, that concern myself and the Commissioner. I have read the Lugard diary, of course, and sight of the All Ports and Interpol circulations on Frazer damned soon brought Kyriacou shuffling into my office bearing his docket and a tale of woe. Then, while he is busy explaining his long-standing neglect in failing to discover an abuse of the Interpol network, we have this former D.I. Marrasey conducting a sniping skirmish with you and a woman sergeant on Cobb Common as though it was the North-West Frontier.' Fairchild was struck by a sudden divergent thought. 'Just what were you doing on the Common with a woman sergeant?'

'Marrasey lured me up there on a stumer. Sergeant Elstow just happened to be with me.'

'And why the rifle fire?'

'A diversion to give him time to get hold of Frazer and tell him it was coming down on top. They were both heading for a rendezvous but in case Frazer was late on parade, he had to buy him time to clear home base. So he fed me a line about a cartridge-case seen lying on the Common and when I got there he put a bullet in my arm.'

'I wonder why he didn't put one between your eyes?' Fairchild seemed greatly interested in the answer. Smith made no effort to supply one. Disappointed, Fairchild took another grape. 'You realize an All Ports won't bottle up a chap with Frazer's experience?'

'I don't expect it to, sir.'

In the face of such a non sequitur, Fairchild demonstrated considerable restraint, content merely to purse his lips. 'And what put you on to Marrasey?' he enquired.

'I was never really on to him until he gave me the bullet last night.' Smith was sure it was Marrasey who had fired at him, but he had no definite proof. One of the rifles from his flat would tie him in with it, not very tightly, nothing a good lawyer couldn't talk his way around. Still, early days, he had plenty of time to add more rope. He addressed himself further to the A.C.C.'s question. 'There was something about the job, right from the off, that made me think copper. No,' he admitted, 'I wasn't that clever, I only felt it in my gut and kept pushing it down the tubes. You may remember, I reported something had left two closely parallel indentations on the seat-belt release of Loach's car. A couple of days ago, I found similar marks on the arm of the charge-room bench downstairs. It seems they had a stroppy prisoner in for burglary and had cuffed him to the bench. I tried it out. With a pair of handcuffs snapped tight over the seat-belt release, there isn't enough of the button left exposed to press it down. After that I began to think copper, and going back to Lugard's covering letter with the diary, "I am, sir, Your obedient servant," I began to think old copper. Remember how that salutation was stereotyped on the old report forms?'

'Hardly enough to take you specifically in Marrasey's direction. It was once common to all Government correspondence.'

'When I rang through here last evening and he answered the phone he clicked as a possible. So I fed him the fact I was close to Frazer to see what would happen.'

Fairchild drew a deep incredulous breath. 'Deliberately?'

Gasping painfully, Smith adjusted the sling supporting his wounded arm. Fairchild was unimpressed. 'Well?' he asked, ominously insistent.

'About as deliberately as I would stick a pin into a list of forty runners in the Grand National and hope to come up with a winner . . . It was a sudden inspiration, sir,' he concluded lamely.

'Smith, the consequence of inspiration is grandeur.' The A.C.C. was coldly pedantic. 'The word you should have used is impulse, preceded by rash. And the consequence of that, is what we have; a bloody disaster.'

'No, sir,' Smith's face was alight with . . . sudden inspiration? 'You see, I not only have Marrasey and Frazer, I have the entire firing squad. I know the rendezvous and they will all be there.'

'How clever of you.' Each word from the A.C.C. was a parody of astonished admiration. 'You will tell me, won't you?' he went on, egregiously beseeching.

Smith told him. Adding, 'Kyriacou's docket will bear me out. Frazer's contact number, for a leave period beginning 30 May, must be the same each year.'

'I wonder why it is,' reflected Fairchild with the gravity of a meditating monk, 'we tend to think those placed in authority above us are deprived of reason, incapable of logical thought, that their minds contract in ratio to the increase in the size and quality of their office carpets.' He fed Smith a face, blandly opaque. 'For instance, did you consider, for one moment, the possibility that I just might have arrived at the same rather obvious conclusion from a reading of Kyriacou's docket?'

'I didn't think you had come out all this way on a Saturday morning just to bring me a bunch of grapes.' Smith would be toyed with no longer. All right, Fairchild was entitled to have a go at him, to put the needle in, but enough was enough.

'If it's blood you want, sir, I lost about two pints up on the Common last night. I am keeping what's left. Have you eaten all those grapes? I've been so damned hungry lately.' Fairchild shook a ganglion of stalks from the bag. Bare, but for a few squashed fruits oozing pulp and seeds.

'You would be advised to make no reference to givers of pips,' cautioned Fairchild. 'Now, you are coming with me back to the Yard. We have to conduct some delicate international negotiations. I presume you are fit enough to travel?'

Sixteen

✦✦✦✦✦✦✦✦✦✦

At seven next morning, Smith was waiting at Ramsgate for the first of the day's cross-channel hovercraft. The tide was out and a breeze, rich with the pleasantly unpleasant smells of sea ordure, set his nostrils twitching as he drew in appreciative lungfuls to dispel the analgesic effects of the capsules he had taken in order to get a night's sleep. He had rung Elstow before settling in for an early night, but she had refused to come to his flat, saying she was unwell, suffering delayed shock. Well, maybe she was. No, be fair, probably she was. Or was she backing away from trouble? Seeing him as a danger to her career. He knew the stroke. You rope on to a fast climber and get yourself pulled up the promotion mountain along with him. But you have to unhook fast if he comes a tumble or you go down with him. No, that wasn't fair either. Elstow must have known the shutter was down on him the moment he arrived on the district, his card marked, 'a competent investigator, but not destined for further promotion.' Still, funny she didn't come over last night. They could have greatly consoled one another, bad arm or no bad arm.

Five minutes after he had settled in his seat, the hovercraft heaved itself upwards on a cushion of air and went wallowing in to the sea. He had suggested to Fairchild that the force helicopter might be a more expeditious way to travel. The rebuff was acerbic. 'With perhaps the Belgian Police Band to greet you on arrival? In case it has escaped your notice, the object is to achieve our purpose as peacefully and inconspicuously as possible.

Indeed, I have serious reservations about the whole exercise. Were it not for your ham-fisted attempt to bring things to a head, we could, and maybe we still should, sit tight and hope they might favour us by kindly returning home.'

But ultimately, no one, least of all Fairchild, was prepared to take the chance, and so Smith found himself roaring across the Channel on a big bag of compressed air, and in sufficient comfort to read the first instalment of Lugard's diary in the Sunday paper. As he had anticipated, the sensitive names had been replaced by an initial letter. It would provide a temporary respite for Commander Hessen, until a trial or the ulcers on his conscience got the better of him.

Commissaire Eugène Caniers of the Belgian Police shook hands with his French counterpart, who protocol demanded be on hand while he and Smith were on French soil. Not that it was normally observed with such formality, but in Smith's presence it was thought seemly. They had driven together in Caniers' Renault along the N40 beyond Dunkirk, where after coffee on the French side of the frontier at Ghyvelde, and an exchange of *Bonne chance*', the Frenchman joined his own following car and departed. Smith's slung arm had raised eyebrows on arrival, the cause was politely established, and significant grimaces exchanged as a result. Caniers was a few years younger than Smith, one of the new breed of North Gauls, an E.E.C. model. Lean in body, progressive in mind, dynamic in an unpredictable on-and-off fashion. He spoke coherent, if somewhat stiff and formal English. 'And now, Mr Smith, we will proceed to the Colme Canal, which the Sergeant Lugard calls in his journal the Bergues-Furnes Canal.'

'You have read the diary?' Smith said, surprised.

'Of course. Le Monde has carried it since last Thursday.' 'That bastard Kepple,' thought Smith, 'just how long did he have the diary before getting in touch? Long enough for him to make sure there would be no time to do anything about its publication.' He cursed himself for being so engrossed in acting the smart-arse as to fail to ascertain such an obvious point. He caught Caniers giving him sly sidelong glances. 'Very controversial,' said Caniers when sure of his attention. 'This diary, it has brought much comment in the papers here, and on the radio and T.V. Many old wounds have been reopened in old bodies. But that need not concern us, eh?' He spoke as if prodding for further discussion.

It was not an area into which Smith wished to enter. He held up his own paper and said, 'We only got it today. You're a bit ahead of us.'

'*Naturellement*,' replied Caniers, complacently gratified.

Smith took to studying the countryside, as he had done from time to time during the journey from Calais. So this was where it had all happened, in 1940 and again in 1944, although of the destruction there was no visible sign. The earth had absorbed it, the hand of man had rebuilt that which he had destroyed, leaving no unhealed scars, except in certain minds. He had somehow expected at least a lingering aura, a ghostly remnant of those who had fled in terror along these roads, who had fought and died here. How could Lugard, Bruce, and their still unknown comrades, have kept their hatred alive in such a *normal* place as this?

They had turned south at Ghyvelde and were now going east from Hondschoote along narrow secondary roads. 'I am told by the local policeman,' Caniers was saying, 'that it was many years ago the house was purchased. At the time it was severely damaged and was bought with two hectares of land for very little money. The British came every year for a week, sometimes two, to rebuild. Occasionally, they paid workmen for the building to be progressed.' He paused to ask, 'Is that correct? Progressed?'

'It will do,' replied Smith.

'So when it is completed by 1952, they occupy from time to time. At week-ends. One family, maybe two families. Throughout the summer time it is the same every year, a *maison de vacances*, a house for holidays. But . . .' A strong theatrical inflexion stressed the importance of what he was about to say. 'At this particular time of year, only the men come. Some only to stay for three or four days, some for a week. They drink beer, they sing English songs, they work in the garden, they explore the countryside. On one day, they put out flags as if *en fête*, but they are solemn, subdued on that day as if with sad memories. At least, so my local policeman tells me.'

'What day is that day?'

'Tomorrow, the 2nd June. On that day, they are all together. When they first come, maybe ten or twelve men. As the years pass the numbers decrease; last year only six come. They are greatly liked by the people here, who know them to be former British soldiers with a regard for Belgium. It was no secret. But now they will know them to be the men of Sergeant Lugard's journal.' Caniers raised his hands from the wheel to signify apprehension. 'The men who killed the officers who betrayed them, who be-

212

trayed the Allies. Pouf. Who knows what the outcome may be?' He steadied the car as it slid towards a ditch. 'I have fifty men standing by.' A reproving finger wagged under Smith's nose. 'Fifty men called out for duty on a Sunday. Scotland Yard is not very popular with my men.'

'Your fifty men, are they similar to the C.R.S.?'

'Nothing is similar to the C.R.S.,' said Caniers, and he was not being complimentary to the Compagnies Républicaines de Sécurité, the brutally tough public order police of France. 'No, they are men of my department; criminal police. I have had to bring them in from Ghent, Courtrai and Ostende, plus my people from Brussels.'

By now, they were driving along what was little more than a farm track under the lee side of a high bank containing the canal. They came to a bridge and from the centre of it, a man was optimistically fishing the water below. Caniers stopped the car and called to the fisherman. Carefully propping his rod against the parapet, the fisherman casually approached, hitching up a pair of baggy corduroys. He was a squat, sallow-complexioned man, with a fleshiness that did not quite conceal powerful, rolling musculature. Caniers listened to his hoarse, staccato report, inserting an occasional nod and an assertive question. '*Très bien*,' he said, when his man had finished, and introduced him to Smith; who got a suspicious glance at his wounded arm, a brief but painful handshake, a truculent inclination of a dark, balding head, and abrupt sight of a broad back as it turned and made its way again up to the bridge.

Caniers unhooked the transmitter in his car and began calling round for other reports. The replies came in; some succinct and negative, others voluble and prolonged. Smith sat himself down on the grass at the foot of the embankment and struggled out of his jacket, hoping the sun's warmth would ease the hurt in his arm. Beneath the stitches it felt as if the flesh was gnawing at itself in an endeavour to reunite and heal. In the distance, a tractor-hauled harrow crawled over a late-ploughed field. Behind it seagulls rose and fell like snowflakes in the wind. From a church close by, a repetitive, unmelodic clangour, the sound flawed and impure as though the bell was cracked. Caniers joined him on the grass.

'The position is this,' he said. 'One left on a motor-cycle fifty minutes ago, rode into Dunkirk, purchased some English newspapers and made a telephone call to a recipient not yet ascertained. The motor-cyclist returned to the house a few minutes ago. Earlier, three sat at breakfast in the garden. At the moment all are inside the house. Do you have a suggestion to make as to how we should proceed?'

Smith squinted into the sun for a few moments. He had been ordered to stay on the sidelines – be helpful, assist with the background, but do not initiate action, do not intrude. 'I am your guest, Commissaire,' he finally said, 'it is not for me to tell you your business.'

'Naturally not,' said Caniers, accepting Smith's words as a statement of the obvious. 'Nevertheless, I will consider what you have to say. If this were England, how would you proceed?'

'I would walk up to the house, knock on the door, go inside and tell them they are under arrest.'

Caniers permitted his uncertainty to show. 'Knowing you are dealing with murderers who may be armed. Or is it the English joke you give me?'

'I would not joke about such a matter. I would do as I said, knowing I am dealing with soldiers who possess great pride and honour.' Caniers pointed to his arm. 'Of which you have a token.' Smith responded with a shrug as Gallic as anything Caniers had produced. 'A necessity of war,' he said, suppressing a wince. 'They would not surrender, of course, but it would give us a chance to assess their mood and the situation. We are dealing with men who have a plan, an eye to the future, their future. They are gambling on something. What? I don't know. But I would be inclined to give it a go.'

The Belgian took a long time over selecting and lighting his Gauloise Bleu and was well into his third exhalation before speaking in a cloud of smoke. 'Very well, we will, as you say, give it a go.' He prodded Smith's chest with a denunciatory forefinger. 'But if we find ourselves hostages in a siege situation, my career is finished.'

'Yours and mine both, Commissaire,' Smith acknowledged. Caniers returned to the radio to warn his surveillance posts of his intentions. From the bridge, Smith could see the house. It lay to the left about four hundred yards along the opposite bank and fifty yards back from the canal. The exterior had been painted white, the shutters green, and red tiles adorned the roof. It looked pretty, but ordinary, no different from the many other houses he had seen in the vicinity. There was a circular plastic table outside on the lawn and a few unoccupied chairs. A short distance from the house could be seen the overgrown stumps of what had once been other buildings. At last a sign of war. He tapped the butt of the Browning automatic protruding from Caniers' waistband. 'Just one other suggestion, Commissaire, I would leave that with your friend.'

Caniers threw back his head as if seeking advice from the heavens, then phlegmatically murmured, '*Merde*,' and handed his gun to the fisherman, who shoved it in his pocket without taking an eye from his stagnating float. Silently, they walked together along the canal-side until they drew level with the house and turned towards a waist-high wrought-iron gate separating the garden from the uncultivated ground outside. Lupins, peonies and pansies grew in colourful profusion along the neat borders. 'Tum tiddily um tum, tum tum tum,' hummed Smith as they strolled up the path to the tune of Country Garden, and to Caniers' evident dismay at such frivolity. Marrasey, smiling a welcome, opened the front door as they approached. 'Good morning, sir, please come in. It is a most pleasant day, is it not?' To Caniers, he gave a slight bow and a cordial, '*Bonjour, monsieur. Entrez, s'il vous plâit.*'

Inside Frazer stood, tall and erect, by the fireplace. It must have been three years since Smith had last had sight of him, the quirky twist was still present on his lips and the face, as menacingly expressionless as ever. 'Hello, Owen,' Frazer said. 'Good to see you again.' He offered no hand but there was a note of sincerity in his greeting.

'And you likewise, Dougal,' Smith replied.

'Forget the Dougal.' The command was flatly emphatic. 'From now on, it's Bruce. Alex, if you prefer, in our present informal circumstances.'

'Not Sanny?'

'It's not that informal, Owen.'

Smith turned to the former controller of his System. 'And with you, it will be Michael Lugard?'

'It will, sir.' Lugard was every bit as neat as Marrasey, but his attire was relaxedly casual. A thin polo-necked sweater, light twill slacks and a pair of blue canvas shoes, made him look quite sprightly, almost light-hearted. 'Allow me to introduce the others.' Lugard indicated three men seated about the room, newspapers in their hands. 'Desmond Chivers, retired deputy assistant Chief Executive, Gosport Borough Council.' A bald head, rubicund cheeks and a portly body half-rose from behind the *Observer*, pulled a pair of spectacles down to the tip of a snub nose and clipped out a 'How do you do.' Lugard waved to another chair, 'Percy Reeves, who owns the Merrymaid Fish restaurant chain.' The *News of the World* was lowered for a moment, and a gruffly jovial voice said, 'How do, squire,' before the paper was lifted once again.

'And this is Ronnie Ayliffe. We haven't got Ronnie's name in the System. Indeed, Ronnie's name is not in any system, he is a founder-member of the black economy. Ronnie is a plumber, terms strictly cash.' The *Sunday Express* was put aside and from within an imploded face, collapsed like a toothless bulldog, a grin emerged. 'Coppers get a discount,' said Ayliffe.

Smith reciprocated by introducing Commissaire Caniers. This time Bruce did offer a hand. 'How is Roger Veldegem these days?' he enquired.

A startled Caniers pulled at his ear-lobe as if to regain his balance. 'You are acquainted with Monsieur Veldegem?' The question was put tentatively and respectfully.

'He stayed with me for a week at St Andrews last year.' Bruce's lips almost parted. 'I managed to correct his backswing. His eighteen handicap was entirely due to his backswing.' Bruce gave Smith the benefit of an explanation. 'Roger Veldegem is a . . . a something in the Ministry of the Interior.' Then to Caniers, 'I hope you take no offence at my reference to Monsieur Veldegem as a something. He is a man I respect and admire.'

'Oh, no,' said Caniers, enduring the perplexity of a foreigner alone and outnumbered by the British, unable to fathom if they were being serious, cynical or sardonic, or merely amusing themselves at his expense. 'That is O.K. Monsieur Veldegem is a very large . . . something.' He had played it safe, rightly assuming Bruce was being serious.

'Good.' Lugard intervened briskly. 'That gets rid of the formalities. Drinks, I think, are in order. Something light and refreshing. Percy! Could you oblige?'

Without a word, Reeves put his paper aside and went into the kitchen. Smith took to admiring a wooden board, flat but with handsomely carved edges, mounted above the fireplace. Gold lettering proclaimed, 'Roll of Honour. 1404th Independent Ammunition Platoon, RASC.' The names of the dead were italicized in black, followed by the date and place of their dying . . . Skiller, Quarrie, a few on 31 May 1940, many more on 1 and 2 June, others in March and April 1945. Still others beyond the end of the war from 1948 until 1980. But no Turnbull, no Loach, and certainly no Boswell or Pyrnford. Honour was clearly prerequisite for a place on the board. Lugard was at his elbow with a glass of light Belgian beer. Smith grasped it and waved it at the post-war names.

'Death in action doesn't seem to be a necessary qualification?'

'To us, all our dead were in action. We may be in action again.' Lugard walked the length of the room pulling aside the full-length curtains beside each window to expose three Bren guns, a Lewis, and two Boyes A/Ts. Smith heard Caniers spitting 'Merde' as each weapon was revealed. And Lugard was not finished. From the recesses of a deep cupboard, he selected from several others, a Lee Enfield rifle. With smooth fluidity of motion, the bolt was opened and two clips of five cartridges rammed into the magazine. The bolt slid forward carrying a cartridge into the breech. A forefinger applied the safety catch. And at no time had Lugard's steel grey eyes left Smith's face. In the challenge of the ensuing silence, he was reminded of the drill instructor he had once seen at work in Chelsea Barracks many years ago, when investigating a loss of mess silver. 'Don't look down, you dozy man. Do it like you was with your bird in the back seat of the pictures. Feel for it, you dozy man. Feel for it.' Lugard had the feel for it all right.

'You came to discuss something with us, sir?' Lugard held his rifle loosely in the crook of his arm and waited for an answer. Smith pulled up a chair and sat down.

'Subject to the usual conditions; you are not obliged, etc. I thought we might talk about Boswell, Pyrnford and Loach. Oh, and incidentally, this as well.' He raised his injured arm.

'I am afraid these are matters we are not prepared to discuss. Although I am sincerely sorry about your arm.'

'Is that an admission of responsibility?'

'No, I merely extend my sympathy.'

Caniers had had enough. 'Just what do you people intend to do?' He bestrode the room aggressively, hands on hips, thrusting a belligerent chin at the five survivors of the 1404th. Demanding a reply with each outward projection. 'Well? Well? Well? Well? Well?'

'We intend to do absolutely nothing, Commissaire.' Bruce answered for his comrades, attempting to sound placatory. 'Nothing!' Caniers gestured at the weapons, speaking with ridicule. And with perhaps a trace of disappointment, repeating,

'Nothing?' Then going on to enquire, 'So, you surrender to my authority?'

'No, Commissaire.' A firm shake of Bruce's head. 'Surrender is not a term we readily accept. I mean we will do nothing providing we are left undisturbed. We merely seek a few days, a week at the most, to enjoy one another's company, talk over old times. To discuss our future.' Smith's involuntary, barking laugh brought him a long malevolent glare from Bruce that almost had visible substance. It certainly had the strength to force Smith to avert his gaze. Bruce continued, 'We will make no demands, Commissaire. You and Smith are free to leave any time you wish. Indeed, it was good of you to call as you did. Hopefully, it will avoid any misunderstanding. Any unpleasantness. As you see, we are prepared for unpleasantness.'

'And unpleasantness you may receive, gentlemen,' said Caniers, stiffly upright, sternly dignified. Not prepared to succumb to the blandishments of reasonable discourse or the consequences of an implied threat. Smith watched the others. Chivers; his newspaper laid aside, primly attentive. A neutral observer, as becomes a town clerk. Ronnie Ayliffe; up on his feet, circling the room, movements shambling, apelike, eyes embedded in a facial concavity, peering through each window in turn. Alert, like a sentry baboon. Reeves; still seated, guzzling the dregs of his beer, belching loudly, still seemingly engrossed in his paper but his eyes also busy, ferreting round the room, now cupping a hand over his right ear to dredge in every word.

'You see, Commissaire,' Lugard broke in, throwing his rifle to Ayliffe, as if to indicate he was not negotiating with a gun in his hand. 'Despite our ages, perhaps because of our ages, we are men of tradition, of pride and purpose. Our tradition was established here many years ago. It was here we were betrayed, and out of that betrayal arose our pride and our purpose. In the garden, many of our comrades lie buried, we cannot desert them now. I admit we are not invulnerable to heavy weapons, but otherwise we have a strong position. Our walls are solid stone, our field of fire excellent, and reasonably clear for two hundred metres in all directions.' He gave way to a frown of disquiet. 'Except, as is obvious, from the far side of the canal. We cannot counter mortar fire from below the bank. That was how the Germans finally crippled us in 1940, after they had wiped out my forward positions.' He spoke in the crisp detached way of a retired general recounting a former battle. One who was prepared to fight the battle again, over the same ground . . . unless his terms were met. 'As Mr Bruce has said, we have no wish to initiate aggression, but we will strongly resist an attack. Grant us an honourable truce and in a few short days we will comply with such reasonable conditions as you may impose.'

'*Incroyable*.' Only in slow articulated French could Caniers express the full extent of his amazement. Recovering, he snapped at Lugard, '*Pourquoi?*'

Lugard paused to consider his reply. 'To satisfy our honour, Commissaire,' he eventually answered.

Smith and Caniers walked back to the bridge, as slowly and silently as they had come. There, they joined the squat fisherman still leaning over the parapet. 'Any luck?' Smith asked, interestedly. By way of reply the fisherman spat at his float with sufficient force and accuracy to set it bobbing about in the water. Without a word, and for quite a time, the three of them watched the float, Caniers pondering imponderables, breaking the silence to slap the steel parapet in frustration, gazing at the house, the fortress of the 1404th, and muttering from time to time, '*Incroyable*.'

Their pensive meditations were interrupted by the arrival of a large mobile crane, easing its way along the track under the canal bank. Following the crane were two cars. The crane stopped, a man got out, climbed to the top of the bank and looked over towards the house, then signalled to the occupants of the cars. Out they poured, one climbing to the crane platform. The long folded arm began to extend upwards.

'*Qu'est-ce que . . .?*' a bemused Caniers asked himself. Smith supplied him with a convoluted answer. 'I think the recipients of the telephone call that could not be ascertained have now been ascertained. Look . . .' He pointed to the man atop the crane who was removing the cover from a T.V. camera. 'The eyes of the world are now upon us, Commissaire,' said Smith joyiessly.

Apart from a vociferous, but fruitless, altercation between Caniers and the television crew, nothing disturbed the remainder of the day until about four in the afternoon, when the crowds from the beaches east of Malo-les-Bains, having by now heard that the men from *le journal de Sergent Lugard* were again besieged nearby, decided to leave early and witness their last stand. By six in the evening a thickening throng had assembled from miles around, which Caniers' few uniformed gendarmes could not quite control. Especially when some twenty or so young Flemings came roaring in from the east, anxious to seize any opportunity to display their placards and banners demanding autonomy and bi-lingual status before the cameras. Breaking through the police lines, the Flemings rushed towards the side of the house, above which they could see the crane-mounted T.V. cameraman. Sight of a Bren-gun muzzle protruding from an upstairs window brought them to a hesitant halt. While they held their banners aloft, one of their number cried out in English, 'We wish to join you, we will fight with you, we will die with you.' And without waiting to see if their presence was acceptable, they again moved forward. A burst of machine-gun fire ripped up the ground at their feet and sent them scampering backwards, banners and placards abandoned. The other spectators, mainly Walloon, cheered. Some shouting, 'Aim higher, Tommies; aim higher!'

Darkness had descended before the crowds fully dispersed, and by then Caniers had three hundred gendarmes with vehicular back-up on scene, to help them on their way. Day one of what was to be called, after the nearest village, The Siege at Buiskamp, was over.

'For the time being it is not our intention to mount a direct attack.' So announced Caniers next morning to the journalists assembled at the Press Centre set up under canvas in the dead ground under the canal bank. He went on to give them the official word from Brussels. 'As long as these sadly deluded old men do not attempt to commit further acts of aggression or endanger lives, we shall endeavour to resolve this incident by peaceful means.'

Nevertheless, a military detachment was brought in and manned positions facing the house from the far side of the canal. At 10.15 a.m., movement by the front door brought the soldiers to the alert and the T.V. cameras into action. Smith saw Reeves and Ayliffe come out and, ignoring the guns trained on them, proceed to remove the table and chairs from the garden and carry them into a low shed at the side of the house. From the shed they emerged carrying a long pole. This they inserted into a prepared slot in the lawn. Twice more they repeated this operation, until three poles were set up in line. Half an hour later, Bruce, Lugard and Reeves appeared, each carrying a folded flag draped across forearms presented horizontally to the ground. They wore the khaki battledress of 1940, each waist girded with an immaculately whitened web belt, brass clips and buckles gleaming in the sunlight. Gaiters, similarly whitened, adorned their ankles, contrasting sharply with highly polished black boots. Chivers and Ayliffe, also uniformed, fell in on either side of the flag party, Lee Enfield rifles at the slope. Lugard's sharp command broke yet another strange silence to fall on the canal, and in slow time he and his men marched towards the flagstaffs. The flag-bearers stepped forward and the flags of France, Britain, and Belgium went streaming to the mast-head, bright colours fluttering bravely above the green lawn and flowering borders. The three flag-bearers saluted, the escort presented arms and even the portly Chivers and the grotesque Ayliffe seemed soldierly.

Then the standards were lowered to half mast, a change of position by the escort, while the flag party returned to the house, marching out again carrying arms. In the quiet, the cocking of a rifle action could be clearly heard from the Belgian line. An officer's voice called for caution, '*Pas de feu,*' no firing. Bruce and Reeves took post facing Chivers and Ayliffe; Lugard, his sergeant's stripes clearly visible, centred himself at the head of the files. Further orders were given, Present Arms, then into a slow and solemn Reverse Arms. And while they stood, heads bowed over the butt plates of downward-pointed rifles, an amplified bugle sounded the Last Post through an open window. Slowly, and without orders, the Belgian soldiers climbed to the top of the bank to join in the salute to the fallen. And there they remained even when Lugard's command brought the five rifles to the port and his orders produced a synchronized rattle of rifle bolts to send skyward a three-round volley of controlled musketry.

Back went the flags to the mast-head, another present of arms, and the ceremony was over. It was just a few minutes after 11 a.m. on the second of June.

At Smith's side, Caniers was shaking his head and whispering, '*Incroyable,*' as the remnants of the 1404th returned to their fort. A British T.V. reporter came up to them, brandishing his bulbous length of electronics like a phallic flasher and aggressively demanded oral intercourse. Caniers obliged whilst Smith took the opportunity to fade into the background, afraid of what he might say.

The only other thing of note to occur that day was at six in the evening when the flag party came out again to formally lower and remove the flags. Afterwards Smith returned to his hotel for dinner and to phone in his report to the A.C.C.

'Did you see the circus performance, sir?' he began. 'The clowns were very good.'

'According to the press and T.V. reports it was a simple, moving and poignant ceremony,' replied Fairchild, in his contradict-me-if-you-dare voice. 'And from my view of it, I would not quarrel with that description. That being said, a circus might aptly describe the juggling the Commissioner and I are having to do to satisfy the Home and Foreign Offices. Then there are the insatiable demands for us to put our heads in media mouths, every hour on the hour. We appear between a procession of Dunkirk veterans, ex-P.O.W.s and extracts from Lugard's diary, as read by a distinguished knight of stage and screen. It is not a particularly edifying position to be in, Smith.'

'I am sorry about that, sir.'

'Contrition does not compensate. You, Smith, are being marked up according to St Matthew, Chapter 10, Verse 30.'

'I never got very far beyond the Old Testament, sir.'

'The very hairs of your head are all numbered,' quoted Fairchild, and hung up his phone.

Dawn on day three of the siege saw a strange figure rise out of the ground mist at the rear of the encircled house. It was of an old man with a walking stick, wearing civilian clothes but with his breast ablaze with decorations and on his head a *poilu's* steel helmet. The besiegers, wondering how he had managed to slip through their cordon, saw him hobbling toward the house, alternately propelling himself forward with a little skipping jump, then a wave from his stick, and calling out, '*Mes amis, mes amis, je suis Robert. Robert Deschamps.*' They saw someone scamper from the house to help him, watched them clasp each other in a fervent embrace and afterwards disappear inside. That night they heard much singing of 'Madelon', 'Roll out the barrel', and other wartime songs; for ex-Caporal Robert Deschamps of the 12th French Mechanized Division had rejoined those with whom he had shared the desperate defence of a small section of the Bergues–Furnes Canal line, in 1940.

Throughout the next day, little of note occurred beyond continuing attempts to negotiate a surrender by telephone, all of which were politely refused. An approach by military emissaries under a white flag to present an ultimatum was halted by a stream of tracer bullets, placed far enough in front of their feet to be taken as an honourable rejection of terms, rather than an intention to defile a flag of truce. It was intended as an exploratory stratagem based on a reasonable surmise from the content of the diary, that while the defenders might have dug up their old weapons, they had little ammunition. It failed because the 1404th had re-stocked their supplies at the end of the war simply because military logic dictated there was little point in keeping weapons without ammunition.

Attitudes at the scene hardened as a result, and that night four 105mm recoilless cannon were placed in position, their barrels trained to converge on the house. The defenders were told they had forty-eight hours to surrender, as from 9 a.m. on Thursday 4 June.

Back in Britain, an application by the Director of Public Prosecutions to obtain an injunction against publication of the final instalment of the Lugard diary on the grounds of sub-judice interference with possible criminal charges, was surprisingly rejected. 'No,' said Mr Justice Springer-Field, who held a D.S.O. from the battle of Arras. 'It is not sufficient to say that persons at present outside the jurisdiction of English justice, and against whom no extradition proceedings have as yet commenced, may be subject to criminal charges should they return, or subsequently be returned, to this country. That is altogether too vague and ill-defined.'

In Parliament, questions from both sides of the House demanded to know what the Prime Minister was doing to ensure that the Belgian Government did not fulfil its reckless threat to slaughter the British subjects. Amidst the usual caterwauling accompaniment, she replied that every effort was being made by Her Majesty's Government in its endeavours to obtain a peaceful settlement. From France also came official protests on behalf of Robert Deschamps, who, it transpired, had escaped his German captors after being segregated from his British comrades, and had gone on to become a Resistance leader. Recaptured, this time by the Gestapo in 1944, he lay crippled by torture in Fresnes Prison until released by the Paris uprising prior to the liberation of the city by the Allies. Later he was decorated by De Gaulle himself.

Outside the Belgian Embassy in London, the demonstrators' placards were hastily amended to read, 'Save the Buiskamp Six.'

Before the intervention of Deschamps, the whole business had been viewed in Paris with amused interest, another diverting symptom of the English disease, although *Le Figaro* tended to see it as a devious British prelude to a withdrawal from the Common

Market. However, now the French had their own demonstrators in the streets, brandishing the words, *Secours Robert Deschamps et les Cinq de Buiskamp.*

During Friday afternoon, the cannon were withdrawn.

The siege ended at 8 a.m. the following Sunday, but only after sounds of prolonged hammering from inside the house had brought the encircling forces to a state of alert. Then Lugard was seen to come out and push his old Norton Commando motor-cycle away from the side of the house, where he drove a chisel through the petrol tank and set the machine on fire. Shortly afterwards the five Britons and the solitary Frenchman emerged, all wearing civilian clothes: the Britons carrying suitcases. It was as if old friends, taking a pleasant holiday together, had reached the end of their stay and were, regretfully, about to depart on their separate ways. Deschamps was embraced by each of his comrades in turn, as Smith, Caniers, and a number of other Belgian police officers came up. Inside the house, they found the Roll of Honour of the 1404th Independent Ammunition Platoon still in place, and piled beneath were the platoon's weapons, every one of them thoroughly and completely spiked, the barrels split and ruined.

As the defenders were marched away, the soldiers on the opposite side of the canal cheered. Perhaps more in relief that their long, boring vigil was at an end than as a mark of approbation.

Seventeen

✦✦✦✦✦✦✦✦✦✦✦✦✦✦

'It is a pity the Belgians didn't hang on to them a bit longer, Smith.' Archibald Yallope, Deputy Director of Public Prosecutions, had taken it upon himself to personally supervise preparation of the brief for Treasury Counsel, in the case of *The Queen*-v-*Ayliffe, Bruce, Chivers, Lugard and Reeves*, and spoke moodily as he pressed himself into the corner of a window in an endeavour to follow the flight of a solitary tern to touch down in the lake of St James' Park.

'I got the impression they were only too glad to be rid of them when they offered no objection to immediate deportation,' said Smith.

Yallope went a-tiptoe in his efforts, 'And you couldn't get an admission out of them at all?' His voice came high-pitched from a stretching neck. Yallope was well aware of the answer, seeking only a lawyer's confirmation.

Smith dutifully supplied it. 'Each of them said the same thing. "I plead not guilty to murder and will say nothing more." '

'Not very imaginative of them.' Satisfied, Yallope turned away from the window; the tern had gone beyond his line of vision without alighting. 'Well now,' he said, seating himself behind his desk, 'let's see what we can make of the eventual indictment. And by the way, it was wise of you to confine the charges simply to the Pyrnford murder at this stage of the game. Although if you had loaded everything on the sheet, possibly these silly magistrates at Cobb Common would not have granted bail.' Praise and reproach came to Smith in two sentences. 'Do you think the beaks were influenced by all the brouhaha that went on beforehand?' Yallope kindly offered him an out. 'I am sure they were,' said Smith, taking full advantage.

'Hmnn.' Yallope scrutinized the validity of his own excuse on the wall behind Smith's head. 'Well, let's look at the bird in hand,' he went on, taking hold of the case papers Smith had spent long hours preparing. 'For the Pyrnford count, we have the diary and the covering letter with all its limitations. Then we have the rifles and the bullets. I see Palmer is not all that strong on this. Is he? I mean, he states the striations and markings on the bullets used to kill Pyrnford are identical with the test shot from the rifles found in Lugard's flat. That's fine. But he goes on to qualify it by saying he cannot refute the possibility of weapons of similar make producing the same peculiarities, other than asserting the probability of such a happening being extremely remote.' Yallope thrummed fingers against his lower lip to produce a dismal tune. 'You know Paddy Wimperton, defending, positively thrives on remote possibilities?' Again the question was rhetorical, requiring only an acknowledging nod from Smith.

'Ah, well,' Yallope continued, 'Fishy Dickie has overcome higher fences.' He was referring to Richard Plaice, Q.C., Senior Treasury Counsel, who would prosecute. The pages were flicked over under Yallope's scratching fingers. 'Now let's dive into the bush and see if we can flush a pheasant. The Boswell killing. Ye gods, one solitary living witness. The no doubt estimable former Detective Sergeant Horace Slawthorpe, plus of course Lugard's diary and the similarity of method.' The finger-induced burbling again gave indication that much was lacking. 'Not a soul extant to give medical evidence on the cause of death. Still, the jury are entitled to assume the cause from the circumstances. Yes, let's run it and see where it finishes.' Yallope heaved over a sheaf of statements and said, 'Once more into the bush dear friends.'

Smith well knew the file had been thoroughly studied days before, and that minds had been made up as to what form the prosecution would take. But he was being accorded the courtesy of Yallope's legal assessment of his case and was not unappreciative of the fact. 'The lewd and licentious Loach and the murder thereof,' Yallope looked across at Smith, the curve of his mouth giving a thumbs down. 'Not really there. Is it? I mean your prognosis is no doubt spot-on, but it has no legs. Has it? Your theory about the handcuffs is all very fine, but it is not capable of proof. Is it? All that in the letter about him being dealt with for killing the boxing person, Bailey, is mere taradiddle, unless we can put the typewriter in someone's hands. What do you fancy happened to it? The typewriter?'

Smith was glad of the opportunity to answer at least one of Yallope's questions. 'I fancy it's somewhere at the bottom of the English Channel,' he said.

'Then you can understand why we won't stick that particular bird in the oven?'

'Yes, I do understand, but the facts had to be reported.'

'Indeed they did. And I am greatly obleeged,' said Yallope, expansively generous, only to change quickly to a low rumble of sympathetic rejection. 'And I am afraid your arm is not on either, legally speaking, I mean. How is it, by the way, healing nicely?' Smith assured him it was. 'The trouble is,' said Yallope, 'we are again devoid of specific hands; on the gun this time. Your most thorough enquiries have established that persons answering the descriptions of Aycliffe, Chivers and Reeves were seen separately arriving at Lugard's flat during the day when you were later shot. And Mr Marrasey, as the neighbours then knew him, was seen to return shortly after seven. You postulate that it would be a simple matter for him to again leave the flat unseen and with a rifle concealed under a voluminous motor-cycling coat he then possessed, make his way by one of several footpaths to the Common, to lie in wait for your arrival. In the meantime, the other three made for Dover in Reeves' car, and that can be supported by the finding of the car in the long-term car park. Then, it is most reasonably supposed by you that after inflicting his wound on your person, Lugard returned to the flat, succeeded in tracing Bruce and warned him to depart with greater alacrity than he originally intended. With Lugard then doing much the same. You know what dear old Paddy Wimperton will do to that interesting but highly speculative body of attack?'

Smith knew only too well. Wimperton would derisively amputate the legs, arms and head and the burden of proof would crush the torso. But Yallope had omitted to mention his original contention. 'I had suggested there was enough to do all four for conspiracy. If not to murder me, then inflict G.B.H. Palmer ties the bullets to the rifle, Exhibit 16. One of the five found in the flat. I would have thought there was enough to support a conspiracy.'

Yallope stirred uneasily in his chair. 'Yes,' he grudgingly admitted. 'But we are going on two substantive counts of murder for all five. Fishy Dickie is averse to clouding the consommé with a thin conspiracy. Apart from the fact that there is judicial distaste for conspiracy charges when a substantive offence has been committed, it would mean leaving out Bruce from that particular count. Dickie feels it is all rather risky. Gives the defence a chance to launch a shoal of red herrings into the well of the Court. For the same reasons we are not going ahead with the relatively minor crimes, such as possessing firearms with intent to endanger, etcetera.' The thrust of Yallope's reasoning broke through his previous argument like the point of a drill. 'Against the background of all this highly charged twaddle we have had to endure as a result of the diary and the siege, we don't want to give an emotionally motivated jury the soft option of convicting on only the lesser charges.'

Smith had been there many times before; at the opening moves of the contest, the legal game. Knowing that in this case the game had already begun. A new and original opening had been made in the form of the Lugard defence.

Yallope was being careful, cautious, and objective. The opponents careful, cautious, but subjective. Yallope staying completely inside the limits of prosecution policy. Did the evidence support an odds-on chance of conviction? If, in his opinion it did not, then no go; there are better things to do with the money. In most fifty-fifty cases, a strong-minded copper could subvert what was, to his mind, an equivocal wishy-washy attitude by sticking an alleged offender straight on the charge sheet at his own responsibility, without reference to the D. of P.P. or anyone else. So what, if when his case papers reached the prosecutor's desk there was much weeping and wailing about the strength of the evidence; he would sit pat and say, 'Well, I think it's a goer. Let's leave it to the court to decide. That's what it's there for, isn't it?'

And as there is no good answer to that, the prosecutor would farm the brief out to counsel, who would happily give it a go – for to him, win or lose, it was money in the bank. But the copper had to judge it carefully. There had to be some powder in the keg, enough to make more than a fizz and splutter, enough to make a reasonably loud bang. Otherwise the Director's man would come trotting along to Court and offer no evidence. And in the repercussions, it would be costs against police and a helluva lot of imaginative explanatory writing to do afterwards.

So, for once, Smith had played it carefully, realizing that everybody else was doing the same. He had not loaded the charge sheet with everything in sight. Because a good copper knows as much about the criminal law as most criminal lawyers, he recognizes the flaws and weaknesses, he knows the rules of evidence that can confine and restrict the whole truth. He knows the game. And he knew he was up against the Lugard defence. Prepared when Lugard was Marrasey and running the System. For Marrasey would realize it was coming on top sooner or later with Lady Lowderton's identification of her brother's body. Just as he and Bruce, who was once Frazer, had known all about her existence, long before her intuition, her curiosity, had made her pick up the phone at the sight of a dead face on the television screen.

Fairchild had used his weight to go rampaging in to S.B. archives and discovered that Bruce, when he was Detective Constable, Special Branch, had got her mail and phone intercepted for six months in 1949; on the very acceptable grounds of her provable pre-war association with prominents in the British Union of Fascists. Plus a contention, purporting to come from a source in Vienna, that she was giving aid and comfort to war criminals. There was nothing in the transcripts to lend credibility to that contention, but ample evidence to suggest she genuinely believed her brother to be dead.

Frazer, who was now Bruce, had given her another three months on the bell in 1952 just to make sure. The only significant item was a demonstration of the peculiar love-hate relationship that had existed between Lady Lowderton and her brother. In conversation with a cousin, now deceased, she mentioned changing the name of her house to Beaucourt, '. . . the last time I saw dear Antony was when he was stationed there. We went up from Paris, with the de Roches.' Then later, in the same conversation, replying to a pitiable suggestion that the dear boy might be wandering about somewhere in Europe suffering loss of memory, she had snapped back irascibly, 'Then if the silly ass has lost his memory, he might as well be dead for all the use he will be to me.'

'I wonder why they did not remove the possibility of her identifying her brother?' Yallope had asked.

'Because it would dishonour their quest with innocent blood. As Loach did,' Smith replied, and had drawn an amusedly tolerant smile from Yallope for such archaic sentiments and beliefs. So he continued in the clipped reportage of policemen, interspersed with a few phrases of criminal patois to which lawyers love to be made privy. 'It was a chance they were prepared to take, a gamble on a memory faded by age, an appearance altered by age. It came unstuck and they knew Kyriacou's file would bring in the tumble. But they didn't bottle out, they made contingency plans, holding onto the possibility Kyriacou would be the one to bottle out when he realized he had been lumbered with a right stumer that could blow him back to a barber-shop in Islington. They hoped he might decide to sit on it, file it under "F" for forget. The only trouble was, Kyriacou didn't realize at first just what a hot potato he had in his hand. And when it began to warm up he looked around for a lap to dump it in . . . and chose mine.'

'And you think this . . . charade on 2 June was all part of that contingency plan together with publication of the diary?' Yallope sought support for a proposition Fishy Dickie would put to the jury in his opening address.

'They had never paraded in that fashion before,' Smith confirmed. 'They had raised the flags, certainly. But no uniforms, no rifle drill. They just stood around with their heads bowed for a couple of minutes. Yes, I think it was part of a plan to influence a future trial. Yet at the same time they wanted to go out in style, according to their own concepts of justice and honour. It was a parade, not a charade. It was no more a charade than the execution of Pyrnford.'

This time, there was no tolerant smile from Yallope. He had leaned across his desk, frowning. 'Then they really are very dangerous people,' he said. And Smith knew he was not referring to the people, but the concept.

He went straight to his flat from the D. of P.P.'s office. Elstow had said she would be there: but she wasn't. Maybe he was too early for her, but he had no intention of returning to the nick at Cobb Common, or of phoning her at the office. Now that the case papers had been submitted, he could relax, wait for the committal and subsequent trial. Despite his resolution he lifted the phone to reach Elstow, then hardened himself against the impulse. She *had* been affected by the shots in the sandpit. Not against the marksman, against the target. He himself, who had drawn down the fire. She had since distanced herself from him, flinching at the sight of his wound as if she had never seen the results of violence before. As if she imagined it on her own flesh. His arm, he kept telling everyone, was healing nicely. Even though whenever he lifted it to present his whiskers to the razor, the puckered red raw scar stretched its lips to leer and mockingly say, 'All that fuss over little old me. You'll never be a hero, take three bullets in the belly, a lump of shrapnel in the skull, have one eye blown out and get back on your feet to man the gun. You couldn't march from Cracow to Regensburg on three square meals a day, let alone through a war with only a few turnips and a couple of mouldy potatoes to keep you going. You're no Sergeant Lugard.'

Elstow arrived just after eight with Chinese food in tinfoil containers. 'You haven't eaten, have you?' she asked. He had, but said he hadn't, glad that his compulsive bachelor domesticity had made him wash up immediately afterwards. She noticed he ate without enthusiasm and remarked on the fact. More for something to say than for any other reason, he asked her to come away with him for a week. 'We could get a late booking to Majorca, or anywhere you fancy. Sit in the sun for a bit.' She refused. As he somehow expected she would.

'It wouldn't be wise,' she said. 'You know what they are like. If we take leave at the same time, there would be talk. Some of them have got ideas already.' Then to change the subject she said, 'By the way, what have you been doing to Commander Hessen? Did you know he has applied to go off pay for a year to enter a religious retreat?'

Reacting as if stung, he shouted at her. 'What makes you think I'm responsible?'

Taken aback by his vehemence, she said, 'It was just a joke. Mr Hessen was so grandly jovial before . . . the murders.' She intended to say 'before you arrived on the District,' but his darkening face made her change the event. But not to be browbeaten, she went on dispassionately. 'Haven't you noticed how morose he has been lately? I think Loach's death and Marrasey's involvement must have shaken his faith. According to Vince Ogden, his clerk, he wants the time to prepare a thesis on Kierkegaard's Christian existentialism, its relationship to Crisis Theology, and how the concept may be used to improve policing in an increasingly atheistic society.' She delicately stripped the meat from a spare rib. 'Do you understand what he could be trying to get at?' The bone lay bare between her fingers.

'The important thing is, does Hessen understand what he is trying to get at?'

They prodded through the rest of the meal in a desultory silence, broken only by isolated comment on the result of his conference with Yallope, and the decision to proceed only on the substantive murders. Finally, pushing her plate aside, Elstow leaned across the table and said with determined seriousness, 'I think we should get things absolutely straight between us –'

'Don't waste your time,' Smith interrupted. 'Nothing in nature is absolutely straight, and what we have is natural. Be content with that, for you'll never make Commissioner of Police if you don't know anything about Kierkegaard's Christian existentialism and its relationship to crisis theology. Just be happy to know I'll never call you *woman* detective sergeant ever again.'

Reluctantly, she put down the knife she still held, and went over and kissed him. 'There is a village up in the mountains in Majorca,' she said. 'It's called Deya. They say it's particularly beautiful.'

Eighteen

✦✦✦✦✦✦✦✦✦✦✦✦✦

Not so many years ago, as recently as the early fifties, there were but four courtrooms within the precincts of the Central Criminal Court, lying just to the west of St Paul's, in a street called Old Bailey in the City of London. The City of London, the anachronistic square mile of commerce and capital, new flesh on its ancient bones, defending its traditions and privileges with symbolic sword and mace. Jealously aloof and independent of a spreading megalopolis beyond its confines, that can only call itself, like some itinerant showman, 'Greater' London. The City provided and maintains the Central Criminal Court with the wealth of its institutions and merchants. Sitting as judges therein, its Recorder and Common Serjeant, ancient and honourable offices of Law. And, as is the way of things, the Court became known as the Old Bailey, or more simply, to lawyers, policemen, and criminals, as the Bailey. And the lawyers and policemen who attended with their cases were the superior of their breed, the criminals the more notorious of theirs.

The Bailey, again until recently, was a Court of Assize for all London. Trying only grave treasons and most heinous felonies. Sir Roger Casement; Irish patriot. Altruistic rebel. William Joyce; alias Lord Haw-Haw, of Deutschsender Hamburg. Haigh: who reduced the bodies of the women he killed to a sludge of sulphuric acid. Christie; the gasman, asphyxiating his victims and storing them tidily in his mean little house; bringing them out every now and again to be fondled in his necrophiliac embrace.

All these, and many others had gone from the dock of No. 1 Court to the gallows, under the nod of a black-capped red judge. Red, because always sitting in that Courtroom was a Judge of the High Court wearing the crimson robes of his rank. And he was, as were the three other judges, given daily escort to his seat by the Sheriff of London, his Tipstaff and City Aldermen. The Sheriff, resplendent in cut-away coat, lace jabot, silken knee-breeches, silver-buckled shoes, and short sword at his side; his retinue, less exotic, in severe morning dress. Amid an exchange of bows between the Judge and escort, the usher would demand silence, and command all to rise whilst he intoned the ritual 'Oyez Oyez! All manner of persons having anything to do before my lords, the Queen's Justices of Oyer and Terminer and general gaol delivery, draw near and give your attendance. God save the Queen.'

Little wonder that detectives with cases at the Central Criminal Court would attire themselves in what they called 'the Bailey lot.' Their newest, darkest and most sober suiting, for a rare and awesome occasion.

Today, the ceremony is still carried out on the old mezzanine floor where the original four court-rooms are located. But elsewhere in the building increasing lawlessness brought about the hurried erection of further courtrooms in every cavity and crevice of the once spacious foyer, followed later by the joining of an ugly, squat extension to the original edifice until the number of courtrooms was quintupled, and still more well hived away to annexes in the Strand. The additional courts are devoid of such ceremony. The law of expediency had overcome the majesty of justice; mediocrity prevailed. The distinction between felonies and misdemeanours was abolished, the Courts of Assize and the lower Courts of Quarter Sessions intermingled into a commonality called Crown Courts which, to meet still greater lawlessness, were housed in any vacant hall, church or school that happened to be spare. Crown Courts sprang up in every borough High Street, like betting shops, with the business of both establishments not entirely dissimilar.

Thus, on a boisterously wet Thursday in November, Smith, having youthful links with the past, was soberly clad when he turned into Old Bailey from Newgate Street, and head down against the wind, went by force of habit into the main entrance, above which some sanctimonious Victorian had inscribed in contradictory terms, 'Defend the children of the poor and Punish the wrongdoer.' Smith found the doors closed against him, having forgotten that since 1973 when the I.R.A. bombed the building, the main entrance had been closed, compelling those with business inside to enter by the smaller door of the extension. There his identity was checked and his briefcase examined. Once inside he went straight to the mezzanine to look for his witnesses. There was Tom Palmer, sitting alone on a bench abstractedly perusing his notes. Ethereal. Peacefully unconcerned, like a man about to die. His coat wrapped about him like a winding-sheet. Brandy for breakfast? Horace Slawthorpe, thumping him on the shoulder from behind, made his presence felt as he boomed, 'By gum, lad, Ah niver thought Ah'd see the day. Reet proud Ah' am. Cleared the bloody thing oop after all these years. And givin' evidence at Owd Bailey into bargain. Niver thought Ah'd see t'day.'

Lady Lowderton was critically examining the statue of Elizabeth Fry, Prison Reformer. M'lady wore a veiled pink toque, pearls, a long dark purple coat and looked not unlike the late Queen Mary. A large gold-embroidered bag, hung from her arm. Close by, Sam Jones washed unctuous hands as the silver-topped cane was imperiously raised to summon Smith to her side. 'They *can* hang the lying swine, can't they?' She wanted to know, watery blue eyes drenching Jones with contempt. She had obviously been in argument with him on the subject. Over her shoulder, he smiled resignedly at Smith. 'I'm afraid they can't, Lady Lowderton,' said Smith.

'But isn't it high treason or some such thing for lower ranks to kill their commanding officer?' She would not be appeased.

'I'm afraid not, Lady Lowderton. Only if he happened to be a King. Besides, they are not in the army any longer.' He turned to seek his other witnesses, only to be brought up short by a whack on his left arm from the cane. The wound had healed nicely, as he kept telling everyone, but the nerves were still acutely tender. He winced quite loudly.

'I have not finished, young man.' Lady Lowderton took no notice of his pain. 'Surely in the case of that poor young subaltern, his killing can be dealt with . . . What's that word you used, Sam?'

'Retrospectively,' said Jones wearily.

'Yes, why can't they hang the swine retrospectively?' The rubber ferrule went plopping impatiently across the tiles as she waited for Smith to stop rubbing his arm.

'Nobody gets hanged these days, Lady Lowderton,' he said at last. 'Retrospectively or otherwise.'

Her chagrin escaped in a vexatious hiss, then she lapsed into dismissive frailty and meekly allowed Jones to lead her to a seat. Smith went to find the rest of his witnesses.

Amongst the throng, he spotted Mr Victor, disconsolately trying to reset wind-rumpled waves against his reflection in the far window. Needed in court to prove the existence of Green Briars, its connection with Albert Loach, and by association, with the 1404th. And coming from the cafeteria, cheerfully waving his subpoena was Mr Kepple, now appropriately in dark-blue velvet. There to produce the original Lugard diary, his client having two weeks previously relinquished the right of confidentiality. Elstow came through the swing doors with the arthritic Colonel in tow. The one who had so precisely timed the volley of controlled musketry. Hanging on to Elstow by the upper arm, close to her breast: not for support – just enjoying himself. Elstow was definitely mellowing, and the thought pleased him.

There was no Alfie Joss, of course, because under the rules of the legal game, what his boy, 'Bin Bam' Bailey, had told him was actress-and-bishop stuff, hearsay and inadmissible. And there was no Professor Simonson; because Simonson would only attend when a phone call to his laboratory told him the time was nigh for his appearance. Smith had often wished Simonson might be delayed by traffic, or another of the minor calamities that intrude on the affairs of normal people, to cause him to keep a red judge waiting. The outcome would have been very interesting. But it never happened: for no sooner would the witness usher return from the lobby, face woebegone to indicate his absence, than the doors would swing open and in would come Simonson, striding boldly to the witness box just as the preceding witness was stepping down. And the judge, counsel and those who had seen it all before would exchange rueful, admiring smiles, for Simonson had done it once again.

Satisfied his witnesses were all present, Smith went looking for Richard Plaice, Q.C., and found him descending the stairs from the robing room in the company of Paddy Wimperton, defending. Plaice was well named, for he was a flat man, 'so skinny he could hide behind a bus ticket . . . Edge-on,' O'Brien had once described him. And for all his winter weekends in the hunting field, and his occasional forays over the sticks, he still retained the dusty, leaden pigmentation common in lawyers whose time was spent mainly in court and chambers. Not so Wimperton, a bustling, short-sighted little man, mottled by Burgundy, carrying an over-large head between elephantine ears as large and thin as pancakes. By all the laws of nature his ears should have flapped and furled like sails in the wind yet they remained plastered tight against the side of his skull as if set with glue . . . Smith thought perhaps they really were. In an age when criminal law was practised with something between the quietly mannered ritual of a Japanese tea ceremony and the persistence of a fully automated assembly plant, Wimperton was an anachronism, a throw-back to Marshall Hall and beyond. The last remaining practitioner of cross-examination by ribald disparagement, or, as an alternative, by fawning obsequiousness before a witness, leading him or her with honey-voiced blandishments and cajolery into his lair, where simulated sympathy transformed to roaring vilification, where gentle whispers became whips of scorn, and flattery turned to flagellation. O'Brien said of him, 'He could take ten gallons of piss out of a dehydrated donkey, ride it to a zoo and sell it as a furry, four-footed rattlesnake.' In spite of, or perhaps because of, a wife and seven children, he was also a blatant womanizer of vulgarly candid impropriety.

'Wotcher, cock,' he growled, as Smith came up the stairs. 'Had it in lately?' Smith grinned and gave the obligatory reply of not since the last time. Wimperton went dancing on down, bellowing, 'Don't overdo it, leave some for the old uns.' The face of Richard Plaice registered the blank uninterest of a man in whose company a brief conversation had occurred in an unintelligible language. 'Well, Mr Smith?' The enquiry coldly civil.

'The witnesses are all here, sir.'

'A matter of little consequence. The defence are agreeing the evidence.'

'They're pleading guilty?' Smith's surprise was momentary.

'I did not say they were.' The insult of trying to put words in the mouth of a lawyer was met with asperity. 'No, they are not pleading to anything, they are only agreeing the evidence. Wimperton is endeavouring to have the depositions read by some mumbling junior, but I will not permit it.' Plaice progressed in stately dignity down the stairs. 'I foresaw this little ploy before the committal. I told Yallope not to allow the salient witnesses to be conditionally bound over. That is why they are all here . . . And they will all be called. Wimperton can cross-examine or not, just as he pleases.'

Mr Justice Kingston settled in the great chair to the right of an even greater chair in the centre of the judicial bench. No judge sits in that chair, for it is the traditional preserve of the Lord Mayor of London, who rarely attends as Senior Commissioner, but whose seat is never otherwise occupied. Although on the wall immediately behind it is placed, point upwards, the Sword of Justice.

'How say you?' the Clerk of the Court asked the five men stiffly at attention in the dock. 'Do you plead guilty or not guilty to the murder of Antony Pyrnford?'

'Not guilty,' each snapped in turn as if answering to a roll call. And in the same way they answered to the second count in the indictment, alleging the murder of Derek Boswell. Then as the jurors came to the Book to be sworn, Wimperton swung into action. 'Object,' he thundered at the sight of a frosty matron in conservative tweeds, who, puzzled and upset, was removed from the jury box, to be replaced by a young man, bushy-bearded, clad in denim, wearing an anti-nuclear symbol on his lapel: and on whom Wimperton smiled benignly.

While occasional jury vetting by the prosecution has been a source of contentious argument, the right of each defendant to challenge up to three jurors, and have them dismissed without stating cause, has been ignored. Wimperton used seven of his fifteen potential challenges effectively. Objecting to those of whatever age, whose appearance suggested middle-class affluence, prejudices and sense of duty, nodding courteously in acceptance of those whose dress implied a working-class background, and whose age gave rise to a possibility of service in the ranks during the war. Raising no objection to the young, however outrageous their apparel; the more anarchistic they seemed to be, the more he nodded approvingly.

Once it was considered, if not bad form, then certainly a waste of time for defence counsel to exercise his right of pre-emption: it only meant one righteous middle-class householder or small businessman would be replaced by another from the same mould. But since the jury lists had been enlarged to include almost any adult, defence vetting by appearance, instinct and perception, to secure a jury whose sympathies might lie with a defendant, had become an increasingly popular gambit. Throughout it all, Richard Plaice sat stoically noting his brief, for there was nothing he could do about it. Eventually a jury was sworn, the bushy-bearded young man giving only affirmation, to the tight-lipped disapproval of Mr Justice Kingston.

Barely had Plaice reached his feet to begin his opening speech, than Wimperton was on the offensive again; rising in a flourish of waving documents.

'M'lord, I apologize to my learned friend for interrupting at this early stage.' A now-seated Plaice ignored a grandiloquent bow. 'But I must make application to you, touching upon the manner in which the prosecution clearly intends to present its case. M'lord, it is an application you may feel best be made in the absence of the jury.'

'Yes, Mr Wimperton,' said the judge. 'Most of your applications are best made in the absence of the jury. Let them withdraw.'

After a jury that had barely settled in its place had shuffled away, muttering in its perplexity, Wimperton addressed himself to the judge and the task in hand.

'M'lord, it will not have escaped your notice that the indictment has been drawn in a way most disparate in time and space; the defence in fact are faced with a reversal of chronological sequence of a most sinister kind. Count one in the indictment alleges a murder that occurred in the spring of this year, whereas in count two, we have yet another murder that took place over thirty-five years ago, and in support of which, unhappily, only one witness lives to tell the tale. Now, M'lord, it seems crystal clear that the prosecution intend to support their weakness in count two with their strength in count one; that is to say, by relying almost entirely on the apparent similarity of the method used to kill. My learned friend may well argue Boardman's case, and others, may permit him to infer a similar act in one count, may sustain the possibility of similar acts in another as being the work of the same persons. But M'lord, after nearly four decades? Does not in that great span of time the law of probability, or even of chance, supervene? Demanding an unrelated repetition of even the most remote of happenings . . .'

'Such as the sinking of a second *Titanic*, Mr Wimperton?' The judge intervened smoothly. 'I cannot recall such a recurrence. Neither can I recall such another unrelated murder committed in a like manner, by tying the victim to a chair and barbarously shooting him to death. As was said in Boardman's case, it would be an affront to commonsense to assert the similarity was explicable on the basis of coincidence.' Eyebrows raised almost to the rim of Mr Justice Kingston's wig told Wimperton to talk his way out of that.

He tried.

'M'lord, I follow your lordship's most cogent examples with

great respect and due consideration. But, and again with great respect, M'lord, I must point out certain flaws in such an otherwise most pertinent and relevant rebuttal. Ignoring, as I certainly do, M'lord, the scale of the first disaster in relation to the puny tragedy before us, I must ask you to consider what part the speedy advance of science played in preventing a second, coupled of course with the regulations and directions laid down to ensure the unlikelihood of a repetition.'

Satisfied only that the *Titanic* remained sunk, Wimperton gathered his gown about him to refloat another vessel. 'M'lord, I fully accept what you say about Boardman's case, but the events therein were confined to a matter of months, not aeons of time, not separated by hundreds of miles. Consider, M'lord, if you will be so kind, these facts. The deceased, Boswell, was associated with the ill-fated 1404th Platoon for little more than six months, whereas while its survivors endured the horrors of prison camp and mine, Boswell was serving with various other units in the Home Forces for at least five years prior to his unfortunate demise. M'lord, in that time of war, consider just how large the number of disaffected soldiery he may have antagonized to a degree that made them wreak vengeance upon him. Ah, but the method, I hear you say, the exotic, the esoteric, the flamboyant and original method!' Here Wimperton allowed his voice to drop to a lower register, gloomily, morbidly, serious.

'M'lord, my instructing solicitors have endeavoured to obtain from the Ministry of Defence, the number of occasions in both World Wars in which the method you so rightly describe as barbarous was used in executions for many peculiarly military crimes. M'lord, it is a subject the Ministry has been reticent to discuss and adamantly refuses to disclose. In consequence, I am obliged to rely purely on your lordship's wide knowledge of life and history which will doubtless tell you that such executions did happen, and happened frequently, particularly in the Kaiser's war. M'lord, you will also know, I am sure, that large numbers of soldiers from that war also served in the Hitler war. If not so many in the standing army, then certainly a large number in the Home Guard, with which the deceased Boswell had some dealings during the latter period of his service. M'lord, far be it for me to suggest any of that honourable body of men were responsible for his murder. I only say that the executions I mentioned earlier were carried out by ordinary soldiery; the method of execution, the formalities, if they may be so called, were commonly known among them.'

Up in the crowded public gallery, Smith saw an old man nod in vigorous agreement, grabbing his companion's arm, holding up two fingers as if to indicate the number he had seen or carried out.

Wimperton went on, 'M'lord, at that time in 1945, the country was still at war, soldiers in their millions were under arms, the possibility exists, I put it higher, the *reasonable* possibility exists that other undiscovered hands may have slain the unfortunate Boswell.' Taking the edges of his gown in his hands, Wimperton flung his arms wide and stood like a large bat for a moment of final appeal. 'M'lord,' the arms slowly dropped as his voice grew more powerful, 'I need not say, but say I will; my friend cannot pray in aid the diary of Sergeant Lugard to bolster his case on count two. The ambiguous reference in the so-called postscript of that tract to Boswell may be given many different meanings, other than an admission of murder at the hands of my clients.' Still louder now, he declaimed. 'For I know, and my friend knows and you, M'lord, most certainly know, the diary is only evidence against the person who made it, the accused, Lugard.'

Wimperton leaned forward, supporting his short frame with elbows splayed out over the little portable desk he used on top of the lower table to hold his brief, the large head peering incongruously over folded arms, his words now soft as silk. 'M'lord, concerned as I am not to delay these proceedings, anxious as I am not to be a party to a profligate waste of the court's time, I am obliged to say, that should I have to meet such a grossly prejudicial juxtaposition of evidence then I will have little alternative but to apply for separate trials on counts one and two and further . . . that on count two, my other clients be separately tried. Apart from the defendant Lugard.' The gown swirled defiantly, and the large head disappeared like some conjuror's illusion behind the small collapsible desk.

For a time, Mr Justice Kingston remained slouched in his chair in a state of judicial cogitation, eyes closed, red sleeves, erminetrimmed, folded across his breast. A cardinal in a quandary. Almost lazily he came forward, the eyes opening, arms stretching out before him, fingers entwined, 'Mr Plaice,' he said. 'The submission made by your learned friend did indeed disturb me before the matter was raised, although not to the extent we have so . . . forcefully heard. I am, however, of a mind to say it would be unfairly prejudicial to admit the association of evidence on count one to influence the jury on count two. What are your views?'

Plaice gave up without a struggle. 'M'lord, if the counts are heard in isolation, then clearly the prosecution would fail on count two. I, of course, concede that Lugard's diary is only relevant as evidence against him alone. However, it would be invidious, contrary to natural justice, to try Lugard alone on that count, especially when the absence of associative evidence makes the outcome dubious. I cannot offer substantive argument against my friend's proposition and therefore place myself entirely in your lordship's hands.'

Wimperton had tried . . . and succeeded, as he knew he would.

Seated at the solicitors' table in front of him, Smith heard him whisper to his junior. 'One down, one to go, Charlie.' The judge was speaking to Plaice. 'That being so, I will give the jury certain instructions at the appropriate time.' To the crowded press gallery went a stern warning. 'For the benefit of the many strange faces I see among you, who are possibly ignorant of what may, or may not be published respecting submissions made in the absence of the jury, the short answer is, nothing . . . Absolutely nothing may be published in this country, at any rate respecting the matters raised, or the comments made, until this trial is concluded. And I will deal very severely with anyone foolish enough to ignore my directions. Is that quite clear?' Not expecting an answer, he swiftly addressed himself to counsel, saying, 'Now for heaven's sake, let us have the jury back and get on with it.'

Scene One of Act I in another comedy of legal manners was over. It had been well rehearsed beforehand in the judge's chambers by the characters taking part. It needed a public showing, of course, for justice must be seen to be done.

Richard Plaice opened his long-delayed speech to the jury, carefully omitting any reference to the killing of Boswell – the judge had already told them they could forget all about Boswell; later on he would give them certain instructions as to his disposal.

The lunch adjournment coincided with the end of the prosecution's opening. The judge withdrew and Wimperton, scribbling at his desk, reached out with his free arm to grab the hem of his retreating junior's gown, all the while continuing to write; then jerking the young man backwards he said, 'Not so fast, Charlie, post-prandial instructions for you. Going to slip over to Margie's flat, give her one, have a glass or two of claret, bit of lunch. Or maybe the other way round. Might be a little late.'

'I'll keep the pot boiling,' the young man promised faithfully.

'You damned well will not. You just sit here looking bright, but not a peep out of you. They'll open with Colonel Whatsisname who heard the shots, assorted bluebottles who went to the scene, then this estate-agent wallah. No cross, d'ye hear? No kerfuffle. I should be back in time to sort out what's left for the day.' He closed his notes and squirted towards the door, bellowing, without troubling to turn his head, 'Remember, not a peep out of you, Charlie.'

Smith went to look for Elstow, only to be told she had left word to say she was accepting the colonel's invitation to lunch. Mellowing too much, thought Smith. Tom Palmer, withdrawal symptoms showing in twitching shoulders and trembling hands, said he was going to the Magpie; regarding Smith's refusal to join him as churlish, stamping off in high dudgeon. Smith made for the cafeteria; Slawthorpe was at a far table preaching the immaculate conception of Geoff Boycott to some young uniformed officers. Smith settled for solitude, coffee and a meat pie, only to have the solitude devoured by Mr Kepple; orange juice, cream crackers and cheese.

'Mind if I join you?' Mr Kepple seemed distinctly uncomfortable. 'Hanging about here is ab-so-lute-ly nerve-racking. The place is pos-i-tive-ly Ho-garthian; such aw-ful people. Nasty, but I do mean *nasty*.'

'We haven't had anyone mugged inside the Bailey so far, Mr Kepple.'

'It's only a matter of time, I should think. And I do not wish to set the trend.' Little fingers brushed cracker-crumbs from his lapels. The rest of the packet is going to keep Mr Kepple very busy, thought Smith.

'I mean, look at those two over there,' Mr Kepple slid his eyes towards the corner table without moving his head. 'In front of me in the queue, bold as brass, one saying to the other, "What are you going to do with the snouting bastard, Dave?" And the other one, the one with the scar down the side of his neck, replied, "Give him a faceful of mallet, before I do his bollocks." ' Mr Kepple sent his eyes on another surreptitious journey, shuddered, and said again, 'Nasty, but I do mean nasty.'

Smith made no attempt to follow the elliptical orbit of Mr Kepple's gaze; minor digressions he could do without. Still, the emasculation of informants, real or imagined, was becoming a bit prevalent lately. A lot of good snouts with squeaky voices and spreading hips had high-tailed from hospital and town to remote non-violent crime-free communities where sheep, and everyone else, may safely graze. Snouting had always been a high-risk occupation: it was fast becoming a dying art. He turned his chair slightly to catch the ghosts reflected in the window. Youngsters; he didn't know them. Couple of young slags. Loudmouths. They had had a good tickle though; it was apparent in the dark tight-fitting Mayfair gambling-club suits; sharp, but well made. Expensive. Like the austerely sculpted West End hairstyles. They probably had the silver Merc or the electric blue B.M.W. stashed in the multi-storey down in Farringdon Road. Yes, they had had if off big and had spread it round the clubs; that was how they came unstuck: but as they imagined themselves to be the self-confident shrewd boys who always boxed clever, ego demanded their fall be put down to a grass, and some poor bastard was going to get his testicles tenderized.

A few years ago it would have been no problem; slags like that would have dwelt in Brixton from the moment they were nicked. But with the Bail Act as it is today, you would have a job to keep Heinrich Himmler in custody. Still, old Kingston had come up to scratch and put the block on extended bail for Lugard and his men. 'Certainly not,' he had said firmly, in reply to Wimperton's application for renewal when he rose for lunch. 'They are charged with murder, and will remain in custody. This court is not an assembly of amenable magistrates.'

Mr Kepple was clutching at his wrist, the two young slags were on the move, giving him, and everyone else the stone face, the narrow eye and the dead pan. Method actors, four-line villains. 'Drop the bag and grab a handful of clouds or you'll be grabbin' the clouds that come from the front of this twelve-bore sawn-off.' Sometimes having to go for a retake: 'Put your fucking brains on the counter or I'll blow your fucking money all over your fucking bank.'

There were at least thirty others like them wandering about the building waiting for their cases to come up: giving each other the forefinger across the snitch, the big aye-aye, or the jerking thumb, as they passed in search of briefs who were going to unscrew the fit-up, demolish the verbals, fracture the forensic, and give the filth a faceful of shit. Like everyone else in the building, himself included to a certain extent, they were perfor-mers, posturers, but playing their parts for real. That was the trouble with slags nowadays, they used real people, played with real bullets . . . Bang bang and you were dead – for real. At least Lugard had brought a touch of class into the game.

'Do you think I'll get it over with in the old witness thingie this afternoon?' Mr Kepple still clutched his wrist as he watched the double-vented black jackets disappear into the lobby. 'I mean, all this waiting about is so anxiety-making.' Gently Smith released himself and assured Kepple the chances were pretty good, then idly wandered after the two slags. He would see which courtroom they came to rest in and find out who was dealing. Have a word in case a valuable snout was involved; leave it to whoever had them in to put the frighteners on . . . if he could. It was the best he could do and it passed the time until they resumed in No. 1 Court.

The afternoon sitting droned on, with Mr Wimperton's junior beginning to squirm in his seat as the clock went beyond three-ten. Witness followed witness with no sign of his leader. Lady Lowderton was in the box, having nearly finished identification evidence of her brother's corpse with glowing details of his early life. Simonson was due in next. Smith had phoned him thirty minutes previously to let him know. The clerk was speaking into the internal phone. Maybe that was it, Smith thought, he tucks himself into the clerk's office and probably into his sherry as well, while he waits for the buzz. The usher came back in from the lobby, downcast and empty-handed. Lady Lowderton was turning to leave the witness box, Charlie, the junior, was chewing the hem of his gown, when in one door at the back of the court came Simonson, and in the other came Wimperton.

'Pray remain where you are, Lady Lowderton.'

Simonson stopped in his tracks to thrust a shaft of outraged indignation at Wimperton, who, taking no heed, came crabbing forward down the long steps, uttering effusive apologies to the judge: sincerely regretting his tardiness; other matters; other courts demanding his presence; unforeseen delays . . . do most earnestly beseech the Court's pardon. Mr Wimperton had cut it very fine.

Up in the witness box, Lady Lowderton stared defiantly at the goblin who had suddenly appeared, huffing and puffing before her. She had earlier responded to her surroundings with haughty composure, brusquely spurning the judge's offer of a chair as she would the advances of an impoverished suitor. Answering Plaice's questions with the testy impatience the intolerant reserve for half-wits and idiots. Any fool should know the body she had identified was that of her brother, Captain Antony Pyrnford.

'I will detain you but a little while longer, Lady Lowderton.' Wimperton gently fanned himself with the pages of his brief. 'Would it be correct to say that, back in those happy carefree days before the war, you and your brother had the astuteness, the sagacity, to recognize the rising menace of international communism?'

Richard Plaice was on his feet in a trice, only to be stayed by the judge's upraised left hand, while his right brought Lady Lowderton's opening mouth to a silent closure.

'Where are you going, Mr Wimperton?' He asked with ominous simplicity.

'In search of provocation, M'lord,' replied Wimperton briskly. The eyes of the judge and Mr Plaice exchanged unspoken questions and reached unannounced conclusions. Plaice resumed his seat.

'You may answer the question, Lady Lowderton,' said the judge.

Bridling at his temerity in shutting her up in the first place, she stomped her cane on the floor of the witness box before speaking. 'Well, of course we did. Anyone with half an eye could see what was happening; what is still happening.'

'And what did you do about it?'

'We helped those who were doing something about it.'

'To wit, whom?'

'Patriots.' A euphoric screech. 'British patriots.' A shrill paean. Wimperton nodded encouragingly, seductively.

'And did your acumen, your insight, your privileged circle of social acquaintances, assist you and your brother to recognize other sources, then placing the traditions and standards of the nation in deadly peril?'

She hesitated warily, cane lightly tapping as if probing the ground; she saw the stakes beneath the succulent grass, sniffed the air seeking a way out, decided on a sideways leap.

'Such as what?'

It was Wimperton's turn to hesitate: he could have said, 'It is for you to answer my questions,' but that would only have prolonged the sparring. He presented the sting in the tail.

'Did you and your brother not consider that an even greater threat lay in the power of what was then being described in certain quarters as the Jewish conspiracy?'

'No. Mr Wimperton.' The judge again stopped Lady Lowder-

246

ton's opening mouth, and took Wimperton sternly to task. 'You will go no further in that direction. I am always prepared to allow the defence certain licence in matters of relevance, but you go too far, and I will not have the privilege so wantonly abused.'

Wimperton bowed obsequiously, 'M'lord, my profound apologies. I withdraw the question entirely and conclude my cross-examination.' He had got the question in, that was more than half the battle; had to take it round the houses, up hill and down dale, to be sure the old boy didn't see where he was going, but he had got it in. The old sow wasn't going to cough to it in any case, but the jury got the drift. A good question was always better than a bad answer. Sometimes better than a good answer; jurors remembered the question that went in below the belt. Gave it an answer of their own.

With terse precision Simonson gave evidence in-chief, and at its end waited with teeth bared for Wimperton to pick up the gauntlet. He received only an airy wave of dismissal, Wimperton had no questions for him or any other witnesses during the remainder of the trial.

Promptly at four, the court rose and all persons having anything further to do before the Queen's Justices, did, as commanded by the usher, depart hence, to give their attendance at half past ten in the morning.

Slawthorpe became downright melancholy when Smith told him the Boswell murder was going to be chucked without even coming to trial. He wouldn't have minded if it had at least gone to the jury. If he at least had his day in the witness box, got in a last tussle with defence counsel, given the buggers a run for their money. Gone down fighting. Even Smith's assurances, that arrest and charging justified treating the crime as cleared up, failed to restore his spirits. Refusing Smith's offer of a bed for the night, he said he would make his way to King's Cross and get the five-fifteen for York. 'Lads'll gie me a run ower to Scarborough. See thee owd son, tek care.' A gentle hand on Smith's shoulder, then he slewed like a tank into the path of an oncoming taxi; bringing it to a grinding halt but receiving no abuse from the driver, for Horace Slawthorpe had finally retired from the police and his expression gave notice of the fact that he did not like it.

Friday saw the second day of the trial with Richard Plaice taking his witnesses through their evidence, patiently articulating his questions, in the deliberately studied, low-keyed, almost offhand manner now long adopted by prosecuting counsel. No hand-on-hip histrionics, no extravagant gestures; occasionally the telling pause, the quietly penetrating repetition of a significant answer. But boring. And through it all Wimperton sat playing with a gold pencil, uninterested as though what was being said was of no significance. It was all deadly dull, as he intended it should be, and within an hour after lunch three of the jurors had been rebuked by the judge for nodding off.

Up in the dock, the survivors of the 1404th sat in graven dignity, uttering no word, for no words were required of them in the tactics adopted for the game. They were aloof and impervious to the monotonous murmurings below. Impassive, they had no part to play, except by their presence. They were on view as trophies, to be won or lost by the adversaries engaged beneath them; eloquence for lances, rhetoric for swords. Weapons that would only be fully and finally wielded when both contestants came to sum up . . . Afterwards the judge would cleave down the middle, with probably a subtle cut favouring the one side or the other.

Nineteen

++++++++++++++

The week-end supervened, and although they had only been sitting for two days, the jury seemed to welcome the break. Friday had been a tedious day; relieved only by an overlong application by Wimperton that the jury be permitted to take their copies of Exhibit 21, the Lugard diary, away with them 'to peruse at leisure, to fully assimilate the contents, to assess and understand the true characters of the defendants, to enable them to grasp the nature of the cataclysm that bound them in an enduring affinity.' This, and much more at greater length.

Plaice objected strongly, and Mr Justice Kingston refused the application, giving a significant indication as to the form his summing up would take: 'Lugard's diary has, as I see it, little relevance to the defence. It is not exhibited for individual members of the jury to study in isolation, it is a matter for their joint deliberations and their cohesive findings, on such of the passages as have relevance to this case.' Wimperton knew his application would be rejected. But it had served its purpose. Another little reminder to the jury, another little point on his side of the board.

Throughout the day, Lady Lowderton had sat in court perched upright on the hard benches; listening avidly to every word, lowering blackly at anything to Antony's detriment, pecking greedily in agreement with words illustrating the callous savagery of his destruction.

Just before noon the next day, a wet chilly Saturday, Smith was in his office at District H.Q. dealing with a few administrative odds and ends when Commander Hessen came in to bid him farewell. The Murder Room had long been wound down, and Smith was but lightly saddled with humdrum routine. Hessen was on his way to Norfolk, to his religious retreat. And had already donned a hair shirt. At least a pair of thick flannel trousers, a fibrous roll-neck sweater and bare feet, blue-pink, in open-toed sandals. And he was going to get there the hard way, as evidenced by the bicycle clips around his ankles and a yellow oilskin cape draped over his shoulders.

'I am tremendously looking forward to the next twelve months, Owen. The Commissioner was most understanding; really approved the idea.' Rain glistening on his face enhanced a spiritual radiance. 'I shall return much wiser, regenerated, if not reborn. Come on, walk with me down to the station yard.' An arm within the damp cage clammily encircled Smith's shoulders and he was heaved along the corridor. 'One thing I learned from you, Owen. One lesson I will put into practice when I return: spend more time among the lepers. Evil can only be fought with clean hands, but they must not be the fumbling hands of a blind man. The hands must know that which is evil, they must strike with the certainty of knowledge. That was my failing, Owen, I looked down on evil but never descended into the pit to clean it with my own hands.'

'They get dirty that way. I should know.'

'We can cleanse them with the purity of our thoughts. God didn't create the world without getting his hands dirty.'

'I wish I could be sure of that. It would make me feel better.'

'You can, Owen. You can. Have faith. Think clean. I must away, must make Cambridge at a reasonable hour. There is a spot by the river. Fond memories. I shall spend the night there, in the open. Possibly a little exhausted, for I am out of condition. But then exhaustion cleanses the mind, one can meditate the better.'

'Won't it be rather wet?'

'I have a bivvy in the pannier. All I need.' Hessen buttoned up the collar of his cape and swung a long leg over the saddle. 'Adieu for now, Owen. Remember. Think clean.' One powerful thrust on the pedal took him as far as the open gate where he wobbled for a few moments, waiting for a break in the traffic, then, head down, he turned right and disappeared. Smith called after him. 'Give my love to Kierkegaard.' And rather than go back to the office, he made his way along to the Cock and Hen. He didn't feel much like working any more. Get a few pints under his belt; afterwards O'Brien could come with him to Selhurst Park. Crystal Palace were playing Spurs. Should be a good game. Elstow had gone to spend the week-end with her mother in Somerset. There was a surprise awaiting her when she got back. She would find herself in Orders, transferred to the National Drugs Intelligence Unit at the end of the month. Maybe she wouldn't mind; it was a good posting, she could make a name for herself. No one had said anything about their relationship but obviously it had come a tumble, someone had put the squeak in, moved her out of it. Still, she knew where he lived.

Immediately after lunch on the following Tuesday, Mr Justice Kingston began summing up to the jury.

Unhindered by lengthy cross-examination or further applications from Patrick Wimperton, Q.C., it had been one of the speediest 'sensational' trials on record. Smith had over an hour in the witness box; a relatively short time for the officer in charge of a murder enquiry. Giving his evidence with the steady precision of a professional witness, one eye on the judge's pen, waiting for him to get it down before going on. Occasionally looking up from his notes to be transfixed by Lady Lowderton's watery gaze. Eyes enlarged by tears that never actually ran, something to do with the strength of the surface molecules of water, he had once read. Wondering, with slight inward alarm, what the defence had up its sleeve when at the end of his evidence Wimperton got to his feet, going through all the predatory rituals of defence counsel about to launch a scathing cross-examination. Pinning him with the long gimlet of implied omniscience, the purposeful flap of his brief, the oppressive pause, then the sibilant utterance of: 'Is it not a fact, officer . . .' Only for him to impishly throw a soft squelchy tomato . . . 'that my clients, the five accused in their entirety, are all persons of impeccable character?'

He acknowledged that they were and Wimperton sat down again. Shouldn't have let him get away with that so easily; it was something he should have anticipated. Evidence of good character is always admissible, and if it exists defence counsel always want to get it in.

But 'impeccable'? That was a bit strong, even for Wimperton. Should've simply given him: 'There are no convictions recorded against them.' Then if he wanted to pursue 'impeccable', given him an argument that he didn't know them *that* well. Wimperton would have only come back at him though. 'You have no reason to think the characters of my clients are anything other than impeccable, have you?' And he would have to give him a 'No, sir' on that one. Evidence of bad character is not admissible. Never? Well, hardly ever. Just as you should not say, 'No previous convictions are recorded' before a guilty verdict. Counsel, and some judges, can get a bit snappish on that; it implies the accused is about to get one. But 'impeccable' was a bit strong.

For him it was practically over, he could be a spectator for the rest of the trial, no longer concerned about witnesses failing to put in an appearance, about exhibits going adrift, or his laxity in covering some unforeseen eventuality. He answered Wimperton's whispered 'Got you going that time, cock,' with a disrespectful 'Bollocks.' One was entitled to take liberties with Wimperton, he was the biggest liberty-taker in a liberty-taking business.

Like a double shelf of busts in half-profile, the jury faced the judge. The precise eloquence of Richard Plaice, Q.C., had been finally heard in a brief but effective closing speech. The emotive oratory of Wimperton had continued longer, but he too was now silent. The one, using only provable facts, had endeavoured to establish certainty. The other, needing only to cast reasonable doubt, had assailed them with conjectural possibilities and speculative hypothesis. It was now up to the judge . . . and the sown seeds of the Lugard defence.

Mr Justice Kingston laid aside his pen. All had been noted, the account was complete; accountability remained. 'Members of the jury, if you adhere to your oath you should find little difficulty in reaching a verdict in this case. Remember this, you have sworn or affirmed, that you will give a *true* verdict according to the evidence. Not as some misguided people are apt to say, a *just* verdict. Justice is nothing to do with you. That is my prerogative. You are the judges of the facts, assessing the weight and preponderance of the facts, distributing them without prejudice, and according to their value in favour of one side or the other. And they must be facts only revealed within the walls of this court, coming only from the mouths of witnesses that have appeared before you and given evidence. Nothing that has appeared in what are called the media should influence your verdict in any shape or form. Some of my brother judges would say to you: put everything you have seen, read or heard before this trial out of your heads. I will not insult your intelligence by a futile attempt to dislodge what has been irrevocably and insidiously planted. If you are so stupid as to permit such weeds to grow in a garden of reason, so be it. The great pastures of English justice are too broad and wide to be blighted by the occasional bed of nettles.

'Are you so stupid, members of the jury? I do not think so. There is a tendency today to refer to the broad spectrum of our population as the mindless masses; I spurn such an iniquitous calumny, for I have stood in the well of the court, and sat on the judicial bench, for too many years, and seen too many juries to have anything other than the highest opinion, the deepest respect, for the mass of our people from whom you have been chosen. I am quite convinced you are the equal of all who preceded you in that jury box, and that your verdict will be a response to the evidence placed before you, and to nothing else.'

The Lugard defence tottered on its foundations. Smith looked at the jury. The busts shone as though the judge had gone over them with wax polish and a duster. Except for one, the young man in denim, no longer watching the judge; his beard lay on his chest, the subject of his pensive eyes . . . like a youthful Shaw. What did he do for a living, Smith wondered. An eternal student? A lecturer at some polytechnic? Was the knot between his brows indicative of anger, cynicism, or mere cogitation? Still, if he had rumbled the judge's platitudes, he would certainly have seen through Wimperton's rhetoric . . . The judge was asking the usher to pass up one of the rifles; maybe he was going to shoot him.

Holding the Lee Enfield with some dexterity in the palm of his hand, the judge presented it to the jury. He had the point of balance right, just in front of the magazine.

'Consider this weapon, members of the jury. The deceased, Pyrnford, was shot by this and four other similar rifles, all of which are before you in court. I think you need have little doubt of that fact. Quite properly, Mr Wimperton has drawn your attention to the evidence of Palmer, the ballistics expert, who told you – and we need not go into his technical jargon – that each of the five bullets alleged to have penetrated the body of the deceased bore marks that allow him to say, with a high degree of probability, that each of the five bullets recovered at the scene must have passed down a specific barrel of each of the five rifles. Mr Wimperton has rightly, for that is his job, pointed out that Palmer offers some qualification to this by saying that with so many millions of rifles having been manufactured, he cannot discount the remote – and he does say remote – possibility, of such characteristic detail being repeated in another gun some-where in existence.'

Kingston returned the rifle to the usher, as if now glad to be rid of it.

'Members of the jury, were only one such weapon before you, you might have some small difficulty. But you have five! Well, in fact, six, but let us content ourselves with five for the moment. A remote possibility, multiplied by five, vanishes into the infinity of mathematical absurdity . . . Leaving only the certainty that the deceased was murdered by the guns now before you. Four of the guns used to kill Pyrnford were found within rooms occupied by the accused Lugard and situated only a mile or so from the scene. Rooms frequented by the other accused, Ayliffe, Chivers and Reeves: all expert handlers of similar weapons, as you have seen from the recorded repetition of the largely irrelevant episode in Belgium the defence obliged us to watch. The fifth gun was surreptitiously deposited at the home of a man named Loach, known to have served with the accused in the 1404th platoon. Loach is dead and you need not concern yourselves unduly with him. The sixth rifle has no corresponding bullet to fit it. The prosecution explain that omission by saying it was carried by the commander of the firing squad. A reasonable assumption in relation to the military method of killing and the proclivities of the accused.'

Mr Justice Kingston went on remorselessly: the Lugard diary. 'Not a very inspiring document you may feel, the ramblings of a disillusioned upstart, nothing there that was not endured, and worse, by thousands of other gallant, uncomplaining men. Evi-dence only against Lugard certainly . . . but why did the others join him in flight, when it became apparent arrest was imminent? And why did they participate in what you may think was a men-dacious humbug, this, so-called by the press, second stand on the Bergues—Furnes Canal?'

The Kyriacou docket: 'Evidence only against Bruce, certainly . . . But did not the record of phone calls from Lugard's flat show a succession of calls to the St Andrews area at the time when he, Ayliffe, Chivers and Reeves were present. At a time before their hurried flight to avoid arrest.'

He swooped like a hawk on Wimperton's hyperbole for the defence. Making liberal use of phrases and questions like: 'What do you think of that contention?' 'Well, use your common sense.' 'Do you accept this? It is a matter for you, of course.' 'Is such a hypothesis likely? You must give it every consideration.' Reasonable words in any cold transcript before the Court of Appeal, but when spoken with the stress of incredulity and the emphasis of ridicule, they have other meanings, different connotations. But all recognized moves in the game.

'You may be surprised, as indeed I was surprised, that none of the accused has given evidence in their own defence. They have not even chosen to say a single unsworn word from the dock, where they would be free of cross-examination. But you must not take your feelings beyond surprise; for they are perfectly entitled to remain mute, and in remaining silent you must not infer anything to their detriment. It is not an indication of guilt. The defence are rightly saying to you that it is for the prosecution to prove their case beyond all reasonable doubt. Not for us to prove our innocence. You must not think this a proud conceit. If it is, it is one they are entitled to display . . . whatever the consequences may be. They say they are innocent, and so they remain, until and unless you decide otherwise.

'However, that is not the end of it. Mr Wimperton, acting on their behalf, and more by intuitive sophistry than by a declaration of intent, invites you to suppose, should you decide they did in fact kill Pyrnford, they did so because they were so provoked by events in the past as to be beyond the constraints of reasonable men. This . . . is what might be called a fall-back device; a lesser of two evils. An invitation to find – should you be convinced they killed Pyrnford – that they did so under provocation, and are guilty only of manslaughter. It is a matter for you to decide, but let me say this to you. It may well be that in that fateful year of 1940, Pyrnford was the murdering brute he is said to be in Lugard's diary. That he truly was a vile, treacherous and untrammelled traitor to King and country; responsible for many known deaths and unknown defeats; the cause of these men suffering long years of privation and captivity. Even if he were guilty of all that, and ten times more, none of these crimes . . .'

Kingston's words faltered as a feline mewling began to fill the courtroom. Stronger than a hiss, lighter than a snarl, it had pervasive audibility. Heads turned, some people half-rose from their seats, the usher bawled for silence, but the noise went unabated. It came from the drawn lips of Lady Lowderton, sitting at the rear of the court, voicing her anger and anguish at the awful suggestions coming from so distinguished a source. By her side Sam Jones, trying in vain to shake her into silence, was white-faced at his proximity to a client responsible for such appalling contempt.

'Have that *woman* taken outside.'

The judge's order was moderate and calm, the omission of Lady Lowderton's title the only indication of his fury. She was on her feet and stomping to the door before the usher reached her, stopping as she passed the dock, to screech at those inside. '*Canaille* . . . Jew-lickers . . . Bolsheviks!' The only heads that did not turn were those of the prisoners. Running anxiously ahead of her, Sam Jones held the door open to facilitate Lady Lowderton's stately exit.

'She is not to be readmitted to this courtroom.' With that Mr Justice Kingston took up his thread, quickly splicing it, making an invisible mend.

'None of these crimes can excuse the killing of the person responsible for them outside the lawful exercise of judicial authority. Provocation, to be a successful defence to murder, must first of all be strong enough to cause a reasonable man to lose all vestige of self-control. You may think such provocation once existed; that is a matter for you. But it is for me to tell you – and I give you a solemn direction in this – it is not an emotion that can be stored and cherished over the years to be periodically renovated and recharged until the day of retribution arrives. For then it becomes vengeance, a gratification of bloodlust, a base indulgence. Provocation may only reduce murder to manslaughter if the reaction to it is immediately consequent to the provocative words or deeds. To put it simply, if sufficient time has elapsed for hot blood to cool, for tempers to subside, then provocation becomes dust beneath your feet. Do not allow that dust to be thrown in your eyes, members of the jury, for a great deal of it has been flying about before and during this trial.'

Kingston turned the pages of his register, giving time for his words to sink into the minds of the jury. Smith watched the faces in the dock, going from left to right. Ayliffe, emotion buried in the recesses of his face, fingers scrubbing the base of his neck. Bruce as hard and as dead as a granite statue awaiting some incantation to bring it to life. Chivers, the lights over his head scintillating on his scalp like beacons, his chubby cheeks paler now. Lugard sitting stiffly at attention, fighting back with his eyes; drilling them straight into the judge. Reeves, sweat creeping from his brow, trickling down the dried-up river beds in his face. They all knew the mortar shells were coming closer. Mr Justice

Kingston ranged in on them once again.

'Those representing the accused are of course aware of the limitations time places on provocation, and have tried to give it immediate significance. They have suggested something occurred in the cellars of Green Briars, where the deceased is said to have been held and given some travesty of a trial before being put to death. Perhaps, said Mr Wimperton, Pyrnford reviled the accused as being cowardly scum for failing to obey his orders and die at their posts. Maybe, said Mr Wimperton, he gloated over his wartime treacheries, revelled in recounting atrocities committed against the Jewish race ... and so on and so forth. Thereby causing – to use Mr Wimperton's words – the dismemberment of reason, the eruption of irresistible wrath. All very fine, members of the jury. But it is incumbent on the defence to support these suppositions with evidence, and you have not heard a single word to reinforce the flimsy structure they have tried to erect.'

As if responding to the pressure of Lugard's eyes, the judge looked at him, frowning at the temerity of his resolution. 'Lugard, you will stop staring at me in that challenging and impertinent manner.' Lugard rose to reply but was held by a further command. 'Do not attempt to address me, Lugard. Simply comply with my instruction.' A slight inclination of Lugard's head signalled compliance but not submission. The intensity of his gaze, now fixed on the sword of justice, was undiminished. Almost reluctantly, Mr Justice Kingston broke off the encounter and came back to the jury.

'It boils down to this, does it not? Are you satisfied, beyond all reasonable doubt, that the accused, waiting patiently over the years until Pyrnford fell into their grasp, took him to the cellars of Green Briars and there, like the farcical mountebanks they seem to be, held a kangaroo court culminating in the deliberate killing of their former commanding officer. If you are so satisfied, members of the jury, that is murder and nothing else. And you should so convict ... Should you have a reasonable doubt, you will acquit.

'Remember this, a reasonable doubt is not some vague or fancied emotional caprice. It must have substance. Consider it akin to a serious decision you would make in your personal affairs. For instance, the purchase of a new car. You may like its styling, the engine is sound, the suspension strong, the seats comfortable, but when you take it on the road there is a disturbing whine from the transmission. You have a reasonable doubt about its ability to provide you with reliable transportation. Did you hear any disturbing whine coming from the prosecution's gearbox? I cannot say that I did. But if you did, then by all means acquit. Now let me . . .'

Kingston went on to particularize, dealing with each of the accused individually, 'You cannot take an excess of guilt in one and apply it to another in whom you may think it lacking. You must consider them separately . . . Consider one with another, only when interlocking facts bind them irrevocably together . . . You may find one or more guilty, one or more innocent . . .'

At four o'clock, Mr Justice Kingston suddenly broke off; saying he would conclude his address to the jury in the morning. There was little more he could say to them, but very few judges allow a jury to retire in the late afternoon. That would mean remaining on hand, possibly late into the night, until the jury reached a decision. A sensible measure, as all connected with the courts agree; for they too would have to hang around.

Wimperton watched the jury, heavy-laden with thought, struggling out of their wooden compound. Turning to Plaice, he said, 'Lap of the gods, Dickie?'

'You really are a supreme optimist, Paddy.' Plaice wrapped the red ribbon round his brief and tied a precise bow.

'I know. I even bet on the nags you ride. Have you anything good for Sandown this Saturday?'

Smith made his way out to the lobby. Lady Lowderton was standing by the window in her old-fashioned ankle-length coat, legs astraddle, leaning forward on her cane, as if watching for something out in the street. With a feeling of apprehension, Smith realized she was unconcernedly piddling on the floor. Stepping daintily over the little round puddle, Lady Lowderton saw him and waved her cane. 'Has that sanctimonious cretin finished blackening my family name?' Smith gently parried the cane prodding at his belly, looking over her shoulder for the restraining influence of Sam Jones. There was no sign of him.

'The subject never came up again,' he told her.

'You and your fucking promises of confidentiality. You have destroyed me. You realize that, do you? Just as those fucking bastards destroyed Antony.' She was in full control of herself, cursing with a well-bred fluency, rendering it the more effectively offensive. He could do little in reply but offer his arm to assist her down the stairs to the street. Behind them a plaintive cleaner wanted to know 'Ooo did this then?'

He could not help feeling sorry for her; a raddled remnant of privilege and prejudice, as much a survivor as any of the 1404th. She was his responsibility, his witness. Without her he would still be plodding around trying to find Lee Enfield rifles to fit unknown hands.

Reporters hovered outside eyeing her ravenously. While the trial was still alive, she was protected prey, not yet dead meat. A Rolls swept to the kerb and the uniformed chauffeur held the door as she climbed in. He recognized the driver, one from a hire company in Knightsbridge. 'To the Savoy,' she said, too loudly. Someone was already in the back seat, face behind the evening paper. Not Sam Jones, the hips were too narrow, the paunch too flat. As the car drove away, he got a glimpse of a handsome, swarthy profile turning to speak to her. Maybe she was into escort hire as well? He went back inside to satisfy himself Sergeant Blake had the exhibits put away safely for the night. They were stored in an old cell in the basement. The Roll of Honour of the 1404th, Exhibit 27, was lodged on its side on top of a cracked toilet bowl.

Sending Blake back on his own to Cobb Common, he walked along the Embankment and on past the Abbey into Victoria Street and New Scotland Yard. He had to fill in Fairchild on the progress of the trial. Later, back to Cobb Common where Elstow was putting on a bottle or two in celebration of her move. She reckoned the move; the traipse along the corridors of power, the chance to say 'Good morning, sir' to the Commissioner. Sour grapes, Smith? The girl was good. Hadn't she just come out top in The Inspectors exam? She was going places! Would she ever again come to his flat in Kennington?

He took a throbbing head with him to the Bailey next morning. Should have known better, beer and spirits never mixed well with him. Should have stuck with one or the other. Still, he had the nous to get himself out of it before he got too pissed. Leaving Elstow behind . . . and she never came over to Kennington afterwards. Well, maybe she was a little stewed herself.

Lady Lowderton was there ahead of him, still regally attired, although in a different outfit. Loose-fitting coat in crimson silk with a huge ermine collar. One-upping Kingston? She was in fierce argument with the City of London police sergeant on the street door. At least it was fierce on her part.

'I would not be found dead inside the damned courtroom, but I have every right to be present inside the precincts of this abominable place. You have allowed whores to pass in the company of criminals up for trial, and yet you try to refuse entry to the widow of a baronet, a witness for the Crown. Fetch your superior here this instant.'

The crowd behind grew impatient. Reluctantly, the sergeant let her through. After all his P.C. on the door of Court 1 had strict instructions to keep her out. Let him handle her or, even better, let the old cow kick up another rumpus and get herself jailed for contempt.

Mr Justice Kingston sent the jury out at ten forty-five, after telling them to return a verdict of not guilty on Count 2 – the murder of Boswell. A formality, he told them, as the accused were in the charge of the jury it was for them to return that verdict on his direction. They did as they were told, the bearded young man in denim acting as their foreman.

'I wish he had given them that direction before his summing up. Not at the end of it,' complained Plaice to Smith. 'I don't like them getting a practice run in saying not guilty just before they retire.'

A sweepstake initiated by one of the reporters was set running on how long the jury would be out, coupled with a stab at the verdict. Of those unaccustomed to court reporting, none went for a time later than three in the afternoon and all plugged for guilty. The older Old Bailey hands went for later times, between four and five, but still going for guilty. One or two of the even older ones stipulated not guilty.

Smith wandered the corridors and lobbies, knowing it would be at least two hours, but the uncertainty kept him within the precincts of the courts. Chatting with former Yard colleagues there with other cases. Catching sight from time to time of Lady Lowderton; tottering about on her own, apparently deserted by Sam Jones. She too was at the chat; haughtily intercepting Prison Officers, attendants, policewomen, and junior counsel, giving them the frailty act, the condescending smile, the interested ear. Getting in return the obliging explanation, the understanding nod, the directing finger. Maybe she is trying to find the ladies room, Smith thought idly. He steered clear of her; he had told her, after she had given evidence, that she was released as a witness, there was no further need for her to remain. But she was going to stick around till the death – or what would have been the death less than twenty years ago.

The morning dragged on with no sign of the jury. Mr Justice Kingston had begun a fresh trial in No. 1 Court, a domestic murder, a Saturday-nighter. The wife had taken a club hammer to her husband's skull as he lay in a drunken stupor. She was going for diminished responsibility on the grounds of menopausal depression. It was a D.C.I.'s job, one for the middle pages of their local paper.

By lunch-time most of the sweepstake tickets had been torn up and the holders were heading for the nearby water-holes of Fleet Street. Telling himself it was more for the exercise than anything else, Smith took a walk over to Hatton Garden, the once exclusive centre of London's jewel and diamond trade. Tom Street, the villains called it – from jewellery – tomfoolery. It used to be a seedily anonymous thoroughfare, but they had smartened up the bottom end a few years ago, shark-jawed office windows over-hanging the street, the shops moving in with fake marble façades and enticing come-ons. 'Twenty-five percent discount on diamond rings', 'Wholesale prices', 'Highest prices paid for gold.' The old street dealers were gone, Benny, Lou, Syd, Jack and the others, with their kerbside deals, their tissue-paper 'parcels' of diamonds exchanged on a handshake. The Globe pub they used to frequent had been demolished. The top end of the street, the class end, was much as it used to be, small basement workshops, with three or four tiny offices on each of the floors above where the quietly dressed men from Amsterdam, Zurich and New York would occasionally call. Just outside this one, the villains had blagged poor old Myer Weinstein for a quarter of a million in diamonds; across the road, half-blind Sam Beckman had been swagged away in a Transit and left for dead in Epping Forest minus a hundred and eighty thousand in emeralds. The villains always went in brutally strong on those defenceless old men, knowing full well that they would not deliver on a threat, that the gear had to be forcibly taken from them. Over in Grenville Street, he had nicked Harry the Rat busily punting the Creighton stones to Glasses Dwyer. He knew now he hadn't come up here for exercise, he was on a Memory Lane kick. For all that was a long time ago, when the C.I.D. was The Department and people knew how to take a joke.

He had a salt-beef sandwich and a cup of coffee in the Nosherie for old times' sake, and got back to the Bailey shortly after two. The group of pressmen and counsel outside No. 1 Court told him the jury was still out. Lady Lowderton was over by the window, her backside perched on the inside ledge. Giving the fish eye to the copper on the door. He wondered if she would respond to a circuitous chat leading to the identity of the swarthy fellow he had seen in her hired Rolls. But noting her churning jaws, he decided against it. Like Sam Jones, he didn't want to be in the middle of one of her outbursts, and she could be working herself in that direction. In any case, she had now slid to her feet and was off on another meander round the building.

At four, Kingston adjourned the domestic, part-heard, and had the outstanding jury back in.

'Not that I wish to hasten your findings, but should you be in any difficulty I will do what I can to clarify matters.'

'No,' said the young foreman with the beard. 'It is just that we are not yet unanimous.'

'Very well,' Kingston accepted it with prim fortitude. 'Take your time. If you are still undecided, I will call you back later and instruct you on a majority verdict.'

Smith looked for the tight mouths on the jury. There was one on a nondescript young woman with a huge bust, like a bolster under her jumper. Another on a middle-aged man trying to replace lost hair and lost youth with a curly, but very obvious toupee. Yet another on a young three-piece-suited executive type. He knew where the dissension lay. But in what direction, guilty or not guilty? A lot more sweep-stake tickets were torn up. The older Old Bailey hands went looking for the guy who held the kitty.

At eight-thirty in the evening, Kingston had them back to enquire if at least ten of them were agreed on a verdict. The tight mouths were still firm, although the lips of the man with the toupee sagged a little towards the corners. 'No,' said the foreman, 'that number are not in agreement.' Kingston expelled a breath of testy resignation. 'Oh, very well, you will have to be found accommodation for the night. Remember, you must not discuss . . .'

He again assisted Lady Lowderton down the stairs and out to her hired Rolls, hoping for another sight of her swarthy companion, but the back seat was empty. She climbed in clutching her abdomen as though in pain. He asked if she was feeling unwell, for she had had a tiring day, but a hectoring snort told him his concern was not wanted. He was mildly curious about the swarthy man. Could she be paying for it? At her age? He was in the grip of euphoric fatigue himself, brought about by the fact that the end was in sight, his responsibility for everything was over, it was out of his hands. He had a fit of the giggles, imagining her scrawny bones with a hired lecher. 'Stompin' at the Savoy,' he laughed aloud.

She was at the Bailey again next morning, long before Smith arrived. The men on the door told him she had got there before ten. Sitting perched on the window ledge in her loose-fitting crimson coat and ermine collar, she looked, from a distance, like the Dowager Empress of China at the time of the Boxer Rising. There was a stiff implacability in her posture as if she were concealing great pain. Leaning on her cane from time to time, using one hand to claw at her ribs as if trying to ease an inner ache. He went over to her. 'Good morning, Lady Lowderton. Wouldn't you be more comfortable on one of the benches?'

She declined with a gracious ethereal smile. 'No thank you, Mr Smith. They are rather low, and it is difficult for a person of my years to rise from them.'

He hoped her tranquillity would last the day. Maybe there was nothing much wrong with her. He remembered seeing her occasionally clawing at her ribs yesterday. Perhaps it was just that her corsets were too tight.

'They're coming back in.' Just before noon the word went about the lobbies and corridors, and there was a general surge to the doors of Court No. 1, where a tide-race developed between those wishing to enter and those being hustled out from the case currently in progress, now temporarily adjourned.

Smith watched the jury as they took their places. The woman with the massive breastworks seemed sullenly reconciled behind them. The toupee was slightly askew on the head of the middle-aged man, raffishly pushed to one side as if he had too much to drink at an office party. Angry red patches stained the cheeks of the executive in the three piece suit.

There is a popular myth in being that if the jury look at the accused as they return with their verdict, it means they are going to acquit. This jury was no different from the hundreds of others Smith had seen. Some looked – others did not. The clerk asked the foreman to rise and the young man in denim got to his feet. Mr Justice Kingston hovered grimly above, not seeing him, pen at the end of a long arm making abstract notes in his register like a recording angel. Waiting. The foreman suddenly lost some of his earlier self-assurance, uncertain now if he had done the right thing, but knowing it was too late to change his mind. The accused were on their feet waiting for the verdict; staunchly at attention. The foreman glanced towards them and the sight seemed to steady him. The Clerk of the Court led him into the preliminary exchanges.

'Are you all agreed on a verdict?'

'No.'

'Are at least ten of your number agreed on a verdict?'

'Yes.'

The Clerk looked up to the judge for approval. A brief nod gave him sanction.

'How say you, do you find the prisoner, Ronald John Ayliffe, guilty or not guilty of the murder of Antony Corbin Pyrnford?'

'Not Guilty.'

And to the same question put in respect of Bruce and Chivers, Lugard and Reeves, he gave his answers with increasing hoarseness as though the breath was freezing in his throat. Four more times he said, 'Not Guilty.'

Feet scuffled noisily in the press gallery, a cacophony of whispers, a reporter at the end trying to squeeze past his colleagues. The usher screamed for silence. The Clerk took issue with the foreman yet again, seeking a verdict on manslaughter. Five times he received a small, but clearly audible reply: 'Not Guilty.'

Mr Justice Kingston loomed over the jury, placing one bent forearm over the other as he came forward on his desk pouring his bitterness on them, all the more terrible for being unspoken. The Lugard defence had held. The five of them were still to attention in the dock, faces almost as stern as that of their judge. He flung an arm at them and said, 'Let them be discharged.' Then after exchanging perfunctory bows with counsel he abruptly left the bench.

'The ultimate in perversity,' said Plaice dismally. 'A black day for Law.'

'Absolutely lousy,' agreed Wimperton. 'But not a bad one for Justice.'

'Are you advocating an open season on fascists?'

'Good God, no. I'm a bit of a bloody fascist myself. Just like my clients. Takes a bit of a fascist to remember great betrayals, to sustain a great hate.'

'Then as to your conduct of their defence, Paddy, you had better trust no similar qualities exist in your Benchers.'

Smith eased himself through the discursive crowd in the lobby. Lugard and his comrades would be down in the cells reception area getting their property back. He wanted a few words with them before they let them loose, before the media carnivores got their teeth into them. In particular he wanted a word with Lugard.

Billy Fowler, the Principal Prison Officer, was on reception; he knew him well. 'Bit of a turn up for the book, that one, worn't it?' said Billy, who spent his working day underground shuffling prisoners between the various dock entrances below the courts. 'Bleeding good luck to them, I say. I read the diary. Known the likes of that bastard Pyrnford myself. Bleeding good luck to them. They're in the solicitors interview room, down the passage, door facing you on the left.'

Smith made for the passage. 'Here, hold on a minute, Guv.' Billy Fowler called him back. 'Give them a couple of minutes. I let the sister of one of them go in a few seconds ago.'

'Sister?' He had never heard of a sister. Which one had a sister? 'Whose sister?' His chest felt empty. Drained.

'Lugard's sister.' Billy Fowler was smiling fondly. 'A charming old duck. Looked like Father Christmas's missus. Give her a couple of . . .'

Smith was at the top of the passage when he quite distinctly saw a heavy door flying across the bottom end to crash against the wall. A roaring monster, baulked by the wall, came thundering towards him, grey-black and swirling, filling the passage from floor to ceiling, searing his skin with a fiery tongue, throwing him back against Fowler and discarding them both in a corner like crumpled paper. He could feel Fowler coughing beneath him, chest heaving with the spasms. But there was no sound, the monster had thrust glutinous tentacles over his ears and was squeezing, compressing; horny talons now ripping into his brain. He wanted to scream but only had the breath to howl, crouched miserably on his knees like a sick dog. Somehow he got to his feet, reeling drunkenly through the thinning smoke, retching with the acridity of it, feeling the pain ease in his ears as he did so, and went lurching on down the passage rolling from one side to the other, trying to cling to walls that seemed only loosely solid, like thick mud. Hearing noises now Fowler still coughing. Half-way along he paused to try and lessen the still-present pain in his head, fingers probing at his scalp. Finding only crisp stubble where his hair had been. A fire began to rage in the flesh of his face. But he went on – he had to see them, and he could see. Thank God, he could still see.

Water dripped from broken pipes, drumming flatly on a severed thigh. The upper third of Lady Lowderton lay in the arms of a headless, legless torso. Tatters of crimson silk hid the emptiness beneath. Her ermine collar, remarkably still white, had turned upwards delicately shrouding what was left of her face. A sound, mouselike, plaintive, took him behind a heavy upturned table. Bruce lay there, still alive, the half smile erased from a blackened face, lips a puckered circlet, whispering in tiny sibilant squeaks. The wall of his stomach had burst, needing the full span of his broad hands to hold it together. From an aloof disembodied place near at hand he saw himself kneeling at Bruce's side, peering into blind, sundered eyes, seeing his finger thrown at the ermine collar, the one third of Lady Lowderton, hearing himself wail in petulant resentment. 'Why didn't you see it, you stupid bastard. She drew an ace to her queen. Pontoon beats a five-card trick. You pay pontoon you stupid bastard. You pay pontoon.' And then he was back inside himself again, a fist of self-reproach stuffed in his mouth, teeth deep in unfeeling flesh. The squeaking ceased abruptly, the hands fell away and that which was held in slithered to the floor. Through a gap blasted in the ceiling sunlight gave life to seething dust motes; plankton in a rich ocean. Nothing else – no one else – remained whole . . . alive. He saw Lugard's forearm, knowing it was his because a trick of the blast had inverted the face of a gold watch without removing it from the wrist. He could read the inscription: 'Presented to Det. Inspr. John Marrasey on his retirement.'

There were voices at the end of the passage now. He could hear Billy Fowler saying: 'Just like Father Christmas's missus she was. Done up like Father Christmas's missus.' The thought had never occurred to him before.

They kept him in hospital for a week, assuring him his hair would grow back, the skin would heal on face and hands. O'Brien came to see him, smuggling in a bottle of scotch. Elstow came with flowers and sympathy; saying of Lady Lowderton, her eyes shining, 'You must admit it was somehow grand. Superb.' The next day she went away to the Police College on the Inspectors' Course. Fairchild came with grapes and explanations. As they had reconstructed it at the Lab, Lady Lowderton had had approximately four pounds of explosive together with the batteries wrapped round her middle. The wiring was fed down her right arm. All she had to do was slip the little copper electrodes over a finger and thumb and, at the appropriate time, snap them together. The explosive? 'Semtex-H' made by East Bohemia Chemicals, Semtin, Czechoslovakia. Composition? About 44% R.D.X. + 40% P.E.T.N., the rest plasticizer. End-users? A little to the I.R.A., some to the Red Brigade in Italy, quite a bit to E.T.A. in Spain, but most favoured client, Black September and those other splinter groups purportedly outlawed from the P.L.O. Fairchild ate most of the grapes again.

He got a fortnight to recuperate by the sea at the Police Convalescent Home, in Brighton. A week after he resumed duty he called in at Cobb Common nick. O'Brien was preparing the trial exhibits for submission to central property stores; standing back, chin cupped in hand, solicitously reverent, studying the Roll of Honour of the 1404th Independent Ammunition Platoon.

He turned to Smith and spoke with synthetic piety. 'Y'know, Guv, it would be a nice gesture if I got that signwriter to add the names of Lugard, Bruce and the others at the bottom. What do you reckon, Guv?'

All Futura Books are available at your bookshop or newsagent, or can be ordered from the following address:
Futura Books, Cash Sales Department,
P.O. Box 11, Falmouth, Cornwall.

Please send cheque or postal order (no currency), and allow 45p for postage and packing for the first book plus 20p for the second book and 14p for each additional book ordered up to a maximum charge of £1.63 in U.K.

Customers in Eire and B.F.P.O. please allow 45p for the first book, 20p for the second book plus 14p per copy for the next 7 books, thereafter 8p per book.

Overseas customers please allow 75p for postage and packing for the first book and 21p per copy for each additional book.